Critical Praise for Lion Feuchtwanger's
The Oppermanns

"The story of the Oppermanns appeals to our reason, our sense of justice, our indignation. But [the novel] appeals to our emotions as well; those emotions, detached but profound, which it is the problem of pure artistic creation to arouse. . . . Feuchtwanger, no more than Voltaire or Zola (in the Dreyfuss case), is concerning himself with the literary values of his material.... And so this novel is addressed to the German people, who will not be allowed to read it, urging them to open their eyes. And it is addressed to the world outside bearing the message, "Wake up! The barbarians are upon us!"   —*New York Times Book Review*, 1934

"The book is a loosely imaginative commentary on the course of events in Germany from the period of General von Schleicher's brief Chancellorship to a few months after the appointment of Herr Hitler as Chancellor. Inevitably the result is something both less and more than a novel. . . . "
          —*Times Literary Supplement* (London)

"There are few novelists living today who can compete with Feuchtwanger's rare gifts of historical observation and understanding of individual character."   —*Booklist*

"A powerful, gripping appeal to the world on behalf of a declassed minority which has lost its right to the quiet enjoyment of life and liberty."   —*Boston Transcript*

"Solid and exciting, conceived and realized by an artist, the best novel Feuchtwanger has written." —*The New Republic*

"Feuchtwanger is a brilliant enough writer to know how to plead his cause popularly and incomparably."
          —*Chicago Tribune*

The OPPERMANNS

LION FEUCHTWANGER

Translated from the German by JAMES CLEUGH

With an introduction by
RUTH GRUBER

CARROLL & GRAF PUBLISHERS, INC.
NEW YORK

Reprinted by arrangement with Viking Penguin, Inc.
Translated from the German by James Cleugh

First Carroll & Graf edition 1983
Second Carroll & Graf edition 2001

Carroll & Graf Publishers, Inc.
A Division of Avalon Publishing Group
19 West 21st Street
New York, NY 10010-6805

Library of Congress Cataloging-in-Publication Data is available.
ISBN: 0-7867-0880-8

Manufactured in the United States of America

INTRODUCTION

He sits on the sofa in his hotel suite, his head hunched forward as if he is reading a book. He is a small man with a gentle voice, a giant among the German Jewish novelists rescued from Nazi terror. He is Lion (pronounced Leon) Feuchtwanger. It is 1947, and I meet him while he is in New York on a lecture tour.

He speaks to me the way he writes; with cool logic and a carefully controlled passion. He tells me that he writes to shake the world, as he did with his novel *The Oppermanns,* as timely and riveting in 2001 as when he published it in 1933, the very year Hitler rose to power.

I had come to interview him, but almost at once he was interviewing me.

"What do you do," he smiled, "when you're not cross-examining your willing victims?"

I hesitated, and said, "I'm writing a novel."

He waited for me to go on. "It's about a young couple who meet in the Bergen Belsen Displaced Persons Camp."

"And what's the problem?" he asked.

"Mrs. Ogden Reid, the owner of the *New York Herald Tribune,* has asked me to cover the voyage of UNSCOP—the United Nations Special Committee on Palestine. It means giving up the novel and traveling some four months through Germany, Austria, Palestine, and the Arab world. I'm in full swing with the novel and I don't know whether I should continue or take on this new assignment."

His blue eyes behind huge glasses seemed to ignite. "Of course you must go. The novel can wait. You can always go back to the novel. This is a chance of a lifetime. How many young women—even men—are given such an assignment?"

I never regretted taking his advice. Soon, our conversation returned to the subject of his own life and work. He told me he was fortunate to be living in Sanary, near Marseilles, France, in 1933, when he was asked by the British to write a play about life in Germany under Hitler's emerging shadow. Had he then been in Germany denouncing Hitler, he would probably have been arrested, tortured, even murdered, for what already was a substantial outpouring of his anti-Nazi articles and speeches. He accepted the commission and wrote the play entitled *Die Geschwister Oppenheim* (*The Family Oppenheim*). However, as soon as the British gave diplomatic recognition to Hitler's new regime, they cancelled any plans to perform it. In six months, from April to October 1933, Feuchtwanger turned it into the historical novel called *The Oppermanns*.

In the epilogue to the German edition of *Exit*, a later historical novel by Feuchtwanger, he explained that he had written *The Oppermanns* in white heat: "I wanted to enlighten the readers of the world as soon as possible about the true face of the Nazi regime and its dangers."

It was an early wake-up call. Too many people were apathetic about Hitler and the evil that was National Socialism. Too many looked upon Hitler as a clown with a Charlie Chaplin moustache. In essays and plays, and in *The Oppermanns*, Feuchtwanger tore open the curtain of anti-Semitism in Germany.

"How did you escape from the Nazis?" I asked him.

"I owe it to my wife, Marta."

Marta Loeffler Feuchtwanger, famous in Munich for her beauty, twice saved his life.

In 1914 they were living in Hamamet, a small place south of Tunis, when the first Great War of the twentieth century broke out, and they were caught by surprise. They became "enemy aliens" and were imprisoned in primitive conditions. Marta managed to escape, smuggled him out, and hurried them aboard an Italian ship. They landed in Palermo, Italy, and then went home to Germany, where he enlisted in the German military and fought for a few months in the war.

The second escape occurred while they were living in Sanary, in southern France. In May 1940, France fell to the Nazis. Captured by the Vichy French, Lion and Marta were again arrested as "enemy aliens" and thrown into separate prison camps.

I sat mesmerized as he told me how he was forced to carry bricks up a hill, then carry them down again, and repeat the process until he was exhausted. "It was one of the Nazi tricks to dehumanize us with useless labor."

"Did I think I was going to die?" He repeated my question. He shook his head. "No man believes in his own death. That's what kept me alive."

Marta again escaped from her camp. She learned that Lion was ill and so mistreated that he was close to death. Desperate, she forced her way into the office of the American Consul, Hiram Bingham, Jr., who then hid her in his own home. A coterie of Americans—among them Varian Fry, the diplomat the world now knows was rescuing hundreds of Jewish writers and artists—worked to save him. Feuchtwanger and Marta crossed the Pyrenees on foot to safety.

The Oppermanns, though he had written it seven years earlier, captured the trauma and emotions of their hazardous escapes. It was an instance of art imitating life and life, in turn, imitating art.

* * *

In the novel, the Oppermann family, successful middle-class German Jews who own a chain of furniture stores, are robbed of their business, their homes, and their money, as the Nazi laws take hold. Some escape to Switzerland, among them Lion's autobiographical literary hero, Gustav Oppermann, who finds temporary haven in Lake Lugano. Back in Germany, some commit suicide, others are trapped.

"Their homeland, their Germany," Feuchtwanger writes, "had proved false to them. For centuries they had felt secure in that homeland and now everything was suddenly crumbling to bits . . . neighbor spied on neighbor, son on father, friend on friend."

Like many German Jews, several of the characters in the book live in denial, refusing to see the danger that is soon to engulf them; others see the violence, the lies of the Nazis, and the misery of the Jews as they are tortured in concentration camps—their faces and skulls battered, their limbs broken, their bodies starved, their lips thirsting for a drop of water.

He did not consider *The Oppermanns* his best work, though the historical novel won rave reviews when it was published around the world in 1933 and 1934, and again, many years later when it appeared in America as a feature film on public television. "It is his most prophetic book," Herman Graf, who first republished it in English in 1983, told me. "He wrote it in 1933 with Hitler just in power, yet it reads as if he had written it in 1938, with all the details of the Nazi's later and most horrendous atrocities."

Every book one writes carries within it a fragment of autobiography. *The Oppermanns* mirrors a piece of Feuchtwanger's life in Germany. Born in Munich in 1884 to an Orthodox Jewish family, he rebelled against the orthodoxy of his handsome but cold and distant father and morose mother who rarely smiled. Timid, mocked by eight siblings for his diminutive stature, he soon surpassed them all by his writing.

Still in his teens, he began publishing plays and critical essays and at twenty-four, received a Ph.D. from the University of Munich. He married Marta in 1912 and moved to the Riviera to write novels. Marta gave birth to a fragile little girl who died before she was one. Feuchtwanger was so depressed that he vowed they would never have another child.

In 1925 he wrote *Jew Süss* (retitled *Power* when it was published in the United States a year later) which made him an instant success in Europe and America. It was produced in England as a motion picture, and in 1939 was distorted by the Nazis into a violently anti-Semitic movie.

Words, books, history—they were his life. Wherever he settled, he created a library, though he twice lost connection with his precious volumes. His Berlin library was destroyed when Nazi thugs broke into his apartment, stole his unfinished manuscript about the Roman historian, Josephus, and burned his books in a funereal pyre. He was forced to abandon his second library in Vichy France when he escaped with only the clothes on his back. In America, he created a third library with over 30,000 volumes in various languages. They are now at the University of Southern California and supported by the Lion Feuchtwanger Memorial Fund.

Though he had rebelled against religious orthodoxy, he never denied his Jewishness. He once said that even though his mind was intellectual, his heart was Jewish. In fact, his orthodox Jewish training was the core of many of his novels. His book *Raquel: The Jewess of Toledo*, the thirteenth-century story of the beautiful daughter of King Alphonso the Eighth's Jewish Finance Minister, is one of his masterpieces. He based it on the Biblical story of Queen Esther and King Ahasuerus, and dedicated it to two women: Marta, the wife he loved, and his loyal secretary, Hilde Waldo. Some thirty years later, by coincidence, I wrote a book about another Raquel called *Raquela: A Woman of Israel*.

Each time he came to New York on a lecture tour or to discuss a new book with his publisher, Ben Huebsch of Viking Press, I interviewed him; and when he moved to Southern California, I visited him at his home overlooking the hills of Pacific Palisades. Often, as we talked, I felt his blue eyes studying me—warm, penetrating, filled at times with sadness, and other times squinting with mischief and fun.

When Herman Graf visited Marta, still erect and elegant in her nineties, he drove round and round the house unable to find the hidden entrance, until at last he found the Spanish stairs leading downward to the mansion. Marta Feuchtwanger was amused by his dilemma. "You couldn't find the stairs," she laughed, and then more seriously said, "That's why nobody can murder me."

Lion's secretary, Hilde, helped me understand how he wrote his historical novels. Early mornings, he'd swim in the Pacific Ocean, take walks with Marta, then eat breakfast and begin working. He'd spend the morning dictating to Hilde, who typed as fast as he spoke. Often in the afternoon he'd read and research voraciously, studying original documents, letters, and speeches to find all the material to make his historical novels authentic. Frequently, he'd work until seven or eight at night. Later, he and Marta would relax, dining and socializing with Thomas Mann and others in the colony of German exiles and émigrés who found not only success in America but also that for which they yearned most—freedom.

Lion had long been an admirer of American writers and artists, especially Walt Whitman and Mark Twain, and continually sought to link Europe and America. His admiration for America had intensified knowing that Americans had helped save his life and President Roosevelt had arranged the visas that brought him and Marta to safe haven.

He died in 1958 at the age of seventy-four, having survived wars, revolutions, imprisonments, and through it all he had remained cheerful, courageous, and life-loving, a novelist whose hauntingly prophetic work, *The Oppermanns,* stands as a moving testament to man's innate capacity to transform the stuff of our lives into redemptive art.

Ruth Gruber
February 2001
New York City

Not one of the characters in this book existed as an actual individual within the boundaries of the German Reich during the period of 1932–1933; however, they did exist collectively. In order to attain an accurate picture of the type, the author had to forgo any photographic representation of the individual. The novel *The Oppermanns* does not describe actual but historic people.

The material for the descriptions of the views, customs, and methods of the Nationalists in Germany can be found in Adolf Hitler's book *My Battle,* in the reports of those who escaped from Concentration Camps, and, particularly, in the official notices appearing in the 1933 series of the German *Reichsanzeiger*.

The author chose the name "Oppermann" because it brings to mind similar, generally Jewish, names such as Wassermann, Friedmann, Goldmann, Silbermann, etc. . . . and at the same time has a German sound. A parallel instance occurs in the name Hitler, which is borne by a Jewish family in Moravia as well as by the Chancellor of the Reich.

After the type of this volume had already been set, a family by the name of Oppermann advised the publisher that Oppermann is a strictly Christian name and that they would, therefore, like to have it avoided that bearers of the name Oppermann be branded before the general public as belonging to a Jewish family. In view of the existing circumstances, the publisher readily understands this attitude on the part of the Oppermann family and herewith advises the readers of this novel of the facts which the Oppermann family wishes to have definitely understood.

L. F.

November 1933.

CONTENTS

The OPPERMANNS

Book One: Yesterday

YESTERDAY

WHEN Dr. Gustav Oppermann awoke on the sixteenth of November, which marked his fiftieth birthday, it was long before sunrise. That was annoying. The day would be a strenuous one and he had intended to sleep late.

From his bed he could distinguish a few bare tree tops and a bit of sky. The sky looked distant and clear, there was no sign of the fog that is so common in November.

He stretched and yawned. Then, resolutely, now that he was well awake, he threw back the clothes from the broad, low bed, swung both his feet lightly to the floor, emerging from the warmth of the sheets and blankets into the cold morning, and went out on the balcony.

Below, his little garden sloped, in three terraces, down to the woods; to right and left wooded knolls rose, and beyond the more distant tree-covered area further hills and woodlands appeared. A pleasantly cool breeze ascended from the little lake, which lay out of sight to the left, and from the pines of Grune-wald. In the profound silence that precedes daybreak, he breathed the forest air deeply and with enjoyment. The strokes of an axe came faintly from the distance; he liked the sound; the rhythmic blows emphasized the stillness.

Gustav Oppermann, as he did every morning, rejoiced in his house. No one, if he were suddenly transported here without warning, could suspect that he was less than three miles from the Memorial Church, the centre of the West End of Berlin. Really, he had chosen the prettiest spot in Berlin for his house.

He had here all the peace of the countryside and in addition, every advantage of the great city. It was only a few years since he had built and furnished this little place in Max Reger Strasse, but he felt as though he had grown together with the house and the woods, as though each one of the pines surrounding him were a piece of himself. He, the little lake, and the sandy street below, which, fortunately, was closed to motor vehicles, belonged together.

He stood for a time on the balcony, drinking in the morning and the familiar landscape, without thinking much about anything. Then he began to shiver. He was glad he still had a short hour before his daily morning ride. He crept back into the warm bed.

But he could not sleep. That damned birthday. After all, it would have been wiser to leave town and escape the whole bother.

As he was here, he might at least have done his brother Martin the favour of going to the office today. The employees would be vexed, considering the sort of people they were, that he would not be there to receive their congratulations personally. Ah, well. It was too much of a bore to mope about and listen to people's clumsy congratulations.

A self-respecting senior partner ought to take that sort of thing for granted. Senior partner. Rot. No doubt about Martin being the better business man, to say nothing of his brother-in-law Jaques Lavendel and the chief clerks Brieger and Hintze. No, he was quite right to steer as clear of the business as possible.

Gustav Oppermann yawned noisily. A man in his position should damned well be in a better mood on his fiftieth birthday. Hadn't those fifty years been good years? Here he lay, the owner of a fine house that suited him exactly, of a substantial bank account, of a valuable business partnership; he was a collector and acknowledged connoisseur of fine books, a gold medallist in sports. His two brothers and sister were fond of him, he had a friend whom he could trust, a host of entertaining acquaintances, as many women as he wanted, an adorable mistress. What ailed him! If anyone had reason to be in good humour on a day like this, it was he. Then, damn it, why wasn't he? What was to blame?

Gustav Oppermann snorted peevishly, threw himself on his other side, determinedly closed his heavy eyelids, and kept his strong, virile head motionless on the pillow. He would go to sleep now. But his fretful resolution was of no avail, he could not sleep.

He smiled like a mischievous boy. He would try a remedy that he had not used since childhood. "I am doing well, better, superlatively well," he thinks. Again and again, mechanically: "I am doing well, better, superlatively well." By the time he will have thought this two hundred times, he should be asleep. He thinks it three hundred times and remains awake.

Nevertheless, he really was doing well. Physically, materially, and spiritually. He had, he could honestly say, in spite of his fifty years, the appearance of a man in the early forties. And that was how he felt. He was not too rich and not too poor, not too wise and not too foolish. Achievements? Gutwetter, the author, could never have succeeded without him. He also had put Dr. Frischlin on his feet. As for what he had published himself, those few essays on eighteenth-century life and literature, they were decent enough books, written by a cultivated man. No more, he didn't deceive himself. All the same they were pretty good for the senior partner of a furniture store. He was a mediocre man without any particular talent. To be mediocre was best. He was not ambitious. At any rate, not very.

Ten minutes more, then at last he could get ready for his morning ride. He ground his teeth together lightly, closed his eyes but he no longer thought of sleep. To be quite honest,

there were, of course, a few things he still wanted. Wish number one: Sybil was a mistress many people justifiably envied
him. The beautiful and clever Ellen Rosendorff was fonder of
him than he deserved. Nevertheless, if he didn't get a certain
letter from a certain person today, it would be a bitter disappointment to him. Wish number two: he really could not expect the Minerva Press to undertake the publication of his biography of Lessing. Nor was it important in these times
whether the life and works of an author, who died a hundred
and fifty years ago, were described all over again or not. But
all the same, if the Minerva Press refused the book, it would
be a blow to him. Wish number three:

He opened his eyes. They were brown and deep-set. He did
not feel as peaceful or as resigned as, scarcely a moment ago,
he had believed himself to be. Deep, vertical furrows above
the strongly moulded nose, thick eyebrows angrily drawn together, he scowled gloomily at the ceiling. It was remarkable
how his keen face instantly reflected each change in his impetuous, ever-changing moods.

Should the Minerva people accept the Lessing book, there
would still be a year's work on it. If they refused it, he would
lock the manuscript, just as it was, in some drawer. In that
case, what could he do all through the winter? He might go
to Egypt, to Palestine. For a long time he had intended going
there. One should have seen Egypt and Palestine.

Should one really?

Rot. Why spoil this beautiful day by thinking about such
things? Thank goodness, it was time for the ride at last.

He walked through the little front garden towards Max
Reger Strasse. His figure was rather thickset, but in good training. He walked with precise, quick steps, his entire sole firmly
pressing the ground, but he carried his massive head high.
Schlüter, his servant, stood in the gateway and wished him
many happy returns. Bertha, Schlüter's wife, the cook, came

out too and wished him the same. Gustav, beaming, acknowledged their greetings in a loud, hearty voice. They all laughed.
He rode away, knowing that they were standing looking after
him. They would have to admit that he kept himself in
damned good form for a fifty-year-old. He looked particularly
well on horseback, too, taller than he actually was, his legs being a little short, though his body was long. "Just like Goethe,"
as his friend of the Bibliophile Society, Headmaster François
of Queen Louise School, remarked at least once a month.

Gustav met several of his acquaintances along the road,
waved cheerfully to them, without stopping. The ride did him
good. He came back in high spirits. It was fine to have a rub-
down and a bath. He hummed lustily and out of tune a few
not altogether easy melodies, and snorted mightily under the
cold shower. He ate a hearty breakfast.

He went into his library and paced up and down a few
times with his precise quick step. He felt pleasure in the
fine apartment and its tasteful furnishings. At last he sat
down before the massive desk. The large windows scarcely
separated him from the landscape, he sat as though in the open
air. Before him, a bulky pile, lay his morning letters, the birthday letters.

Gustav Oppermann always looked at his correspondence
with pleasurable curiosity. One had, from one's first youth, put
many feelers out into the world. What was the reaction?
There were birthday greetings and congratulations. What
else? He rather hoped that perhaps among these forty or fifty
letters there might be something to bring excitement into his
life.

He did not open the letters, but arranged them according to
their senders, those he knew and those he was not sure of.
Now, at last, he felt a sharp little thrill. Here was the letter
from Anna which he had expected. He held it in his hand for
a moment. His eyelids twitched nervously. Then a boyish

smile spread over his face, he put the letter to one side, quite
out of reach. He was going to postpone reading it, like a child
who leaves the most coveted morsel to the last. He began to
read the other letters. Birthday wishes. It was nice to have
them, but they were hardly exciting. He reached for Anna's
letter, balanced it in his hand, took up the paper-knife. Then
he hesitated. He was really glad that a visitor came in to disturb him.

The visitor was his brother Martin. Martin Oppermann
came towards him, a little heavy on his feet, as usual. Gustav
loved his brother and wished him well but this did not prevent his quietly noting that Martin, though he was two years
younger, looked the elder. The Oppermanns resembled one
another; everyone said so, it must be true. Martin had a large
head, like his; his eyes also lay rather deeply in their sockets.
But Martin's eyes had a slightly dull, oddly sleepy expression.
Everything about him was clumsier, fleshier.

Martin stretched out both hands to him. "What shall I say?
I can only hope that everything will stay just as it is for you.
I wish this most heartily." The Oppermanns had deep voices.
With the exception of Gustav, they disliked showing their feel-
ings. Everything about Martin was reserved and dignified.
But Gustav was well aware of his sincerity.

Martin Oppermann had brought his birthday gift with him.
Schlüter fetched it in. The coverings were stripped off a big
parcel, revealing a picture. It was a bust portrait, oval in shape.
Above a stiff collar in the fashion of the eighties, a large head
rested on a rather short neck. The head was fleshy and the
brow, above deeply set rather sleepy eyes—the Oppermann
eyes—was heavy and protruding. The expression was shrewd,
thoughtful, and kindly. It was the head of Immanuel Oppermann, their grandfather, the founder of the furniture firm of
Oppermann. This was his likeness at the age of sixty, shortly
after Gustav's birth.

Martin placed the picture on the big desk, and held it there in his fleshy, well-kept hands. Gustav looked out of his own brown, pensive eyes into the brown, shrewd eyes of his grandfather Immanuel. No, the picture was not very remarkable. It was old-fashioned and had little artistic value. But the four Oppermanns prized it. It had been dear and familiar to them from their early youth, undoubtedly they saw more in it than there actually was. Gustav liked to keep the light walls of his house undecorated. Only one picture hung in the entire house, in the library. But it had always been one of his dearest wishes to have this portrait of Grandfather Immanuel for his study. Martin, on the other hand, believed it should hang in the private office of the business. Gustav, well as he got on with his brother in other respects, had taken it amiss that he had been denied possession of the picture.

Thus the sight of the portrait filled him with joy and satisfaction. He knew it had been a wrench for Martin to part from it. Beaming, he expressed his pleasure and gratitude volubly.

When Martin had gone, Gustav called Schlüter and instructed him how to hang the picture. He had long made up his mind where it should go. Now it was really going to be put there. Gustav waited impatiently for Schlüter to finish. At last it was ready. The study, the library, and the third room of the ground floor, the breakfast-room, led into one another. Slowly and thoughtfully Gustav let his eyes pass from the portrait of Immanuel Oppermann, his grandfather, his past, to the other, the hitherto unique picture in the house, the one in the library, the portrait of Sybil Rauch, his mistress, his present.

No, the picture of Immanuel Oppermann was really not a work of art. The painter, Alexander Joels, who had executed it on commission for the friends of Immanuel Oppermann, had at that time been grotesquely over-rated. Today he was forgotten. But what Gustav Oppermann liked about the picture was actually something apart from its artistic merit. He and his brothers and sister could see in this familiar portrait the man himself and his work.

The life-work of Immanuel Oppermann was nothing great in itself. It was merely successful commerce. But it meant more in the history of the Jewish inhabitants of Berlin.

The Oppermann family had been established in Germany from time immemorial. They originally came from Alsace. There they had been bankers on a small scale, merchants, gold- and silver-smiths. The great-grandfather of the present generation of Oppermanns had come to Berlin from Fürth in Bavaria. The grandfather, Immanuel Oppermann, had filled important contracts as purveyor to the German armies operating in France in the years 1870–1871. A framed document hung in the private office of the Oppermann firm, in which the taciturn Field-Marshal von Moltke attested that Herr Oppermann had rendered the German army good service. A few years later Immanuel had founded the furniture firm of Oppermann. It was an undertaking which manufactured household furniture for the middle classes and, by standardizing its products, was able to give good value. Immanuel Oppermann took a personal interest in his customers, sounded them, tempted their obscure desires into the light of day, created new needs for them, and then proceeded to supply these needs. His jokes were repeated everywhere. They were an excellent combination of lusty Berlin common sense and his individual brand of genial scepticism. He became a well-liked personality in Berlin and soon his popularity began to extend beyond the city. It was by no means due solely to personal vanity that the Oppermann brothers later registered his picture as the trade-mark of their firm. Through his integrity and manifold connexions with all sorts of people, he contributed towards making the emancipation of the German Jew a fact, not a mere printed paragraph: giving them a real home in Germany.

Young Gustav had known his grandfather quite well. He used to go three times a week to his house in Alte Jacobstrasse in the very centre of Berlin. The sight of the rather stout gentleman sitting at his ease in his black wing-chair, his little cap on his head, a book in his hand or on his lap, and often a glass of wine at his side, had made a deep impression on the boy, inspiring him with respect and, at the same time, with confidence. In his grandfather's house he felt himself to be both on his best behaviour and yet at perfect ease. He was allowed to rummage freely in the gigantic library: here he had learned to love books. His grandfather did not mind explaining to him what the lad did not understand, blinking slyly and enigmatically at him out of his sleepy eyes, so that one never knew whether he was joking or in earnest. Gustav never, in later life, understood as clearly just what these books meant: that statements might be lies and still appear more real than facts. When he asked his grandfather questions, he received answers which seemed to be about something entirely different. But in the end they proved themselves to be the answers, in fact the only right and proper ones.

Gustav Oppermann, as he stood before the picture, did not think of all this. But he saw it all in the portrait. In the painted eyes there was so much of the good-humoured, calm wisdom of the old fellow that Gustav felt himself small but secure before them.

Perhaps it was not advantageous for the other picture, for the one in the library, the portrait of Sybil Rauch, to be confronted by such a neighbour. There was no question but that André Greid, the painter of that portrait, was worth ten times as much, artistically and technically, as simple old Alexander Joels. There was a great deal of white in his picture. He had known that the portrait was to hang on a light wall and had visualized the entire wall as a background for it. From that

bright surface Sybil Rauch emerged, clear-cut, self-willed. She
stood there slim and resolute, one leg slightly advanced. The
slender head was poised on a long neck, the wilful eyes of a
child peered forth under a long, narrow, headstrong brow;
the outline of the cheeks was emphasized. The long lower section of the face receded and ended in a childlike chin. It was
an uncompromising likeness, a definitely striking picture.
"Striking to the verge of caricature," Sybil Rauch would pout
when she was in a sulky mood. However, the portrait did not
minimize the things that made Sybil Rauch attractive. In
spite of her undeniable thirty years, the woman had a childlike, though shrewd and self-willed expression. "Self-centred,"
thought Gustav Oppermann, still under the spell of the other
portrait.

It was now ten years since Gustav had met Sybil. She had
then been a dancer with many ideals and little sense of
rhythm, but she enjoyed some success. She was well off and
lived in comfort, pampered by a worldly-wise, patient mother.
The ingenuous, South German esprit of this dainty girl, so
strangely mingled with a sharpness and shrewdness far beyond
her years, had attracted Gustav. She had been flattered by the
obvious devotion of this substantial, distinguished man, and a
sincere and unusual devotion quickly developed between the
girl and the man twenty years her senior. He was at once her
lover and her uncle. He sensed her every mood, she could be
perfectly frank with him, his advice was at all times understanding and well considered. He had discreetly made her
realize that her dancing, with its lack of musical values, could
never lead to real, self-satisfying success. Convinced of this, she
changed hobbies with quick determination and began to train
herself, under his direction, for authorship. She had the knack
of expressing herself vividly and newspapers willingly printed
her sketches and short stories. When her private fortune was
swept away through the economic changes in Germany, her

earnings went far towards her support. Gustav, himself without creative talent but a good critic, gave her assiduous and sensible advice and through his extensive connexions helped her to a good market. They had often thought of marriage, she more persistently than he. But she realized that he preferred not to harden the relationship between them by a legal union. Taking it all in all, the ten years together had been good years.

Good years? Say rather, agreeable years, reflected Gustav Oppermann, contemplating the clever, lovable, wilful child in the picture.

And suddenly he became conscious again of the letter, of the unopened letter on the big desk, Anna's letter. There would not have been ten comfortable years with Anna. There would have been years of quarrelling and upheaval. But on the other hand, if he had been Anna's lover, he would hardly have needed to ask himself that morning what he should do with himself during the winter, in case the Lessing biography were rejected. He would have known well enough, then, what to do and where to go. He would probably have had so much to do that he would have groaned aloud if anyone had mentioned Lessing.

No, he hated the hectic restlessness as he observed it in many of his friends. He liked his own respectable, well-ordered idleness. It was good to sit in his fine house with his books and his assured income, among the pine-wooded hills of Grunewald. It was good that he had finished with Anna in those days, after two years with her.

Had he finished with her or had she finished with him? It is not easy to find one's way through the history of one's own life. This much, however, was certain. He would miss Anna if she disappeared from his life altogether. To be sure, there were always rancorous after-thoughts whenever they met. Anna was so quarrelsome. She had such an outspoken, cutting way of pouncing on every fault, on every tiny little weakness. Whenever he had to meet her, even when he read one of her letters, he had the sensation of being before a judge.

He held the letter in his hand, reached for the paper-knife, and cut it open with a single stroke. His thick eyebrows drawn sharply together, deep vertical furrows above his powerfully moulded nose, tension in ever line of his big face he read the letter.

Anna sent him her best wishes in a few cordial words. In her beautiful, even handwriting, she informed him her holidays would begin at the end of April and she would be glad to spend its four weeks with him. If he would like to see her, please to advise her where.

Gustav's face relaxed. He had been uneasy about that letter. It was a good letter. Anna's life was not an easy one. She was secretary to the board of directors of the electricity works at Stuttgart, extremely absorbed in her work. Her private life was limited to her four weeks' holiday. The fact that she had offered to devote those four weeks to him proved that she had not given him up.

He read the letter a second time. No, Anna had not done with him. She was saying "yes" to him. He hummed, carefully and out of tune, the morning's difficult melody. He inspected, half consciously, half mechanically, the picture of Immanuel Oppermann. He was sincerely delighted.

2

Martin Oppermann, meanwhile, drove to his office. Gustav's house was in Max Reger Strasse, on the boundary between Grunewald and Dahlem. The original office of the

Oppermanns was in Gertraudten Strasse in the centre of the city. Franzke, the chauffeur, would need at least twenty-five minutes to get there. In favourable circumstances, Martin would get to the office at ten minutes past eleven. If he should have bad luck with the traffic lights, not until after a quarter-past eleven. He had an appointment with Heinrich Wels at eleven. Martin Oppermann did not like to keep people waiting. And to keep Heinrich Wels waiting was doubly undesirable. The interview would not be a pleasant one in any case.

Martin Oppermann sat stiffly in the car, bolt upright, in a not particularly easy or natural attitude. The Oppermanns were heavily built. Edgar, the doctor, was slighter. Gustav, too, had reduced his weight to some extent by training. Martin had no time for that sort of thing. He was a business man, the father of a family, and had responsibilities of all kinds. He sat upright, his big head thrust forward, his eyes closed.

No, the interview with Heinrich Wels would not be pleasant. Pleasant occasions in business were rare nowadays. He ought not to have kept Wels waiting. He ought to have presented the picture to Gustav that evening at dinner. It had not been absolutely necessary to take it to him that morning. He was fond of Gustav, yet he envied him. Gustav had an easy time of it, too easy. Edgar, the doctor, had an easy time, too. He, Martin, was the only one who had had to succeed Immanuel Oppermann in the business. It was damned difficult in these times of crisis and rising Anti-Semitism to make that succession a meritorious one. Martin Oppermann took off his top-hat, ran his hand through his scanty black hair, and sighed a little. He should not have kept Heinrich Wels waiting.

They had reached the bustling Dönhoffplatz. In another moment they would have arrived, at last. There was the building already. It stood, jammed between its neighbours, narrow, old-fashioned but solid, built generations past for generations to come. It inspired confidence. The car passed the four big

show-windows and stopped at the main entrance. Martin
would have liked to jump out quickly, but he restrained himself, mindful of his dignity. Leschinsky, the old doorman,
stood at attention before he swung the revolving doors in motion. Martin Oppermann put a finger to the brim of his hat,
as he did every day. August Leschinsky had been employed in
the business ever since Immanuel Oppermann's time. He
knew every detail. He certainly knew that Martin had just
come from congratulating his brother Gustav on his fiftieth
birthday. Did the old man find an excuse for his late arrival
in this fact? Leschinsky's face with its grey, bristling moustache, was always surly, the man's attitude was chronically unbending. Today he was standing particularly erect and stiff:
he evidently approved of his chief's conduct.

Martin was less satisfied with his conduct than his doorman.
He took the elevator to his office on the third floor. He used
the rear entrance, he did not want to catch sight of Heinrich
Wels sitting there, waiting for him.

On the wall above his desk hung, as in all the Oppermann
business offices, the portrait of old Immanuel. He felt a slight
pang at the thought that it was no longer the original, but a
copy. It was of course fundamentally a matter of indifference
whether the original hung here or at Gustav's. Gustav had, no
doubt, more appreciation of it. He certainly had more time to
look at it, and it was hung in a better position in his house. At
bottom, too, Gustav really had a better right to it. Still, it was
annoying to feel that from now on he, Martin, would no
longer have the original before his eyes.

His secretary entered. Mail submitted by the chief clerks.
Papers to be signed. Telephone calls. Oh, yes, and Herr Wels
was waiting to see him. He had an appointment for eleven.
"Has Herr Wels been there long?" "Just about half an hour."
"Please ask him to come in."

Sitting erect in stiff dignity was a matter of habit with Mar-

tin Oppermann, he did not have to assume a pose. But today
he did not feel in top form for this interview. He had carefully weighed the proposition he intended putting before
Wels, had discussed everything with his chief clerks Brieger
and Hintze. It was essential that Wels be in a good humour,
the matter was a delicate one, it was too bad that he had kept
Wels waiting.

The case was as follows: At the very beginning Immanuel
Oppermann had not manufactured the furniture which he
sold, but had left its manufacture to Heinrich Wels, senior,
then a trustworthy young workman. When branch shops were
established in Berlin, one in Steglitz and one in Potsdamer
Strasse, it became more difficult to continue the arrangement
with Wels. Wels was reliable but he had to charge too much
for his work. Soon after the death of Immanuel Oppermann,
the firm began, at the instigation of Siegfried Brieger, the present chief clerk, to have part of the furniture made in cheaper
factories. When the management of the business passed on to
Gustav and Martin, they opened a factory of their own. For
more complicated jobs and for special orders they had recourse, as before, to Wels's workshop. But the principal needs
of Oppermann's Furniture Stores, which had meanwhile
established another branch in Berlin and five provincial
branches, were now filled by their own workshops.

Heinrich Wels, junior, regarded this development with bitterness. He was a few years older than Gustav, a hard-
working, reliable, slow-thinking man. He linked his factory to
retail shops, model enterprises run with infinite care, in order
to compete with the Oppermanns. But he was not successful in
this. His prices could not compete with those of the standardized Oppermann furniture. Countless people knew the name
of Oppermann. The trade-mark of the Oppermanns, the picture of old Immanuel, had penetrated into the most distant
provinces. The simple, old-fashioned slogan of the Opper-

mann advertisements, "Oppermann customers buy good goods cheaply," was a household phrase. All over the Reich Germans worked at Oppermann desks, ate off Oppermann tables, sat on Oppermann chairs, and slept in Oppermann beds. One might sleep more comfortably in Wels beds, and the Wels tables might be more durably constructed, but people preferred to invest less money, even if what they bought was a bit less substantial. Heinrich Wels could not understand that. It hurt his craftsman's pride. Had the recognition of solid merit died out in Germany? Could not these misguided purchasers see that at one of his, Wels's, tables a single man had laboured for eighteen hours, whereas the Oppermann stuff was merely the product of a factory? They did not see it. They only saw that a Wels table cost fifty-four marks and an Oppermann cost forty, so they made their purchases at Oppermann's. Heinrich Wels could not understand people nowadays. His bitterness steadily increased.

However, during recent years, things had taken a turn for the better. A movement was making headway which spread the idea that hand-made articles were better suited to the character of the German people than standardized products of factories run on international lines. This movement called itself National-Socialism. It freely expressed what Heinrich Wels had long secretly felt, namely that the Jewish firms with their cut-price methods were responsible for Germany's decline. Heinrich Wels associated himself wholeheartedly with the movement. He became a District Chief of the party. He saw with delight that the movement was gaining ground. It was true that people still preferred to buy cheaper tables, but at least they abused the Oppermanns while they did so. The party also managed to put a higher tax rate on the larger stores so that the Oppermanns gradually had to advance their prices for tables, for which Wels charged fifty-four marks, from forty to forty-six marks.

Anti-Jewish circulars arrived in quantities at all the nine Oppermann shops, anti-Jewish posters were pasted on the show-windows at night. Old customers stopped coming. Prices had to be at least ten percent lower than those of non-Jewish competitors; if they were only five percent cheaper some of the customers went to Christian shops. Chicanery from official quarters increased under pressure of the growing National-Socialist party. Heinrich Wels profited. The difference between the price of his merchandise and that of the Oppermanns steadily decreased.

In spite of this, the furniture firm of Oppermann continued, outwardly at least, to maintain friendly relations with the Wels concern. In fact Jaques Lavendel and chief clerk Brieger had hinted to Wels that he should suggest a consolidation of the two firms or, at any rate, a closer co-operation between them. If such an arrangement were concluded, the firm of Oppermann would be relieved of the odium attaching to a Jewish house. Further, as soon as Wels had a share in the business, certain official steps would undoubtedly lose much of their harshness as far as that firm was concerned.

When the success of the Oppermanns had outstripped that of Heinrich Wels, he had been wounded more keenly in his pride than in his purse. He was happy now that his workshops were gaining ground. After a few verbal soundings on the part of Brieger, he had actually received a most courteous note from the Oppermann firm stating that they understood he had certain suggestions to make conducive to an even more pleasant co-operation than in the past. The firm was keenly interested and requested the favour of his call, to take up these matters in person, on the sixteenth of November at eleven o'clock in the office of the manager of the firm in Gertraudten Strasse.

Heinrich Wels, accordingly, sat in the ante-room of the head office of Oppermann's and waited. He was a stately man

with a frank, determined face. He was a righteous man and a
stickler for precision. Which of them had first approached the
other? At a meeting of the Association of Furniture Manu-
facturers, chief clerk Brieger had spoken to him about the increasing difficulties of his firm. Brieger had deliberately led
him on to ask certain questions. It was no longer possible to
figure out who had made the first advances. As usual, he was
sitting here to make a proposal which was not of disadvantage
to himself but which would, most likely, prove still more prof-
itable to the other party.

They did not want to admit that. He looked at the clock.
He had been an officer of the Reserves at the front during the
whole of the war and had learned punctuality from his military service. He had arrived a few minutes before eleven. Now
he was sitting there and that stuck-up crowd were keeping
him waiting. Ten minutes past eleven. His strong face darkened. If they let him wait another ten minutes, he would clear
out and they could get themselves out of their mess without
him.

Who was it he would have to deal with? Heinrich Wels
was not a judge of men but he knew well enough where in the
firm of Oppermann those in favour of his project were to be
found and where its adversaries. Gustav and Martin Oppermann were both unbearably arrogant, typical Jews; it was
barely possible to get on with them. Chief clerk Brieger was a
whole synagogue in himself, but at least one could talk to him.
They would probably turn up five or six strong. They might
even have called in their legal adviser. They wouldn't make it
easy for him. He would have to fight alone against five or six.
No matter. He would manage it.

Eleven twenty. He would wait another five minutes. They
were letting him sit there till he took root. Another five minutes, and then he would regard his proposals as lapsed. You
can kiss my backside then, gentlemen.

Eleven twenty-five. He could recite the issue of the *Furniture Dealer* which lay on the table by heart now. Those people in the private office were taking a deuce of a long time over their deliberations. Was that a good sign? There was no secretary here he could send in. It was a damned nuisance. But he would make them pay for this.

Eleven twenty-six. He was asked to go in.

Martin Oppermann was alone. It suddenly occurred to Herr Wels that he would have preferred to deal with five or six, as he had expected. That Martin was the worst of the lot. He was the most difficult one to deal with.

Martin Oppermann stood up as Herr Wels entered. "I ask your pardon," he said politely, "for having kept you waiting." He had intended to be still more polite and explain the reason for his late arrival. But Wels's big, harsh face repelled him, as it always did, and he changed his mind.

"Unfortunately," replied Herr Wels in his sulky, rasping voice, "time is the only thing which a business man can afford to waste nowadays."

With sleepy eyes Martin Oppermann gravely and coolly regarded the big man seated facing him. He tried to make his voice sound as agreeable as possible. "I have considered your proposals thoroughly and with the greatest interest, my dear Herr Wels," he said. "Fundamentally we are inclined to go further into the matter but we have some misgivings. Our balance sheet is better than yours, Herr Wels, but I will frankly tell you it is not satisfactory. In fact, it is unsatisfactory." He did not look at Herr Wels, he glanced up at the portrait of Immanuel Oppermann and regretted that it was only a copy. His tone was not the right one to adopt with this embittered and irritated man. At the moment there was no need to come to terms with Wels. The political situation seemed quiet. Probably there would be no such need for months or even years to come. But there was no guarantee of security, it was as well to be cautious. The only sensible scheme would be to temporize with Wels and keep him in a good humour. His, Martin's, manner was not the right one for such an interview as this. Old Immanuel would certainly have known better how to handle this stiff, obstinate fellow.

Herr Wels was also ill at ease. One got no further, talking like this. "Things are not going well with me," said he, "and they are not going well with you either. We girls needn't be afraid to tell each other that." He twisted his grim mouth into a smile. The waggish phrase, uttered by his grim voice, sounded twice as gloomy.

They went into details. Martin took out his eyeglasses, which he very seldom used, and polished them. Herr Oppermann really found it difficult putting up with Herr Wels to-day, and Herr Wels had the same difficulty with Herr Oppermann. Each found the other overbearing. The conference was a torment for them both. Herr Wels felt that the Oppermanns were not taking the matter seriously. What they wanted to embark upon was an enterprise that committed them to very little. They wanted to merge one of the Berlin and one of the provincial branches with two corresponding establishments belonging to Wels. This proposal did not interest Herr Wels. If things went badly, the Oppermanns would lose two of their eight branches. That would not worry them much. But he would lose two out of his three branches and be ruined.

"I see that I have made a mistake," said Herr Wels tartly. "I thought we might be able to come to terms. Agree to an armistice," he corrected himself, with a thin, grim smile. Stout Martin Oppermann assured him courteously and glibly that he had no idea of regarding the negotiations a failure. He was certain that if the matter could be more thoroughly discussed, an agreement would be reached.

Herr Wels shrugged his shoulders. He had persuaded himself that the Oppermanns were done for. It now appeared that they thought that he, not they, was done for. They wanted to put him off with an appetizer and then devour the dinner themselves. He departed gloomily, in a rage.

"Those gentlemen are going to burn their fingers some day," he thought, as he went down in the elevator. He did not merely think it, he muttered the words. The elevator-boy looked at the scowling man in amazement.

3

After the interview Martin sat down at his big desk. Wels had scarcely left the room before he shed his gracious, confident manner. He had not reached his goal. He had made a mess of it. He sat there glumly, vexed with himself.

He sent for the chief clerks, Siegfried Brieger and Karl Theodor Hintze. "Well, did you get on with the fire-eating 'goi'?" Siegfried Brieger shot the question at him right away, after a perfunctory greeting. The brisk little man, in his early sixties, lean, irascible, distinctly Jewish in appearance, drew up a chair close to his chief. His big nose, over a growth of muddy-grey moustache, made a sniffing sound. Karl Theodor Hintze, on the other hand, remained on his feet at a respectful distance, with a reserved demeanour, obviously disapproving of the informal haste of his colleague.

Karl Theodor Hintze disapproved of everything that Herr Brieger did and Herr Brieger made a joke of everything that Karl Theodor Hintze did. Karl Theodor Hintze had been, during the war, captain of the company in which Brieger was serving as an ordinary conscript. Their mutual relations were the same then as now. They had already discovered, in those days, how very dependent they were upon each other. After the war, when things were going badly with the elegant Herr Hintze, Herr Brieger had found him a job in Oppermann's Furniture Stores. Under his guidance, the indefatigable, conscientious fellow had quickly reached a position of trust.

Martin Oppermann made his report to his two assistants. The three knew one another well. The result of the interview had been a foregone conclusion. No one had believed that Wels would accept. The only question had been how he would take it. After Martin's report everyone realized that it would have been wiser to have let Herr Brieger deal with Herr Wels. Brieger could have made Wels an even less favourable offer than Oppermann, and yet Wels would have gone away more satisfied.

What had to be done now was obvious. Wels would have to be shown that the Oppermann business could discount the odium attaching to Jewish enterprises without his help. A lesson of that kind would make him more tractable. The present political tranquillity was the best chance they had to take some necessary and long-premeditated steps.

All that was required was to turn the Jewish firm of Oppermann into a stock company with a neutral name that was beyond suspicion. Other Jewish firms had done well after changing their names in this way. What happened was that purchasers who wished to boycott a certain Jewish firm supplied their needs by having recourse to an apparently non-Jewish company, which was in reality nothing more nor less than a subsidiary of the hated Jewish firm. As Wels did not choose to join them, the Oppermanns would themselves float a stock company under the name of "German Furniture Company" and, to begin with, merge one of the Berlin and one of the provincial branches into it.

That was technically easy to do, promised success, was the best solution. All the same it required a certain amount of courage to carry it through. "German Furniture Company," what meaning did that convey? Something vague, indefinite, as colourless as "railroad car." Oppermann's Furniture Stores, on the other hand, could not be disassociated from the picture of Immanuel Oppermann, from stout, respectable Martin, from brisk, big-nosed Herr Brieger. Cutting the Berlin branch in Steglitz and the Breslau branch away from the main business and calling them "German Furniture Company" was like amputating a finger or a toe.

But was not just this necessary if they were to save the whole business? It was.

Once their minds were made up, quick action was imperative. Martin was to speak to the other Oppermanns and would that very day get in touch with Professor Mühlheim, the legal adviser of the Oppermanns.

When he was alone, Martin rested both his arms heavily on the sides of his chair. His shoulders drooped. Perhaps it would be a good idea to do some exercises every morning, as his wife had advised him. Forty-eight is not a great age, but if one does not look after oneself, one will be an old man in two years. Gustav looked delightfully young and fresh. Gustav had an easy time of it. To exercise successfully would take up at least twenty-five minutes each morning. Where was he, Martin, going to find those twenty-five minutes?

He pulled himself together, sighed, and reached for his mail. No. That was not so important. The difficult job must come first, that had been his invariable rule. He must notify his brothers and sister at once. He would not spoil Gustav's day for him. It was out of the question that Gustav would have any objections. He would sigh, make a few comments of philosophical nature, and sign. It would be still easier with Edgar. He would have his chief difficulty with Jaques Lavendel, his brother-in-law, the husband of Klara Oppermann. He would not make any objections either. On the contrary, that experienced business man had long been urging that the name of the firm should be changed. The only thing was, Jaques Lavendel's manner was so extremely blunt. Martin had no objection to people speaking their minds. But Jaques Lavendel was a bit too outspoken.

He requested his secretary to get him the two telephone numbers, that of Professor Edgar Oppermann and that of Jaques Lavendel. Professor Oppermann, the secretary informed him, was in the clinic. That was where he always was, of course. One would have to leave him a message to ring up. Of course he never would. He had far too much work in his clinic and was far too little interested in business. Well, Martin had, as usual, done his duty in that direction.

Jaques Lavendel was on the line now. He never stood on ceremony. In his rather hoarse but friendly voice, immediately after Martin's first introductory sentences, he announced that he would like to have an opportunity of discussing the matter personally with Martin. He would, as he did not live far from Martin, call, if the latter had no objection, at his home, after lunch. Martin replied he would be delighted.

He was not delighted. Lunch with his wife and son and the brief subsequent hour of freedom was Martin's favourite time of day. He could not always avoid having guests, some things are more easily settled at home than in the office. But he did not like these occasions. They spoiled the day for him.

Immanuel Oppermann looked down on his grandson with his sleepy, shrewd, kindly eyes. The latter did not consciously think it but he subconsciously felt: this is a copy, the original is gone.

4

Punctually at two o'clock, as he did every day, Martin entered his house which stood in Cornelius Strasse in the Tiergarten district. He changed his coat and collar. There must be some distinction between his private and his business life. Then he went into the morning-room. It was large, impressive, but somewhat conventionally furnished. Martin made it a point to use the Oppermann furniture even in his private residence.

He found his wife and his son in animated conversation. Like his father, the seventeen-year-old Berthold was often rather silent and, although he could talk interestingly and facilely, he was inclined to be reticent about the things that meant most to him. Martin was glad to find him in a talkative mood today.

Liselotte interrupted her son as Martin entered. There was a smile on her large animated face, showing above a high-necked dress, as she turned to him with "How are you, my dear?" "Quite well, thanks," answered Martin. "Hallo, my boy," he added to Berthold, and smiled too. But Liselotte's grey, almond-shaped eyes had learned, during the eighteen years of her marriage, to read her husband's face. He did not like discussing business matters in the family circle. But although he did not speak, she knew that he was immersed, that day, in weighty affairs.

They sat down to table. Berthold talked excitedly. The seventeen-year-old boy had his father's fleshy face and his mother's fearless grey eyes. He was already nearly as tall as his father, when he reached his full height he would overtop him by half a head.

He spoke of what was happening at school. The class-

teacher, Dr. Heinzius, had been killed, some days ago, in a
motor-car accident, and the headmaster of the school, Rector
François, was temporarily instructing the Lower Sixth in the
dead man's subjects, German and History. These were Berthold's favourites. He loved sport and books, like his uncle
Gustav, and he had got on uncommonly well with Dr. Heinzius. The point now was that Dr. Heinzius had given him a
particularly difficult subject for the lecture which every member of the Lower Sixth had to deliver once a year. It was "Humanism and the Twentieth Century." Would he be allowed
now, after the death of his beloved teacher, to deliver this
talk? And would he be able to manage the idea of "Humanism" without the help of the kindly Dr. Heinzius? Rector
François had told him that he personally had nothing against
the subject, but that he did not want to anticipate the decision
of a new class-teacher, who was to begin his duties next week.

"I certainly have undertaken a lot," observed Berthold. "Humanism is a devilishly hard problem," he assured them
gravely. "Suppose you choose a less abstract subject," suggested Martin. "Something about a modern author," Liselotte
proposed, flashing her son an encouraging look out of her
grey, almond-shaped eyes. Martin was astonished. Talking of
modern literature at school would be a ticklish business,
wouldn't it? Fundamentally Martin and Liselotte were usually
of the same opinion. But she, the Christian, the daughter of
the old Prussian civil-service family of the Ranzows, often
took a more liberal view of things.

Martin changed the subject. He told them he was expecting
Jaques Lavendel after lunch. The news at once took Berthold's
mind off "Humanism." Perhaps he could use the car now?
His father was a busy industrialist and drove about the whole
day. It was very seldom that Berthold could get hold of the
car for himself. He must not let the opportunity slip. For instance, he could drive out to the ball-field on the Sachsen-

damm for football practice. That would be a good excuse. His fun would, to be sure, make a hole in the three hours he had set apart for "Humanism." Oh, rot. He could always dig up time for "Humanism." When he would get another chance of digging up the car, goodness only knew.

As soon, therefore, as lunch was over, Berthold took leave of his parents. He telephoned to his school friend, Kurt Baumann, and asked him to meet him at the Halle Gate to go out to the ball-field on the Sachsendamm. Kurt Baumann was not very keen. His radio set was out of order, he had taken it to pieces, he wanted to find out exactly what the trouble was: that took time. But Berthold persisted. He spoke of a surprise he had for Kurt Baumann. There was something so triumphant in his tone that Kurt Baumann guessed and burst out: "You've got the car! Oh, say, that'll be great!" Berthold Oppermann was really a good sport, he was decent about sharing, he copied Baumann's mathematics and let Baumann copy his German essay, and when Franzke the chauffeur handed over the wheel to the boys, he only drove two-thirds of the time and let Kurt Baumann drive the other third.

At last they got to the point when Berthold sat next to Franzke the chauffeur at the steering wheel. He was thick with Franzke the chauffeur. Franzke, of course, had his moods and did not always encourage conversation. But today he did. Berthold saw that at once. He would be sure to let him take the wheel, in spite of the fact that people under eighteen were not allowed to drive. He was in a fever of impatience to reach the suburbs. But it would be unmanly to show his impatience. So he started a serious, manly conversation with August on the present state of affairs, dealing with economics and politics. August Franzke and the boy understood each other excellently.

When Franzke, later, as was only fair, let Kurt Baumann take the wheel and Berthold sat at the back of the car with nothing to do, he suddenly remembered a certain experience immediately after the funeral of Dr. Heinzius. He had been allowed to drive out to the distant cemetery in the car, and on the way back he had taken Kurt Baumann and his cousin Heinrich Lavendel with him. He had been very much impressed by the gloomy grey cemetery in the woods at Stahnsdorf and by the funeral proceedings. However, the other two, only five minutes after the burial of Dr. Heinzius, seemed far more interested in the car than in the dead man, above all in the question whether Franzke the chauffeur would in the end allow them to take the forbidden wheel. Berthold did not understand how his friends could so quickly forget their recent experience. Even now, while Kurt Baumann sat at the wheel, it made him feel puzzled and pensive.

When, however, he himself was allowed to take the wheel, all such thoughts vanished. Within and without him, nothing existed but the Berlin traffic of the south-western district.

5

Meanwhile, in Cornelius Strasse, the arrival of Jaques Lavendel was expected. Frau Liselotte anticipated it with pleasure. Martin, she knew, did not exactly see in his brother-in-law Jaques a man after his own heart. It was a trial to him that his younger sister, Klara Oppermann, had married this man from Eastern Europe. Jaques was, of course, an excellent man of business, he was well off, knew the world, and was always agreeable. But he lacked a sense of dignity, of formality, of reserve. It was not that he had noisy or boisterous manners. But he referred to unpleasant matters so baldly, and that mocking, gentle smile of his, when anyone spoke of honour, dignity, and so on, irritated Martin.

It did not irritate Liselotte. She liked her brother-in-law Jaques. She belonged to the conservative Ranzow family. Her father, who had an impressive title but a poor salary, had made up for the lack of material comforts in his life by high principles and a strict code of behaviour. Liselotte Ranzow, who was then twenty-two, had been glad to exchange the narrow mode of life in her father's house in Stettin for the liberal outlook of the Oppermanns. She had encouraged the taciturn, awkward wooing of young Martin by every means in her power.

"Shall we wait for Jaques before we have coffee?" she asked, showing the large teeth between her long, well-shaped lips in a slight smile. She saw that Martin was hesitating as to whether he should see Jaques alone or ask her to be present. "Have you got something important to discuss with him?" she asked.

Martin reflected. He and Liselotte were good comrades. Naturally, he would tell her today about the decision to change the name of the two branches. That was not easy. He had, so far, seldom had occasion to mention disagreeable things. Perhaps it would be better to tell her and Jaques at the same time. "I should be very glad if you would stay," he said.

Jaques Lavendel, then, sat between them. The little, deep-set eyes under the broad forehead were keen and kindly. The heavy, reddish-blond moustache emphasized the sparseness of his hair. The gentle, rather hoarse voice got on Martin's nerves, as usual.

While Martin explained matters, Jaques listened with his eyes half closed and his hands folded over his waistcoat, his head a little on one side, without any movement in his face or attitude, apparently indifferent. Martin would have preferred him to interrupt and ask questions, but he did not interrupt.

Even when Martin had finished, he was silent. Liselotte watched Jaques Lavendel excitedly. She was more excited than distressed. Martin, relieved as he was that the matter had not affected her more deeply, thought with bitterness: she is not taking it seriously, she doesn't take my affairs seriously. You wear yourself out and get no thanks for it.

Jaques was persistently silent. At length Martin asked: "Well, what do you think about it, Jaques?" "Good, good," said Jaques Lavendel and nodded his head several times. "I think it's a good thing, I say. The only pity is that you didn't do it long ago. And a still greater pity is that you didn't complete the job and take this Wels in with you."

"Why?" asked Martin. He was trying to speak calmly. But both Liselotte and Jaques Lavendel noticed his irritation at this suggestion. "Do you believe we have so little time left? I know these people. He would become insolent the moment we consented. You know we have nothing to lose by waiting."

"Perhaps. And perhaps not," said Jaques Lavendel, shaking his big, reddish-blond head. "I am no prophet. I don't pretend to be a prophet. But isn't everyone always too late? It might last another six months, it might last another year. Who can tell how long it will last? But if things go wrong, it might possibly not last more than another two months." He jerked up his head suddenly, looked at Martin with his little deep-set eyes, winked slyly, and continued in a very matter-of-fact tone: "Grosnowice changed masters seventeen times. Seven times the changes brought pogroms with them. Three times they seized a certain Chayim Leibelschitz and told him: 'Now we are going to hang you.' Everyone said to him, 'Be sensible, Chayim. Leave Grosnowice.' He did not leave. They seized him a fourth time and again they did not hang him. But they did shoot him." He had finished speaking, he cocked his head to one side again and closed the lids over his blue eyes.

Martin Oppermann knew the story. He was peeved. Liselotte, also, had already heard the story once before. But it interested her to hear it a second time.

Martin took out his eyeglasses, polished them, and put them back again. "We certainly can't be expected to throw the Oppermann shops at him," he said, and his brown eyes were by no means sleepy now. "Well, well," said Jaques soothingly, "I am sure you have done a good thing already. Besides, if you would really like to bring in some American capital, I volunteer to arrange the matter within a week and to such good effect that no one will be able to touch you. And no one will dare to talk about 'throwing things at people,'" he added, smiling.

The question of transferring Oppermann's Furniture Stores to Jaques Lavendel, who was a naturalized American citizen, had been under consideration on several occasions; but the idea had been abandoned for various reasons. Curiously enough, Martin did not now advance any one of the many practical objections but said rather spitefully, "Lavendel would not be a good name for our stores." "I know that," replied Jaques quietly. "As far as I know there never was any question of it," he added, smiling.

The transformation of the two branches into the German Furniture Company was really not quite as simple as it appeared. There was a mass of details to be discussed. Jaques Lavendel had many useful suggestions to offer. Martin had to admit that Jaques was the more resourceful of the two. He expressed his thanks. Jaques stood up and took his leave with a firm, hearty handshake. "I, too, thank you sincerely," said Liselotte warmly in her strong, deep voice.

"I don't understand anything about your business," she said to Martin, after Jaques had gone. "But why, if you really want to bring this Wels in, don't you do it at once?"

6

Gustav Oppermann had worked all the morning with Dr. Frischlin. Dr. Klaus Frischlin, a tall, lean man with a poor complexion and very thin hair, came of a wealthy family. He had originally studied the history of art. Engrossed in his work he had hoped to become a university professor. Then his money melted away, and he starved pitiably for a time. Gustav Oppermann had discovered him when his total possessions consisted of a threadbare suit, cracked shoes, and the manuscript of a remarkably thorough study of the painter Theotokopoulos, called El Greco. In order to give him something to do, Gustav had started an art department in Oppermann's Furniture Stores and had made him its head. Gustav, in his blind optimism, had at first dreamed, through the presence of Klaus Frischlin, of having the firm handle such modern styles as steel and architectural furniture. However, he very soon realized that the art department had to bow to the middle-class demands of the Oppermann customers. Klaus Frischlin still endeavoured in devious ways, but in vain, to smuggle in his own fastidious taste. Gustav was amused and touched by these attempts. He was fond of the tenacious fellow and often employed him as a private secretary and research worker.

Gustav had sent for Frischlin this Wednesday as he always did on that day. He did, in fact, intend working at his biography of Lessing. But wasn't it tempting envious fate to busy himself with it on such a day as this? Accordingly, he gave up the idea and applied himself instead to a brief examination of his life from a chronological point of view. Had it not occurred to him that very morning how difficult it was to find one's way about one's own life? A fiftieth birthday would be the ideal day to introduce some sort of order.

Gustav was well versed in the biographies of many men of the eighteenth and nineteenth centuries. He knew the decisive experiences in the lives of these men. It was curious how difficult it now seemed to decide what was important and what irrelevant in his own destiny. Yet he had lived through many exciting experiences, influencing his own fate and everyone else's: he had known war and revolution. What had fundamentally affected him? He was shocked to realize how much had left him indifferent. This self-examination was making him nervous.

He ceased his meditations abruptly and smiled. "Please take a postcard, my dear Frischlin," he said. "I want to dictate." He dictated:

"Dear Sir:
   Take note of this for all your life:
            It is upon us to begin the work,
            It is not upon us to complete it.
                         Yours very sincerely,
                         Gustav Oppermann."

"A fine sentence," observed Klaus Frischlin. "Isn't it?" said Gustav. "It's out of the Talmud." "To whom is the card to be addressed?" asked Frischlin. Gustav Oppermann smiled boyishly and mischievously. "Take it down," he said. "To Dr. Gustav Oppermann, Berlin-Dahlem, Max Reger Strasse, 8."

Aside from the dictation of this postcard, the morning remained unproductive. Gustav was glad when he found a plausible excuse to stop work. This excuse materialized charmingly in the person of his mistress, Sybil Rauch. Yes, Sybil Rauch drove up in her funny, disreputable little car. She had a

certain air of importance about her, as usual. Gustav came to
meet her at the front door. Unembarrassed by the presence of
Schlüter, the servant, who had come to open the door for her,
she stood on tiptoe and kissed Gustav on the forehead with her
cool lips. That was not exactly a simple matter for under one
arm she clutched a large parcel, her birthday present.

This present proved to be an old-fashioned clock. Above the
dial-face it had a movable eye, a so-called God's Eye, an eye
which moved, every second, from right to left, and was never
still. Gustav had thought for a long time of installing such a
clock in his workroom, a kind of constant reminder, which
would incite its rather easy-going owner to regular work. But
it had been difficult to find a case which would harmonize
with the room.

He was pleased that Sybil had discovered the right one. He
thanked her boisterously, sincerely, charmingly. At bottom he
was a little disappointed. This wandering eye that was to keep
him under observation, wasn't it a kind of criticism of him
when she put a thing like that in his room? He would not
permit this unsympathetic feeling to become a definite thought.
He kept on talking, affectionately, animatedly. But Sybil's
gift had again aroused in him, against his will, that subcon-
scious feeling which he would never admit to himself, namely,
that Sybil, in spite of the fact that they both had the best intentions of being entirely absorbed in each other, would always remain on the outer fringes of his life.

Sybil, meanwhile, was standing in front of the portrait of
old Oppermann. She knew how much Gustav thought of the
picture, was glad to see it there at last, and commented in a
few apt phrases on how well it looked in the study. She examined it closely, summing up, in her characteristic way, the
shrewd, kind, happy man of the portrait. "They all go well
together," she said finally, "the painter, the man, and the
period, and they all fit nicely in here. I wonder how this Im-

get on in our times?" she added

:upid remark. It was interesting to
.nuel's type might fare nowadays.
Sybil's gave Gustav another slight

that in which Immanuel Opper-
:he fact that it was still very much
rifling their anxieties seemed, how
v slow, regular, and dull was a
:l Oppermann in comparison with
f today! Sybil's observation had of
t came automatically to the mind in
And yet Gustav had, quite unjusti-
fiably, the impression that it was directed against himself. The
clock ticked, the God's Eye moved from side to side and
watched how they spent their time, Sybil stood before the picture of the dead man. He experienced again the feeling of
uselessness, that slight, disturbing uneasiness, the feeling of
futility, which he had had that morning.

He was glad when Schlüter announced that luncheon was
served. It was a cheerful meal. Gustav Oppermann was a
judge of good food. Sybil Rauch was full of amusing ideas and
knew how to express them charmingly and aptly. Her South
German accent sounded pleasantly in Gustav's ear. He was
fifty years old and still very young. He beamed.

His happiness was complete when Professor Arthur Mühlheim, his friend, dropped in during dessert and brought Friedrich Wilhelm Gutwetter, the novelist, with him. The two were
excellent foils to Gustav and Sybil.

Arthur Mühlheim, a brisk little man with a wrinkled, cheerful, and clever face, was a few years older than Gustav. He was
never still, was ready for any number of practical jokes, was
one of the best lawyers in Berlin, and had similar tastes to

Gustav's. They belonged to the same club, liked the same books and the same women. Arthur Mühlheim was also interested in politics, Gustav Oppermann in sport, so that they always had plenty to talk to each other about. Mühlheim had sent Gustav a large consignment of special cognac and brandy, vintages which were actually of the year of Gustav's birth. He considered it beneficial to drink liquor of the same age as oneself.

Friedrich Wilhelm Gutwetter, a small man of about sixty, very careful of his person, wore noticeably old-fashioned clothes and had huge, childlike eyes in his placid face. He was the author of scrupulously polished tales, highly praised by the critics, but read and valued by very few people. In the rare moments when Gustav worried about the bristling emptiness of his life, he would tell himself that he had not lived in vain because he had helped Gutwetter to get on. The fact was that Gutwetter, without Gustav's support, would have had to endure the bitterest privation.

Friedrich Wilhelm Gutwetter sat quietly and happily, looked admiringly and covetously at Sybil out of his big eyes, often had to have Mühlheim's nimble sallies explained to him before he could understand them, and interjected slow observations of a general poetic character into the others' noisy and lively talk.

He had brought a present for his friend, but he did not mention it for twenty minutes or half an hour; the rapid talk of the others and the sight of Sybil had made him quite forget about his present. It was this: he told them he had had an interview with Dr. Dorpmann, his publisher, the head of the Minerva Press. They had spoken of the Lessing biography. Dr. Dorpmann, as is the way of publishers, wanted to give an evasive answer. But he, Gutwetter, stuck to his point. It was a fact, it was as certain as death, the existence of the soul, and the resurrection, that the Minerva Press would bring out the Lessing biography. In his quiet, gentle voice, he told them the

whole story and looked at his friend Gustav in a calm and exceedingly friendly manner.

"What do you mean by certain as the existence of the soul
and the resurrection?" asked Mühlheim. "Do you mean hundred percent certain or hundred percent uncertain?" "I mean
certain, absolutely certain," answered Gutwetter with imperturbable amiability.

But they had some difficulty in understanding each other.
For Gustav had jumped up with a shout, seized the stout and
placid Gutwetter by the shoulders, shook him and slapped him
on the back with noisy expressions of joy.

Later, when Herr Gutwetter was alone with Sybil, he said
in his quiet, pleasant tones: "How easy it is to make people
happy. A biography. What is a biography? As if anything else
mattered but creative work. And yet here a man goes rum-
maging round among odds and ends, so-called reality, among
faded, worn-out things, and is quite happy. What a child our
friend Gustav is." Sybil looked pensively into his big, shining,
childish eyes. Friedrich Wilhelm Gutwetter was ranked as one
of the foremost of German stylists. Many thought him the
finest. Sybil, who was conscientiously painstaking over her
little tales, asked him to help her with a certain sentence which
she could not get right. Gutwetter gave her his advice. He
gazed at his docile pupil with joy and admiration.

Gustav meanwhile was in the highest of spirits. He found
the world a magnificent place and wanted to do everyone a
good turn. He even gave his servant Schlüter a minute account of the glad tidings that Friedrich Wilhelm Gutwetter
had brought with him. He was happy.

7

When the first of his guests had arrived and were standing talking to one another in a rather formal way, Gustav had been afraid it would be a boring evening. It had been rash to bring people of so many different types together. But it was just that which charmed him most in his manner of living, the fact that he made an organic whole of separate units. He desired—in fact he had set his heart on it—to gather about him this evening all those who meant something to him: his family, his business associates, his friends from the Bibliophile Society, from the Theatre Club, from the sporting world, his women. Now, after dinner, he was glad to see that the excellent dainty courses of the carefully planned menu had raised the spirits of everyone and that all the previous formality had vanished.

There they stood or sat together, his guests, about twenty of them, in groups, and yet in such a way that no group was quite separate from another, and chatted amiably. They talked of politics. That was, unfortunately, inevitable nowadays. Jaques Lavendel, as usual, was the most at his ease. Stout and sluggish, he sprawled in the most comfortable armchair, his shrewd, kindly eyes half shut, and listened with ironical indulgence while Karl Theodor Hintze condemned the Nationalist movement lock, stock, and barrel. According to chief clerk Hintze, its adherents were without exception dunces or swindlers. Herr Jaques Lavendel's broad face smiled with provoking forbearance. "You are unjust to people, my dear Herr Hintze," said he, in his hoarse, amiable voice, shaking his head. "It is the very strength of this party that it disregards reason and appeals to instinct. It needs intelligence and will-power to proceed as consistently as those fellows do. The gentlemen understand their customers, as every good business man does. Their goods are shoddy, but saleable. And their propaganda is first-class, let me tell you. Don't under-estimate their leader, Herr Hintze. Oppermann's Furniture Stores could congratulate themselves if they had such a good director of publicity."

Herr Jaques Lavendel did not speak in a loud tone. However, without effort, his hoarse voice compelled attention. But the others were reluctant to agree with him. Here, in the charming rooms of Gustav Oppermann, people were not inclined to concede that a thing as imbecile as the Nationalist movement had a chance. Gustav Oppermann's books were ranged along the walls, the library and study formed a unit of good taste and comfort, the likeness of Immanuel Oppermann, shrewd, kindly, tremendously life-like, watched the company. One's foundations were firm, one was equipped with comprehensive knowledge, enjoyed the fine things bygone centuries had developed, had a substantial bank balance. It seemed ridiculous to imagine that the tame, domesticated beast—the common man—threatened to revert to his wolfish nature.

The brisk chief clerk Siegfried Brieger made merry at the expense of the leader of the party and his movement. The leader was not a German, he was an Austrian, his movement was Austria's revenge for the defeat she had suffered at the hands of the Germans in 1866. Was it not an impossible undertaking to make a law of Anti-Semitism? How was one to know who was a Jew and who was not? "They can spot me all right, of course," said Herr Brieger coolly, pointing to his big nose. "But have not the majority of German Jews so merged themselves in the nation that it really only rests with them whether they admit that they are Jews or not? By the way, do you know the story of the old banker Dessauer? Herr Dessauer thought his name too Jewish. He changed it. He announced: 'From now on I am no longer Herr Dessauer but

Herr Dessoir.' Herr Cohn met Herr Dessauer in the tram. 'Good morning, Herr Dessauer,' says he. Says Herr Dessauer, 'Excuse me, Herr Cohn, but my name is now Dessoir.' 'Pardon, Herr Dessoir,' says Herr Cohn. Two minutes later he calls him Herr Dessauer again. 'Excuse me, Dessoir,' Herr Dessoir corrects him emphatically. 'Pardon, pardon,' says Herr Cohn, excusing himself volubly. The two gentlemen leave the tram and walk a little way together. Herr Cohn asks, after a few minutes: 'Could you tell me, Herr Dessoir, where I can find the nearest *Pissauer?*' "

Herr Jaques Lavendel relished this anecdote. The author Friedrich Wilhelm Gutwetter did not understand it at first and had to have it repeated. Then a cheerful smile spread over his quiet face. "After all," he said, pointing to Herr Lavendel, "this gentleman expressed in a concise way what is coming to a head among people of that sort. The authority of sober reason is being undermined. The paltry varnish of logic is being scraped away. An epoch is at hand during which the large, partially hyper-developed animal, known as man, will revert to his fundamentals. Aren't you thrilled to be living during these times?" Quietly, he turned his head with its shining, childlike eyes around the group. His ample necktie covered the opening of his waistcoat; in his old-fashioned apparel he resembled an ascetic priest.

The others smiled at the author. He figured in centuries. They were obliged to figure in shorter terms: in years, in months; to them the Nationalist movement merely stood for a brutal agitation, stirred up by military and feudal elements who hoped to derive a profit from the low instincts of the small citizen. This was the view of the cynical Professor Mühlheim, who made frivolous and clever jests about it. It was the view, expressed with all caution, as befitted clever business people, of the Oppermanns; it was the view of the ladies Caroline Theiss and Ellen Rosendorff. But suddenly one of the guests upset the pleasant mood of the evening and translated into the sober speech of every day, disconcertingly, what Jaques Lavendel had expressed with cool prudence and Friedrich Wilhelm Gutwetter in general poetic terms. It was the girl Ruth Oppermann, aged seventeen, who had been silent the whole evening and now suddenly burst out: "You all have such excellent theories, you explain everything so cleverly, you know everything. The others know nothing, they don't care a rap if their theories are stupid and all contradictory. But they know one thing. They know exactly what they want. They act. They do something. I tell you, Uncle Jaques, and you, Uncle Martin, *they* are going to do the trick and you will get left." She stood there, a little awkwardly, the blue dress hanging badly on her body. Her mother, Gina Oppermann, did not understand how to dress her. Her black hair looked dishevelled, despite the careful coiffure. But her large eyes peered passionately and resolutely out of her tan face; her speech was maturer than that of a child.

The others had stopped talking, there was absolute silence when she had finished; only the loud ticking of the clock was audible, and the God's Eye moved from left to right, from right to left. Professor Edgar Oppermann, smiling a shade ironically, was at the same time proud of his spirited daughter. But Gina Oppermann, her mother, a small, insignificant woman, was completely enchanted by Ruth. Ruth was just like her father, she would certainly one day be as great as he, the great doctor. She was very different from the other girls they knew. She had only two interests, politics and medicine. She was a Zionist and already spoke Hebrew fairly well. She intended to study in Berlin, London, and Palestine and then establish herself as a doctor in Palestine.

Gustav Oppermann was pleased with his niece Ruth. He often made fun, in a genial way, of her Zionism. But he considered it a good thing that this type existed in the Oppermann family. If it had not been for her passion and intensity, something essential would have been lacking. Her fanaticism made her seem actually beautiful. She was young enough to be pardoned for her absurdities.

The pretty, blonde, sharp-nosed Caroline Theiss watched the impetuous, plain girl with amusement. Ellen Rosendorff, however, did not smile. Gustav Oppermann had certainly invited some curious people to meet one another. Ellen Rosendorff, tall, slim, and dark-skinned, with almond eyes, had met Gustav Oppermann at the Red and White Tennis Club. She was fond of society, sport, and flirtations. Her sophistication was a piquant contrast to her biblical appearance. She had a sharp tongue and enjoyed small, malicious jokes. She was one of the young Jewesses with whom the Crown Prince flirted, and the remark she had made when the Prince's car, which he drove himself, had had a narrow escape from an accident, was known all over town. "You must drive carefully, monsieur. Just think of us two lying underneath the smashed car in a single unrecognizable mass. One can't conceive Jewish bones in the mausoleum at Potsdam, and those of a Hohenzollern in the Jewish cemetery at Weissensee." She had scarcely ever changed her tone with Gustav Oppermann either; they talked of nothing but the thousand little things that rich and idle people talk about. And yet it was more than a superficial pleasure in each other's company that bound the two together. He realized that her sophistication was a defensive mask, that actually she was melancholy, tortured by the futile activities of her existence. And she was aware of similar traits in him, which, however, were less apparent and which he would not admit. She watched Ruth Oppermann now with a serious and inquisitive expression. If anyone would take the trouble, he could turn Ruth Oppermann, without difficulty, into a fashionable Berlin lady; but it would, in most cases, be useless to attempt to make Ruth Oppermanns out of fashionable Berlin ladies.

Professor Edgar Oppermann, the doctor, was standing talking to Rector François, headmaster of the Queen Louise School. Edgar, like all the Oppermanns somewhat stout, but possessing at the same time a certain elasticity of movement, was midway between dark and fair. He merely smiled at the foolish, arbitrary character of all race theories. How many blood tests had been made, how many skulls had been measured, how many hairs had been examined, all to no purpose! Edgar Oppermann talked animatedly, not at all dogmatically, using many swift gestures. His hands were sensitive, slimmer than those of the other Oppermanns. They were the hands of a great surgeon. "I have never noticed," he concluded, smiling, "that the larynx of a so-called Aryan reacts to a certain stimuli in a different way from that of a Semite." He was neither Jew, nor Christian, nor Semite, nor Aryan; he was a throat specialist, a scientist, so sure of his ground that he did not think it worthwhile to show either scorn, anger, or pity for the race-theorists.

Rector François agreed with him enthusiastically. He, too, was in the first place a scientist, a philologist. A passionate devotee of German literature, a member of the Bibliophile Society for many years, he was a great friend of Gustav Oppermann. Human nature, he declared, had not changed in the least within the memory of man. If one were to consider the movement started by Cataline, one would be astonished to find how closely it resembled, to all appearance, the Nationalist movement. Exactly the same methods were employed in those days: mass meetings, wild talk, unscrupulous statements, vilest ignorance.

"Let us hope that we too may soon find a Cicero in our midst," he concluded. The lean gentleman with his delicate, rosy complexion, his strong rimless spectacles, and his white, trim, upturned moustache spoke fluently, neither too quickly nor too slowly, in well-turned, printable sentences. He would certainly have preferred to devote himself to the volumes in the library rather than to the idly conversing people about him. However, more often than at the books, he cast furtive glances at a large, stocky lady in a dark silk dress, his wife. He was under her strict observation. If Frau François lost sight of him for a moment, she would be sure to find him again the next.

She had by no means an easy time of it with her husband. He was so careless, always blurted out just what he thought. The political situation was, of course, quiet for the time being, but Frau François put no faith in this tranquillity. Envious colleagues had their ears wide open everywhere, they carefully treasured each chance word. The moment the Nationalist party got the upper hand, an imprudent word, uttered today, might rob a man of his position, of his bread-and-butter. What would happen to her and their three children then? No one would pay him a cent for his treatises on the influence of the ancient hexameter on the vocabulary of Klopstock. But the thoughtless man would not listen to such arguments. He always believed everything was all right as long as one could prove one's statements. If she tried to explain to him that now-adays accuracy meant nothing and became a little heated on the subject, he would patiently raise his eyes to heaven in mild protest. He would call her "Little Thundercloud." Oh, he didn't understand that it was only for his sake that she was worrying. He had no sense in practical matters. Frau François pressed her lips together, looked gloomy. Rector François glanced at her, then nervously looked away at once. "Little Thundercloud," he thought.

François officiated at the Queen Louise School, to the Lower Sixth form of which Martin's son Berthold belonged. Martin joined them. He knew François as a man of liberal views, easy to talk to. Yes, François agreed, in most schools nowadays the Jewish boys did not have an easy time. But he had been able, so far, to keep his own establishment free from political influence. Now, to be sure, he was to be given a senior master from Tilsit, regarding whom he felt a certain uneasiness. He stopped at a look from Frau François, who could, however, hardly have heard what he was saying.

Jaques Lavendel, meanwhile, was further expounding his theories to his sister-in-law Liselotte and his wife Klara. Klara, like all the Oppermanns, was stout and thick-set. Her large head with its light brown hair and massive brow gave an impression of calmness; she might be stubborn but was not stupid. When she had decided to marry the Eastern Jew, Jaques Lavendel, everyone advised against it. But she had made up her mind. The very traits that appeared unmannerly to others: the frankness with which he bluntly expressed the conclusions at which his commonsense had arrived, his kindly shrewdness—all these things attracted her. She was silent by nature but she had decided opinions and, whenever it came to an issue, she stood by her convictions. She was listening now, in silent, smiling agreement, to what Jaques was explaining to her and her sister-in-law Liselotte. It was to the effect that the growth of all dangerous movements had been watched for years, often for decades, without the logical inferences ever having been drawn from them. What history had taught him was Amazement. A tremendous amazement that each time those in jeopardy had been so slow in thinking about their safety. Why, in the devil's name, had so many French aristocrats been so asinine as to be caught in the Revolution, whereas any schoolboy nowadays knows that the writings of Rousseau and Voltaire, decades earlier, had indicated precisely what would happen.

Martin Oppermann watched the two women who were listening attentively and with amusement to Jaques Lavendel.

Liselotte's large face, with its almond-shaped grey eyes, seemed
very fair beside the broad, heavy head of her sister-in-law. She
sat there, alert and radiant, her neck white and very youthful
as it rose out of the shallow opening of her black dress. She
smiled swiftly at him, showing her big teeth, then turned
again to Jaques Lavendel. Martin was a little jealous of his
brother-in-law. He felt Liselotte's approval of Jaques as a kind
of mild reproach against himself. He was well aware of the
ability of these Eastern Jews, of their boundless energy. Real
qualities, no doubt. But didn't Jaques's hoarse voice, his per-
sistence, repel her? The hoarseness had originated during
the war, when a glancing bullet had wounded Jaques in the
throat. That was too bad, naturally, but it did not make the
man the more attractive. At least not to him. It was, of course,
better that Liselotte got on well with Jaques than that she
felt repulsion for him. Could anyone imagine a more successful
marriage than theirs? Perhaps it was because he took such
pains to keep his business away from his private life. In
Cornelius Strasse he never mentioned Gertraudten Strasse.
Why, indeed, should Liselotte care whether he sold a chair for
thirty-six or forty-three marks? All the same, it was a pity that
she did not care. She had received the information about the
merging of the two Oppermann branches into the German
Furniture Company with pleasant coolness. Just the same, it
was too bad.

His brother Edgar, too, had received the information pretty
coolly. Gustav would take it harder than Edgar, Jaques, and
Liselotte. It was a blessing he had so many other interests to
divert him. Gustav was really a charming fellow. He had
surely only invited the two chief clerks to give him, Martin,
pleasure. Gustav did everything easily. He was a happy man.

Martin did not begrudge him his happiness. He also rejoiced
deeply in Edgar's happiness and fame. Things did not come so
easily to everyone. All right, let it be he, Martin, who had the

harder lot. He pulled out his eyeglasses, polished them, and put them away again. In a sudden gust of emotion he went over to Gustav, touched him lightly on the arm, and drew him across the room to Klara and Jaques Lavendel. Then he fetched Edgar in the same way.

There they sat together, the Oppermann brothers and sister, solid, secure. It was a stormy time, they too had had their share of the deluge, but they could stand that, they remained firmly on their feet. They and the picture of old Immanuel belonged together. They could justify themselves to the picture, its colours had not faded on their account. They had won a place for themselves in this country, a good place; but they had paid a good price for it. Now they sat there firmly, contentedly, securely.

The others noticed the family group and detached themselves from it, so that the Oppermann brothers and sister sat alone.

The chief clerk Siegfried Brieger was particularly pleased with this emphatic evidence of family feeling. Every type of solidarity pleased him. "Unity," he said to Professor Mühlheim. "Everything depends on that. It's lucky that we Jews stick together. Like monkeys. That's why nothing can happen to us. You can cut the tree away from under us a hundred times. There's always one of us that climbs up to the top again and we others, like the monkeys, catch hold of his tail and he pulls us up with him." Frau Emilie François envied the Oppermann women, from the bottom of her heart, their husbands' sense of family solidarity. It was certain that none of them would risk an imprudent remark and endanger wife and child. Ruth Oppermann stared at her uncle out of her big, intense eyes. She was sure that in the end she would be able to explain to a man, who so obviously felt his unity with his family, the unity with his tradition.

Sybil Rauch, too, was watching the Oppermann group. She

stood there, slim and resolute, her eyes looking resentful under the high, headstrong, childlike, brow. No one could have said that the picture by André Greid was a caricature. It was a curious idea of Gustav's to stage these family scenes for his friends. Sentimental. Silly. He was young for his age, he looked well, he loved her, and she was fond of him. He helped her, he understood a good deal about her affairs, she hardly knew how she could get on without him. But it was coming out now, he was really nothing but a sentimental old Jew. She looked across at Friedrich Wilhelm Gutwetter, comparing them. Gustav was ten times as clever, ten times as much a man of the world. But the author, with his big eyes, in his obsolete dress, at once ridiculous and touching, was all of a piece. Everything about Gustav was involved, multiple, divided, there was layer upon layer of him. There was his family, his intellectual interests, his sport, his feeling for her, his strange affection for that person Anna in the background. Where was the real Gustav?

Gustav himself was completely happy. He had drunk, not too much, he never did that, but enough to feel exhilarated. The only pity was that the others did not see how completely and unconditionally happy he was. That he enjoyed women, friends, his family, and his house was perfectly obvious to everybody. That he enjoyed books, his efforts on behalf of the author Gutwetter, his Lessing biography, was known to a few. But the happiness that came from uniting the two, from this two-fold possession—that was a joy which, at most, only Mühlheim and François understood.

But even if the others could not understand, he wanted to do his best to make them as happy as possible. He decided to treat them to some of the cognac, which Professor Mühlheim had sent him, the cognac which had been distilled in the year of his own birth, 1882.

Schlüter brought the bottle, a gigantic bottle, and the big, bulging glasses. But a further ceremony was necessary before people would drink. Chief clerk Karl Theodor Hintze was a stickler for formality. It would be a shame to gulp down such splendid stuff as this gloriously fragrant old French cognac without a few suitable words of introduction. In his sharp military tones, in the midst of a universal silence, he gave eloquent expression to the wish that the brothers and sister Oppermann and the firm of Oppermann might endure for many more decades in the flourishing and thriving position, in the prosperity, so to speak, in which the company saw them now. Not until he had finished did the guests begin to drink.

8

Sybil Rauch took her departure with the rest. Her disreputable little car came in for the jesting comments it always did. As soon as the others were out of sight, she drove back. She had promised Gustav to spend a little more time with him alone.

The room was full of smoke. Schlüter and Bertha had gone to bed. The temporary staff of assistants had left. They went out on to the terrace overlooking the garden. It was very cold, there was a cloudy moon, the Grunewald pines stood stiff and motionless. Sybil was astounded at the change in the view, but Gustav knew it in every phase.

He shivered in the chill evening. They turned back, and soon went to bed. Gustav, Sybil's long, narrow head on his breast, lay tired and happy. Yawning, at peace, he told her, for the fourth time, how glad he was that the contract for the Lessing biography had given him a task for the ensuing year.

Sybil lay awake. As she wanted to get home before daybreak it was not worthwhile going to sleep. As though he were a stranger, she looked at the sleeping man, with curiosity, without pity. Did he really believe that the Lessing biography was "a task"? The Lessing biography would be a thick volume. There was a slim little volume by Friedrich Wilhelm Gutwetter entitled: *The Prospects of Caucasian Civilization.* Sybil Rauch thrust out her underlip scornfully, like a naughty child.

She got up and dressed, shivering a little, quietly. Gustav slept on.

She went into the study. She had left her handbag lying there. On the desk lay a lot of papers covered with writing. Sybil was an inquisitive girl. She rummaged about among them. She found a postcard.

"Dear Sir:
    Take note of this for all your life:
          It is upon us to begin the work,
          It is not upon us to complete it.
                  Yours very sincerely,
                  Gustav Oppermann."

Sybil looked at the address and the signature, read the card twice, and smiled. Her friend Gustav was an amusing man. He knew many useful truths. She carefully put the papers back again into the disorder in which she had found them.

She drove home in her little, open, shabby car, through the cold night. Her friend Gustav was one of those who had "arrived," there was no doubt of that. It had been very easy to see that today, when he had arranged that exhibition of the things that made him rich and happy. Sybil Rauch was a shrewd, sceptical girl. She was sceptical also regarding herself, she did not over-estimate her talent. She knew that her pretty little stories were more scrupulously devised than the average productions. She took a lot of trouble over them, she had developed her individual style. But her secret ambition was to

write something on a bigger scale, a big, epic work, a mirror of
the age, a novel:

> "It is upon us to begin the work,
> It is not upon us to complete it.

Take that to heart, my girl. Take that to heart, Sybil."

9

In the Lower Sixth of the Queen Louise School, during the
five minutes' recess between the mathematics and the German lesson, the boys stood about and talked excitedly. The
authorities had now at last made up their minds who was to
succeed Dr. Heinzius, the master who had come to so lamenta-
ble an end. Their choice had finally fallen upon Dr. Bernd
Vogelsang, hitherto senior master at Tilsit School, the man
whom Rector François had referred to at Gustav Oppermann's
birthday party as causing him a certain amount of uneasiness.
The boys were anxious to see their new form master. Much
depended, for each one of them, upon what type of man the
new teacher was. As a rule, it was a snap for the Berlin boys to
have to deal with provincial schoolmasters. They felt themselves superior to them from the very start. What could a man
from Tilsit know about life? Was there a sports pavilion
there, or a subway, or a stadium, or an aviation field like the
Tempelhof or a Luna Park or a Friedrich Strasse? Besides the
boys knew already that Dr. Vogelsang was tainted with Nationalism. In the Queen Louise School, under the mild and
liberal Rector François, Nationalism was not popular.

Kurt Baumann, one of the boys, related for the hundredth
time a case which had occurred in the Kaiser Friedrich School.

The fellows there had found a peach of a way of showing the Nationalist senior master, Schultes, which side his bread was buttered on. As soon as he got going with his nonsense they started humming with their mouths shut. They had practised for days, so that the combined humming drowned out the voice of the master, without anything being noticeable on the boys' faces. At first the senior master Schultes thought the reason for the noise was an aeroplane. He had been encouraged in this belief. When, however, the aeroplane regularly turned up every time he started his sickly rot about the Fatherland, he smelt a rat. But they kept their secret. Immense pains were taken to discover the reason for the noise, a thousand conjectures were made. Was it the central heating, the water supply, or men in the cellar? They kept the fellow guessing. He was a nervous, sensitive man, that Nationalist senior master Schultes. When the humming started for the fourth time, he burst into tears and turned his face to the wall. Later, to be sure, when the board of trustees took up the investigation, the Nationalists in the class gave the game away and the ring-leaders were punished. All the same, what the boys at the Kaiser Friedrich School had managed to do had been pretty good. The idea might also come in handy at the Queen Louise School, in case the gentleman from Tilsit tried to abuse them.

Heinrich Lavendel did not consider the idea practicable. He was sitting on his desk opposite his place, fair-haired, sturdy, swinging his legs alternately as though he were doing gymnastics. Heinrich Lavendel, in spite of the fact that he was rather short, looked healthier and stronger than most of his companions. They were nearly all pale and had an indoors look about them. His delicate skin was fresh and bronzed. He devoted all his spare time to taking exercise in the open air. Gazing with interest at the tips of his swinging legs as they flashed in and out, he said thoughtfully: "No, that's no use at all. It might work the first and second time, but we would be caught the third time." "What can we do, then?" asked Kurt Baumann, slightly hurt. Heinrich Lavendel stopped swinging his legs, looked round, opened his extremely red lips, and said lightly, shrugging his broad shoulders: "Passive resistance, my lad. That's the only sensible line to take."

Berthold looked thoughtfully with his piercing grey eyes at his cousin Heinrich Lavendel. That chap had an easy time of it. To begin with he was an American. Sometimes, even now, an English word often rose to his lips out of memories of his early years. Secondly, he was the indispensable guard of the Lower Sixth's football team. These were two facts which were bound to make an impression on a Nationalist teacher. His, Berthold's, position was more difficult. Not only because the new man was to teach German and history, Berthold's favourite subjects, but, above all, because it depended on this man whether he would be allowed to make his speech on "Humanism."

A group had gathered round another of the boys, Werner Rittersteg. There were six or seven of them and they were the Nationalists of the class. They had not had an easy time of it so far, they were coming into their own now. They held their heads together. They whispered and laughed and put on important airs. The senior master Vogelsang was a member of the executive committee of the "Young Eagles." That was important. The Young Eagles were the secret society of the youth of Germany, the atmosphere around that society was full of adventure and secrecy. They formed blood-brotherhoods, they had a secret court. Whoever betrayed their slightest plan was cruelly punished. The whole thing was enormously exciting. The senior master Vogelsang would certainly let them join.

This senior master Vogelsang, meanwhile, was sitting in Rector François's office. He sat erect, not leaning back, his reddish hands, covered with downy fair hair, resting on his thighs, his pale blue eyes fixed unwaveringly on François, de-

termined to get this interview over with with as few gestures
as possible. Involuntarily, Rector François looked for the sabre
at the side of his new senior master. Bernd Vogelsang was
not tall, but he made up for his lack in stature by an excess of
vigour. The upper and lower parts of his face were separted
by a flaxen moustache. A long scar divided his right cheek
into two sections and a straight parting divided his hair.

Already, two days ago, when he reported to Rector François,
Bernd Vogelsang had received no favourable impression of the
establishment. Everything he had hitherto seen confirmed all
his previous gloomy forebodings. Of the entire staff of the
place he only approved of a single person, Mellenthin the
porter. He had stood at attention to the new senior master.
"Were you in the Service?" Bernd Vogelsang had asked.
"In the 94th," Mellenthin the porter had answered. "I was
wounded three times." "Right," Vogelsang had replied. But so
far that had been the only good mark he had been able to
give. That milksop, Rector François, had let the school go to
the dogs. It was a good job that he, Bernd Vogelsang, had
turned up in time to put new life into the thing.

Rector François gave him a friendly smile from under his
white, trim moustache. Frau François had told him to be sure
and make himself agreeable to the new master. The new master was not making it easy for François. His curt way of speaking, the concise, sharp, and at the same time banal arrangement
of his phrases, his hackneyed, editorial style, were all deeply repugnant to him.

The new man had turned, with a sudden jerky movement,
to contemplate a fine, old marble bust. It was an ugly, profoundly shrewd head, that of the author and scholar, François
Marie Arouet Voltaire. "Do you like that bust, my dear colleague?" asked the Rector politely. "I like the other better,"
declared the new master bluntly in his broad, squeaking East
Prussian accent, pointing to the opposite corner, at the bust of

another ugly man, the head of the Prussian author and king, Friedrich von Hohenzollern. "I can understand, Herr Rector," he went on, "why you have placed the great king's antithesis facing him. On the one side the man of spirit in all his grandeur, on the other the creature of intellect in all his paltriness. The dignity of the German is emphasized by the contrast. But allow me to confess frankly, Herr Rector, that I should find it disagreeable to have that grinning French rascal before my eyes all day long." Rector François continued to smile, doing his best to be polite. He found it difficult to make contact with the new teacher. "I believe it is time," he said, "for me to introduce you to your class."

The boys stood up as the two gentlemen entered. Rector François spoke a few sentences. He spoke more of the dead Dr. Heinzius than of Dr. Vogelsang. He gave a sigh of relief when he had closed the door between himself and the new master.

Dr. Vogelsang had stood stiffly erect during the Rector's speech, with his chest thrown out and his pale blue eyes staring straight before him. He now sat down, smiled, and did his best to be genial. "Well, boys," he said, "now we're going to see how we shall get on with one another. Show me what you know." Most of the boys had disliked the new teacher at first sight. The high collar, the affected air of smartness, did not impress them. Provincial, from the darkest corner of the provinces at that, they had said to themselves. But his first words were not clumsy ones, that was not a bad tone to take with the Lower Sixth.

It was a lucky chance for Vogelsang that they happened to be reading just then "Arminius's Fight," by Grabbe, a piece by a semi-classic poet of the first half of the nineteenth century, crude, weak in ideas, but full of genuine passion, at times extremely picturesque. The battle fought by Arminius, the magnificent entry of the Germans into history, this first great vic-

tory of the Germans over the Romans was a favourite theme
of Bernd Vogelsang's. He compared the poems written about
Arminius by Grabbe, Klopstock, and Kleist. He asked few
questions himself, he gave his tongue free rein. He was no
lover of subtleties, he did not care for shades of meaning as
the dead Dr. Heinzius had, his object was to infect the boys
with his own enthusiasm. He occasionally allowed them to put
in a word. He assumed the tone of a comrade, wanted to find
out at the start to what extent they were familiar with patriotic
poetry. One of them mentioned Kleist's wild hymn, "Germania to Her Children." "That's a magnificent poem," cried
Vogelsang with enthusiasm. He knew the piece by heart and
recited some of the powerful lines of insane hatred against the
foreigner:

> "Every biding-place and meadow
> Colour with their bones ash-grey;
> Whom the fox and whom the raven
> Scorned, let them be fishes' prey;
> Choke the Rhine with their foul corpses,
> Let it—heaped with their dead bones—
> Change its foaming course and circle
> The Palatinate's proud stones.
> 'Tis a frolic when the huntsman
> Finds the wild wolf's hidden lair.
> Strike him dead! The law of nations
> Questions not your reasons fair."

Vogelsang recited the hate-verses with ecstasy. The scar which
divided his right cheek turned red, but the rest of his face remained as rigid as a mask, while the words issued from between his high collar and his small, flaxen moustache. They
had a particularly odd effect in his broad East Prussian accent.
The entire man was a little ridiculous. But Berlin boys have a
delicate ear for what is honest and what is put on. The boys of
the Lower Sixth were well aware that the man who stood be-

fore them, ludicrous as his appearance was, spoke from the
heart. They did not laugh. They looked, instead, with a certain
abashed and inquisitive air at this fellow, their teacher.

When the school-bell rang, Bernd Vogelsang had the impression that he had won all along the line. He had got the
Lower Sixth of a liberal, hostile Berlin school well in hand.
Rector François, that milksop, would be astonished. The class
was, of course, already deeply corrupted by the subversive
poison of Berlin intellectualism. But Bernd Vogelsang was full
of confidence: he would manage to rock his nurseling's cradle.

In the quarter of an hour's recess which followed he sent for
the two boys who were scheduled to give the next lectures.
Talking is more important than writing. He considered that
thesis of the Leader of the Nationalist party sacrosanct, he
took the lectures very seriously. He soon came to an understanding with the first boy, who intended to speak on the
Nibelung legend, on the subject: "What is the lesson for
modern times of the struggle of the Nibelungs with King
Etzel?" "*Bon!*" said Vogelsang. "We can do a great deal with
that."

But what was the intention of the other boy, that grey-
eyed one? "Humanism and the Twentieth Century"? He took
a good look at the grey-eyed boy. A tall chap, of striking appearance. The black hair and the grey eyes didn't go together.
A boy like that might fit all right in Berlin: in a band of
young men, marching in step, he would be incongruous. "I beg
your pardon?" asked Dr. Vogelsang. "Humanism and the
Twentieth Century? How can one usefully discuss such a
gigantic theme in a mere hour?" "Dr. Heinzius gave me a
few tips," said Berthold modestly, his fine, deep, manly tones
much subdued. "I am surprised that my predecessor approved
of subjects of such an abstract character," continued Dr. Vogelsang. His voice sounded sharp, squeaky, and pugnacious.
Berthold was silent. What could one answer? Dr. Heinzius,

who would certainly have had something to say, lay in the cemetery at Stahnsdorf. Berthold himself had thrown a shovel of earth on the coffin. Dr. Heinzius could not help him now. "Have you been working long at the subject?" the squeaky voice asked again. "I have pretty nearly finished the lecture," Berthold answered. "I was to give it next week," he added almost apologetically.

"I'm sorry for that," said Vogelsang, courteously enough. "I don't like such abstract subjects. I should like to forbid them on principle." Berthold pulled himself together, but he could not prevent his chubby features from twitching just the tiniest bit. Vogelsang noticed it, not without a certain satisfaction. To conceal it, he repeated: "I am sorry you have gone to so much trouble. But, *principiis obsta*. After all, work is its own reward."

Berthold had really grown a little pale. But the other was right. One could hardly explain humanism in an hour. Vogelsang was not a sympathetic figure to Berthold; but he was a devil of a fellow, he had shown that during the lesson. "What subject would you suggest to me, sir?" he asked. His voice sounded hoarse.

"Let's see," meditated Dr. Vogelsang. "What's your name, by the way?" he asked. Berthold Oppermann told him. Ah, thought the teacher, that explains it. That was the reason for choosing that odd subject. He had already noticed the name, particularly, in the class-list. There were Jewish Oppermanns and there were Christian Oppermanns. No need for a long investigation. The Jew, the despoiler, the enemy, betrays himself to the expert at a glance. Humanism and the Twentieth Century. They always hide themselves behind masks of long words.

"How would it be," said he lightly, in the tone of a comrade—in dealing with this dangerous boy it was worth while taking double precautions, "how would it be if you took Arminius the German as the subject for your lecture? What do you say, for instance, to the theme: 'What can we learn today from Arminius the German?'"

Senior Master Vogelsang sat motionless at his desk, his eyes fixed inflexibly upon the boy. Is he trying to hypnotize me? thought the latter. Arminius the German, indeed. His name was Arminius the Cheruscan, man. Anyhow, whether it's Arminius the Cheruscan or Arminius the German, that makes no difference to me. It doesn't interest me. He stared hard at the teacher's scarred face, at the precise parting of his hair, at his staring, pale blue eyes, at his high collar. It doesn't interest me. I don't care a hang about it. But if I say no, he'll think me a coward, for certain. Humanism is too abstract for him. Arminius the German. He's only trying to provoke me. I get you, my boy. I shall say I'll think it over. Then he'll answer, yes, do, my boy. And it'll sound as if he said: shirker. Am I a shirker?

" 'What can we learn today from Arminius the German?'" came the squeaky voice of Vogelsang once more. "What do you say, Oppermann?"

"All right," said Berthold.

The sound of his answer had not yet died away, when he wanted to take it back. He ought to have said: I'll think it over. He had wanted to say that. But it was too late. "That's fine," Vogelsang approved. He was having a good day of it. He had emerged the victor from this interview too.

Berthold, when the others asked him during the next recess how he was getting on with the new chief, was monosyllabic. "He's just half and half. We'll have to see." He did not say more.

He generally went a good part of the way home with Heinrich Lavendel. The two boys rode their bicycles, their books and notes fastened with leather straps to the handle-bars, now close to each other, one's hand on the other's shoulder, now separated by the traffic.

"He's messed up my lecture for me," said Berthold. "That's tough," said Heinrich. "The swine. He just thinks to himself: 'I'm master.' It's simply personal spite." Berthold did not answer. They were separated by passing cars. At the next red light they found themselves side by side again. They kept close together, each with a foot on the roadway, hemmed in by cars. "He suggested to me: 'What can we learn from Arminius the German?'" said Berthold. "Did you agree to it?" asked Heinrich, amid the hooting of motor-horns. "Yes," said Berthold. "I wouldn't have," said Heinrich. "Look out, he's trying to put you in a tough spot." Yellow light, green light, they rode on. "Have you any idea what he may have looked like?" asked Berthold when they found themselves together again. "Who?" asked Heinrich, who was thinking about the afternoon's football practice. "Arminius the Cheruscan, of course," said Berthold. "I expect he looked just as much a wild Indian as the rest of them," was Heinrich's opinion. "Think it over a little, will you?" begged Berthold. "O.K.," said Heinrich. Often, when he wanted to speak heartily, the words he had used as a child came to his lips. Then the boys' roads separated.

10

Berthold wrestled with his subject. The whole thing was one great battle and Dr. Vogelsang was the enemy. Vogelsang had had the luck to choose the ground. He had the sun and the wind in his favour and knew the lie of the land better than Berthold. Vogelsang was wily. But Berthold was plucky and tenacious.

He sat brooding over the books which dealt with his subject, Tacitus, Mommsen, Dessau. Had Arminius the Cheruscan actually accomplished anything? His victory had been precious little use to him. Only two years later, the Romans were across the Rhine again; they recovered two of the three lost eagles of their legions. The whole thing was only a colonial war, a kind of Boxer rebellion, which the Romans soon settled. Arminius himself, when he had been conquered by the Romans, was slain by his own countrymen. His father-in-law looked on from the Emperor's box while Arminius's wife and son walked in chains in the Roman triumphal procession.

What can we learn from Arminius the German? General considerations were no use to Berthold. He had to have striking pictures: The fight. Three legions. A legion means about six thousand fighting-men. With its baggage-train and other appurtenances, ten to twenty thousand. Swamps, forests. It must have been very much like Tannenberg. A camp of fortified baggage-wagons, the thickening fog. Above all, the Germans hated the Roman law-makers. They temporarily spared their lives so as to put them to death later on with exquisite tortures. The Germans, Berthold read in the book by the nationalistic historian Seeck, believed that common law was inimical to personal honour. They did not want any law. That was the chief reason for their rebellion.

It was essential to know what Arminius had looked like. That point had struck Berthold at once. Again and again, with concentrated effort, he tried to get an idea of him. The monument in the Teutoburg Forest, a tall pedestal with a conventional statue upon it, didn't help at all. "Look here, man, that Arminius of yours was no fool," Heinrich Lavendel said to him. "Those boys must have had a different kind of intelligence from ours, a sort of American Indian point of view. He was a cunning devil, that's certain." No doubt he had that Nordic craftiness, Berthold meditated, about which everyone talked nowadays. Dr. Vogelsang had it too.

Berthold lay awake during the night, he often did now. He had only the small lamp on his bed-table switched on. The wallpaper had a delicate design, repeated a hundredfold: an exotic bird sitting on a drooping twig. If one half closed one's eyes, the line which formed the bird's breast, taken with the line of the suspended twig, produced the contour of a face. Ah, now he had it. That was the face of Arminius. A broad forehead, a flat nose, a big mouth, a short but strong chin. Berthold smiled. Now he had got his man. Now he had got the better of Dr. Vogelsang. He went peacefully to sleep.

Up to now, Berthold had not confided his difficulties to anyone except Heinrich Lavendel. From then on his taciturnity left him. Only in the presence of his parents did he keep silent. They noticed that the boy was excited about something, but they knew from experience that if they asked him what it was, he would only get stubborn. So they waited for him to speak of his own free will.

But Berthold talked to a good many others, and collected a good many opinions. There was, for instance, that experienced man of the world, the chauffeur Franzke. For him, the battle in the Teutoburg Forest held no problem. "The whole thing is clear," he decided; "in those days there might have been some justification for National Socialism." Jaques Lavendel, on the contrary, declared that the barbarians had made the same mistake at that time that the Jews made seventy years later, that is to say, they had blindly revolted against a brilliantly organized stronger power. "That sort of thing never succeeds," he concluded, putting his head on one side, and drawing his lids far down over his blue eyes.

Much more sympathetic to Berthold than this sober interpretation, was his uncle Joachim's opinion. Berthold regarded his mother's brother, Joachim Ranzow, with reverence and affection. Government Director Ranzow, tall, slender, and elegant, precise in speech and character, had won the boy's heart by treating him as an adult. What Uncle Joachim had to say on the problem of Arminius the German was romantic. Berthold did not quite understand it, but it made an impression on him. "You know, my boy," said Uncle Ranzow, carefully pouring him out a strong schnaps with his long hand, "the fact that the affair ended badly doesn't prove anything.

> "One man may ask: 'Is this thing safe?'
> The second: 'Is it right?'
> Their queries show us in one phrase
> Which free man is, which wight."

Arminius was right. It was only by means of revolt, even at the risk of defeat, that the Germans came to understand their own natures, crystallized themselves, learned to live. If they had not revolted in those days, they would never have entered history, they would have had no history and would have vanished into obscurity. It was only through Arminius that they won a name and arrived. Name, reputation, is all that counts. What sort of a man the real Cæsar was, is without interest: what lives is the legendary Cæsar.

If Berthold understood that correctly, it was not alone a true likeness of Arminius that was important. The face of the statue in the Teutoburg Forest might also have a part to play. It was therefore not enough for him to have an idea, now, how Arminius looked. That was confusing. He was still far from his goal.

A chance conversation with his cousin Ruth Oppermann did not help to simplify matters. Ruth patronized him, treated him as a small boy who had grown up with misguided ideas. Well, he was young, it was necessary to free him from his prejudices, to make the truth clear to him. It was such a simple truth, too. She did her very best to rescue him. Whenever Berthold saw that plain girl with her high-strung manner, he got annoyed. But in spite of that, he was always looking for fresh opportunities to quarrel with her. It was true that she was weak in logic; but her aims harmonized with her, she was a personality, she was sound.

To Ruth Oppermann, Arminius's procedure was the only possible one. He did what a few centuries before the Maccabees had done, he rose against the oppressors and drove them out of the country. What else could one do with oppressors?

As she stood there, the great eyes flashing in her olive-tan face, her hair a bit dishevelled, as usual, Berthold was reminded of the Germanic women who went into battle with their husbands, to defend their wagon-camp. They were fair-haired, those German women, of course, their skin was white, their eyes were blue. But their hair, too, must have been dishevelled, their eyes big and wild, their whole expression probably identical.

His cousin Ruth was right, Uncle Joachim was right. He himself, Berthold, admired Arminius. The only confusing thing was that, unfortunately, Uncle Jaques, too, was right, that, in the end, nothing whatever had come of the victory of Arminius.

II

In any case the enemy, Senior Master Vogelsang, behaved himself, in the weeks that preceded Berthold's lecture, in a perfectly unexceptionable manner. Bernd Vogelsang did not want to be in too much of a hurry about anything. The Queen Louise School was dangerous ground, it was necessary to advance carefully, with Nordic craftiness. Vogelsang suspected adversaries all through the school. He classified them. Out of the entire Lower Sixth, he could find, for the time being, only two boys fit to join the ranks of his Young Eagles, Max Weber and Werner Rittersteg.

Werner Rittersteg had a pale and unhealthy complexion and a high, piping voice. He was the tallest boy in the Lower Sixth. His classmates had nicknamed him "Long Lummox." He had found Dr. Vogelsang an impressive figure from the start. He had fixed his bulging eyes on the new teacher with such doglike submissiveness, that the latter had at once noticed him. Bernd Vogelsang approved of blind subjection to authority, he interpreted it as manly loyalty. He considered the boy Rittersteg worthy of acceptance into the ranks of the Young Eagles.

The only son of wealthy parents who wanted their boy to go far, Werner Rittersteg had never hitherto, in spite of his height, distinguished himself among the rest. Of average intelligence, slow of judgment, he had not got on well under senior master Heinzius. His reception into the Young Eagles was the first great success of his life. His narrow chest swelled. It was he whom Dr. Vogelsang had chosen, and he had, with one single exception, rejected the others.

There was no doubt that the air of secrecy which hung over the Young Eagles, over their blood-brotherhood, their extraordinary, mysterious rites, their secret court was extremely attractive to the other boys, so that they envied Weber and Rittersteg. Even the level-headed Heinrich Lavendel, when he heard of the enrolment of these two, had said, "Lucky dogs!" The Long Lummox wished that Heinrich Lavendel had said more. It was precisely that boy, among all his companions, upon whom he would have liked to make an impression. He envied and admired the strength and skill with which the other was able to whirl, turn, and twist his short, sturdy body

about. In a groping, clumsy way he constantly sought to win
Heinrich's approval. He had actually learned English in his
honour. But even when he had greeted him, one day, with the
words: *"How are you, old fellow?"* Heinrich had remained
perfectly cool. It was a torment to Rittersteg that even his great
success did not alter this indifference.

Apart from the appointment of the two Young Eagles, nothing sensational occurred in the Lower Sixth. The boys quickly
came to terms with their first Nationalist teacher. He was not
particularly popular and not particularly unpopular. He was
a master like any other, nobody got excited about him any
longer. Soon the phenomenal performances of Heinrich Lavendel at football again became more interesting than Dr.
Vogelsang's occasional Nationalist utterances.

Rector François, too, calmed down. He sat mildly and peacefully in his big study between the busts of Voltaire and Frederick the Great. Nearly three weeks had now passed without
the occurrence of any untoward incident. There was only one
thing that worried him. Herr Vogelsang's frightful German,
that stiff, trite, editorial, Nationalist New German. At night
when he retired, he would sit on the bed, carefully unfastening
his suspenders, and lament to his wife: "He is ruining everything I've given the boys. Thought and speech are identical.
We have struggled for seven years to get the boys to use
straightforward, lucid German. Then the Ministry of Education lets this Teuton loose on them. You can train the skull of
a new-born babe to any shape you like, make it long or broad.
Is the careful speech of our boys sufficiently drilled into them
to withstand the influence of this cramped, affected, early-
Germanic jargon? It would be a pity if the boys were to go
out into the world lacking clear ideas as well as clear speech."
His kindly eyes gazed with a worried look through the strong
lenses of his rimless glasses. "Those are not the things to worry
about now, Alfred," Frau François declared in a resolute tone.

"Be thankful that you have gotten along with him all right so far. One can never be careful enough these days."

Frau Mellenthin, the porter's wife, was disappointed. From what her husband had said, she had expected that the new man would at once distinguish himself by some great deed. Mellenthin, the porter, however, did not allow himself to be dissuaded so soon from his first opinion. "Tannenberg was not won in a day either, he'll do something yet," he declared emphatically. Frau Mellenthin took heart and repeated her husband's opinion to others; for he had a good nose for changes in the weather, and could scent every storm two days before it came.

12

At eleven twenty-five Herr Markus Wolfsohn, salesman at the Potsdamer Strasse branch of Oppermann's Furniture Stores, had begun to serve Frau Elsbeth Gericke, who wished to buy her husband a chair for Christmas. She was not quite sure whether she wanted an ordinary chair or an armchair. All she was certain of was that it must be some piece of furniture, something just for her husband. Herr Wolfsohn had shown her all sorts of chairs and armchairs. But Frau Gericke was a lady who couldn't make up her mind. Further, a purchase of this kind was a great occasion for her, which she wished to prolong to the full; she was delighted to be the object of such painstaking attention. And it was painstaking attention that Herr Wolfsohn gave her. Herr Wolfsohn was a good salesman, serving customers was his lifework.

At eleven forty-five, matters had reached a decisive stage. She was hooked, Herr Wolfsohn recognized it with the practised eye of a trade-psychologist, with many years of experience behind him. Frau Gericke, notwithstanding the time and eloquence that he had bestowed upon her, was a windfall for him. For what had hooked her was Model 483. Five years ago a large quantity of this baroque-style armchair, Model 483, had been manufactured in the Oppermann factory. Incidentally, matters had very nearly come to a crisis between the partners on its account. The senior partner, Dr. Gustav, otherwise an affable gentleman, who took no share in the conduct of the business, had claimed the chair to be in such bad taste as to compromise the reputation of the house, and it was actually this very baroque armchair, Model 483, that had caused the establishment of the art department and the appointment of Dr. Frischlin. However, Markus Wolfsohn liked Model 483. It was showy, and the petty-bourgeois customers of the firm of Oppermann liked a certain amount of ostentation. As usually happens, the model had not caught on. The chair took up a great deal of space, people's houses were small, there were less bulky and cheaper armchairs in which one could sit more comfortably. In spite of every effort, all attempts to interest customers in the baroque armchair were unsuccessful. The number was sold at a loss, for half the original price, and the salesmen who got rid of them received a five percent commission.

Herr Wolfsohn, then, was now on the point of disposing of one of these models. In glowing terms he pointed out that a note of elegance at once pervaded any room adorned by this baroque armchair. He had invited Frau Gericke to prove for herself how comfortable the chair was. He could not forbear to add, quite incidentally, how very distinguished she looked in it.

At twelve-eight he had pulled it off. Frau Gericke declared herself prepared to acquire the baroque armchair, Model 483, for the sum of ninety-five marks.

Herr Markus Wolfsohn had therefore forfeited eight minutes of his lunchtime, which began at twelve and ended at two. But he did not mind that. On the contrary, he felt quite elated. He had known in his bones that this difficult customer would in the end be hooked by Model 483, that venerable fixture. Twelve-eight, that was eight minutes lost. But four marks seventy-five earned. That was fifty-nine pfennigs a minute. A splendid profit. If every minute of his time were paid for at that rate he would be glad to sacrifice the whole of his lunchtime.

Herr Wolfsohn hurried to get to Lehmann's Café, where he was accustomed to spend his noonday leisure. But first he bought the *Berliner Zeitung*. This was provided free at Lehmann's, but it was always in use, and today, after the windfall supplied by the purchaser of the armchair, he could afford to buy his own paper. He found his favourite seat by a window, unpacked the sandwiches which his wife had prepared for him, and sipped his hot coffee. Herr Lehmann, the proprietor, came over in person to his table. "Everything satisfactory, Herr Wolfsohn?" he inquired. "Everything satisfactory," confirmed Herr Wolfsohn.

Chewing and sipping, he scanned his newspaper. Unemployment figures were rising; this crisis was terrible. He personally, to be sure, had nothing to fear from it. He had held his position in the firm of Oppermann for twenty years. He was safe. He had, in spite of the crisis, earned a commission, that very day at noon, of four marks seventy-five. It was the seventh time that November he had earned a commission. He was pleased with himself.

Herr Wolfsohn, as he turned the paper, caught sight of his reflection in the mirror. He had no illusions on the subject. He was tolerably decent-looking. But some of his colleagues were better-looking. In the mirror, there confronted him a gentleman who was more on the short side than on the tall, with a dark-skinned face, lively black eyes, heavily greased, neatly parted black hair, and a black moustache that aspired, without much success, to be dashing. Herr Wolfsohn's principal worry was his small, irregular, defective teeth. It was especially the gap in the middle of the upper row that was annoying. The Health Insurance Fund had agreed to put a tooth in for him. A fellow-member of the Savings Society "Old Pickled Herrings," Hans Schulze, who was a dentist, had explained to him that the job could be much better done by means of a so-called bridge. But the insurance people wouldn't do that. He would have to fork it out himself. About eighty marks was the usual charge. "Old Pickled Herring" Hans Schulze, would do it for seventy, out of pure brotherly feeling for his fellow-member. Herr Wolfsohn might even be able to beat him down to sixty-five. Seventy marks was a lot of money. But one's bodily expenses were the most important. What they would put in his mouth he would carry about with him his whole life long, and even beyond that, until the Last Judgment. Supposing he still had thirty-five years to live, the cost would be reduced to about two marks a year, at simple interest, to about eight marks at compound. Four marks seventy-five was a fine premium and he had earned seven premiums that November. The bridge business would require six or seven attendances. Owing to lack of time, he could not think of undergoing such a lengthy treatment before Christmas. It would be fine to have his frontage fixed up again like new.

However, Herr Wolfsohn was clear on one point: that he did not owe his success in life and business to his appearance. He had wrested it from fate by ability and tenacious energy. He had studied salesmanship from the ground up. Above all, one must never shirk any trouble. Not make a mess of things. Never let a customer go, no matter how disagreeable he might be. The Oppermann stocks were well-assorted. A customer might refuse twenty models. One could always find a twenty-first. The great thing was never to appear to be tired.

Herr Wolfsohn's sandwiches were finished. But he could

still, in view of the four marks seventy-five, treat himself, today, to a chocolate *éclair* with whipped cream. He ordered one.

His pleasant anticipation was clouded for a moment by a
paragraph in his paper. He read with indignation that National Socialists had wanted to throw a Jewish-looking gentleman out of a moving train on the subway, because he was alleged to have made a disgusted face when, as they sang their
hymn, they came to the lines:

> "When Jewish blood spurts from the knife,
> Then things go right again."

But they had come up against a strong man. The other pas-
sengers helped him. The rowdies could not carry out their intention. They were, on the contrary, as the newspaper stated
with pleasure, arrested and faced with the punishment they
deserved.

Herr Wolfsohn read the news with uneasiness.

However, his uneasiness did not last. It was an isolated case
of violence. On the whole, the political outlook was more re-
assuring than it had been for a long time. Schleicher, the
Chancellor, kept a firm hand on the Nationalist party, the
peak of the movement was past. Herr Wolfsohn read that
three times a day; in the morning the *Morgenpost,* at noon the
Berliner Zeitung, and in the evening the *Acht-Uhr Abendblatt*
published irrefutable information to the effect that the National Socialists could under no circumstances achieve further
successes.

Herr Wolfsohn was in complete accord with himself and the
world.

Had he not reason to be quiet and happy? If Moritz
dropped in this evening, his brother-in-law Moritz Ehrenreich,
he'd give him a sound calling-down again. Moritz Ehrenreich,
type-setter in the firm of the United Wholesale Printing Com-

pany, Zionist, member of the Makkabi Sports Association, had a black outlook on German affairs. What was the matter with people like Moritz Ehrenreich? A few rowdies wanted to throw a Jew out of a subway train. Well, what of it? They were arrested and would get the punishment they deserved. Herr Markus Wolfsohn had not had any unpleasant experiences himself. He stood on an excellent footing with his colleagues, was popular in Lehmann's Café, in the Savings Society "Old Pickled Herrings."

He was, which was perhaps even more important, popular with Krause the superintendent. It was a bit of luck, getting that comfortable three-roomed flat in the apartment unit in Friedrich Karl Strasse at Tempelhof. Eighty-two marks. It was a gift, my dear sir, a positive, absolute gift. The unit had been erected with the aid of a subsidy from the municipality. The rents were less than the ordinary rate of interest charged on the cost of building. A gift, my dear sir. Oppermann's Furniture Stores had been able to procure dwellings at this cheap rate for twenty of their employees. He owed his to chief clerk Brieger; in other words, to his own business efficiency.

Unfortunately, rent agreements were only concluded for a period not exceeding three years, and twenty months were already gone. But Herr Wolfsohn was thick with Krause the superintendent. He knew how to manage him. Herr Krause was fond of telling jokes, which were very old and always the same. It was not easy to maintain an attitude of suspense when listening to them, not to laugh too soon, not too late. Markus Wolfsohn could do it, though.

He licked some whipped cream out of his moustache and called for his bill. His good humour increased as he took out his purse. It wasn't only because of the seven commissions. It was because the entire balance for the month of November was first class.

Herr Wolfsohn was paid, during a month, after all due deductions, two hundred and ninety-eight marks. In addition to that, commissions and percentages averaged fifty marks. He gave Frau Wolfsohn three hundred marks to cover the entire household expenses of the family of four. After deducting the price of his commutation ticket on the subway, therefore, he had left, for noonday coffee and pocket-money, about forty marks. Herr Wolfsohn was in the habit of going, once a week, to the "Old Fritz" restaurant to play skat with the "Old Pickled Herrings." He was a good player, and his winnings, in spite of the fact that twenty percent of them had to be paid over to the Society, often enabled him to increase his monthly income by six or seven marks. This November he had had marvellous luck. At the monthly audit of accounts he would be able to hold out fully eight to ten marks from Frau Wolfsohn.

While he waited for his bill, he meditated gloatingly over possible ways in which the secret surplus he had kept back might be spent. He could, for instance, buy a few ties, which he had had his eye on for a long time. He could ask Fräulein Erlbach of the bookkeeping department to go out with him. He might again back a foreign horse in Meineke's cigar shop. Back a horse. Of course, man, that was it. Eight or even twelve marks is a fine sum to have, but the morsel becomes really juicy when it grows into eighty or one hundred marks. Markus Wolfsohn goes the whole hog, they knew that in his business, and so did the "Old Pickled Herrings." He would pop in at Meineke's straight away, now, before he went back to business, and back that horse.

Herr Meineke greeted his old client with pleasure. "You're quite a stranger, Herr Wolfsohn. Well, what is the hunch to-day?" he went on. "Marchesina is pretty well thought of," he declared. "But as you know, my dear Herr Wolfsohn, I never express an opinion myself." No, Marchesina was no go so far as Herr Wolfsohn was concerned. There was a horse running called Quelques Fleurs. Herr Wolfsohn was proud of his elegant French accent. "No," he said, "I'm all for Quelques Fleurs."

After the excitements of the morning and noon, it was a quiet afternoon. And then came the best part of the day, the evening.

Markus Wolfsohn during his trip home, though the air in the subway was smoky and stuffy, already felt the thrill of the snug security which would surround him in his home. He went up the steps from the station. Here, already, were the familiar trees. Here the strip of meadowland which was going to be built up next year. Now he was in Friedrich Karl Strasse. And here was his beloved block of apartments. Yes, Markus Wolfsohn was fond of that block, he was proud of its two hundred and seventy flats, each as like the other as so many tins of sardines.

And Herr Wolfsohn belonged in his flat just as the sardine does in its tin. *My home is my castle* was one of the few English sentences he remembered from his three years at the technical school.

He climbed the stairs of the house. The smell of cooking met him on every floor. Radio music sounded through the doors. His door was the one on the right on the third floor.

Before he opened it he had the slight sensation of fury he experienced every day. For on the door next his own was a visiting card, which read: Rüdiger Zarnke. Herr Wolfsohn looked at the visiting card grimly. He was a mild man, but he was often possessed of a furious desire to tear that card down. He felt himself on common ground with all, or at least with the great majority, of the inhabitants of the block. Their joys, their sorrows, and their opinions were his own. They were his friends. Herr Zarnke was his enemy. It was not only that Herr Zarnke's brother-in-law had made frantic efforts to obtain possession of the flat next door to Zarnke's, which was his, Herr

Wolfsohn's flat. Herr Zarnke was also in the habit, every chance he got, of hanging three flags with the hooked cross on them out of his three windows. Herr Wolfsohn had continual reason to be irritated by Herr Zarnke. The walls were thin, he could hear Herr Zarnke's loud, grating voice from morning till night. He often met him on the stairs, too. He could not help noticing that Herr Zarnke had big, strong, white teeth.

With a baleful look of suppressed fury, then, at the visiting card, Herr Wolfsohn opened the door of his flat. From the kitchen came the sound of his wife's clear, sing-song voice: "Is that you, Markus?" He often made jokes about that foolish question. "No," he answered, full of good-humoured sarcasm. "It's not me." She went on bustling about the kitchen. He took his collar off, exchanged his brown business suit for an old, threadbare suit, his shoes for well-worn, comfortable slippers. He shuffled over into the other room, took a smiling look at his sleeping children, the five-year-old Elschen and the three-year-old Bob, and shuffled back. He sat down in the black wingchair, acquired in Oppermann's Furniture Stores at a special price, a real bargain, a windfall. He sniffed with relish the odour of the pickled cutlet, the so-called Kasseler Rippespeer. There was no need for him to turn the radio on. He could listen in to Herr Zarnke's radio. It was pleasantly noisy music today. He looked it up in the paper: aha, *Lohengrin*.

Frau Miriam Wolfsohn—he called her Marie—bustling, with fair, reddish hair and a rather plump figure, brought in the meal. There was a bottle of beer with it, cold and tempting. Herr Wolfsohn took up his newspaper, ate, drank, read, and listened to the radio while his wife talked to him. He enjoyed his evening peace with all his senses.

However, what Frau Miriam Wolfsohn had to tell him in her garrulous way was not altogether pleasant and she expected him to make a fuss about it. She spoke of the necessity of buying a new winter coat for the five-year-old Else. It was

really a shame that Elschen had to run about in such an outgrown coat. Frau Hoppegart had already made pointed remarks about it. The child had outgrown the coat all around.
"Your young one looks like a bursting sausage," Frau Hoppegart had pertinently observed. It was time that Elschen's coat
be passed on to Bob. Frau Wolfsohn had begun her story before Telramund had accused Elsa of Brabant. When Lohengrin challenged Telramund to battle, she was dealing with
the amount that Elschen's coat would probably cost. She esti-
mated it at from eight to ten marks. Naturally, Herr Wolfsohn made a fuss. But Frau Wolfsohn saw at once that he was
not taking it tragically. By the end of the first act of *Lohengrin,* they had agreed on buying the little coat by Christmas.

Frau Wolfsohn cleared away the meal. Markus Wolfsohn
sat down again in the black wingchair, finished reading his
newspaper, let it fall, and while Lohengrin and Elsa celebrated their wedding and the smell of the Kasseler Rippespeer
and the sauerkraut still lingered pleasantly in the room, he
looked thoughtfully at a certain greyish-brown stain on the
wall near the ceiling. Very shortly after the Wolfsohns had
taken possession of the flat this stain had appeared on the wall.
It had been quite tiny to begin with. But now it had got bigger. It was just above a remarkable picture called "The Waves
at Play," which represented gods and goddesses swimming
about and playing tag. The picture came from the art department of Oppermann's Furniture Stores. Herr Wolfsohn had
been allowed to have it extraordinarily cheap in spite of the
fine frame. A month ago the distance between the picture and
the stain had been at least as wide as two fists. Now it was, at
most, only as wide as one. Herr Wolfsohn would have given a
good deal to know whether, and if so to what extent, the stain
showed itself on the other side of the wall too, in Herr
Zarnke's flat. But that was unfortunately impossible. There's
no dealing with people like that. They throw one out of mov-

ing subway trains. When Herr Wolfsohn had spoken to Krause the superintendent about the stain, the latter had informed him that all necessary repairs would be carried out in the spring. Besides, that sort of damp stain did not mean anything. A decent flat needs a spot just as a spinster needs a child. That might be. But, in any case, the stain was a blot on the appearance of the room. Herr Wolfsohn would have to have another talk with Krause the superintendent tomorrow.

His meditations were interrupted by the arrival of his brother-in-law, Moritz. Frau Wolfsohn brought in a second bottle of beer, and the two men had a conversation on world affairs and economics. Moritz Ehrenreich, the type-setter, was small and sturdy, had a stern, animated face, full of wrinkles, with brown, keen eyes, and tangled hair. He stamped up and down the room, his legs wide apart, quarrelsome as usual, full of the most gloomy presentiments. He was not inclined to regard the assault on the Jew in the subway as an isolated case. Such occurrences were going to be the order of the day in Germany, he proclaimed, just as they were at one time in Tsarist Russia. Fire and sword would come to Grenadier Strasse, to Münz Strasse, and even the Kurfürstendamm would not escape. People were going to see something.

Markus Wolfsohn had another bottle of beer brought in and listened with pleasure to the popping noise it made when it was opened. He regarded the squat, boxer's figure of his brother-in-law with quiet irony. "Well, and what are we going to do about it, Moritz?" he asked. "Shall we all join the Makkabi Club and learn to box?"

Moritz Ehrenreich did not approve of such silly jokes. He knew exactly what ought to be done. One had to have five hundred English pounds, in order to emigrate to Palestine. Because of the fall in value of the pound he had got much nearer to his goal during the last few months. He already had four hundred and forty pounds. "If you were wise," said he, "you, Markus, and you, Miriam"—he called his sister Miriam just as obstinately as Herr Wolfsohn called her Marie—"if you were wise, you'd come with me." "Must I learn Hebrew in my old age?" Herr Wolfsohn jested good-humouredly. "You'd never manage it," jeered Moritz Ehrenreich. "But you ought to make the children learn Hebrew. As a matter of fact, there is a girl by the name of Oppermann in our class who is getting on very well with it."

It gave Herr Wolfsohn something to think about, an Oppermann learning Hebrew. He listened, too, with interest, to the statistics with which Moritz Ehrenreich supplied him. Palestine was one of the very few countries which had escaped the crisis. Exports were increasing. They were also going ahead with sports in that part of the world. Herr Ehrenreich expected to be able, in not such a very long time, to watch the Olympic Games there. He spoke with violent emphasis, pacing excitedly up and down. His words tumbled over one another. His enthusiasm was infectious.

All the same, Herr Wolfsohn did not have the faintest intention of leaving Berlin. He was fond of the city, he was fond of Oppermann's Furniture Stores, he was fond of the block of flats in Friedrich Karl Strasse, of his family, of his dwelling. *My home is my castle.* He gazed in comfortable assurance at the picture in the fine frame, where the gods and goddesses were playing tag. If it were not for the stain above it, and Herr Zarnke next door, he would be completely happy.

13

Resting his elbows upon it, Professor Edgar Oppermann sat at his desk in the director's room at the throat hospital. He was staring sternly at the piles of printed and written papers that lay before him. Much as he loved every other task connected with his activities, he hated this room, the office work, his administrative duties. Senior Nurse Helene, who stood near the door, with determination in every line of her stout person, appraised him anew each morning, as though he were an interesting case which had just been brought in. She knew that the two faces which Edgar Oppermann most frequently showed to the world, one serious, austere, calm, and the other brisk and confident, were masks. Yes, he was, by nature, an indomitable and cheerful worker, he was by nature confident. But it was a strain for him to show that confidence, that energy, all day long, to hundreds of people, one after another. She knew that his brisk air was often artificial, put on.

Nurse Helene generally got on well with her Professor. But when he was at his desk, he was difficult to deal with. She observed, above his nose, those vertical furrows which were so familiar to her. Not a good sign. It was just after eleven o'clock in the morning. Professor Oppermann had finished his consultations, made two or three visits to private patients, but a strenuous day's work still lay before him. However, she knew that his first energy had already been used up, and that he would have to crank himself up again. He was overworked. Her Professor was always overworked. If only Frau Gina Oppermann were not quite such a ninny, thought Nurse Helene. Here, at the hospital, she could protect him. People were always on his trail. They had even begun telephoning the Professor at his home, and Frau Gina, the poor cluck, could never say "no" to anyone.

Edgar Oppermann looked at his mail today with particular reluctance. Things got more and more tangled up every year. Details which used to settle themselves automatically now required tedious and vexatious consideration. Sternly, as though they were poorly prepared examination papers, he glared at the letters.

Nurse Helene stepped resolutely to the desk. She pointed to a piece of paper upon which something was written, underlined three times, heavily, in red. She asked him bluntly: "Have you seen that, Professor?" Professor Oppermann, in his doctor's smock, not altering the position of his head and propped elbows, squinted at the note and said crossly: "Yes."

On the paper was written: "Privy Councillor Lorenz will stop by at twelve. He requests Professor Oppermann to be in, if at all possible."

Edgar Oppermann snorted. "Of course it's about Jacoby." "What else should it be about?" Nurse Helene asked sternly. "The Jacoby case has been dragging on quite long enough."

"The Jacoby case," Edgar Oppermann reflected. Was there, in fact, a Jacoby case at all? The whole affair was really so simple. Dr. Müller, second of the name, hitherto chief physician at the throat hospital, had accepted the professorship at Kiel. Edgar Oppermann would very much have liked to see Dr. Jacoby, his favourite assistant, appointed to the vacancy. Six months ago the appointment would have been made, within a fortnight, in accordance with Oppermann's wishes. Dr. Jacoby was scientifically particularly well qualified to hold the position, he was a splendid diagnostician and indispensable to Oppermann in the laboratory. But he was a clumsy fellow, born of a poor family in the Berlin ghetto. He was insignificant-looking, ugly, inhibited. Formerly such things would not have mattered. Edgar Oppermann knew that, as soon as Dr. Jacoby, who had endured the hardships of starvation in order to complete his studies, was free of the more pressing of his financial anxieties, as soon as he could set to work without hindrance, he would go very far indeed. It had to be admitted that Dr. Jacoby reminded one of the caricatures of Jews in the comic papers. But what was, after all, more important to a patient, the fact that the doctor had a pleasant face, or that he diagnosed his disease correctly?

Edgar sighed. So Privy Councillor Lorenz wished to speak to him. Lorenz was the presiding physician of all the clinics in the municipality. He was not very strong in theory but he was a hard-working practitioner, and he did not despise theory, as many such practitioners do. He respected learning and gave it his humble support to the best of his ability. He had also agreed, in principle, to support the candidacy of Dr. Jacoby. Nevertheless, Edgar felt a certain uneasiness at the prospect of this interview.

Lorenz was coming at twelve. Edgar had, therefore, to leave his round of visits in the wards to Dr. Reimers. "All right," he sighed. "I'll be here at twelve. If I should be a few minutes late, please ask Privy Councillor Lorenz to wait for me." Edgar was always late. Nurse Helene always allowed for that. It was convenient today. She had certain things to discuss with Privy Councillor Lorenz which concerned her Professor.

Edgar turned towards her. Now that he had come to a decision, his face changed. It was again the brisk, confident face of Edgar Oppermann as the world knew it. "At any rate, I still have time to go to the lab, haven't I, Nurse?" he smiled. "And as for all this," he pointed to the papers in front of him. "As for all this, you can let me off it today, now that I have consented to see Lorenz." He grinned slyly, like a schoolboy sneaking off from an unpleasant task, stood up, and was out of the room in a moment.

With a rapid step, toes turned in, he sailed through the long, linoleum-covered corridors to the laboratory. Dr. Jacoby sat over the microscope, a little man with stooping shoulders. Edgar Oppermann gave him a quick sign not to disturb himself. But Dr. Jacoby rose. The slim, worried-looking, awkward fellow gave Edgar the soft, dry hand of a child. Edgar knew of the trouble he had, being naturally inclined to excessive perspiration, to keep his hands always dry so he would not be

hampered in his professional work. "We must not deceive ourselves, Professor Oppermann," said Dr. Jacoby. "The outcome
of case 834 is hopeless. It was in its third stage."

Edgar shrugged his shoulders. The Oppermann treatment,
that surgical operation which had made him famous, could no
longer be applied, after a certain stage, without the risk of a
fatal result. He had never denied that. With Dr. Jacoby, he
became absorbed in a discussion of the cases. It was important
to define the various stages of the disease minutely, to know
precisely when the second phase passed over into the third.
Some means had positively to be found to reduce the coefficient of uncertainty.

Dr. Jacoby argued with his chief passionately yet haltingly.
The conviction forced itself upon the latter more persistently
than ever, that if anyone was the right man to perfect the Oppermann treatment, it was this fanatic for precision. To that
fellow Jacoby, the figures of the statistics of the disease-charts
were really more important than the figures of his income. He
had completely forgotten that he was speaking to the one man
who could give him an assured livelihood. And the other, too,
completely forgot that he would very shortly have to engage
in an interview which would be decisive for the fate of his
partner. Humped up in his white doctor's smock, as if he were
freezing, the little man squatted in his seat, crouching in a stiff,
clumsy attitude. The other, however, paced up and down with
his brisk, precise stride, his toes turned in, the white smock
flapping about his legs. Both men had their minds closed to
everything which had no bearing on the vitality and fertility
of a certain bacillus.

Suddenly Edgar gave a start. He took out his watch. It was
ten minutes past twelve. The thought came to him seething
hot, that old Lorenz was waiting for him. He stopped short in
the middle of a sentence. Little Dr. Jacoby, who had been, the

moment before, still the brilliant scientist, became insignificant as soon as he no longer spoke about his microbes, and turned into the grey, ugly dwarf he really was. Should Edgar tell him that he had to leave on his account? Out of the question. Old Lorenz was a decent fellow, but there was always a coefficient of uncertainty in official business, at least as high as that in the Oppermann treatment. What a sight the lad was, sitting there, a regular Schlemihl. Edgar hurriedly gripped his hand. His own hand was not large, but the other's tiny one disappeared inside it. "You must come and dine with me one evening soon, my dear Jacoby. I want to have a real talk with you. This confounded Berlin bustle." He smiled. His face grew quite young when he smiled.

He sailed off again through the corridors. He must tell Gina he had invited little Jacoby to dinner and fix the exact time. Nurse Helene would have to remind him. If possible, it had better be an evening when Ruth was free too. Why did he suddenly think about his daughter? Obviously in connexion with little Jacoby. But why? Perhaps it was the earnestness, one really had to say, the frenzy, with which both pursued their aims. He, Edgar, smiled at Ruth's Zionism. He ought to spend more time with her. Reason, reason, my daughter. Get thee not to a nunnery, Ophelia. It was a pity that the simplest things were the most difficult to understand. He was a German doctor, a German scientist. German science and Jewish science did not exist, the only thing that existed was Science. He knew it, Jacoby knew it, old Lorenz knew it. But apparently Ruth did not know it, and certain others who mattered were still less aware of it. He thought with some uneasiness of the conference he was going to. In the end, little Jacoby would have to be sent to Palestine, he thought, smiling.

14

Matters had gone just as Nurse Helene expected in the director's room. Privy Councillor Lorenz was punctual, her Professor was late. She had time to consult with the Privy Councillor.

The Oppermann treatment, famous throughout the world, had lately been the object of particularly vindictive attacks in the Berlin newspapers. Oppermann was accused of using patients of the third class, the poor non-paying patients from the municipal clinic, as subjects for his dangerous experiments. The Jewish doctor, it was stated in the coarse jargon of certain Nationalist newspapers, did not shrink from shedding streams of Christian blood for the sake of self-advertisement. Nurse Helene was of the opinion that it was time something was done about this filthy slander. Her Professor should not let any impudent scoundrel insult him. She stood, stout and strong, at the desk. "I think it's really time I called his attention to it, Herr Privy Councillor," she declared in her quiet, energetic tones. "It's time he did something about it."

Privy Councillor Lorenz sat facing her. He was a colossus in build, with a red face beneath extremely white, short hair, a small snub nose, and rather bulging blue eyes under his thick, white eyebrows. "I should not care a hang, if I were he, my girl," he blurted out in his blunt Bavarian idiom. The words tumbled from his big mouth, with its many gold teeth, like bits of rock. "Pigsty," he grumbled, and struck the newspaper with the underlined paragraphs with his red, thick-veined hand. "The whole of politics is nothing but a pigsty. Unless one cannot help doing otherwise, one should simply ignore them. That's what annoys the pigsty crowd most." "But he holds a government appointment, Herr Privy Councillor," grumbled Nurse Helene. "If you ask me," old Lorenz grumbled back at her, "that's no reason to take action against that gang. Anyone who deals with them only soils his own hands. Don't let such things turn your hair grey, my girl. As long as the Minister leaves me in peace I shan't stir. All that"—he brushed the newspapers aside—"doesn't exist so far as I am concerned. You may rest assured of that." "Well, if that is your opinion, Herr Privy Councillor," Nurse Helene shrugged her shoulders and, as she heard Edgar coming, took her leave, her anxiety by no means allayed.

Edgar Oppermann excused himself for being late. Privy Councillor Lorenz did not rise, but stretched out his big hand and assumed a particularly hearty air. "Well, my dear colleague, I'll come to the point at once. Permit me. I should just like to go over this Jacoby affair with you thoroughly." "Is it so complicated?" asked Edgar Oppermann in his turn, instantly feeling cross and nervous.

Privy Councillor Lorenz licked his gold teeth, endeavouring to assume a still heartier tone. "What isn't complicated in these days, my dear Oppermann? The mayor is a fool. He is always licking the Ministry's boots. He scents every wind that comes from that quarter. The subsidies for the clinics, in any case, are getting more and more difficult to put through. As for the requirements in your department, my dear Oppermann, theoretical and laboratory work, they'll whine over every Reichsmark before they'll come across with it. We must take all that into consideration. Your friend Jacoby is, of course, the right man. I can't say that he is particularly agreeable to me as an individual, that would be a lie. But he's a scientist, there's nothing wrong with him there. Varhuus hasn't dared, either, to ignore him completely. But do you know whom he wants us to consider seriously? Reimers. Your friend Reimers, my dear colleague Oppermann."

Edgar Oppermann paced up and down with his short rapid

strides, automatically trying to put springiness into his heavy body. As usual, Professor Varhuus, his colleague at the University of Berlin, would be bound to object to any suggestion that came from him. To propose Dr. Reimers was deucedly clever of him. Dr. Reimers was Edgar's second assistant. He was very popular with the patients and a frank, agreeable fellow. Edgar was not against Reimers; he was for Jacoby, however. His position was a difficult one. "What is your opinion, my dear colleague?" he asked, still walking up and down.

"I have already explained to you, Oppermann," said Lorenz, "that I am fundamentally in favour of that Schlemihl of yours. But, frankly, I foresee difficulties. There are now, in certain important circles, gentlemen who value an imposing appearance higher than genuine merit. Pigsty politics again. At any rate, Reimers is ahead of your little friend Jacoby by a nose. I don't think the board will ask for sectional photographs but, after all, they may want to see what the candidates look like and may ask them to call. I doubt whether a personal appearance would improve the chances of our friend Jacoby."

Edgar came to a halt at some distance from Councillor Lorenz. "Do you wish me to withdraw Dr. Jacoby's candidacy?" he asked, and his heavy voice sounded strangely hard and determined in contrast to the grumbling of the other.

Lorenz turned his bulging eyes towards Edgar. He wanted to make a vehement reply but did not do so. On the contrary, he said in a surprisingly mild tone: "I wish nothing at all, Oppermann. I only wish to speak candidly with you, that's all. Personally, I confess, I like Reimers better but, as a scientist, I prefer your friend Jacoby."

Edgar Oppermann slowly pulled a chair into a convenient position and sat down heavily. Like all the Oppermanns, he appeared larger when seated. He looked gloomy, the artificial briskness had vanished. Old Lorenz suddenly got up and stretched. His red face with its crown of white hair looked gigantic on his huge body. Clumsily, his white smock billowing about his mighty figure, he approached Edgar. A true doctor, Lorenz had once said to a faint-hearted student, understands everything and can do everything. He fears God and nothing else in the world. His students had called him "Feargod" ever since. But today he was not an angry Jehovah. "I have no illusions about myself, my dear Oppermann," said he as mildly as he could. "At bottom I am nothing but an old country doctor. I understand my patients and I can smell out things about them that you younger people know nothing of. On the other hand there is very much that you young people know and I do not. Reimers is, on the whole, nearer my type. But I prefer your friend Jacoby."

"What's to be done, then?" asked Edgar.

"That's what I wanted to ask you," said old Lorenz. And as Edgar Oppermann still remained silent, with an unwontedly ironical expression hovering about his lips, he added: "I freely admit I could fix it up for your friend Jacoby without more ado. But that would be bad for the subsidy. Shall I risk it? Do you wish me to?"

Oppermann made a growling noise, a peculiar mixture of bitter laughter and negation. "Well, then," said Lorenz. "There's only one alternative: postpone the decision. The political situation may have altered for the better in a month's time."

Oppermann growled out something. Lorenz took it to be an assent. He breathed heavily, glad to have done with the unpleasant subject, and laid a hand upon Oppermann's shoulder. "Science is long-winded. Jacoby will just have to wait a bit." The white smock swirled around his broad hips. He was leaving. "It must be someone who combines the appearance of Reimers with the ability of Jacoby. Otherwise they won't do it. The shallowness of human nature is to blame, my dear colleague. It's a filthy thing," he added, already at the door, sounding like a departing storm. "Human nature, I mean."

When Lorenz had gone, Edgar rose, vertical furrows above his nose, feet turned in, and paced to and fro with an unwontedly slow step. Then, curiously enough, he persuaded himself that the interview had not gone so badly. Old Lorenz was in favour of little Jacoby, at any rate, and old Lorenz was a real man. His ill-humour vanished rapidly, like that of a child. When Nurse Helene came in, the sun was already shining again in his face.

Nurse Helene, in contrast to Oppermann, was less satisfied by her interview with old Lorenz. She had thought over, in her stolid way, everything he had said. He had promised not to induce the Professor to take legal action until the Minister forced him to. The Minister would, however, be certain to force him to. She would have to warn her Professor. I really think it would be better if I showed him the article.

But when she saw Edgar's beaming face she decided, in spite of her energetic character, to put it off. "Was it very unpleasant?" she contented herself with asking. "No, no," Edgar Oppermann gave her his sly, friendly smile. "The score was two-three."

15

In the five minutes' recess before the German lesson Berthold assumed a manly attitude, behaving as if he had forgotten what lay before him and talking on indifferent subjects to his companions. Senior Master Vogelsang also behaved as if the forthcoming event were not of any consequence to him. He came in, sat down stiffly at his desk, and turned over the pages of his notebook. "What was it we were going to do today? Ah, I have it. Oppermann's lecture. Now then, Oppermann."

And as Oppermann came forward, Vogelsang added, obviously in a very good humour today, in a kindly bantering and encouraging tone: "Wolfram von Eschenbach, begin."

Berthold, standing between the teacher's platform and the boys' benches, showed no sign of nervousness. He appeared unconcerned and casual, his right foot advanced, his right arm hanging down, and his left hand resting lightly on his hip. He had not chosen the easiest road, he had not shirked any of the difficulties. He had seen it through. He was quite certain now what we, or at any rate what he, could learn from Arminius the German. From the standpoint of a rationalist, the achievement of Arminius might appear useless. But such an interpretation became meaningless in view of the unbounded admiration which the heroism of this man, in the cause of liberty, had kindled in the heart of every German, especially in a German of today. Berthold wished to pursue this train of thought in accordance with the good old rules he had been taught: general introduction, statement of subject, point of view of the lecturer, the objections, the refutation of the objections, then finally, once more, the lecturer's thesis. Berthold had set down in writing, to the last comma, exactly what he wished to say. But speaking came easily to him, so he had disdained to learn his manuscript by heart in parrot fashion. He wished, while keeping to his fundamental design, to leave the wording of the individual points to the inspiration of the moment.

He stood there, then, and spoke. He saw the faces of the other boys before him: Max Weber's, Kurt Baumann's, Werner Rittersteg's, and Heinrich Lavendel's. But he was not speaking to them. Only to himself and to that fellow behind him, the enemy.

For Senior Master Vogelsang had taken up a position at Berthold's back. He sat there stiffly, uncompromisingly, and listened. Berthold could not see him, but he knew that Vogelsang's gaze was fixed hard upon him, exactly on the nape of

his neck. He felt the place underneath his collar that Vogelsang's gaze was set upon. It was as though someone were
pressing the tip of his finger there.

Berthold took pains to think of nothing but his phrases. He
was to speak for fully thirty minutes. He had got through
about eight minutes. The introduction was over, the subject
had been stated, and his thesis outlined. He had got as far as
the "proof." Then he became aware that Vogelsang's gaze was
no longer upon him. Yes, Vogelsang had risen, very quietly,
in order not to disturb the lecture. He was advancing. Berthold saw him, next, against the wall to the left. He walked
along the left-hand row of benches on the tips of his toes with
measured but careful steps. Berthold heard the slight creaking
of his boots. Vogelsang went to the rear of the room and stood
in the left-hand corner. He wished to have Berthold in front
of him, watch the words come out of his mouth. There he
stood, behind the last bench, very upright (was not one hand
resting on the pommel of an invisible sabre?), his pale blue
eyes fixed unwaveringly upon Berthold's mouth. Berthold began to feel uncomfortable under his scrutiny. He turned his
head for a moment in the teacher's direction, but this made
him still more uneasy. He looked straight in front of him,
made a slight movement, and tossed his head as if he wanted
to drive away a fly.

He finished the "proof." He was not talking so well now as
he had at first. It was very warm in the room; the rooms in
the Queen Louise School were, as a rule, overheated. His upper lip was perspiring slightly. He came to the "objections."
The achievement of Arminius, he said, had perhaps not, from
the point of view of sober reason, resulted in any permanent,
external consequences. It had to be admitted that the Romans
were, a few years later, in exactly the same position as they had
been in before the battle. Indeed——

He stopped for a moment, suddenly realized that he could

not go on. He tried to concentrate. In his mind's eye he could see the narrow pages of his Latin edition of Tacitus, the large Roman type of his fine German edition of Tacitus. He glanced again at that corner on the left. There stood Vogelsang, still motionless, attentive. Berthold opened his mouth, closed it and opened it again, looked down at the tips of his toes. It must be at least eight seconds since he had stopped speaking. Even ten. What was it he had said last? Oh, yes, that the achievement of Arminius had really had no external consequences. There was no question but that Luther's translation of the Bible and Gutenberg's discoveries had been more important to Germany and to her position in the world than the battle in the Teutoburg Forest. The achievement of Arminius, we must admit, remained, practically, without significance.

Did he want to express himself quite like that? No, he wanted to give the idea much more discreet, less blunt, less harsh expression. Well, anyhow. Get on, Berthold. Get it over. Only, no more pauses, the first had already lasted an eternity. But now he had the threads again. Now nothing more could happen to him. He would get into his stride after the "refutation." A second stop? No, Herr Doctor, impossible.

He smiled triumphantly across the room towards the far corner. "But all the same," he began again. Hallo, what was this? Why was Vogelsang's face suddenly changing in such an extraordinary manner? Why was the scar which cut through his cheek getting so red? Why was he opening his eyes so wide? None of that will do any good, Herr Doctor. I've got hold of the threads again now. You can't faze me now. "But all the same," he began, in a brisk and vigorous tone, "admitting all that——"

At that point he was interrupted. A sharp, squeaking voice issued from the corner: "No, not admitted. I do not admit that. No one here admits that. I am not going to put up with it. I refuse to listen to such a thing any longer. Who do you think

you are, young man? What sort of people do you suppose you
have sitting here before you? Here, in the presence of Germans, in this time of German need, you dare to characterize
the tremendous act which stands at the beginning of German
history as useless and devoid of meaning? You admit that, you
say. You have the effrontery to utter arguments of the rankest
opportunism and then you say: you admit that. If you, yourself, have lost every spark of German feeling, you might at
least spare us, who retain our love for our Fatherland, your
foul abuse. I forbid it. Listen to me, Oppermann. I forbid it,
not only for my sake, but for the sake of this institution, which
still remains, for the present, a German one."

A deathly silence had fallen. The thoughts of most of the
boys had been wool-gathering in the warm room. They were
sprawling, day-dreaming, but now, at the sharp, squeaking
voice of Vogelsang, they looked up at Berthold. Had he really
said something so awful? And what was it, actually, that he
had said?

It had been something about Luther and Gutenberg. They
did not quite understand Vogelsang's rage, but probably Oppermann had really gone a little too far. In these lectures one
ought to say just what was in the lesson-books, no more and no
less. It looked as though he had got himself into a nice mess.

Berthold himself, when Vogelsang had interrupted him, was
at first deeply astonished. What was the matter with the man?
Why was he shouting so? He might have had the decency to
let him finish. It had not hitherto been the custom to interrupt
the lecturer. Dr. Heinzius had never done so. But he was now
under the ground, in the cemetery at Stahnsdorf. And that
fellow was shouting. The "objections" had to be stated. They
ought not to be suppressed, they had to be refuted. That was
what we have been taught, such were the rules, Dr. Heinzius taught us that.

I didn't say anything at all against Arminius. The thing was

an "objection." I was going to refute it. There's my manuscript. I stated my own attitude quite clearly at the beginning
of Part B. He really ought to stop, he ought not to go on
shouting so.

I had an uncomfortable feeling as soon as he suggested
Arminius to me. I ought to have stuck to "Humanism." Heinrich said straight away that he was a swine, that it was pure
personal spite.

He's talking utter nonsense. My manuscript is on the desk,
in my satchel. Anyone who read it would realize that the
swine is talking utter nonsense.

What was it I really said? I don't remember exactly. It was
not in the manuscript. Nevertheless, I could cite it as evidence.
Then everyone would see what I meant to say.

I won't cite my manuscript as evidence. Arminius was a
wild Indian. I can't bear him. The "objection" was a fair one.
I have said so, that ends it.

He had abandoned his unconcerned attitude. He stood very
erect, his fleshy head held high, his grey eyes looking straight
ahead. He let his enemy's words patter over him.

The fellow at last seemed finished talking rot. Berthold
stood there, gnawing his underlip with his big white teeth.
Now he should pull out his manuscript and say: "I don't know
what you mean, Herr Senior Master. Here is the manuscript."
But he did not say it. He remained silent, embittered and im-
penitent. He kept his grey eyes fixed unwaveringly upon the
other's pale blue ones. Finally, after a pause that seemed to
last an eternity he said in a clear but quiet voice: "I am a good
German, Herr Senior Master. I am as good a German as you
are."

This colossal nerve on the part of the young Jew struck Dr.
Vogelsang dumb for a moment. Then he felt an impulse to
give his fury rein. But he held all the trumps in his own hand.
He did not want to throw them away in a burst of temper. He

controlled himself. "I see," he contented himself with saying, as quietly as the other. "You are a good German, are you? Well, will you be so good as to leave it to others to decide who is a good German and who is not? A good German, indeed." He gave a scornful snort. And then, at last, he came out of his corner, but not quietly. Every step was loud and firm. He came straight up to Berthold. Then he faced him, eye to eye. Before the tensely silent class, amidst breathless excitement, with simulated calm and moderation, he inquired: "Will you, at least, apologize for what you have said, Oppermann?"

Berthold, for the fraction of a second, had also thought of apologizing. He had said something he had not intended saying. He had said it in an unconcentrated moment and in a crude and unfortunate manner. Why not admit it? Then the whole matter would be settled, he could finish his lecture and everyone would be bound to see that he was a good German and that the fellow opposite was doing him an injustice. But confronted by Vogelsang's stare, by his disgusting, arrogant, slashed face, this impulse vanished before it had become a real thought.

The other boys all stared at Berthold. Vogelsang's attitude had impressed them. It seemed as though Oppermann had bitten off more than he could chew. But, naturally, he must not eat humble pie on that account. They waited, curious to see what he would do.

He and Vogelsang were standing eye to eye with each other. At last Berthold opened his mouth. "No, sir," he said very quietly, even modestly, "I shall not apologize, sir." Everyone was satisfied.

Vogelsang, too, was satisfied. Now he had really won. Now, owing to this attitude of Oppermann's, he would have the opportunity of showing how a German schoolmaster crushed corruptive elements. "Very well," he said. "I'll remember that, Oppermann. Be seated."

Berthold went to his seat. What he had done was certainly not very wise. He could see that by his enemy's attitude, by the light that flashed in his eyes. But if he were to be given a choice again, he would do the same thing. He could not apologize to that man.

The other decided to practise moderation at all costs. But he could not resist calling out to the boy, as he sat down among the others: "Perhaps some day, Oppermann, you will be glad if people are satisfied with such amends." His voice was casual but just this tone emphasized his triumph and his scorn. "We'll go on now with our reading of Kleist," added Bernd Vogelsang and thus concluded the incident in a lofty manner.

16

The report of what had occurred spread rapidly through the whole school. Even Rector François heard of it before the morning was over. He was not surprised when Senior Master Vogelsang paid him a visit.

Vogelsang scarcely allowed himself a disapproving glance at the bust of Voltaire, so full was he of the recent event. But he kept himself in hand, deliberately avoided all exaggeration, and gave an accurate account of the matter. François listened to him with evident uneasiness. His small, well-kept hands stroked his trim moustache nervously. "Unpleasant," he said several times after Vogelsang had finished. "Exceedingly unpleasant."

"What steps do you intend to take to punish the boy Oppermann?" inquired Vogelsang in a restrained tone.

"He's a conscientious lad," was Rector François's opinion,
"particularly interested in German essays and his lectures. No
doubt he had carefully prepared his manuscript. Perhaps we
ought to have a look at it before we come to a definite decision.
It is probably a case of *lapsus linguae*. In that event it would be
a mistake, with all due respect to your feelings, my dear colleague, to punish a slip of the tongue too severely."

Vogelsang raised his eyebrows in astonishment. "In my
opinion, Herr Rector, it would be impossible to punish such a
case too severely. At a time when the shameful peace treaty,
the treaty of Versailles, is creating havoc, a young chap has the
audacity to decry by means of insipid logic one of the most
sublime of German achievements. While we Germans, especially we recognized Nationalists, are having such an immeas-
urably hard struggle to awaken our people, a schoolboy, a
mere child, insults the efforts made by our forefathers to shake
off their chains. Such behaviour would perhaps have pleased
your friend Voltaire, Herr Rector. But how anyone can take
the trouble to look for excuses when a boy belonging to a
school which, after all is a German one, reaches such a height
of presumption, that, I must frankly confess, is more than I
can understand."

Rector François stirred uneasily in his chair. The thin, rosy
skin of his face twitched. He was almost as much disturbed by
the fellow's phraseology as by his topic. The bombastic German, the ranting, mass-meeting oratory made him physically
uncomfortable. If only the chap were nothing more than an
opportunist. The worst of it was that he sincerely believed the
gibberish he was talking. Due to an inferiority complex, he
had encased himself in an armour of the cheapest nationalism,
through which not a ray of commonsense could penetrate.
And he, François, had to listen to all this rubbish with atten-

tion and courtesy. What terrible days these were. Once more Goethe was right: "There is nothing the rabble fear more than *Intelligence*. If they understood what is truly terrifying, they would fear *Ignorance*." Yet he, François, knowing what was right, had to sit there with his hands tied. He was not allowed to protect the clever lad against that bully of a man, his teacher. For, unfortunately, Little Thundercloud was right. If one got carried away, if one dared openly to espouse the cause of reason, then the whole herd of Nationalist newspapers would begin to bellow. And the Republic is weak, the Republic always eats humble pie. It leaves one to the mercy of the bellowing herd. One loses one's job, one's bread and butter, one's children are pauperized, and one loses the best thing life has to offer: a tranquil old age.

Dr. Vogelsang, meanwhile, was explaining his view of the case point by point. *"Lapsus linguae,"* said he, "slip-of-the-tongue, you claim. But does not the importance of these school lectures lie precisely in the fact that they release, through his contact with an audience, the real sentiments of the lecturer?" He was on his favourite topic now. "Talking is more important than writing. The glorious example of the Leader proves it. And what the Leader says on that subject in his book, *My Battle*——"

At this point, however, Rector François interrupted him. "No, my dear colleague," he said. "I refuse to follow you into this field." His mild voice sounded unusually resolute, his friendly eyes flashed through the big lenses of his glasses, his cheeks flushed, he drew himself up—one realized he was taller than Senior Master Vogelsang. "You know, my dear colleague, that since the establishment of this school I have been fighting for the purity of German speech. I am not a fighter by nature; life has demanded many a compromise from me. However, I can make one statement: I have been uncompromising in this fight. And I shall remain so. Of course, I have been shown your Leader's book. Some colleagues of mine have placed it in their school-libraries. But I have not. I know of no other work so disfigured by sins against the spirit of the language as that one. I cannot permit that book to be even quoted within the walls of my establishment. I most emphatically request you, my dear colleague, not to quote that book in this house, not to me and not to my pupils. I will not have the speech of the boys ruined."

Bernd Vogelsang sat with his thin lips compressed. He was painstaking and thorough. He knew his way about the German language and its grammar. He had made a mistake. He ought not to have quoted the Leader's book to this misguided man. It was unfortunately only too true. Rector François was right in a certain sense. The greatest living German, the Leader of the German movement, was not familiar with the rudiments of the German language. He had that in common, to be sure, *mutatis mutandis,* with Napoleon, with whom he also shared the attribute of not having been born on the soil of the realm that he had come to liberate. Just the same, Vogelsang suffered because of the linguistic failings of his Leader. In his spare time he labored at the task of eliminating the most flagrant errors in the book entitled *My Battle*—that most important document of the German liberation movement—and to transpose it into a German which would be grammatically and stylistically perfect. As usual, he would have to swallow the Rector's insolence without comment. There was no counter-argument he could advance. The invisible sabre had fallen from his hands. He sat silent, lips compressed.

Rector François at first thoroughly enjoyed his own indignation. Life often compelled one to sacrifice the intellect. Little Thundercloud had wrested many a concession from him in that direction. But he had not yet fallen so low as to allow anyone to bespatter him with the mud of the book entitled *My Battle* and call it perfume. By degrees, however, the sinister look of anger on the face of his senior master and his ominous silence began to alarm him. Rector François had stoutly defended his beloved German and that was enough. He became again the conciliatory gentleman he was by nature. "Please do not misunderstand me, my dear colleague," he said soothingly. "Far be it from me to say anything against your Leader. You remember how the Emperor Sigismund silenced the bishop who corrected his grammatical mistakes. '*Ego imperator Romanus supra grammaticos sto.*' No one requires your Leader to be an expert on German grammar. But I require it of the pupils of Queen Louise School."

It sounded like an apology. But it remained a piece of impudence on the part of that fellow François to have spoken so disrespectfully of the Leader's failings. What he, Vogelsang, might think, it was not right that this effeminate creature should blurt it out. Bernd Vogelsang would not permit himself, in any case, to be diverted from his object. Not by a long shot!

At that moment vengeance for the crime which the boy Oppermann had committed became Senior Master Bernd Vogelsang's life-work.

"Let us return to the point, Herr Rector," he squeaked. The invisible sabre was back again now. "The case of Oppermann is not only one of a slander against the German race, a slander that borders upon treason in such times as these, it is also an uncommonly impudent breach of school discipline. I must ask you again: what steps do you propose to take to punish the refractory boy Oppermann?"

Rector François sat on, tired, courteous, harmless as ever. "I will consider the matter, my dear colleague," said he.

Rumour travelled swiftly in Queen Louise School. A year ago, the porter, Mellenthin, had saluted young Oppermann, the son of the furniture people, obsequiously. Now he looked the other way when Berthold left the building. However, when saluting Vogelsang, he would remain stiffly at attention even after the senior master had walked past. Who was it who had always said that the new man would, one of these days, show these donkeys what was what? And who was showing them now? Once more it was proved that Mellenthin, the porter, had a good nose.

17

In two hundred and twelve out of the two hundred and seventy flats in the block in Friedrich Karl Strasse at Tempelhof, Christmas trees were lit. They had cost anything from one to four marks apiece; they were for the most part modest little fir trees, ornamented with all sorts of fripperies, little candles and tinsel and with brightly coloured, not exactly wholesome, sweetmeats. Gifts lay beneath them, heterogeneous yet always of the same types: underclothing, wearing apparel, cigars, chocolate, toys, gingerbread. People with particularly grandiose ideas had soared to a camera or a radio. Two bicycles had also been presented on the block in Friedrich Karl Strasse. The price tickets of the various presents had, for the most part, been removed. But the recipient did not have to inquire very long before being informed of the exact cost.

In Herr Wolfsohn's flat, too, a Christmas tree had been lighted. Herr Wolfsohn had had grandiose ideas. He had paid two marks seventy for the tree. It had been marked at three marks fifty but the shopkeeper had made a reduction of eighty pfennigs. Anyway, it had been easy for Herr Wolfsohn to do things on a grand scale. The improbable had happened. The gallant steed, Quelques Fleurs, had won a smashing victory. On the first of December Herr Wolfsohn had a surplus of eighty-two marks that Frau Wolfsohn knew nothing about.

But she was to have her share in this secret hoard. He had spent his money like a lord. Here she was standing before the long-coveted reserve bedspread, astounded at its fine quality. Herr Wolfsohn had only paid twenty-five marks for it. She gazed admiringly at him. She had never come across any shop where she would have had to pay less than thirty-two marks for a bedspread like that. Neither had Herr Wolfsohn, for that matter, since he had actually paid thirty-four marks. Elschen's winter coat was of such a kind, too, that Frau Hoppegart, who had wrinkled her nose so often in the past, would have nothing left to sniff at. Even Bob had received something quite magnificent. It was a bombing plane. If you wound it up, it rose into the air and dropped a rubber ball. On its cardboard box was printed: "First-Class Bombing Plane. The terms of the Versailles treaty forbid Germany to protect her frontiers. The day will come when Germany will break her chains. Remember."

However, Herr Wolfsohn had also thought of himself. The insurance people could keep their silly tooth. He was going to treat himself to the bridge. That very morning he had begun to turn his dream into a fact. He had telephoned Hans Schulze of the "Old Pickled Herrings" and given him the commission to renovate his frontage. He would, of course, tell Frau Wolfsohn that he had finally persuaded the insurance people to supply the bridge. As soon as the work was finished, he would pay Schulze fifty marks down, the balance of fifteen marks he could easily pay in small instalments. The work would be started directly after Christmas, and during the first days of the new year Markus Wolfsohn would be able to introduce his new tooth to his astonished associates. He kept the secret to himself, did not say a single word about it even to Frau Wolfsohn. But, inwardly, he was very proud of himself. He imagined what he would look like with his new frontage. He had visions of posters from which beamed elegant gentle-

men with large white teeth. *"Keep smiling."* As soon as he
had the new teeth, everything would be smooth.

From the radio set came the sounds of bells, choruses, and
hymns. The children sang "Stille Nacht, heilige Nacht." They
were singing it in almost all the flats in the block of Friedrich
Karl Strasse. For quite a while a feeling of consecration hov-
ered over the block. It was as evident in the Wolfsohns' flat as
elsewhere. Then one of the parts of the bombing plane broke
off. Little Bob was scolded, howled, and was put to bed. Then
a twig of the tree caught fire. Elschen was scolded, howled,
and was put to bed.

While Frau Marie was busy with the children, Markus
Wolfsohn sat in the black, high-backed, bargain-price wingchair, day-dreaming and at peace. Thus many others in the
block in Friedrich Karl Strasse sat: day-dreaming and contented. The contentment of each individual increased the general contentment. Herr Wolfsohn was one of these contented
people. He wished everyone well.

Except one person. He smiled broadly, with entire satisfaction, when violent yelling came from the next-door flat, drowning the sound of the radio. Without having to strain his
imagination, Herr Wolfsohn gathered that young Zarnke
had broken part of his bombing plane and was getting a
thrashing. Herr Zarnke indicated, during this scene, how much
the bombing plane had cost him. He had had to fork out two
marks eighty pfennigs. The news heightened Herr Wolfsohn's
gratification. For he had only paid two marks fifty.

In other respects, too, Christmas evening in the Zarnkes' flat,
so far as one could judge by external indications of its progress,
was less peaceful than at the Wolfsohns'. Frau Zarnke had told
her husband three times that a certain pair of brown leather
slippers in the Tempelhof branch of Tack's Stores were extraordinarily cheap. Herr Zarnke had not however made her a
present of those leather slippers, but himself one of the Lead-

er's book, *My Battle*. While professing the greatest respect for her husband's political activities Frau Zarnke considered this behaviour selfish, and was unable to restrain herself from expressing her views in metaphorical, yet forceful language. Herr Zarnke, for his part, replied, as a German man should, without metaphors. The loud and long dispute augmented Herr Wolfsohn's comfort.

He sat smiling in his black wingchair, contemplating the picture of "The Waves at Play" and the stain on the wall, which had now spread to a point below the picture, listened to the solemn melodies of the radio and to the row next door. He felt himself at one with all the other occupants of the block in Friedrich Karl Strasse. His Christmas was a quiet, happy one.

18

The next evening the Wolfsohns were the guests of the Moritz Ehrenreichs in Oranien Strasse in the centre of Berlin. The Wolfsohns did not often visit the Ehrenreichs. In fact, they seldom went out at all. Markus Wolfsohn felt most at his ease in his own flat. But it was Chanukka, the Feast of Lights, the Feast was very late this year, it usually came from two to four weeks before Christmas. It had become a habit with the Wolfsohns to visit their relatives in Oranien Strasse on this holiday.

Markus Wolfsohn, still in the mood which the preceding happy Christmas evening had induced, sat at his ease in one of the two armchairs covered in green rep which adorned the living-room of his brother-in-law Moritz, and smoked one of the twenty cigars with which Moritz Ehrenreich had munificently presented him on the occasion of the Feast. They were fifteen pfennig cigars. What with one thing and another the evening had cost Moritz at least seven or eight marks. He was really a queer old bean, that lad. He was enlightened, read a great deal, and in spite of all that stuck obstinately to old-fashioned nonsense like this Chanukka Feast. Or wasn't it such nonsense after all, for a man in Berlin, in 1932, to light candles to celebrate a victory won by some savage old Jewish general two thousand years ago over some savage old Syrians? Were there any signs visible today of the tolerance which that savage old general was alleged to have brought about? People threw Jews out of moving subway trains. Was that tolerance?

Nevertheless, Herr Wolfsohn looked with good-humoured interest at the strange illuminator which Moritz had kindled in order to celebrate the Feast in accordance with the ancient ritual. It was a horizontal rod, irregular in shape, with eight openings and small spouts for oil and wick and a ninth light in the very front. Behind this rod was a triangular screen, made of very thin silver with embossed images of Moses and Aaron: Moses with the sacred Tablets and Aaron in a tall cap and priestly robes. The Ehrenreichs had inherited the candlestick from the wife's family. It was very old. What might be its actual value? Herr Wolfsohn asked himself that question every year. When one sells such things, one never gets anything but a fraction of what one expects.

They now sang the hymn, "*Moaus zur yeshuosi,*" Rock and Refuge of my Redemption. It was a very ancient hymn, a kind of Jewish national anthem. Moritz always declared that he kept the Feast on national, not religious grounds. The tune was impressive. Moritz set to with a will, the clear voices of the women and children joined in, Markus Wolfsohn himself growled out something. The noise of the singing drowned the sounds of the radio sets from the flats above, below, and next door. When the song was finished, Frau Miriam, nicknamed

Marie, observed that the Chanukka anthem was really finer than the Christmas hymn, "Stille Nacht, heilige Nacht." Moritz Ehrenreich retorted peevishly that he was unable to judge. Herr Wolfsohn's decision was that both songs were equally fine.

After the children had been put to bed, Frau Wolfsohn and Frau Ehrenreich discussed domestic affairs. Messrs. Wolfsohn and Ehrenreich, however, aired their views on politics and economics. The more sceptical and calm Markus was, the more aggressive and violent Moritz became. "Just take a look at this," he stormed, taking a newspaper clipping from his pocket. "A certain Dr. Rost writes here: 'There are still a few Germans who say: of course, everything is the fault of the Jews but aren't there some decent Jews too? That is nonsense. For if every Nazi knew even one single decent Jew then there would have to be twelve million decent Jews in Germany to counterbalance the twelve million Nazis. But in all Germany there are less than six hundred thousand.' No. I refuse to live among a people who permit their leaders the use of such logic."

Markus Wolfsohn thought the argument of Dr. Rost over. A good salesman, too, often has to develop a daring sense of logic. But if he addressed the customers of Oppermann's in terms of Dr. Rost's logic it would be risky. In general, he informed Moritz, the adherents of the swastika were quite nice to him personally. Of course, it sometimes happened that customers refused to be served by Jewish salesmen. But they could seldom tell the difference between the Christian and the Jewish salesmen. Once, indeed, one of them took a Christian salesman for a Jew and declined to be served by him, deliberately requesting to be served by himself, Wolfsohn.

Moritz stamped up and down the room and laughed scornfully. "You'll never get any sense until you are poking your head out of the hospital window with a bandage round it."

Markus smiled. He thought frankly that he, too, knew one of the brotherhood of whom he would be as ready to believe the worst as Moritz. Herr Rüdiger Zarnke. Herr Zarnke would throw him out of a moving subway train without the slightest hesitation. He would then have killed two birds with one stone: he would have done a deed conformable to the world policy of the Nationalist party and obtained a flat for his brother-in-law.

Moritz growled on. Who was it, then, who was responsible for giving German culture its world-wide reputation? The ten million conservative Jews who speak Yiddish, their archaic German. It was they who had believed most profoundly in German culture. They alone, all through the war, kept on the German side. 12,723 German Jews had fallen in that war, 2.2 percent of all the German Jews in existence, far more than the corresponding percentage of the entire population. These figures did not take into consideration baptized Jews and persons of Jewish origin. Counting them one would reach the approximate figure of 5 percent, unquestionably more than double the corresponding percentage of the entire population. Now they were getting their reward, these German Jews. "No, I'll have nothing more to do with these people. Away with risks. I still need eighteen pounds. Then I shall have all I need for Palestine. This is the last time we shall celebrate the Festival of the Maccabees together here. I'm off."

The Chanukka lights were burning low. Markus Wolfsohn listened calmly to his companion, smoked his third cigar, and drank an Asbach Extra Old. He had his opinions and his brother-in-law had his. It would be uninteresting indeed if everyone had the same opinions. If his brother-in-law Moritz really could not sit still, let him be off to Palestine. He, Markus, would see him off at the station and wave good-bye. But he himself would remain in the country and earn an honest living.

19

On the same evening, Jaques Lavendel had also invited two guests to keep the Chanukka Feast with him, his nephew Berthold and his niece Ruth Oppermann. Jaques Lavendel had a connoisseur's love for objects of the old Jewish rituals. He had five particularly fine old Chanukka candlesticks: two were of Italian workmanship of the Renaissance period, one was Polish and had two mythical animals and blessing priests' hands carved upon it, one came from Württemberg and was adorned with figures of birds and a small bell, and one was from Bucovina, of eighteenth-century workmanship, provided, oddly enough, with a clock; it was a piece from which he obtained special amusement on account of its absurdity.

Here, too, they sang the hymn, *"Moaus zur yeshuosi,"* Rock and Refuge of my Redemption. Jaques Lavendel sang it with his hoarse voice, taking a childish pleasure in it. Berthold watched the singing man in some surprise. The lights and the hymn had no meaning for him. The Christmas tree meant more. He looked upon the Chanukka ceremonies as a mere gesture. He had come in the secret hope of discussing, in detail, with Uncle Jaques and Heinrich that case of his, that painful business with Dr. Vogelsang, in which nothing had been done since the day it occurred but which he knew, perfectly well, was far from finished. He had not spoken about it to anyone since then. He hesitated about confiding it to his parents or to Uncle Joachim. The persons who would understand him best were, undoubtedly, Uncle Jaques and Heinrich.

He waited rather impatiently for the dinner to come to an end. One ate well at Uncle Jaques's, long and abundantly. Ruth Oppermann teased Uncle Jaques because it was only when he practised the old customs that he noticed the secret bond which has been keeping the Jews of the world together for thousands of years. Uncle Jaques teased Ruth because she so passionately maintained that political unity was the one and only thing that could assure Jewry of a continued existence.

The evening was already far advanced, and Berthold had still had no chance of broaching the subject he had so much at heart. He was sure he would never get to the point now. It was a wasted evening. He decided to leave soon.

Ruth Oppermann was, just then, relating an experience which had befallen an East-Jewish child. Little Jacob Feibelmann went to a school attended principally by Nationalist children. The majority of his classmates were members of a Nationalist society. The boys were equipped with rubber truncheons. Well, one day one of them announced that his truncheon had been stolen. The teacher, indignant that there should be thieves in his class, ordered all the school-bags searched. The truncheon was found in little Feibelmann's knapsack. It had obviously been put there surreptitiously. There was wild excitement: Sly boots was the thief. The boy had to leave school. He had been deranged ever since, Ruth went on, he was continually crying, no one could do anything with him.

When Ruth had finished, Berthold suddenly spoke. He abruptly began to relate his own case. He told them about that lecture on Arminius the German which had really been forced upon him, of Dr. Vogelsang's interruption, of the latter's demand that he should apologize. He could not prevent his broad, boyish face from taking on a strained, worried look as he told his story. However, he managed to remain calm, manly. In fact he even, now and then, achieved that light and casual air to which he aspired.

It would have been a serious setback for him if the others had received his story with the same sort of casual air, with the damned indifference of adult, experienced people. But they did not do so. Berthold was almost worried that they took it too seriously.

Uncle Jaques put his head on one side, drew his lids far over his blue eyes, and reflected. "When the Romans were in Judea," he said at last, "they exacted very high tribute from the Jews. They asked the Talmudic Rabbis: 'Should a man give a correct valuation of his goods or not?' The Rabbis answered: 'Woe to him that doth and woe to him that doth not.' Whatever you do, my lad, he'll try to put the rope round your neck." He paused for a moment and then continued: "I would say neither yes nor no. I would simply say, 'This is what I meant. But if anyone feels insulted, then I am sorry and I wish I had not said it.' Rector François is a reasonable fellow."

Heinrich was sitting on a high chest—he was fond of sitting in unusual places—swinging his legs to and fro. "Rector François," he said, "is a *good old fellow*. But the *boys* will think it a case of backsliding. Long Lummox, I mean a certain Werner Rittersteg, said at a committee meeting of the football club that 'Berthold ought to be expelled because he has not apologized.' For the time being, I gave him a good punch. Two days later he said that 'If Berthold did apologize he would be pretending.' A man's word is a man's word, it would go against honour."

"Honour, honour," repeated Uncle Jaques, shaking his head. He said no more, but Berthold had never before heard a more bitter indictment of this conception of honour.

"Moreover, I don't believe," Heinrich went on, studying the tips of his toes intently, "that Vogelsang, the swine, will content himself with a half-and-half explanation. The thing can't be done away with except by a full and definite apology." He stopped the rapid swinging of his legs and jumped off the chest. *"Go ahead,"* he turned to Berthold. "Get it over. You can't go against the whole school. You've shown enough civic courage. What you said about the old Indian was undoubtedly right. But there's no point, when you have to deal with a chap like that, in sticking to a statement simply because it's true. In a case like that it's much better to show Nordic cunning than a martyr's courage. I must say," he concluded with a wise air, and suddenly looked the image of his father, "you've learnt damned little on the practical side from your studies of Arminius the German."

"You're wrong, wrong, wrong!" cried Ruth Oppermann in a passion. She shook her head with its tan complexion and black hair, that hair which always looked a little wild and dishevelled. "You'll never do anything with these people if you employ that sort of opportunism. There's just one thing that they respect. And that's pluck, and nothing but pluck."

Berthold looked at his cousin in amazement. Had she not expressed unbounded admiration for the achievement of Arminius? And now she was demanding that he stick to his rationalist criticism of that achievement. That was Ruth all over. Not precisely logical, but a personality.

The Chanukka lights had burned out. Jaques Lavendel brought out some phonograph records. Hebrew songs, an old Yiddish folk-ballad. He hummed the words as he played the record.

> "We used to be ten brothers,
> We traded in luscious wine;
> One of us died, poor fellow,
> And then we were only nine.
> Yossel, come play the fiddle,
> And Tevye, play the bass,
> We'll play a tune so merry
> Here, in the market-place."

When the record stopped, Aunt Klara, who had hitherto been silent, observed: "There's nothing for it, Berthold. You must apologize. Do it while you are still on your holidays, in a letter. Write to Rector François."

20

Sybil had given her maid the evening off. She and Gustav got their cold supper ready together. Busily, charmingly, Sybil bustled to and fro in her pretty two-roomed flat. It always pleased him anew to see her taking his little likes and dislikes into consideration. She had a remarkable understanding of the superficial things that make life pleasant. Slim, childlike, clever, charming, she fussed about him. She chattered precociously. Everything about her person and her quarters was such that, should necessity arise, one could do without. But if Gustav had to do without her, would life be worth living?

Gustav was beaming cheerfully. He very much enjoyed this period between Christmas and the New Year. He sat eating, drinking, chatting.

The contract for the biography of Lessing had arrived. The payment was not on a sumptuous scale. He was to receive it in instalments of two hundred marks each for a period of eighteen months. Rather a scanty wage for about four thousand hours' work. But he had already finished most of the work and now, he remarked jestingly, he had an assured income for one and a half years.

Sybil listened attentively, without smiling. She earned on an average from three to four hundred marks a month from her neat, often cruel, little sketches. No one knew how much trouble these sketches cost her, how diligently she polished them, and how badly she was paid in the end. Gustav had an easy time of it. For him those two hundred marks were a tiny, negligible addition to his income. Men gave flowers, chocolates, and perfume. They often paid sixty or seventy marks for a dinner in an expensive restaurant. They did not know how much happier you would be if they paid twenty marks for the dinner and paid you the forty marks in cash. Gustav was anything but stingy. He regularly deposited a generous amount to her monthly checking account. But to dress well cost money, payments for work came in slowly, one was often in a fix. To go to a sensitive man like Gustav for money was quite impossible.

Two hundred marks. The flat cost money, there was the car, her silk slips. Stockings were cheap. A Russian had just written a good novel about three pairs of silk stockings. She, Sybil, had planned a story about a woman who was a good sociologist, level-headed and reasonable, but forced to earn her living by writing fashion-articles. The working-out of the plot was weak, but now she had got on the track of an idea. The two hundred marks would be a good theme for a secondary plot. She must really talk to Gustav about it. It was in matters pertaining to "plot" that he was able to give good tips. But he was not in the mood today. She, however, was in the mood. Her brain was busy, she would have liked to jot down the plot of the story.

Gustav, meanwhile, was talking about his Lessing. Klaus Frischlin was turning out to be very useful. The question was, should he employ him steadily on this. In that case, Frischlin would have to give up his activities as director of the art department at Oppermann's. He would be able to finish the Lessing work in eighteen months at most. Was it worth while, for that purpose, to take Frischlin out of a not altogether satisfactory but secure settled position?

Sybil listened absently. She was thinking of her story. Gustav noticed her abstraction. A little vexed, he took leave of Sybil earlier than he had intended.

The next day Professor Mühlheim had lunch at Gustav's house. The brisk little man's face was more slyly wrinkled than ever on this occasion. He had put through a splendid piece of business for Gustav just in the nick of time. He had been urging Gustav for years to invest his capital abroad. The outlook in Germany was becoming steadily more threatening. Would he not be a madman who should continue to sit in a train, the staff of which showed unmistakable signs of madness? Mühlheim now had the opportunity, through a certain transaction, to invest money abroad without risk. He gave Gustav circumstantial details. The business had been very shrewdly thought out, everything about it was perfectly legal, the artful tax requirements had been cleverly circumvented.

Mühlheim sipped his black coffee slowly. Patiently, proceeding from one point to another, he explained the whole complicated business to his friend. Gustav listened, fidgeting nervously, tapping a tune on his thigh with his powerful, hairy hand. The God's Eye moved back and forth, Immanuel Oppermann regarded his grandson with a shrewd, kindly, sleepy expression. Grandfather Immanuel had had an easy time. He had never faced such problems as this. Besides, he would probably have accepted Mühlheim's offer with the greatest satisfaction. But he, Gustav, did not approve. His feelings rebelled. Perplexity and mental conflict were reflected in his face, which never hid any emotion.

Mühlheim grew angry. He got into a regular passion. For whose benefit did Gustav wish to leave his money in Germany, then? For the militarists, so that they could make mincemeat of it for their secret armaments? For the big industrialists, so that they could apply it to exceedingly dubious enterprises in Russia, for which it was never possible to get in sufficient capital? For the Nationalists, so that they could pay their storm troops with it and reimburse the Leader's propaganda out of it? For those thirteen thousand members of the Agrarian Party, so that they could put further milliards into their senseless economic policy?

Gustav rose and paced up and down with rapid, rigid strides. Mühlheim was unquestionably right. The money paid over to the State was used for purposes very different from the public interest. It was not used for his, Gustav's, protection, but for attacking him. But, all the same, they served the purpose of maintaining the law, even if that law was misguided, and Gustav agreed with Goethe, who preferred to put up with injustice rather than lawlessness. He held out his powerful, hairy hand. "Thank you for thinking of me, Mühlheim. But I am going to keep my money in Germany."

Mühlheim did not take the hand. He looked angrily at the stubborn fellow. The thing was dead sure. It was strictly legal. The company Gustav was to subscribe to had a number of German Nationalists, even of members of the Party, on its list of shareholders. Such an opportunity of investing money abroad safely would not occur again. The list of subscribers would close tomorrow, on the last day of the year. What was the matter with Gustav? What were his reasons? Where were his objections? He might have the decency to say what his arguments were.

Gustav, embarrassed, continued to pace up and down. Arguments? He had no arguments. He considered it *unfair* to send his money out of Germany. The fact of the matter was that he was attached to Germany. That was all. Sentimental scruples, no doubt, which could not stand against Mühlheim's logic. But the fact was that he was sentimental. Why, he went on, smiling boyishly and mischievously, why could not a man who had half a million in cash assets and at least twice as much invested capital not afford a little sentimentality?

"Merely to enable yourself to afford that sentimentality in

the future, idiot," cried Mühlheim with an excited laugh, "you ought to safeguard a few hundred thousand."

After some discussion, Gustav agreed to subscribe, not four hundred thousand, as Mühlheim desired, but a mere two hundred thousand marks to the corporation. Mühlheim gave a sigh of relief. Now he had arranged at least a certain degree of security for his foolish friend. Gustav signed the power of attorney which Mühlheim laid before him. "Don't forget, by the way," said he proudly, "that I possess, apart from this, two hundred marks' monthly income from the Lessing thing."

This tedious business over, he quickly recovered his good humour; and when Friedrich Wilhelm Gutwetter arrived, his smile was as beaming as ever. Mühlheim could not tear himself away from politics so quickly. "We have seen the proletariat let loose," he proclaimed. "It was not a pretty sight. We have seen the substantial citizen let loose, the agriculturist and the militarist, and that was hideous. But all that will be a paradise to what we shall see when the petty bourgeois is let loose, the Nationalist party men and their Leader." "Do you really believe that, sir?" asked Gutwetter, and gazed at him in friendly fashion with great, childlike eyes. "I have a different idea of it," he added mildly. "I believe that the war was only a curtain-raiser. The century of the great conflict has just begun. It will be a century of destruction. The final generations of the white race will attack each other without mercy. The thunder will mate with the ocean, and fire with the earth. Man will have to develop brains with horns to cope with this struggle. Such will be the character, as I see it, of the future national state. A military power beyond conception, a judiciary power with severe, restrictive laws, and a school system to educate senseless brutes in the ecstasy of self-sacrifice; such is the outlook." He spoke mildly, in gentle tones, his carefully groomed head rose calm-featured from the coat, which resembled that of a priest, the childlike eyes looked dreamy.

The other two, when he had finished, were silent for a time. Then Mühlheim said: "All right, if that's your opinion. But perhaps you'll have another cognac and a cigar before it happens."

21

In the year 1905 there had appeared in Moscow a book with the title, *The Great in the Little, or, Antichrist as an Immediate Political Possibility*. The author of the book was a certain Sergius Nilus, an official of the Synodal Chancery. The twelfth chapter had an appendix with the heading, "Protocols of the Wise Men of Zion." These "Protocols" professed to transcribe the proceedings of a secret meeting of the leading Jews of the world, which was alleged to have taken place in the autumn of 1897, on the occasion of the first Zionist Congress in Basel, in order to determine the general lines of a plan for the eventual conquest of the world by the Jews. The book was translated into many foreign languages and made a deep impression, especially upon German university men. In the year 1921, a contributor to the London *Times* proved that these "Protocols" had been copied, largely word for word, from a pamphlet written by a certain Maurice Joly, which had appeared in the year 1868. In this pamphlet, certain supporters of Napoleon III, Freemasons and Bonapartists, were accused of having concocted an enormous plot to achieve world dominion for themselves. The author of the "Protocols" had simply substituted the word "Jews" for "Freemasons and Bonapartists." In so far as the "Protocols" had not been copied from Joly's pamphlet, they were taken from the novel entitled *Biarritz* which had been published in the same year, 1868, by a certain Goedsche under the pseudonym of John Retcliffe. In this novel a description was given of how, once every hundred years, the princes of the twelve tribes of Israel, which had been dispersed throughout the world, met in the old Jewish cemetery at Prague and debated upon the further measures to be taken for the establishment of Jewish world dominion. A burst of laughter went up from the whole civilized world upon the discovery of this stupid forgery. It was only in Germany, especially in the universities, that the "Protocols" were still believed in.

The "Protocols" and everything that concerned them had always been a particular source of amusement to Gustav Oppermann. He was interested in the documentary evidences of human folly; he possessed a small, special collection, among them editions of the "Protocols" and relevant literature.

On the last day of the year, Rector François was in the habit of lunching at Gustav's. François had picked up a particularly amusing edition of the "Protocols" by one Alfred Rosenberg and had brought it as a little attention.

Luncheon passed off merrily, with plenty of good talk. Rector François came of a French emigrant family. Reason and humanity had become a tradition with this family, whose members were proud to remember the great achievements of the eighteenth and nineteenth centuries. Now, to be sure, under the influence of Frau Emilie, Little Thundercloud, Rector François had grown cautious and only referred to his ancestry in intimate circles. Here, with Gustav, Alfred François was able to speak quite freely. His literary taste was the same as Gustav's, like him, he hated politics and was a fanatical champion of the purity of language. François could discuss his anxieties here. Both men were aware of human folly, which is as deep as the sea. But they also knew that in the end reason always conquers folly with the same certainty that Odysseus conquered the Cyclops Polyphemus, with the same certainty that the men of the Bronze Age overcame the men of the Stone

Age. Gustav Oppermann and Rector François conversed in the same vein as the ancestors of the Rector.

But before the meal had come to an end it occurred forcibly to François that he would have to redeem yet another of the promises which Little Thundercloud had extorted from him. For, when he was telling Frau François what a charming little book he was going to take to Gustav Oppermann, she had said to him: "If you are going to see your friend tomorrow, you might discuss your Oppermann case. He should persuade the young scamp to settle that dispute with Senior Master Vogelsang once for all. Things like that cannot be left in the air nowadays." She had given François such a sermon about it, that he had finally assured her he would talk the matter over with Gustav.

Now, therefore, he mentioned it. Cautiously beginning with a few general observations, he broached the matter. The war had made changes in the German language. It had introduced new ideas and new words and intensified the vocabulary and syntax. If the new turns of expression would be adopted to the exclusion of others, the result would be disgusting. If, however, what was good in the old were united carefully to what is good in the new, a style, less sentimental than the earlier German, would be created. It would be stronger, more austere, more rational, more virile. Many of his boys had a fine ear for this new, and as far as he was concerned, welcome German. Berthold Oppermann had one of the finest. He combined an appreciation of the technical progress of the present century with a lively interest in humanistic matters, in the mind of man. It could only be hoped that the irritating new teacher whom they had planted in his beloved institution, like a potato in a tulip bed, would not spoil things too much. And then he related the Vogelsang affair.

Gustav listened without particular interest. Did François expect him, Gustav, to regard this case as a real problem? Here was a concrete instance of how completely each one of us becomes absorbed in his activities and how we magnify matters that concern our interests. This case was really a most simple one. The lad had made a reasonable statement. The teacher, obsessed by vulgar sentimentalism, refused to admit it. Could François honestly believe that, when a young fellow of the twentieth century made an honest statement in an institution of learning, it could be held against him?

It had not quite come to that, Rector François told him, stroking his trim, white moustache with his well-kept hands. But Gustav really underestimated the influence which the Nationalist movement unfortunately possessed, in schools as elsewhere. François had had an interview with an official, a sensible fellow with whom François got on very well. This official had promised him that, if possible, he would shortly remove the disturbing new master from the school. The official himself, however, was dependent on exterior circumstances and had to make compromises on all sides. The obvious policy for him, François, was to bide his time in dealing with the Vogelsang-Oppermann affair. If Vogelsang were removed, the case would automatically be settled. But that was only, as already stated, a possibility. It would be as well not to rely too much on that. Perhaps Gustav would urge his nephew to make the apology demanded.

Gustav looked up in surprise. He had expected quite a different conclusion to François's introductory remarks. He drew his thick eyebrows together, the deep, vertical furrows appeared above the large nose, the entire face of the emotional man reflected his amazement. The same prudence which had permitted him to invest money abroad, through Mühlheim, was now prompting Dr. François. Such prudence was, certainly, not to be expected from a boy. After a short silence, he said: "No, my dear François, I cannot help you in this affair. I can understand anyone who does not mention a fact which he knows is true. But since my nephew has voiced such a statement, I should not care to advise him to deny it and, in addition, to apologize for it." He sat up erect, his face forbidding and arrogant. He looked very large when sitting down. "Just like Goethe that way," thought François. Little Thundercloud would be vexed, he continued, mentally. But he could assure her, with a clear conscience, that he had done his best. Moreover, he approved of his friend Gustav's attitude.

Both men were glad when they were able to rise from table and go across to the library for their coffee. It was pleasant to talk here, in this fine room, of the eternal folly of mankind, deep as the sea, and its equally eternal defeat by intelligence. Gustav added the little book dealing with the "Protocols" to the other pamphlets in his collection. He took out, smiling, the Leader's book, *My Battle,* which stood rather near to the "Protocols," and read some particularly juicy passages to his friend. Rector François covered his ears. He did not want to listen to the incorrect, distorted German of the book. Gustav spoke to him soothingly. On account of his repugnance for the style, he had evidently missed the comic quality of the content. He refused to be dissuaded from quoting a few passages: " 'The vileness of the Jew is so gigantic,' " he read, " 'that it should astonish no one if, to the German mind, the incarnation of the Devil and all that is evil assumes the shape of a Jew.' . . . 'It was the Jew and it still is the Jew who brings the Negro to the Rhine with the object of destroying the hated white race by the resultant mingling of bloods, to cast the white man down from his cultural and political eminence and to set himself up as master.' . . . 'The Jews,' " he read, " 'do not wish to establish a Jewish State in Palestine in order to inhabit it, all they want is a centre, in which they shall be free to exercise sovereign rights, for the organization of their international crook activities, a refuge for convicted scoundrels and a high-school for future crooks.'" Rector François, disgusted as he was, had to laugh over this accumulation of nonsense. Gustav, too, laughed. He went on reading. Both men burst into gales of laughter.

But Rector François could not stand the reading of this unappetizing matter long. "I can scarcely describe to you, my dear, friend," said he, "how uncomfortable it makes me feel to listen to anything from that vile book. Without exaggeration, it literally turns my stomach." Gustav smiled and asked Schlüter, over the house telephone, to bring some cognac. He put the Leader's book back near the "Protocols." "Is it not strange," he remarked, "that the same epoch should produce men of such diverse potentialities as the author of the book entitled *My Battle* and the author of the book entitled *Civilization and Its Discontents?* An anatomist of the coming century will, no doubt, be able to prove a difference in development between the two brains corresponding to at least thirty thousand years."

Schlüter brought the cognac, iced the glasses, and poured out the liquor. "What's the matter with you, Schlüter?" asked Gustav. "You're looking very strange." It struck François, too, how haggard the quiet, deftly moving man was looking. "The clinic rang up," Schlüter said, a gloomy expression on his calm features. "My brother-in-law is in a bad way. He will hardly last into the New Year." Gustav was startled. "When were you there last?" he asked. "The day before yesterday," said Schlüter. "My wife was there yesterday. He said to her: 'Those curs should not be allowed to get away with everything. The whole country will go to the devil if we all go on holding our tongues. Even if I were sure that all this would happen to me again, I would still give the same evidence.'" "You must go to the clinic, Schlüter," said Gustav. "Go at once. Tell Bertha she can go too. I don't need you any longer. Bring the telephone into this room. If anybody rings, I'll open the door myself. Take the car if you like." "Thank you, Herr Doctor," said Schlüter.

Gustav told François what had occurred. Schlüter's brother-in-law, a certain Pachnicke, a mechanic by trade, a decent fellow who took no interest in politics, had witnessed one of the daily scuffles between Republicans and the mercenaries of the Nationalist party. During the scuffle one of the Republicans was killed. The Nationalists declared that they had acted in self-defence, having first been attacked by the Republicans. It was the usual defence offered by the adherents of the Nationalists after they had assaulted and killed an opponent. During the prosecution of the mercenary who had shot the Republican, the mechanic Pachnicke had been called as a witness and had stated, with truth, that the swastika men had begun the scuffle. His statement, together with those of all the others who had sworn to the same effect, was not, however, believed, and the mercenary was discharged. But Pachnicke himself, shortly after the case, had been assaulted by some swastika men at night and so roughly handled that he had to be taken to the clinic.

"You see, my dear Oppermann," said François, after Gustav had ended his tale, "it is not exactly an easy thing for a man to practise truth and reason in this Germany of ours. Perhaps you will not judge me so harshly for wanting to protect your nephew from the fate of the mechanic Pachnicke." "You are generalizing unfairly, my dear François," returned Gustav rather heatedly. "After all neither you, your staff, nor the gentlemen at the Ministry of Education are mercenaries. No, no. The great majority of Germans are men like Pachnicke, not swastika men. With all their money and soft-soap promises they have been able to take in scarcely a third of the population. After so much costly effort it is an astonishingly meagre result. No, my dear François, the people are sound at heart."

"Tell me that often and as emphatically as you can," returned François. "It is important for us to believe it. But I don't always find it easy to believe. And now, if you will permit me, let us drop the subject. I can still, even now, feel the taste that vile book has left in my mouth. Let's rinse it out with something good." He rummaged among the books, and took out a volume of Goethe. He read, smiling: " 'In times of disorder the masses throw themselves from side to side like a man in a fever.' " They washed their souls clean from the reading of the "Protocols" and the book entitled *My Battle*.

They spent two pleasant hours together. Their uneasiness vanished. A nation which had concerned itself for centuries so intensively with books, such as those they saw around them, could never allow itself to be deceived by the nonsense in the "Protocols" and the book entitled *My Battle*. It had been an excess of caution which had caused Gustav to follow Mühlheim's advice, and François had no reason to regard the issue of the Vogelsang case with any doubt. Gustav had been quite right. The average citizens of the nation were men like the mechanic Pachnicke, who did not belong to the rabble that admired the mercenaries. They remembered the dying man's phrase: "Even if I were sure that all this would happen to me again, I would still give the same evidence." That was the way such people thought, not Herr Vogelsang's way. They stuck to reason, they were not taken in by the hackneyed rhetoric of the Leader. Cheerfully, content, and confident of the future, they jested about the probable fate of the Leader, whether he would end as a barker of a fair or as an insurance agent.

22

On the 30th of January, the President of the Republic appointed the author of the book entitled *My Battle* to the post of German Chancellor.

Book Two: Today

"*The Germans are to blame for the disease which is the most dangerous to culture and also for the greatest absurdity extant, namely* Nationalism, *this 'névrose nationale' from which Europe is suffering; they have robbed Europe of reason and intelligence.*"   —NIETZSCHE.

TODAY

GUSTAV OPPERMANN was on his way to Gertraudten Strasse to attend a meeting in the directors' office at the Stores. Martin had urged him, with unaccustomed importunity, to be present on this occasion, at all costs.

It was a few days after the appointment of the Leader to the post of Chancellor. The streets swarmed with people. Everywhere the brown shirts of the Nationalist mercenaries, and the Nationalist swastika, were to be seen. Gustav's car, driven fast and expertly by Schlüter, could not make very rapid progress.

Still another traffic light. That American expression, *"The lights are against me,"* was an excellent one, Gustav thought. But he had no time to indulge his reflections. The persistent cries of an old woman selling dolls disturbed him. The dolls were likenesses of the Leader. The old woman held one of them to the window of the car. If you pressed the doll's stomach, it stretched out its right arm with open palm, a gesture which the Italian Fascisti had borrowed from ancient Rome and the German Fascists from the Italians. The old woman, caressing the doll, cried: "You sufferer, you hero, you fought, you suffered, you won."

Gustav turned his eyes away from the grotesque spectacle. He too, as well as the whole country, had been surprised by the sudden appointment of the Leader to the post of Chancellor. He had not been so surprised as the Leader himself, but he, too, was unable to understand the course of events. Why was it just now, when the Nationalist movement was on the wane, that a man like the author of the book entitled *My Battle* had been put in charge of the highest office in the land? At Gustav's golf and theatre clubs it had been explained to him that there was no very great danger in the business. The influence of the more moderate, more reasonable members of the Cabinet would hold the Leader in check. The whole affair was a mere ruse to keep the excited masses in hand. Gustav listened to this explanation and was very willing to believe it.

Mühlheim, to be sure, had taken the matter more seriously. The ruling, capitalistic classes, the Agrarian Party at their head, had now, in their abject need, in order to avoid the danger of tremendous graft scandals, called the barbarians to their rescue. Mühlheim did not believe, however, that, once these rescuers had been led to the trough, they could be easily driven away. The sanguine gentleman had even expressed the opinion that the civilization of Central Europe was now threatened by a barbarian invasion, such as had not been seen since the time of the Migrations.

Gustav merely smiled at his friend's pessimism. A people which had reached so high a point of technical and industrial development did not lapse into barbarism in twenty-four hours. And had not someone recently calculated that Goethe's works alone circulated in German-speaking territories to the extent of more than a hundred million copies? Such a people did not listen long to the shouting of barbarians.

Since the appointment of the Leader of the barbarians to the Chancellorship, very little had changed in the quiet streets of the residential section where Gustav lived. Now, during his first drive through the city, Gustav noticed with distaste the extent to which the barbarians were spreading themselves. Their troops dominated the streets. The stiff newness of their uniforms, with the smell of the tailor-shop still upon them, their salutes in the ancient manner, reminded him of supers in a provincial theatre. At the street corners collection boxes, whose contents were destined for election propaganda, were held out to the passers-by. He let down the window of the car to hear what they were shouting. "For awakening Germany, for the one-way street to Jerusalem," he heard. Gustav had been in the army and served for a few months in the field. It was Anna's energy which had saved him from further experiences at the front during that time. His military service, that senseless subservience to the will of others, had been the most disagreeable period of his life. He had endeavoured to wipe it out of his memory, it made him ill to think of it. Now, at sight of those brown uniforms, the unwelcome recollection was reawakened.

They reached Gertraudten Strasse. There stood the main building of the house of Oppermann, wedged between its neighbours, old-fashioned, solid. Here, too, in front of the principal entrance, uniformed members of the Nationalist party were demanding contributions for their election-boxes from the passers-by. "For awakening Germany, for the Leader, for the one-way street to Jerusalem," they cried in their clear, boyish voices. Rigid and sullen, his nut-cracker face with its grey, stiff moustache unmoved, the old porter Leschinsky stood at his post. He saluted Gustav in a particularly surly manner, swung the revolving door round for him with a particularly brusque jerk; he wished to give the senior partner an impressive proof of his loyalty in the face of those young ruffians.

In the directors' office they were already waiting for Gustav. Jaques Lavendel was there, as well as Frau Klara Lavendel, and the chief clerks Brieger and Hintze. Only Edgar was missing. Gustav came in with his precise, rapid stride, his entire sole firmly pressing the ground, and tried to appear unconcerned, beaming, as usual. He pointed to the copy of the picture of Immanuel Oppermann. "Excellent, that copy. I believe you put me off with a copy, Martin, and kept the original for yourself." But it was only the brisk Herr Brieger who responded in the same cheerful, boisterous fashion. "Business is excellent, Dr. Oppermann," said he. "The Nazis are settling down on a great scale just now, and people who are settling down want furniture. And who supplies the furniture for their Brown Houses? We do."

They got to business. Martin said a few introductory words. The Nationalists had used Anti-Semitism as a basis for their propaganda. It was possible, even probable, that now they were in power they would dispense with this expedient as superfluous and economically injurious. However, it would be as well to be cautious. He asked Herr Brieger to give his opinion.

The big-nosed, emphatically Jewish-looking, little Herr Brieger spoke as flippantly as ever. There was now nothing else for it but to combine all the Oppermann branches into the "German Furniture Company." In addition, it would be as well finally to come to an understanding with Herr Wels. He had sounded Herr Wels. It was odd but he was the one who got on best with that fire-eating *goi*. If there was really anything to the scare, and if it was destined to outlast the storm which was almost certain to come—in this particular his outlook was more gloomy than that of Herr Martin Oppermann—then at least fifty-one percent of the stock of the firm must be transferred to non-Jewish holders before the elections. It was essential to prove this beyond the shadow of a doubt, though, of course, the real state of affairs would be quite different. Technically, this could be done with ease. But the necessary transactions were of a delicate and intricate character and required a clear understanding, steady determination, and goodwill from both the partners. Those are three points in which we are strong, but Herr Wels is not. This was Herr Brieger's outline of the situation, described briskly, with many shrewd and witty turns of speech, with an ostensible ease of manner which was not, however, quite convincing.

Martin, after Herr Brieger had finished, observed: "Both projects will have to be undertaken, the transformation of the business into the Furniture Company and the negotiations with Wels. I think that Herr Brieger will be sure to make a success of that." This indirect confession that he, Martin, had spoilt things to some extent in his previous interview with Wels was hard for him to make, but he considered it unsporting to shirk it.

The stately Herr Hintze, sat stiffly aloof, his head held high. "I think," he said, "that if Professor Mühlheim puts his mind to it we can get the German Furniture Company organized within a week. We're not yet at the stage, thank God, where the Oppermanns have to run after a man like Herr Wels. Let us get the German Furniture Company established, gentlemen, and then we can wait quietly until our friend comes to us."

"Well and good," said Jaques Lavendel, directing an amiable glance at Herr Hintze, "but suppose he doesn't come to us? Suppose he listens to what the Leader says every day on the radio? Suppose he believes it? Alas, he's not very strong in the head. Don't credit people with too much sense, gentlemen. Present conditions show that has always, so far, been a bad speculation. Start negotiations with the *goi*. Start them today. Don't be mean. Don't starve the ox that grinds the corn. Give him a big bite to swallow. It's better than giving him the whole thing."

Gustav sat with the air of a man who listens to a discussion out of courtesy but who is secretly bored by it. He stared at the framed document which hung on the wall. He knew the text by heart. "The merchant Immanuel Oppermann of Berlin has rendered good service to the German Army by his supplies to the troops. Signed, von Moltke, Field Marshal." He let his shoulders droop a bit, closed the heavy lids over his melancholy brown eyes. The change in his appearance was hardly noticeable. And yet, suddenly, he did not look young any longer, but resembled his brother Martin.

They had waited, after Brieger had finished, for him to speak first, and it was not until it was obvious that he preferred to be silent that Martin had spoken. Now, as he still remained silent, Martin demanded: "What do you think, Gustav?"

"I am not of your opinion, Martin," said he. His usually amiable growl sounded irritated and determined. "Nor am I of your opinion, Herr Brieger, nor of yours, Herr Hintze, and most certainly not of yours, Jaques. I do not understand why all of you suddenly have the jitters. What has happened? A popular blockhead has been given an important office and has had a check-rein put on him by the appointment of able men as his colleagues. Do you really believe that, because a few thousand young, armed ruffians roam about in the streets, there is an end of Germany?" He was sitting very erect and looked very large; his pleasant face expressed annoyance and excitement. "What do you imagine is going to happen? What are you afraid of? Do you believe they will forbid our customers to buy from us? Do you believe our shops will be shut up? Do you believe your capital will be confiscated? Because we are Jews?" He stood up and marched with stiff and energetic strides about the room, breathing heavily through his fleshy nose. "Don't try to frighten me with your old wives' tales. There are no pogroms in Germany nowadays. That's all over. It's been over for more than a hundred years. For one hundred and fourteen years, if you want to know exactly. Do you believe that this whole nation of sixty-five million people has ceased to be a cultured people because it has conferred freedom of speech upon a few fools and scoundrels? I don't

believe it. I am against paying attention to a few fools and
scoundrels. I am against erasing the good name of Oppermann
from the firm. I am against negotiating with such a dour
person as that man Wels. I am not going to let myself be
infected with your panic. I won't share it. I don't understand
how grown men can be taken in by all that tomfoolery."

The others sat in startled silence. Gustav's self-possession
and courtesy were proverbial. He had never before put up any
serious opposition in business matters. No one had ever seen
him so excited. What was he making such a fuss about? Was
there a single Jewish firm that had taken no precautionary
measures? How could a man as shrewd as Gustav be so blind?
It only showed what came of busying oneself with literary and
philosophical questions.

Jaques Lavendel was the first to speak. "So you still think
that the more liberal view is bound to win?" He gave Gustav
a friendly glance. "God grant you may be right," he added in
his gentle, husky, kindly tones. "If we take things in their
relationship to history, you are certainly right, Gustav. But we
business people are unfortunately obliged to take a more limited point of view. The time of which you speak will certainly
come. I mean, economically speaking. None of us may live to
see it but you will be right then, though the firm of Oppermann will be ruined."

"Your confidence is magnificent," said that stately man,
Herr Hintze. He stood up and pressed Gustav's hand warmly.
"I thank you for what you have said, it was really comforting,
edifying. But as a business man I must say: the heart is the
place for confidence, business is the place for caution."

Martin remained silent, took out his eyeglasses, polished
them, and put them away again. He looked at his brother
with surprise and uneasiness. He suddenly realized that Gustav was fifty years old. His good physical training, his bright,
untroubled life had been of no avail to him. There he stood

and spoke words which had nothing to do with reality. Martin glanced up at the portrait of old Immanuel. In a flash he realized—he was one hundred percent sure of it—old Immanuel would have begun negotiations with Wels a year ago if he had been in his place. He would long ago have come to terms with Wels; smiling and shaking his head, he would have let the name and the portrait disappear. What was there in a name, in a picture? It was a matter of practical policy. He would long ago have settled his family abroad, somewhere among more tolerant, more civilized people. Martin suddenly felt himself immensely superior to his brother. "Gently, gently, Gustav," said he. "We shall find a way out."

Gustav was standing in a corner of the room. Still excited, he was gazing at the others. What had he got to do with them, with these quaking business people? They were repugnant to him, the whole lot of them, with their eternal cheap scepticism. There stood Germany, that great country, from Luther to Einstein and Freud, from Gutenberg and Berthold Schwarz to Zeppelin and Haber and Bergius, and because Germany, racked to the limit of endurance, had lost its head for a moment, those business people gave it up as done for. "There is no need to find a way out," he growled at Martin. "Everything ought to stay as it is. The mere existence of the German Furniture Company is already too great a concession."

The others began to feel angry. "Be reasonable, Gustav," said Jaques Lavendel. "Kant is Kant and Rockefeller is Rockefeller. Kant would not have been able to write books if he had used Rockefeller's methods. But Rockefeller would not have been able to do business if he had used Kant's methods." He gave Gustav a cordial glance. "You can concern yourself with the philosophy of history in Max Reger Strasse, but you must be businesslike in Gertraudten Strasse."

It was Klara, curiously enough, who found a solution for this difficult situation. She was pleased with her brother Gustav, but during his speech she had become doubly sure why she had married Jaques. She had hitherto been silent. They had quite forgotten that she was there. Everyone was astonished when the stout, quiet lady began to speak. "If it is so heartfelt a wish of Gustav's," she suggested, "that the name of Oppermann should be retained, we could continue to run the original establishment here under the name of Oppermann and combine all the branches under the name of the German Furniture Company. And if Brieger negotiates further with Herr Wels privately, I don't suppose Gustav would have any objection."

The proposal of the thoughtful, courageous lady was received favourably by Gustav and the rest. All agreed to it without much discussion. Gustav, to save his face, made one or two further reservations. He was irritated at having let himself go. Finally he, too, duly signed the agreement.

Martin, when the others had gone, dropped both his arms heavily upon the sides of his chair. The incomprehensible attitude of his brother depressed him. "He has much to unlearn," he thought. "Why can't he admit the truth of what is plain to everyone? This 1933 Germany is no longer the Germany of our youth. It has nothing to do with the Germany of Goethe and Kant; we shall have to get used to that idea. He can't learn much from *Faust* about present-day Germany; to do that he'll have to study *My Battle*."

In Cornelius Strasse, at dinner, Martin did his best to maintain an easy flow of table-talk. He had, naturally, no idea of concealing their decision from Liselotte. But it would be hard to bear if she took it lightly. And yet he wanted her to take it lightly. Liselotte sat between her tired and talkative husband and her silent son. She sensed Martin's nervousness and observed with increasing anxiety that Berthold was worrying himself about something which he did not wish the others to know about.

After dinner, briefly, impulsively, Martin informed her that henceforward, with the exception of the original shop, all the Oppermann stores were to be merged in the German Furniture Company. Liselotte sat looking beautiful and stately. She leaned forward a little, while Martin was speaking, her grey, almond-shaped eyes seeking his own melancholy, brown ones. Her smooth face grew serious. "All?" she asked. "All the Oppermann branches?" Her deep voice was noticeably gentle. "It is not easy, Liselotte," said Martin. Liselotte did not answer. She only drew her chair a little nearer to his. Martin had hoped that she would take it lightly. It was a great comfort to him, now, that he had been mistaken.

2

Gustav Oppermann asked Ellen Rosendorff to come into his study. They had been having tea and gossiping. It had been a pleasant afternoon. In the study Ellen stretched on the wide couch, Gustav switched on the lights, not too many, and sat down in the armchair opposite her. "Well, now, Ellen," he said, offering her a cigarette, "what was it you wanted to tell me? What's wrong?" "Nothing and everything," Ellen answered. She lay still, her beautiful, dark-skinned face half in shadow, and puffed at her cigarette. Then she said lightly, "I've put an end to it."

"With whom?" asked Gustav, a little shyly. "With Monsieur?"

"Whom else, innocent lambkin?" returned Ellen. "I was fond of him. I often used to ask myself if I should have cared for him if he hadn't happened to be the Crown Prince. I believe I should have. Besides, his whole character was so consistent. He was just what that particular Crown Prince ought to be."

"And now, all of a sudden, he's inconsistent?"

"It's quite natural," Ellen observed, "that he should be pleased by the present state of affairs. He would be a fool if he did not encourage it. In spite of the fact that he could never have a destiny better suited to him than that of being a Crown Prince out of office. I don't blame him for playing with the idea of mounting the throne. Why shouldn't one use the Nationalists if they are useful to one? There are a number of Jewish firms, too, who supply them with their uniforms, their furniture, and the cloth for their flags. The only thing one must not forget in spite of business is what sort of stuff these contemporaries of ours are made of. One makes use of them and washes one's hands afterwards. He knows that just as well as we do. He has made jokes about the Leader just like the rest of us. He used to go into fits of laughter when passages from his book were read. He's a hearty laugher. And now, just think, Gustav, since the fellow has become Chancellor, he takes him quite seriously. He has actually dared to maintain, in my presence, that the Leader is Somebody. At first I thought he was joking. But he stuck to it. He's lied to himself so long and thoroughly about it that now there's nothing more to be done about it. The world has become a hideous place, Gustav."

Gustav listened to her with sympathy and concern. The fact that he was such a good listener, that he interested himself in their affairs so sincerely, was what made him so popular with women. Under the light flippancy of her manner he could see how very much she had taken the break with the Prince to heart. He could imagine what had happened. She had had a political discussion with the Prince, and he, like the boor he was, had probably made no secret of his Anti-Semitism. Gustav said nothing, seated himself beside her on the couch, took her hand, and stroked the dark, soft skin.

"Isn't it curious, Gustav?" she said after a time. "That man knows the circumstances as well as you and I do. The Nationalist movement was coming to an end, there was no more money to be had out of big business. The Leader was finished. *'He's done for.'* I myself heard Monsieur tell an Englishman that. It was all over. A small group of irresponsible agriculturists have, because they knew of no other way to save themselves, opened the flood-gates to barbarism. The Leader has done no more to achieve this 'success' of his than you or I have. Even old Father Hindenburg, whose consent they squeezed out of him, has done more for it. And he dares to tell me that this success proves there is something to the Leader!

"You know," she continued to lament, "this business has upset all my notions of what constitutes greatness. I ask myself in alarm whether perhaps the greatness of other men hasn't been concocted later, after successes of this calibre. It's dreadful to consider that there may have been nothing more in the greatness of a Cæsar than there is in this fellow." Gustav smiled. "I can calm your fears in this respect, Ellen. In the case of most great men, we have authentic evidence of what they actually did and thought. Cæsar, for instance, left us two books. If you like, Ellen, I will read you a page of Cæsar's *Gallic Wars* and after that a page of the book entitled *My Battle*."

Ellen laughed. "You only have to console me, Gustav," she said. "I need that badly." She quickly turned serious again. "If one only knew how long it would last," she brooded. "It's only a panic," Gustav declared emphatically. "Nothing more." Ellen looked at him thoughtfully and slowly shook her beautiful, biblical head. "Gustav," she said, "you should not try to comfort me in such an unfair way." "Don't you believe it?" asked Gustav in astonishment, unpleasantly taken aback.

"What *do* you believe? Do you imagine this thing will go on?" He put the question eagerly. Suddenly the girl's opinion seemed more important to him than that of his clever friend Mühlheim; in suspense he waited for her answer.

"Do you think I am Hanussen the clairvoyant?" Ellen replied with a smile. "There's only one thing that is certain. I am as sure as we were sure, after America's entry into the war, that the war was lost. I am as sure as that, that this Nationalist business will come to a bad end. But when the end will come and how, and whether the country will go smash over it—" She shrugged her shoulders.

"What are you talking about, Ellen?" demanded Gustav, raising his eyebrows. He was still holding her hand. "Because a fool of a Prince has thrown himself into the arms of the barbarians do you believe that all Germany is going to sink into barbarism?" "I don't believe anything," replied Ellen calmly. "I simply tell myself that it is easy to let the barbarians loose but difficult to get them down again. Barbarism has its charm. I am, myself, often quite strongly drawn to barbarism, I should be telling a lie if I did not admit it. The majority of other people probably have a still more definite leaning towards it." She lay there, beautiful, sad, cynical, shrewd. She had done with that silly adventure with the Crown Prince, through which she had passed with shame and cynicism. Gustav suddenly felt a burning desire. He seized her with his strong, hairy hands. His head quite close to hers, he murmured passionately: "Ellen, let's leave this stupid Berlin. Let's go to the Canary Islands. I'll let the Lessing go hang. Come with me, Ellen. Do, Ellen." She stroked his big, excited head. "You are a child, Gustav," she said. "You're quite all right as you are. You don't need to go to the Canary Islands to prove that to me."

When she had gone, Gustav sat down, tired and happy. He had intended to spend the evening alone, working at his

Lessing. Now he had a desire for people and conversation. He went to the Theatre Club.

Here the general mood was not bad. For the time being, economists had taken the appointment of the Leader with a certain optimism. The Leader, repeating parrot-like whatever was suggested to him, was safe in the hands of the big capitalists. He would avoid making experiments, one was certain of that. The Agrarian Party and the gentlemen of Big Business, who had so long and so well understood how to bottle up the much cleverer Socialists, would not have much difficulty in dealing with the clumsy swastika men. They were well aware why they had come to power. Nothing to worry about. There would be a great outward show of melodrama, but behind the scenes business would go on as usual.

Gustav said little and heard much. He was not very much interested in politics and economics. The change would not encroach upon his own life, upon the intellectual domain. This conviction grew upon him steadily. Now, he could scarcely understand how he had ever been infected by the panic around him. The scene he had made in Martin's office was disgusting. Fifty years old and still as lacking in self-control as a child. But from now on he would keep himself in hand. No more politics. Enough of that senseless, superfluous croaking.

He drank, played a game of écarté. He played rather rashly. He took it as a good omen that he won.

When he left, the old club servant Jean was standing near the entrance to the card-room. It had become a habit of Gustav's, when he was lucky, to keep back a five-mark piece to slip into Jean's hand. He did so today. The dignified way in which the old man thanked him, unobtrusively and yet emphatically, gave Gustav pleasure. He walked part of the way through the chilly winter night. Life was as easy and pleasant as ever.

He slept well and awoke full of confidence. The work was

going on well. Dr. Frischlin, who had given up his position
in the business and now regularly worked with him each
morning, gave him some good ideas. The morning's letters,
too, were pleasing. The one which delighted him most was
from an acquaintance in the Bibliophile Association, a well-
known writer, who asked him to be one of the signers of a
manifesto against the introduction of barbarism into public
life. Gustav smiled; although he was alone, he felt self-
conscious, almost embarrassed. Was his literary work so highly
esteemed that people thought they might derive some benefit
from his signature? He read the letter through again. Signed
the manifesto.

Professor Mühlheim, when he was told of this, received the
news differently than Gustav had expected. "All honour to
your literary ambitions, Oppermann," said he peevishly. "But
personally I should have denied myself the pleasure of signing." Gustav raised his eyebrows, the vertical Oppermann
furrows appeared above his nose. "Would you be so good as
to explain why, Mühlheim?" he inquired sarcastically. "Is
there much explanation required?" asked Mühlheim peevishly.
"What do you expect to gain from a manifesto like that? Do
you believe that such a feeble academic document will make
any impression in any of the government offices?" Then, as
Gustav still obviously did not understand, he burst out: "I
must say, you're impossibly simple-minded. Do you believe
that the result of this proclamation stands in any kind of reasonable relation to the price you will have to pay for it? Don't
you see, man, what a devil of a broth you're cooking for yourself and the rest of the Oppermanns? You're going to come
in for your bit in the Nationalist press. Those gentlemen will
be, in fact, the only ones who will notice the stuff. A year ago
the whole thing would have been a joke. Now they are the
mouthpiece of the Government, and an utterly unscrupulous
Government at that. It will be no picnic for your brother

Martin when he has to read the mud they will throw at you."
Gustav stood before him like a guilty schoolboy. "You really
can't be left alone for a moment, Oppermann," concluded
Mühlheim in a milder tone.

However, Gustav's alarm was soon over. What? Were they
trying to frighten him again? They should leave him in peace
with their silly intimidations. He'd have nothing to do with
them. No one was going to prevent his standing up for Lessing, Goethe, Freud. In God's name, then, let a few idiots buy
the chairs for their precious behinds somewhere else than at
Oppermann's. Mühlheim regarded the excited man with derision. He answered him in a cool, ironic tone. The two friends
parted in a dudgeon.

The effect of the manifesto on Sybil Rauch was very different from its effect on Mühlheim. She was glad to see her
friend's name below the highly respected name of the other
signers. She congratulated him in her childish, cordial way.
It was very decent of Gustav to sign the appeal so unhesi-
tatingly. She was pleased with her friend. Gustav found her
view much more natural, more practically realistic than that
of the politicians, lawyers and business men.

He went on working and living. The work went forward
well, life was fine. The barbarian might be wallowing in the
palace of the Chancellor. It didn't worry Gustav.

3

What Martin Oppermann, Jaques Lavendel, those clever
gentlemen Brieger and Hintze, the experienced Professor Mühlheim, the beautiful, shrewd Ellen Rosendorff had

been unable to accomplish, namely, the shaking of Gustav's rock-like confidence, was effected, curiously enough, by three chairs. To be precise, three chairs at 37 marks, model No. 1184, which had been ordered for a dining-room. Frau Emilie François, Little Thundercloud, had six such chairs standing in her dining-room, and she had long been of the opinion that nine such chairs were necessary. That foolish husband of hers had given Frau Emilie more and more cause for displeasure during the past weeks. The case of that young rascal Oppermann, in spite of the fact that the political situation had become acute, had not yet been cleared up, and the relations of the Rector with Senior Master Vogelsang left much to be desired. Rector François, in order to mollify Emilie to some extent, wanted to present her with the three required chairs for her birthday. Frau François had no objection to this proposal in itself, but she worried over the technical fine points regarding the purchase of the chairs. As it was a case of matching a set, the chairs could only be ordered at Oppermann's. On the other hand it would not look well in these times if a highly placed scholastic official patronized a Jewish firm. The chairs must under no circumstances be delivered in a van belonging to Oppermann's Furniture Stores or by a messenger who was known to be an employee of the firm of Oppermann. She insisted upon François expressly emphasizing this when he ordered the goods. The simplest way would be for him to inform his friend Gustav of her wishes by telephone. Rector François declined to do so. Frau François explained to him that such requests were quite usual, otherwise most of the Jewish shops would have to close down. François, under pressure from her, promised to take an opportunity of arranging the matter with Gustav. He intended to do this jokingly, lightly, incidentally. But Little Thundercloud insisted on being present when François telephoned. It was, no doubt, due to

her presence that the Rector's request did not sound as waggish as he had intended.

Gustav was, in fact, able to manage the telephone conversation in the manner in which Rector François hoped it would
be conducted, lightly and chattily. But after he had hung up
the receiver, his mood underwent a startling change. Were his
friends already beginning to be ashamed of things that came
from him? He grew gloomy, listened to the excited beating
of his heart. Faith and confidence ran out of him like air out
of a defective tire.

4

Dr. Bernd Vogelsang was thirty-five years old. He was
eager and ambitious. The stiff, restrained gestures which
he had acquired in his province grew more graceful in Berlin
without losing an iota of their military precision. His collar
became a centimetre lower. In other directions, too, Bernd
Vogelsang learned a good deal during these weeks. The Leader
had had to struggle fourteen years before he gained the victory. Now, as Chancellor, he did not crow over his triumph,
he restrained himself, he waited until he could dispose of his
enemies once and for all. Bernd Vogelsang, in his own sphere,
imitated the tactics of the Leader. He could wait as well as
the other.

Notwithstanding the strict moderation in his behaviour, he
had now reached the point where the ground was prepared, in
the Lower Sixth of Queen Louise School, for the time when
the genuine German spirit would be able to seize the reins of
power once and for all. Already every one of the boys knew
Heinrich von Kleist's poem, "Germania to Her Children," by

heart, and it did Bernd Vogelsang good to hear his lads repeat the great hate-breeding lines in chorus. Besides this classic the present-day hymn of the Nationalists was also known by heart: the Horst-Wessel Song.

Rector François sat in a weary, melancholy mood in his big office between the busts of Voltaire and Frederick the Great. Of the spirit of Voltaire there was no longer any trace in Queen Louise School and of the spirit of Frederick the Great only its worst side. It was seldom now that any of his assistant masters dared to make open profession of the liberalism which had formerly been the most admirable feature of his school. There was no longer any talk of the possibility of Vogelsang being replaced. On the contrary, François had to look on with folded hands while that man ruined the pliant minds of his pupils for ever.

With all this, Vogelsang maintained a courteous and correct attitude; he gave no grounds for complaint. He avoided, for instance, forcing the issue of the unfortunate Oppermann case. Every week, at most, as opportunity arose, at the close of an interview upon other subjects, he would give a wryly amiable smile, which made an even sharper division between the separate parts of his face, and say in his squeaking East Prussian accent: *"Ceterum censeo discipulum Oppermannum esse castigandum."* * His senior master's witticism made Rector François's blood run cold. He, too, compelled himself to smile under his trim, upturned, white moustache. He stared helplessly through his thick, rimless spectacles at the calm, courteous, superciliously sneering man. He felt as though the other held a promissory note in those reddish hands, covered with their scanty growth of fair hair, an exceedingly troublesome promissory note. "Certainly, my dear colleague," he would hasten to explain. "I haven't lost sight of the affair." And

* "For the rest, I consider that the pupil Oppermann should be punished."

Senior Master Vogelsang never insisted on his point. He only smiled in due acknowledgment. "Good, good," he would say, and take his leave.

Whenever Rector François saw the boy Oppermann, he never failed to address a few friendly words to him. Berthold had matured strikingly during these last weeks. His face was more thoughtful, less soft, more manly. His piercing grey eyes looked preoccupied, pensive under the headstrong brow with its black hair. Women began to notice him. He spoke more and more rarely of his own affairs. Rector François himself, in spite of the fact that the lad knew that he was his friend, could not induce him to make any confidences.

Moreover, Dr. Vogelsang did not plague Berthold. He noticed him no more and no less than the others, and did not dream of disparaging his work. On one occasion, in acknowledging one of Berthold's clever answers, he grinned a polite approval under his thick, fair moustache: "Got a head on you, Oppermann. You've got a head on you." Another time, praising Berthold's fluent prose style, he observed: "A little too fluent, too smooth. Not enough virility, not enough sharp corners. More sternness, Oppermann. 'Sandgrave, be severe.'" Berthold was fair-minded enough to feel that this criticism was well founded.

Heinrich Lavendel observed Vogelsang's calmness with misgiving. A man like Vogelsang does not allow such an affair as that of Arminius the German to lapse. The longer he delayed, the more dangerous it became. "He's only waiting for the steak to be well done. I know all about the swine," said Heinrich to Berthold. "If I were in your place, I wouldn't wait till he jumps on me. *Go ahead,* Berthold. Start things. Take the plunge." Berthold only shrugged his shoulders mutely, rejecting the advice.

Berthold now looked much more grown up than Heinrich.

He was a fine-looking boy. A fine chap altogether. He could prove or disprove anything one asked. But in reality it was he, Heinrich, who was grown up and Berthold who was still a kid. He would have been deuced glad to help him. But all he could do was to stand by and look on while the youngster floundered about. It was enough to make one puke. He did not dare to talk to Berthold a second time. They kept rather quiet while they were cycling home together. But often, now, he went a block further with Berthold, although it was a roundabout way for him, and Berthold quite realized what he was doing.

5

The boy Werner Rittersteg, "Long Lummox," after getting that box on the ear from Heinrich, had at first ceased his courting of the latter's attention. He had even gone so far as to make merry, in his piping, hysterical fashion, over his previously admired fellow-pupil. But when, on one occasion, he asked for a pencil and the invariably obliging Heinrich handed him his own as if nothing had happened, he could not keep up his resentment. The next day he again saluted Heinrich with the English words: *"How are you, old fellow?"* and recommenced his officious manifestations of friendship. Heinrich remained cool. Just as he had previously taken no notice of Long Lummox's attacks, he now merely tolerated his attentions.

When, however, Rittersteg perceived that Heinrich was attaching himself more and more closely to Berthold, he was once more overcome by anger. He, a pure-blooded Aryan, and for that reason superior to all Jews, he who had been admitted

by Bernd Vogelsang into the ranks of the Young Eagles, con-
descended to offer Heinrich his friendship and the ungrateful
chap preferred that stuck-up Oppermann. Who had ever heard
of such insolence? Of course, he shouldn't care a rap what a
Jew boy thought of him. But, unfortunately, he did care. It
riled him, it nettled him to think that Heinrich had no opinion of him. He would have to show him that he was made of
sterner stuff than that dandified Oppermann. He would have
to bring off a great coup, a jolt that would make Heinrich
open his eyes at last.

At this time the election campaign was in full swing and the
prominent journalist Richard Karper, whom the Nationalistic
newspapers facetiously insisted on calling Isidor Karpeles, had
made merry in the Democratic *Tagesanzeiger* at the expense
of the numerous stylistic slips of the Leader. Although the paper was suppressed as a result, the article had had its effect,
particularly on Senior Master Vogelsang. It impelled him, in
his own sphere, to seek a reckoning with this spiteful adversary. He disparaged the petty attacks of Isidor Karpeles, who
called himself Karper, to the boys in his Lower Sixth form. He
explained to them that it was character, not style, that counted
where a statesman was concerned. He expounded his favourite
theory to them, that of the superiority of talking to writing.
He quoted, eliminating therefrom the worst offences against
the spirit of the German language, certain observations of the
Leader on this subject. He branded Karper-Karpeles, the be-
littler of the Leader, as one of those social elements chiefly to
blame for the disintegration, the political and moral decline,
of the German people.

Werner Rittersteg, eyes bulging, gazed humbly on the face
of his respected teacher, from beneath whose flaxen moustache
the stern words issued grandly. But he could not catch the
teacher's eye. The latter's gaze was fixed, Werner Rittersteg
saw plainly, upon Berthold Oppermann. Yes, there was no

doubt about it, Vogelsang's entire bitter attack was directed at Berthold Oppermann.

Long Lummox glanced at Heinrich. The latter had his arms folded upon the desk before him, his broad, fair head bowed, as though prepared to receive a shock. Werner Rittersteg took all this in. But he listened carefully, at the same time, to Vogelsang's words and did not miss a single one of them.

During the midday recess in the school yard he went up to Heinrich Lavendel. It was a fine, warm day. For the first time, that February morning, there was something like spring in the air. *"Look here, Harry,"* said he, and offered him, instead of the pencil he had borrowed, a new one, a big, yellow Kohinoor. He had sharpened it himself with the greatest care. "I've got a pencil-sharpener now, it's an American patent, first-rate, old man," he explained to Heinrich. His prominent eyes were bent dreamily upon the pencil's point, which was long and sharp. "One ought to stick a knife into the guts of a swine like that," he declared suddenly and wildly. Heinrich Lavendel was sitting on the fence, swinging his legs rapidly to and fro in gymnastic fashion. He paused. "Stick a knife into whose guts?" he asked, staring at Rittersteg in astonishment. "That traitor's, of course, that man Karper's, who has been stabbing the Leader in the back." Heinrich said nothing. He merely screwed up his extremely red lips the tiniest bit. Short and sturdy, with his delicate, brownish cheeks, he sat facing the somewhat pallid Long Lummox. The latter, though no judge of men, could read all the thoughts of his hated, admired friend-foe: incredulity, scorn for the braggart, disgust. He could read them all in that little, barely noticeable gesture. Finally, Heinrich took the pencil, fitted the cap carefully over the point, and put it in his pocket. "The one I lent you," he said, "cost five pfennigs. Yours cost at least two groschen, man. But I'm not going to give you the fifteen pfennig change." The Young Eagle, Werner Rittersteg, did not intend to let himself be put off so easily, not he. "You'll see, man," he insisted urgently, unhappily, striving to make the other believe him. "I'll stick a knife in his guts." Then, as Heinrich turned away, shrugging his shoulders, he added, with a disastrous attempt at humour: "If I do it, do I get my fifteen pfennig back?" "You're crazy, man," said Heinrich.

The bell rang. The recess was over. Mellenthin, the porter, supervised his daughter as she put away the rolls which had not been sold during the recess, deliberately ignored the boy Oppermann, nodded amiably to the boy Rittersteg, and stood stiffly at attention as Senior Master Vogelsang passed. Lessons began again.

6

Two days later the newspapers announced that Richard Karper, editor of the *Tagesanzeiger,* had been stabbed in his office by a young hothead. The youth, a certain Werner Rittersteg, who was in the Lower Sixth of Queen Louise School, explained that he had remonstrated with the editor about his notorious article on the Leader and that Karper had then seized and attempted to strangle him, so that he had no choice but to use his knife in self-defence. The papers reported that Rittersteg, after a rigorous examination, as there were no grounds for suspecting that he would escape, had been discharged.

Rittersteg *père,* a wealthy merchant, who held four honorary appointments, gave his son a good box on the ear on the impulse of the moment. Rittersteg *mère* burst into tears on account of the disgrace which the lad had brought upon her. But soon it turned out that Long Lummox was no scoundrel but a hero. The Nationalist newspapers published his photograph. They pointed out that, although the young man's deed could not be unconditionally approved of, it was nevertheless easy to understand that a German youth would be aroused to do violence on account of the dead man's dastardly assertions. Rittersteg *père's* acquaintances rang up to congratulate him. He was appointed to two more honorary positions. After twenty-four hours Rittersteg's parents had forgotten how they had first reacted to what had happened. To them, too, the lad was now a hero. After forty-eight hours Rittersteg *père* would have been able to swear, with a good conscience, that he had always expected his heroic son to accomplish some such patriotic act. In spite of the bad times he rashly promised to let the lad have an outboard engine installed in his rowing-boat for the spring.

Dr. Vogelsang was filled with the deepest satisfaction. The case proved how impressionable German youth was if only one knew how to manage them. A mere hint was enough to set them off in the right direction. Werner Rittersteg was one of those youngsters who would be certain to efface everything evil, corrupt, and disintegrating in Germany.

> What does not suit you
> You must abjure;
> What harms your soul
> Never endure.

These young men knew how to translate their Goethe into action. He, Bernd Vogelsang, had fulfilled his aim in his own small sphere, just as the Leader had in his great one. Eighteen out of the twenty-six boys in the Lower Sixth were now, since Werner Rittersteg's action, avowed Nationalists. Dr. Vogelsang now considered four more of them, in addition to Werner Rittersteg and Max Weber, worthy of admittance to the ranks of the Young Eagles.

However, this very success made him doubly cautious. So long as the victory of the Nationalists was not complete, until the elections were over, therefore, he ran the risk of being persecuted as the intellectual originator of Rittersteg's action. Richard Karper had been a popular author; the newspapers of the Left, in their foolish over-estimation of the importance of the life of an individual, were making a great fuss about his death. Until the elections, a reserved attitude was advisable. After the elections Bernd Vogelsang could announce his part in the affair with redoubled pride. But for the moment the best plan was to keep quiet. Vogelsang scarcely did so much as permit the boy Rittersteg to perceive his appreciation of what he had done. He did not mention the Oppermann case again.

The boys, however, admired their companion extravagantly. He had shown them, by a conspicuous example, how a William Tell, an Arminius the German, would have reacted to the shoddy attacks of a Karper. The fact that he had pleaded self-defence only heightened his glory. Such pleas were permissible against so crafty an enemy. They were an example of that Nordic cunning Dr. Vogelsang was always talking about.

Long Lummox sunned himself in his fame. Although his work was not satisfactory, the masters treated him as if he were made of glass. In the summer he would have a motorboat and cruise about the lake at Teupitzsee with the girls.

There was only one bitter drop in his cup of triumph. He had brought off the great coup. It was a great coup, everyone admitted that. But the person for whose sake he had begun the whole business did not admit it.

He followed Heinrich about, looking at him out of the corners of his eyes, in suspense, in mute entreaty. Wouldn't the fellow now at last say to him: "I was wrong, Werner. I didn't believe you would do it. I ask your pardon. Here is my hand"?

Nothing happened. Nothing happened for a whole week. Heinrich's cold silence drove Long Lummox mad.

On the eighth day, in the yard, exactly at the spot where he had first spoken to Heinrich about his intended action, he walked unexpectedly and rapidly up to him. "Well, man," said he. "Do I get my fifteen pfennig now?" He had pumped himself full of triumph and confidence; he looked steadily at Heinrich, eye to eye, like a superior. But Heinrich returned his look coldly, by no means vanquished. *"No, sir,"* said he. Then, after a short pause, he added maliciously: "If you like, I will deposit the fifteen pfennig as a stake, to be paid out as soon as it is determined whether you acted in self-defence or not." Werner's somewhat pallid cheeks flushed slightly. "Are you playing at detectives, too?" he asked furiously. Heinrich shrugged his shoulders. That was all. Werner, without confessing it to himself, felt that he had been cheated of what he had meant to accomplish by his deed.

Nevertheless, Heinrich had been profoundly affected by Werner's coup. The action of Long Lummox, that *damned fool,* bewildered his judgment and his feelings. What was he to do? He was the only one who knew what had preceded the murder. He could hear quite plainly Werner's high-pitched tones: "One ought to stick a knife into the guts of a swine like that." And then: "You'll see, man, I'll stick a knife in his guts." He perceived that he himself, the pencil, and the fifteen pfennig were very deeply involved in the preliminary steps of this murder. But what else could he have replied except: "You're crazy, man"? They were all absolutely mad, the whole lot of them. The whole country had become a lunatic asylum. Was it not his, Heinrich's duty to tell what he knew, write to the public prosecutor and tell him that this hero was no hero but a scoundrel, that this murder was no act of self-defence, but had been spoken of, was intentional. But if he did give information against the fool, what good would it do? Sensible people knew already and the others were unteachable and would not believe him. He would only make difficulties for himself, his father, the Oppermanns, and Berthold.

His father would certainly advise him not to show up Rittersteg. For good, plausible reasons. Heinrich, even without having consulted his father, knew that well enough. And yet he was perpetually tempted to speak out. One had to give expression to facts. One could not keep quiet when a criminal fool was made into a hero. One was bound, however faint the chance of success, to try to make it plain to others that the chap was a criminal fool. *"Go ahead, Harry,"* he often said to himself. *"Write and tell the attorney what happened."* And directly afterwards, half angry, half smiling, he translated: "Go to it, man." But then reason won the day again. He did not sit down, he did not write, he dragged his knowledge uncomfortably and silently about with him.

Werner Rittersteg did not silently acquiesce in the defeat which Heinrich had inflicted upon him. As he could not make any impression upon him, he proposed at least to show that fellow Oppermann what was what. He wrote a letter to Fritz Ladewig, the President of the Football Club. He again moved, and on this occasion in writing, that Berthold Oppermann, on account of his notorious slander against German civilization, be expelled from the club.

There were nine boys on the committee of the club, one of whom was Heinrich. Ill at ease, Fritz Ladewig made Rittersteg's motion known. The boys looked at one another. No one said anything. Berthold was a good fellow. Why should one start anything before the Rector and the masters had made their position clear? On the other hand Werner Rittersteg was the hero of the school; it was impossible to refuse summarily any motion that he made.

"Well, what do you think?" Fritz Ladewig said after a

while. "You know perfectly well," said Heinrich Lavendel, gazing straight before him without looking at anyone, pale and determined, "that if Berthold goes I shall naturally resign too." A match was scheduled against the Fichte School. Heinrich was guard, whom it was impossible to replace. "We wouldn't consider that," was the verdict. The decision on Werner Rittersteg's motion was adjourned.

Fritz Ladewig reported to Rittersteg what had occurred. He explained that the club took leave to inquire whether he was prepared to insist upon his motion in the face of Heinrich's threat. Werner Rittersteg had accustomed himself, during his membership in the Young Eagles, to give evasive and ambiguous answers to inconvenient questions. "I shall have to think it over privately," said he.

He again approached Heinrich. "I have a suggestion to make to you. I'm ready to swear before anyone that I'm your friend. I declare myself your firm ally. That's worth something, man, the way things are going nowadays. But I can afford to do it. You've only got to promise me one thing. That you'll refrain from voting in the club and will remain a member. If you want to be decent, give me the fifteen pfennig. Say, 'done.' You won't get another chance like it." He tried to be humorous. "Or say 'O.K.'" he entreated smilingly. Heinrich looked him up and down with the impersonal curiosity with which one examines animals in the Zoo. Then he turned his back on him. "Do try to understand me, man," said Werner Rittersteg hastily, with pallid lips. "You need not give me the fifteen pfennig, of course. That was a joke. And you can oppose the motion in the club. But you are not to resign. You have got to promise me that, anyhow." Heinrich turned away in silence. The tall boy laid his hands on the shoulders of the shorter, sturdy figure. He entreated again: "Be reasonable. Don't resign. Stay on."

Heinrich shook the long, pale hands off his shoulders.

7

Rector François spent more and more time in his office. For his private residence was filled with the complaints and adjurations of Little Thundercloud. But even the seclusion of his big office grew more and more gloomy. What did it matter that his book, *The Influence of the Ancient Hexameter on Klopstock's Vocabulary,* was going so well, now that he had to recognize that his life's work had been wasted? In helpless anxiety he watched the rapidity with which the immense, lowering clouds of Nationalism were enveloping his boys. He had loyally done his best to hand on the torch. But now the night was becoming darker and darker, swallowing up his tiny light. Barbarism such as Germany had not experienced since the Thirty Years' War was spreading over the country. The mercenary ruled. His brutal shouts drowned the sweet voices of the poets of Germany.

With cautious fingers, for merely to touch the paper was distasteful to him, Rector François turned over the leaves of the *National-Socialist Anthology.* It was the official song-book of the Nationalist party, whose verses his boys, at Vogelsang's instigation, had now to learn by heart. And what verses they were!

> And when the hand-grenade shall burst,
> The heart within the breast shall laugh——
>
> When Jewish blood spurts from the knife,
> Then all goes well again.

In the classrooms in which formerly the stanzas of Goethe and Heine, the disciplined periods of Kleist's prose, had resounded, they were now blurting out vulgarities of this type. The Rector's face became distorted with disgust. He knew now what it must have been like when the invading barbarians stabled their horses in the temples of ancient cities.

Often he longed to seek consolation and recreation in Max Reger Strasse at the house of his friend Gustav. But he was debarred even from that. Ever since the signing of that manifesto against barbarism, the barbarian newspapers had contained, every second or third day, ugly attacks upon Gustav. He was a marked man and Little Thundercloud had strictly forbidden Rector François to let himself be seen at his house. The masters at his school who were of his intellectual calibre and friendly to him scarcely dared, spied upon from all sides as they were, to utter a single independent word. So it came about that the ageing man generally sat alone in his big study-office; his work was being destroyed before his eyes, together with his friends and his Germany, and he knew that it would not be long before there was as little room for him in this, his last retreat, as for the bust of Voltaire.

During one of these days Rector François met the boy Oppermann in the long corridor that led to the physics hall. Berthold was walking slowly. He looked surprisingly mature. It struck Rector François that the lad, though he was so active in athletics, was beginning to turn his toes in like his father. He gazed at Berthold's keen, melancholy grey eyes, at his worried face. He knew that Little Thundercloud would certainly have scolded him, but he could not do otherwise; he stopped him. He did not quite know what to say. Finally he spoke in his gentle voice, that was now so full of anxiety. "Well, Oppermann, what are you reading in class now?" Berthold answered with more resignation than bitterness in his tone: "The patriotic poet Ernst Moritz Arndt, the patriotic poet Theodor Körner, and more than anything else the *National-Socialist Anthology*, Herr Rector." "Ah, indeed," observed Rector François; he glanced about and, as Mellenthin the porter was nowhere to be seen nor any of the hostile senior masters, but only two little boys belonging to the Fifth Form, he gulped and said: "Look here, my dear Oppermann, that's the way it is now. Ulysses is curious, Ulysses is adventurous, Ulysses has found his way into the den of Polyphemus. That is what happens to every age. But in every age it also happens that in the end Ulysses vanquishes Polyphemus. Only, it often takes rather a long time. I shall most probably not live to see it, but you will." The boy Oppermann gazed at his headmaster. The seventeen-year-old lad actually looked more grown-up than the man of fifty-eight. He said: "You are very kind, Herr Rector." These simple words cheered Rector François; they revived his courage. "Well, now, what I really wanted to say to you, Oppermann, was this," he began again, more eagerly than before. "There is a popular edition just out of one of Döblin's books, called *Giants*. The book as a whole is of a rather baroque type. But there are two fables in it which are worthy of inclusion among the best pages of German prose. They ought to be added to every German reader in use in our schools. Do please read them, my dear Oppermann. One of the fables is about the moon and one is about a dog and a lion. You will be glad to find that even in these times such prose is being written in Germany." The boy Oppermann examined his headmaster with careful attention; then with a strangely far-away note in his deep, precociously mature voice he answered: "Thank you, Herr Rector. I will read the pages you mention." It was perhaps the mysterious tranquillity of the lad's voice which brought it about that Rector François could contain himself no longer. He went close up to the boy Oppermann, who was taller than he, and laid both hands on his shoulders. "Don't lose heart, Oppermann," he said. "I beg of you, in particular, not to lose heart. We all have our parts to play. And the better a man is the more difficult he finds his part. Please tell your Uncle Gustav to show you the letter which Lessing wrote after the birth of his son. I think it was in the year 1777 or '78. Your Uncle Gustav will be sure to know the one I mean. You must grit your teeth, Oppermann, and bear it."

Although Rector François was not exactly Berthold's ideal of virile manhood, this interview nevertheless prevented him for some days from giving himself up to an excessive bitterness of spirit. The next free afternoon he had he went to see his Uncle Gustav and asked if he could see the Lessing letter. "Yes, of course," said Gustav. "It is the letter written on the last day of December, '77. The original is in the Wolfenbüttler library. A fine letter. Düntzer has printed a facsimile of it." He showed Berthold the letter.

Berthold read: "My dear Eschenburg, I am availing myself of a moment in which my wife is lying completely unconscious to write and thank you for your kind sympathy. My joy was so brief. And it was so hard for me to lose my son. He was so intelligent. Do not imagine that the few hours during which I was a father were enough to turn me into a ridiculously fond parent. I know what I am talking about. Was it not the result of intelligence that he had to be brought into the world by the aid of iron forceps? That his suspicions were so soon aroused? Was it not intelligence that prompted him to take the first opportunity of getting away again? It is true that he is carrying his mother off with him. For there is now little hope of my being able to keep her. I wanted, for once, to be as happy as other men are. But the wish turned out badly. Lessing."

Berthold looked through the other letters in the collection. He read one which had been written a week later. "My dear Eschenburg, I can scarcely remember now what I wrote in the tragic letter I sent you. I am heartily ashamed of myself if it gave evidence of the least trace of despair. The hope of my wife's recovery has once more, during the last few days, seriously diminished. I thank you for the copy of the Götz article.

Such material is now the only thing that can distract me. Lessing."

And there was a further letter, again three days later: "Dear Eschenburg, My wife is dead. Now I have also gone through that experience. I am relieved to know that there cannot be many more such grievous experiences for me to go through. Now I must again grope my way alone. Do me a favour, dearest friend, and have a copy made for me, from your large edition of Johnson, of the whole passage on 'Evidence,' together with all the relevant authorities quoted."

Berthold read the letter. It was rather odd that Rector François should have recommended that particular letter about the birth with forceps. But Berthold was touched. The fact that Lessing, at the deathbed of his apparently deeply beloved wife, should have reported his wife's death to his friend and requested him, before the ink was dry, to send him material for his literary work, was a most extraordinary thing. He had not had an easy time of it, that writer Lessing. When he published his *Nathan,* his creed for the emancipation of the Jews, the Nationalists of that day had proclaimed that it would cost him dear. All the same, no one had demanded that he should apologize and recant. In the hundred and fifty years that had elapsed since then, the outlook had grown considerably darker in Germany.

Berthold let his eyes roam over the long and lofty rows of books. All that was Germany. And the people who read those books were Germany. The workmen who, in workingmen's high-schools, spent their leisure grinding away at that difficult writer of theirs, Karl Marx, were Germany. And the Philharmonic Orchestra was Germany. And the motor-car races on the Avus and the workmen's sporting clubs were Germany. But, unfortunately, the *National-Socialist Anthology* was also Germany, as well as the gang in brown uniforms. Could it really be true that this folly was destined to swallow up all the rest? Did people really want to let lunatics rule instead of locking them up? Germany, my Germany. He was suddenly seized by panic. He had learnt self-control; he kept his self-possession even now. Nevertheless, he grew white and red by turns, so that Uncle Gustav approached him, set his powerful, hairy hand on his shoulder, and said: "Keep your spirits up, my boy. In this locality the thermometer never drops under 20° below zero."

8

Edgar Oppermann, in the director's room of the Throat Department of the municipal clinic, signed, without reading them, a number of letters which Nurse Helene had put before him. "There you are, Nurse," he said. "And now I can jump into the lab at last." He looked overworked and harassed. Nurse Helene would willingly have granted him the quarter of an hour's peace in the laboratory. But it was impossible. The situation was too near the danger line. "My goodness," Privy Councillor Lorenz had said to her. "It's high time some strong-minded female took the matter up."

"I'm sorry, Herr Professor," said she. "But I can't let you go just yet. Please read these." And she pointed to some newspaper clippings.

"You get stricter with me every day, Nurse." Edgar tried to smile. He took up the clippings obediently and read them. They were the usual attacks. The only difference was that the tone was now cruder and more vulgar. In every second case, it was alleged, the Oppermann treatment resulted in the death of the patient operated upon. Edgar Oppermann used, almost exclusively, only patients of the third class for his murderous experiments. It was ritual murder on a grand scale which the

Jewish doctor was perpetrating in full view of everybody in order to be able to bask in the flattery of the Jewish press. The eyes of the reader grew dark with fury. "They've been writing that for months," he said sharply. "Can't you spare me these things?"

"No," replied Nurse Helene tersely. Her voice, after Edgar's loud and irritated one, sounded doubly gentle, yet none the less resolute for that. "You should not close your eyes to it any longer, Herr Professor," she said with the sternness with which she was wont to compel a patient to take a disagreeable medicine. "You must do something about it."

"But everybody knows," said Edgar impatiently, "that we get fatal results only in 14.3 percent of cases. Varhuus himself agrees that in more than fifty percent of all the cases which would otherwise be given up as hopeless, the Oppermann treatment is successful." He attempted to master his irritation and smiled. "I am always ready to help people, Nurse. But because the Devil has entered into these swine, must it necessarily be I who must drive him out? You must not ask me to do too much."

But she did not agree. She had sat down. She did not dream of allowing the discussion to end so soon. Stout, powerfully built, she sat before him explaining that articles in these newspapers were certainly not read by medical men, but by a crowd of fanatics. This crowd of fanatics could influence the destinies of the municipal clinic. He could not allow the present state of affairs to continue. He must take action, she went on gently but with determination, he must take action at once. Or did he prefer to wait until Privy Councillor Lorenz told him to?

Edgar Oppermann admitted the logical force of Nurse Helene's argument, but hated the idea of putting it into practice. The people, he declared irritably, who wrote such articles and the people who believed them ought to be put into an asylum, not brought before a court of law. He could not have any dealings with them. No more than with the medicine men of a tribe of aborigines who maintained that consumption could only be cured by placing the dung of an antelope on the patient's eye. "If the Ministry or old Lorenz think it necessary to refute such people, I can't stop them. But *I'm* not going to refute them. I'm not a garbage-remover."

Nurse Helene did not succeed this time. But she did not dream of giving up. She would raise the issue again that evening, tomorrow morning, tomorrow evening. Didn't that great scientist, that child, her Professor Oppermann, realize what was going on around him?

In the hospitals, in the University, on all sides, medical men without ability were seeing signs of hope. An era was beginning in which the requisites were no longer talent and accomplishment but the ostensible consanguinity to a certain race. Nurse Helene had sufficient scientific knowledge to realize that the race theory contained just about as much sense and nonsense as the belief in witchcraft and the Devil. But it was alluring for those whose success had been blocked by the superior attainments of others, to be able to hide their shortcomings by pointing to a non-Jewish ancestry. It was true that, so far, no one had tried to oust her Professor. He was one of the ten or twelve German doctors of world-wide reputation. His students and his patients were devoted to him. But could he not see that already his *protégé,* to wit, Dr. Jacoby, had fallen a victim to the general ill-will? The ugly little man grew daily shyer, clumsier, scarcely daring to go near his patients. And this incomprehensible Professor was unwilling to notice it, was unwilling to grant that little Jacoby's candidacy was hopeless. On the contrary, he consoled him and explained to him, with the most unaccountable optimism, that it could only be a matter of days before his appointment was confirmed.

It was a silly incident which put an end to the voluntary blindness with which Edgar Oppermann had so far protected

himself against the ugly truth. On one of the following afternoons it so happened that a patient of the third class, which
was treated gratis, was caught smoking a cigar contrary to strict
instructions. The man was suffering from an affection of the
throat. The fact of his smoking was not only injurious to the
other patients in the ward but, principally, to himself. The
nurse on duty politely requested the man to stop smoking for
the time being. He made a joke of it and refused to obey. At
last she had to call the physician-in-charge, Dr. Jacoby. The
sight of the ugly little Jew made the man raving mad. In his
sick, hoarse voice he snarled that he didn't care a damn for
what the Jewish doctors told him to do. The whole business,
the Professor together with the others, could go to the Devil.
He was tired of playing the vivisector's rabbit in that place.
He, a man of pure German blood, was going to make it devil-
ish hot for that elegant gentleman, the Herr Professor, in the
German newspapers. The little doctor stood by helplessly, his
face ashen. The other patients joined in. A tumult of hoarse
yelps and barks arose on all sides. They crowded about Dr.
Jacoby in their blue-striped hospital smocks, they shouted from
their beds. He had nothing to offer the shouting, rebellious
ward but the arguments of reason, the least suitable of all seda-
tives. Nurse Helene had the brilliant idea of sending for Dr.
Reimers. He silenced the mutineers with a few strong, obscene
oaths. He did not hesitate to seize the ringleader by the shoulders, give him a good shaking, and eject him from the establishment. He gave the rest a sound talking to in a manly,
robust fashion. The very ones who had originally been the
noisiest partisans of the rebellious smoker, now came to the
conclusion that he was a quarrelsome brute who wouldn't
leave even Hindenburg or God Himself a leg to stand on.
Soon there was nothing more to be heard in the ward but the
gentle voice of Nurse Helene.

The changes in Oppermann's Furniture Stores, the persecution of his brother Gustav in the papers, the vulgar articles against himself, had not disturbed Edgar much. This foolish mutiny completely upset him. He could not understand how sick men, who had been given such diligent scientific attention, could, in spite of its obvious success, turn upon their doctors. The fact that these people, confronted on the one side by their own experience and on the other by a stupid persecution in the papers, decided against their experience and in favour of the persecution, staggered him. He told Nurse Helene that he would now take action.

The very next day he went to see Professor Arthur Mühlheim. He asked Mühlheim whether it was not possible, seeing that he, Edgar, held a public position, to induce the public prosecutor to start legal action. Mühlheim, instead of answering, inquired how old Edgar was. Then he got out a bottle of brandy, distilled in the year of Edgar's birth, poured him a glass, twisted his sly, wrinkled face into a wry smile, and said: "I am afraid, Edgar, I shall not be able to give you much more advice than this."

Edgar, in astonishment, asked how that was and why. Was it not beyond question that the allegations of these newspapers were shameless lies? An enormous weight of evidence could be brought to prove it in a manner which would be comprehensible even to the layman. What could stop him bringing an action, then? Weren't they living in a constitutional country?

"How do you make that out, if you please?" said Mühlheim. And seeing the other's eyes directed upon him in complete stupefaction he explained: "Even if you had come to me a month ago, Edgar, when part of the law was still, at least officially, in force, even then I should have had to advise you, as a conscientious lawyer, against taking action. The writers of the articles would have tried, as a matter of fact, to produce evidence of the truth of their accusations." "But," Edgar interrupted indignantly, "I know—" Mühlheim waved him aside. "The production of such evidence would have been unsuccessful. But the other side would have made a fresh series of insinuations against you, of an increasingly inconceivable and vile character. The court would have permitted inquiry after inquiry into these insinuations, you would have had so much filth piled on your head that you would have died of rage. Don't forget, Edgar, that our opponents have one tremendous advantage over us; their absolute lack of *fairness.* That is the very reason why they are in power today. They have always employed such primitive methods that the rest of us simply did not believe them possible, for they would not have been possible in any other country. They have simply shot down most of the important leaders of the Left, one after the other. They were not punished. To return to the point, you must believe me, Edgar, when I say that you will not find a single judge in Germany today who will condemn the writer of those articles. And after the elections you will not find a single court which will so much as permit you to lodge your complaint."

"I don't believe it, I don't believe it," said Edgar furiously, and struck the table with his fist. But his words sounded like a cry for help.

Mühlheim shrugged his shoulders. He got out a power-of-attorney and asked Edgar to sign it. "The charge will be filed tomorrow," he said. "But I wish you would have spared yourself this disappointment."

"How can my patients put any faith in me when such things are permitted to be said against me?" growled Edgar. "Who asks you to treat your patients? Who tells you that this country wants any such things?" asked Mühlheim bitterly. "But the judges," continued Edgar excitedly, in almost childlike bewilderment, "who have had an academic education, they are sure to know that all this stuff is utter nonsense. Or do they

believe that I sacrifice Christian children?" "They have persuaded themselves," replied Mühlheim, his small, shrewd face
grotesquely contorted with passion, "that, having been born
in the East, you are quite capable of such a thing because of
your blood and natural inclinations."

Edgar, after his interview with Mühlheim, went his way in
a state of utter dejection. Had the world changed so completely within a few weeks or had he grown to be forty-six
years old in utter ignorance of the world around him?

9

Next day he had a rather long conversation with his daughter Ruth. Ruth was used to having her father make fun
of her in an amiable, good-humoured way. He did so on this
occasion, but it was not the same as usual, and the girl was
quick to see that his self-confidence had been shaken. Well as
she knew that he was convinced on scientific principles of the
absurdity of her nationalism, and that her views were a mere
comedy to him, she had not been able to resist advocating her
ideas in his presence with as much wild enthusiasm as ever.
But now, noticing that he was rather shaky, she grew gentler.
Gina Oppermann sat with them without uttering a word. She
was a silly little woman, she had no idea what they were talking about. But she knew every habit, every mood of her husband and daughter, and she was puzzled at Edgar's shy attempts to learn something from his daughter.

During the same week old Privy Councillor Lorenz informed Edgar that Professor Varhuus had finally declared
that he was unable to support the candidacy of Dr. Jacoby.
Privy Councillor Lorenz assumed a particularly gruff manner

during this interview, he was altogether the old "Fear-God" known to his students. Edgar had grown wiser during these last few days, he could see the man's painful embarrassment through his gruffness.

"Give me your advice, my dear colleague," growled the old fellow. The words rumbled out of his gold-filled mouth like pieces of rock. "What am I to do?" He thrust his enormous, white-haired, copper-coloured face towards Edgar. "I can, of course, insist upon its being Jacoby. Then he will follow suit. But then those ——s will cancel the appropriation for your lab. Give me your advice."

Edgar contemplated his hands. "It seems obvious to me how we should treat this case, Privy Councillor," said he. His voice sounded cool and decisive, as it did when he spoke to a patient about the necessity of operating. "You withdraw Jacoby's candidacy and I'll withdraw my action against the ——s, if I may borrow your expression." He laughed. He seemed particularly cheerful.

Old Lorenz felt damned uncomfortable. That chap Edgar Oppermann was a first-class scientist and he liked him. He had made a promise to him. Old Lorenz could do anything, did everything, feared God and nothing else in the world. And now, all of a sudden, for the first time in his life, he was afraid of the ——s who put their noses in his business and obliged him to break a promise. It was a swinish business. But he could not afford to have the appropriation cancelled. He had often been obliged to tell relatives and close friends that an operation had failed and the patient was dead. Old Lorenz was an honest man; this situation was ten times more uncomfortable.

"Don't you think it would be better, Herr Privy Councillor," asked Edgar suddenly, with that wry, frozen smile still on his lips, "if I threw up things here, before they throw me out?"

Old Lorenz's complexion took on a bluish tinge. "You must be mad, Oppermann," he burst out. "Open your eyes. The disease that ails this country, man, is acute, not chronic. I am not going to allow you to diagnose it as chronic. Listen to me, man. Those ——s!" he shouted out suddenly, and brought his great, red fist crashing down upon the table, so that the papers flew about the room. "They're all ——s, those politicians. And I'm not going to do them that favour. If they think I'm going to do them that favour, they're dancing on air."

"Dancing on air," thought Edgar. "What extraordinary expressions these Bavarians use." "Very well," said he. "I am well aware that you have done what you could, Privy Councillor Lorenz. You are a good colleague." "I don't know whether I am, Oppermann," said old Lorenz. "For the first time in my life I really don't know whether I am. And that is what troubles me."

10

The completion of the bridge which was to adorn Herr Wolfsohn's mouth had been delayed rather longer than Herr Wolfsohn had expected. The price had gone up, too. The dentist, Hans Schulze, the member of the "Old Pickled Herrings," wanted to charge him 85 marks, alleging that during the course of his work in Wolfsohn's mouth new and unsuspected difficulties had arisen and further traces of decay had been discovered, to such an extent that in the case of anyone but Herr Wolfsohn he would not undertake the job for less than 100 marks. Herr Wolfsohn had finally, with much difficulty and after several serious and several facetious conversations, got him down to 75 marks. He had paid 50 marks in accordance with the terms of the agreement. Hence the new teeth were still not entirely his own property. But he could have paid the balance of 25 marks at any time and thus have made the teeth his own. If he did not do so, it was because he had heard from many people that the accession of the Nationalists to power would be followed by an inflation of currency, and because he hoped to settle the balance of his debt by paying it in depreciated money.

The new frontage was dear, but it was magnificent. The moustache above Herr Wolfsohn's lips now looked really smart, and his eyes had a doubly alert and lively effect above the new, perfect teeth. Markus Wolfsohn now smiled, more than ever, at business.

However, when he was unobserved by strangers, he seldom smiled, in spite of his new white and gold magnificence. And yet business was better than one might have expected during this rather quiet winter season. The talk of inflation induced many people to spend their money on household needs instead of putting it in the savings bank. Herr Wolfsohn had also earned some money in commissions during this February; not so much, of course, as during November, but he could not honestly complain about business. There were other things that troubled him.

Little things at first, quite unimportant in themselves, but, taken in the mass, enough to spoil one's appetite. Herr Wolfsohn's self-respect, for example, was not impaired by the fact that Herr Lehmann, at Lehmann's Coffee House, no longer inquired whether everything was all right or not. The *Berliner Zeitung,* too, continued, as before, only to be available in a single copy, a perfectly scandalous state of affairs, and unless you bought it yourself, you could take root before you got hold of it. Nor was Herr Wolfsohn's self-respect impaired by the fact that he was not given quite so cordial a welcome at the "Old Pickled Herrings" as formerly. Nevertheless, this circumstance was decidedly more disagreeable than the others, and on one occasion someone had passed a remark which deeply hurt Herr Wolfsohn. At skat they kept a strict watch upon one another to prevent gypping when the winnings were figured, for twenty percent of these had to be paid into the club's treasury. Out of this twenty percent the expenses of the "Old Pickled Herrings" were paid, above all the cost of the great excursion, the "Gentlemen's Outing" which took place every year on Ascension Day. On an occasion when Herr Wolfsohn had been able to win a particularly substantial amount, and his fellow-players were lamenting the fact, he had tried to console them, while paying his twenty percent into the club treasury, by telling them that this money would all come back to them in the pleasures of Ascension Day. "As for you, August," he had said to the chief loser, "you won't get left, you'll drink up half of the punch by yourself anyway." "Don't give yourself airs, man," the other had snapped. "You're dreaming if you imagine that we'll take you along with us this summer." That was of course only a stupid joke, August was drunk, and Wolfsohn behaved as if he had not heard anything. But August's thrust went home, August's words rankled, even today, in Herr Wolfsohn's breast.

Perhaps his brother-in-law Moritz Ehrenreich was right in clearing out now as he was doing. Yes, they had got to that point now: Moritz Ehrenreich was due to sail for Palestine on the third of March, from the French port of Marseilles, on the steamer *Mariette Pacha*. He was to take over the printing and editing of a Hebrew sports newspaper in the town of Tel-Aviv in Palestine. Moreover, he had shown himself munificent up to the last; he had given some of his household chattels to the Wolfsohns. Herr Wolfsohn, however, saw him go with one moist eye and one dry one. He realized, now that Moritz was actually going away, that he would miss him more than he had thought. On the other hand he was glad to be rid of him; for he no longer felt sufficient confidence, in spite of his cheerful talk, to oppose the eternal jeremiads of his brother-in-law.

No, Herr Wolfsohn's self-confidence was being undermined, it was being gradually dissipated in all directions. It was not only those little incidents in Lehmann's Coffee House or in the "Old Fritz" restaurant or in the "Old Pickled Herring" circle. Far more serious was the affair of the superintendent Krause and the damp stain above the picture called "The Waves at Play." Herr Wolfsohn was, unfortunately, by no means as friendly with the superintendent Krause as formerly. The two gentlemen did, of course, still exchange a few words when they happened to meet but it very rarely occurred that Herr Krause told him a funny story. And when, not so long ago, Herr Wolfsohn had asked him straight out when the damp stain, which had already spread quite a long way under the picture, would finally be removed, the superintendent Krause had become cheeky and had said that Herr Wolfsohn had no business to be so particular in view of the cheap rent he paid. There were a lot of people who would be only too glad to take over the flat, stain and all. Superintendent Krause would, of course, extend his lease just the same; Herr Wolfsohn was sure of that. But nevertheless Krause's remarks were a piece of true German *chutspe* * and Herr Wolfsohn would take care not to forget them.

But negotiations with the superintendent Krause were a picnic compared with certain chance encounters with Herr Rüdiger Zarnke. During the progress of the work on the bridge Herr Wolfsohn had drawn a mental picture of the particular satisfaction it would be to him henceforth, in possession of the new frontage, to encounter Herr Zarnke on the

---

* The meaning of this Yiddish word is "impudence," "cheek," and the epithet, "treudeutsch," which precedes it is sometimes used to convey a similar idea. The merit of Herr Wolfsohn's witticism resides in the application of a familiar German epithet expressing something typically Jewish to a Yiddish word expressing something typically German.—*Translator's Note.*

stairs. For hitherto, when the two gentlemen encountered one
another, Herr Zarnke had been in the habit of smiling scornfully to himself, so as to show his strong, white teeth. It had
been a perfect torment to Herr Wolfsohn that he was unable,
because of his own decayed teeth, to return this scornful smile.
The idea of now, in possession of the new frontage, returning
the scorn of Herr Zarnke with a white and gold smile had
made his heart beat high. He had been a bit too previous with
his triumph, however. Herr Zarnke had enlisted in the troops
of the Nationalists and become a troop-leader. Haughtily, ar-
rayed in all the pomp of his brown uniform, with high boots
and two stars on his collar, he went creaking up and down the
stairs. When Herr Wolfsohn saw him from a distance, he
grew weak about the knees. He preferred to turn back, go up
the stairs again, and slink into his flat. But even there he was
not safe now. Herr Zarnke, especially when he knew that
Wolfsohn was at home, was in the habit of bawling out, at
the top of his voice, the Nationalist hymn with the verses
about Jewish blood spurting from the knife. In booming tones,
impossible to ignore, he would tell his wife how the Nationalists, the moment they took over the reins of government on
the fifth of March, would make mince-meat of the Jews. He
went into harrowing details. The Jews would have to get off
the sidewalk the moment even a private of the Nationalist
troops, not to mention an officer, appeared in the distance. If
one of them dared so much as make a wry face about it, he'd
get a smack in the jaw right away. It would be a particular
pleasure to him, Zarnke, to take on the swine next door. He'd
put him through a special course of treatments, and after the
course was over the fellow would have to pick his bones out
of the gutter one by one. Herr Wolfsohn listened to these remarks with some uneasiness. Shrinking, by no means in buoyant mood in spite of the new frontage, the little man sat in
his wingchair without daring to stir. He took the children into

the bedroom, stared at the damp stain, turned on the radio. Perhaps there would be something very loud on, a military march or a Nationalist tune, which would drown the proclamations of his neighbour.

Sometimes, when the music was very warlike, he would draw himself a mental picture of how, when the tide turned, which should be soon, he would give it to Herr Zarnke. He would stop him on the staircase. He would be standing on the upper stair and Herr Zarnke on the lower. "What's the big idea, then, you lousy slob, you?" he would say. "What's the matter with you? You call me a swine, do you, sir? I never heard of such a thing. You think you're superior to me because I'm an Israelite? That's simply ridiculous. My forefathers were already organized and industrialized and completely civilized when your venerated ancestors were still apes climbing about the primeval forest. Understand me, man? And now, get out." People would come out of all the doors and listen, there would be Herr Rothbüchner, Frau Hoppegart, Herr Winkler, Frau Josephson. They would all enjoy themselves listening to the smart way he would sound the right-about-turn to that chap in his high boots. It would be a great occasion for them all, especially, of course, for Frau Josephson. And when Herr Zarnke retired in confusion he would give him a kick in the hindquarters so that he would positively fly down the stairs. Sternly did Herr Wolfsohn elaborate his picture. How Herr Zarnke, when he got to the bottom, would get up painfully, having lost one of his big boots during his rapid descent, how he would dust his brown tunic and slink away, looking small and ugly. Baring his white and gold teeth, Herr Wolfsohn smiled broadly during this pleasant flight of fancy. Softly but distinctly he uttered the splendid phrases in which he would settle the other once and for all. But then the radio music stopped, the voice of Herr Zarnke was again audible and Herr

Wolfsohn slunk back into his wingchair, his bravado snuffed out.

Yes, it was all over with his snug security in the beloved flats in Friedrich Karl Strasse. *"My home is my castle,"* had become a shallow scholastic memory without any tangible significance. The two hundred and seventy flats still remained as much alike as so many sardine tins, but an inexplicable change had taken place as far as Herr Wolfsohn was concerned. Barely six weeks ago, no, barely four weeks ago, he had been one of those two hundred and seventy householders, having the same duties, the same opinions, the same joys, the same sorrows, the same rights as all the others; he had been merely a peaceful taxpayer who wanted nothing from anybody and against whom no one had a grudge. Now, the others still remained what they had always been whereas he —he read it wherever he went, heard it at every street corner —he had suddenly become a rapacious wolf that had driven the Fatherland to destruction. How had that happened? Why had it happened? Herr Wolfsohn sat and brooded, could not understand it.

At the store, matters were still the best. But, even here, things were not quite the same as they had been. Business was active, there was much to be done, but whenever the bustle died down for a short while the men stood about with gloomy, blank faces. Even the active chief clerk Siegfried Brieger was not as brisk as usual; he began to show the weight of his sixty years.

Then something occurred, an incident which, perhaps, made a profounder impression on Herr Wolfsohn than any of the other changes he had experienced. The chief, Martin Oppermann, was a kindly gentleman and treated his employees well, but at bottom he was arrogant; that was a generally accepted fact. During this period it occurred that Martin Oppermann

came into the Potsdamer Strasse branch just when Herr Wolfsohn, as very rarely happened, had to let a customer go without having made a sale. The customer had been a disagreeable
fellow, one of those people, very likely, who would throw a
man out of a moving subway train. At any rate, he was a
swastika man, but Herr Wolfsohn's skill in serving customers
had in the majority of cases been equal to dealing with such
characters. He was deeply mortified that this incident should
have occurred at the very time that his boss was looking on.
And, just as he had anticipated, no sooner was the customer
gone than Martin Oppermann came, with his heavy step,
right up to Herr Wolfsohn. "Did you fail, Wolfsohn?" he
asked. "Unfortunately, yes, Herr Oppermann," said Wolfsohn
and waited for the reprimand that was bound to come. He had
a thousand arguments ready, yet he knew perfectly well that
not one of them would be adequate; the fact was that there
should be no such word as "fail."

And then the miracle happened. There was no reprimand.
Instead, Martin Oppermann looked at him with melancholy
brown eyes and said: "Don't let it worry you, Wolfsohn."

Markus Wolfsohn was a nimble-witted man, of quick understanding, but that remark struck him dumb. Martin Oppermann must have gone mad. "By the way, you look changed
to me," the madman continued, "brisker, younger." Wolfsohn
pulled himself together, groping for the right answer. "That's
due to my teeth, Herr Oppermann," he stammered. The next
moment he realized that it had been stupid to have given the
chief an impression of extravagance, but Herr Oppermann's
lunacy had thoroughly upset him. "I had to go into debt to get
the work done," he hastened to add; "I really could not let it
go any longer." "You have a boy, Wolfsohn, haven't you?"
Oppermann inquired. "One boy and a little girl, Herr Oppermann," replied Wolfsohn. "It's a great responsibility in these
times. One gets so desperately fond of the youngsters but

sometimes one almost wishes they had never been born." He smiled apologetically, a little wryly.

Martin Oppermann looked at him. Wolfsohn expected that he would make some casual remark, some joking phrase, something smart and cheerful. That was in order. And Martin Oppermann did not fail in this. "Keep a stiff upper lip, Wolfsohn," he said. But then he added something astonishing, something altogether out of the ordinary, an unnatural thing, entirely unsuitable to the head of so great and old-established a firm. He added very gently and, as it seemed to Wolfsohn, at once sadly and grimly: "None of us are having an easy time of it, Wolfsohn."

II

Martin Oppermann was really not having an easy time of it. The elections were at hand. The Nationalists were bound to come into power and with them would come arbitrary rule and violence, no one doubted that now. What had been done in Oppermann's Furniture Stores as a safeguard against the impending storm? Within the next few days the Oppermann shops, with the exception of the original store, would be merged into the German Furniture Company. They had done nothing further. As for the bitterly necessary alliance with Wels, which had been stupidly blocked by his, Martin's, own behaviour, was that being taken up on a new basis?

Martin Oppermann sat alone in his private office, his arms resting heavily on the top of his desk, and stared gloomily into space with his melancholy brown eyes. The Oppermanns were already being attacked on all sides. Almost daily the newspapers published tirades against Gustav or Edgar, and they were even beginning to start on the firm now. Was Wels behind it? Martin slowly took out his eyeglasses and with his heavy step walked over to the framed document which proclaimed: "The merchant Immanuel Oppermann of Berlin has rendered good service to the German Army by his supplies to the troops. Signed, von Moltke, Field Marshal." He took the framed document from the wall, turned it over mechanically, examined its blank back. A notice was now being widely circulated, according to which the Oppermann Furniture Stores had made a donation of ten thousand marks to the "Red Sports Club." It was printed in facsimile in all the Nationalist newspapers, it was posted on the walls of their barracks. The note was typed on an authentic sheet of Oppermann stationery and appeared duly signed by himself. The only difference was that actually it had not been the "Red Sports Club" that was concerned but the "Jewish Sports Club" and the sum involved was not ten thousand marks but one thousand. However, it was useless for him to protest. He had no more chance than his brother Edgar, whom they were bespattering with mud in spite of the fact that living witnesses of his scientific knowledge and skill were walking around by the hundred.

Martin hung the framed letter back on the wall, shook his head slowly several times, went back to his desk. Suddenly his big face changed alarmingly. He pounded the desk with his heavy fist. "Damn that gang—" he snarled.

Swearing did no good. He had kept his dignity throughout his forty-eight years. They should not see him lose it now.

Perhaps the negotiations with Wels were progressing? Brieger who, as a rule, was so alert and talkative, that damned Brieger, was obstinately silent, and Martin was reluctant to ask him.

Heavy, portly, irritated, he sat on in silence. Only too soon he would hear about the negotiations with Wels. He suspected, feared, knew it would be so. He would hear about the matter this very evening and from lips much less congenial to him

than those of Herr Brieger. Jaques Lavendel had invited him
for that evening, had urgently requested him to come as there
were important matters to discuss. The discussion could not be
about anything but Wels. How unpleasant the news must be
when Brieger would not tell him personally but had asked
Jaques Lavendel to do so.

That evening Martin found his brother-in-law Jaques as
talkative and outspoken as ever. They offered him sandwiches,
spread with a particularly fine brand of goose-liver, and some
excellent port. They were always eating and drinking in
Jaques's house. Jaques came to the point immediately. "If we
were compelled," he said in his hoarse voice, "to consider
Klara's share in the business as part of our necessary income,
if we could not go on, as thank God, we can, without it, I
assure you, Martin, that I would sell out her share right now
at any price. If, within a few days, you don't succeed in building up a more substantial safeguard than that of the German
Furniture Company, then I can see the end of things for your
business. Yes," he continued with half-closed eyes, absentmindedly taking a large bite of goose-liver sandwich, "Brieger
has requested me to inform you of the state of the negotiations
with Wels. You, Martin, will probably think," he smiled in
his wry, friendly way, "that they are in a bad way: I find they
are not in a bad way." He washed down the remains of the
sandwich with a mouthful of port. Martin watched him, the
seconds seemed endless to him. His nerves were taut, ready to
snap; the sight of the man opposite, eating and drinking, disgusted him. "The fact of the matter is," Jaques Lavendel continued at last, "that that fire-eating *goi* lays less stress upon the
issue itself than upon external formalities, typical *goi* nonsense.
He's standing on his dignity." Jaques made a tiny pause before he uttered the word "dignity" and gave it a slightly ironic
intonation. Coming from his lips in this manner, the idea it
conveyed appeared paltry, hollow, and ridiculous. It irritated

Martin deeply to hear the man before him speak with such contemptuous pity of a quality which lay so near to his own heart. The other continued: "Just think, Martin, Herr Wels has, strangely enough, become quite infatuated with you. He will only deal with you, not with Brieger. He wants you to come and see him. He apparently does not feel quite safe in your office."

Martin was seated in a soft easy-chair. In Jaques Lavendel's house there was neither Oppermann furniture, nor modern furniture, but merely comfortable furniture. Yet Martin felt that he was not securely seated. He was seized with a fit of giddiness; he felt as he had on his first voyage to America in a small boat during a heavy storm. Don't let yourself go. Poise, dignity. That man over there had just made fun of poise and dignity. For him they were—Martin who, in contrast to most people in Berlin strictly avoided the use of slang, suddenly knew exactly what poise and dignity meant to his brother-in-law Jaques Lavendel—for him they were merely *hot air*. But he would not give in. He would not let himself go. He scarcely gripped the arms of his chair a bit more firmly. "I don't think that I shall call on Herr Wels," he said. His voice sounded steady, a bit gruffer perhaps than usual. He saw his sister Klara looking at him and suspected there was pity in her glance. He did not want her pity, he did not care a hang about her pity. His eyes were suddenly no longer sleepy, no longer melancholy, but bright with fury. "I wouldn't think of it," he shouted and stood up. "What is the swine presuming? Does he suppose I am going there to be insulted? That's ridiculous. I wouldn't think of it."

Jaques and Klara looked at the blustering man in silence. In fact, Jaques opened his blue eyes very wide, gazed at Martin attentively in a most friendly manner. When he spoke, there was no trace of irony in his hoarse voice but only the kindly persuasion of an older, more experienced friend. "Rave on to

your heart's content, Martin," he said. "It does one good to
rave. But I feel sure that when you have slept on it you will
realize that raving won't get you out of this mess. I, myself,
can see that there are more attractive things in life than an
interview with Herr Wels. But it would be worse still to
have to close up the business. Have a good sleep on it, then go
and see Heinrich Wels. Go as soon as you can. The best thing
would be to go tomorrow. The very best, tomorrow morning.
Whatever you get out of Wels will be a gain. And the sooner
you go, the more you can get."

Martin had sat down again. "I wouldn't think of it," he
repeated sullenly, but now, after his outburst, his voice sounded
surprisingly subdued.

"*Go ahead*, Martin," Jaques said suddenly in an unusually
hearty tone. "We've got to settle with Wels. *Go ahead*." Oh, to
be able to swear, thought Martin, to give vent to one's fury!
But there would be no sense in it before these two. They were
too reasonable. They looked on quietly, pityingly, and in their
hearts they despised one. He sat sullenly and stiffly in his chair.
He felt weak in his knees. A sudden, ravenous hunger came
over him; yet the sandwiches before him nauseated him.

He rose, thrusting the heavy chair back violently. "Well,"
he said, "I must be leaving now. Thanks for the sandwiches
and the wine. And for your advice," he added grimly.

"By the way," said Klara suddenly in her quiet, resolute
voice, "I would not coerce the boy, Martin." Martin looked up
in astonishment. "I made a mistake," she continued, "when I
advised him to apologize." Martin did not understand. What
on earth was she talking about? What boy? Berthold? What
was the matter now? It developed that he knew nothing whatever about the affair, that Berthold had never spoken to him
about it. This astonished even Jaques, who was never astonished at anything. He told his brother-in-law the story, with
tact and discretion.

This time Martin did not think of poise and dignity. Nor did he lose his temper, as he had a few minutes before in connexion with the Wels affair. These two blows, coming one on top of the other, robbed him of fury just as they robbed him of poise. The Oppermanns were destined to be wiped out, to be beaten; it was Fate, there was no sense in struggling against it. There were the attacks on Edgar, the articles against Gustav. Tomorrow he would have to go and see Wels, the narrow-minded, despised Heinrich Wels, and humble himself. And after that Berthold was to humble himself, his handsome, talented, beloved boy. Berthold had made a true statement, they would not allow him to speak the truth. Because he was his, Martin Oppermann's, son he had to humble himself and say that a truth was a lie merely because it was he who had uttered it.

Martin sat with bowed head. Job, he thought. What was the story of Job? He was a man from the land of Uz and people made silly jokes about that. He was a beaten man. Many plagues descended upon him. His business was destroyed, his children were destroyed, he became a leper, he was angry with God. And Goethe had taken the whole story and used it as a prologue to *Faust*. A beaten man. It had been destined; thus it had been decreed on the first day of the year and thus it had been reaffirmed on the Day of Atonement. This he had been taught. Perhaps he should have closed his stores on the Day of Atonement, if for no other reason than in honour of Grandfather Immanuel. Brieger had always advised it. One had three or four Bibles lying about the house, one should read them sometimes, about Job for example, but somehow one never got around to it. One never managed to get around to anything, not even to one's physical exercises, one grew to be an old man, one grew into a beaten man, and one never managed to do anything.

"I would not coerce the boy," repeated Klara. "I would prefer to take him out of the school." "I'll see," said Martin, and his voice sounded detached and distant. "But I'm not going to Wels," he declared grimly. "Many thanks once again," he added and tried to smile. "You must forgive me. It was rather a lot, coming all at once."

"He'll go and see Wels, naturally," said Jaques Lavendel after Martin had left. "They've done well here in Germany," he added meditatively. "They haven't had to get used to hardships." Below, in the street, a band of Nationalist mercenaries was passing on the way home from an election meeting. They were singing:

> "When the hand grenade shall burst,
> The heart within the breast shall laugh."

Jaques Lavendel shook his head. "That can be reversed," he observed.

> "When the hand grenade shall laugh,
> The heart within the breast shall burst."

He closed the shutters, took out some phonograph records, and played the tunes he loved. The odour of the sandwiches and the wine was in the room. Absentmindedly he took up another, chewed it slowly, and sipped some wine. His broad, fair head aslant, his eyes closed, he hummed in unison with the record:

> "We used to be six brothers,
> Our stocking trade did thrive;
> One of us died, poor fellow,
> And then we were only five.
>
> Yossel, come play the fiddle . . ."

12

Martin, meanwhile, arrived in Cornelius Strasse. He found Liselotte and Berthold still in the morning-room. He noticed how mature the boy had grown during the past few weeks, how worried and old-looking he had become. He was a bad father to have seen nothing of it all this time. He put his heavy hand on the boy's shoulder. His son was now actually taller than he. "Well, my boy," he said. Berthold realized at once that his father knew everything. It was a relief to him that he was about to talk about it.

"Was your conference with Jaques a disagreeable one?" asked Liselotte. She had already guessed from the sound of Martin's footsteps before he had even entered the room that something unpleasant had happened. "To speak in our brother-in-law's jargon, it wasn't a picnic," answered Martin.

He looked at Berthold again, pondering. Should he speak to him now? He was worn-out, dog-tired. What he would like to do most would be to switch off the lights, close his eyes, not even go to bed, just stay sitting where he was, in this chair. It was not as comfortable a chair as the one in Jaques's house. It was an Oppermann chair. He could easily have afforded a much more costly one, it was merely owing to a sense of duty that he used only Oppermann furniture in his home. The reason why he had muddled up the Wels affair was only because he had not been in good form that day. Perhaps it would be better to speak to Berthold tomorrow. But then it might be easier now as Berthold and Liselotte were both there together. Besides, tomorrow he would have to go and see Wels and humble himself.

"You've certainly had your troubles, too, during these last weeks, my boy," he began. His voice sounded calm but not too serious. One had more strength than one supposed; often one thought, "I've come to the end of my rope, I can't do another thing," yet one somehow found further reserve strength. "It was kind of you not to worry us with your affairs. But I would have helped you willingly, Berthold. And so would Mother." Liselotte turned her calm face from one to the other. She had not had an easy time, during these past weeks, between silent husband and silent son. The times made heavy demands upon the Christian wife of a Jewish husband and the Christian mother of a Jewish son. It was a good thing they were about to talk things over now.

"You didn't have good luck with your lecture, Berthold," she said, when Martin had finished the story. "You had been looking forward to it so much." It would have been difficult to express everything that had happened in connexion with the lecture more simply; yet Berthold realized that his mother had said all there was to be said, that she understood the slightest detail of the affair as well as he did. "It was a good lecture," he declared with sudden passion. "I kept the manuscript. You'll see, Father, and you, too, Mother, it's the best I've ever done. Rector François will agree, too. Dr. Heinzius would have been very pleased with it." "Yes, my boy," said Liselotte soothingly.

"But Dr. Vogelsang is there now," Martin said, returning to the point. "There are still two months before the Easter promotions," he went on. "You'll have to put up with him until then." "You mean I am to beg his pardon?" Berthold was trying to speak dispassionately, in a perfectly matter-of-fact tone, without bitterness. "Recant?" he ended dryly.

It was perhaps just that dry tone which irritated Martin. "I'm dog-tired," he said to himself. "I'm in a wretched humour. I should have put off this talk until tomorrow. I mustn't let myself go now under any circumstances." "I don't mean anything as yet," he said aloud. He had intended his voice to sound pleasant but the answer came out somewhat abruptly. "What do you suppose will happen if you refuse?" he continued after a short silence, as though coolly weighing the matter. "I shall probably be expelled," said Berthold. "In other words," Martin said, "you would have to forgo German schools altogether. As well as any future academic career in Germany." He continued to speak in a business-like, matter-of-fact tone. He took out his eyeglasses and polished them. "You will understand, Berthold," he said finally, "that I cannot agree to that."

Berthold looked at his father. There he sat, apparently calm and clear-headed. He was arguing with him as though he were a business associate from whom he wished to obtain some concession. So that was what his father was like when something really mattered. When something mattered, he did not understand the issue. He did not want to understand it. He, Berthold, had been quite right not to have spoken to him before. They were waiting for him to say something. "I would endure a great deal, if I did not have to make this"—he hesitated—"this apology," he added finally. "We all have to endure a great deal at present," grumbled Martin bitterly, without looking at his son. It sounded harsher than he had meant. Berthold grew pale and drew his lower lip between his teeth. Liselotte anxiously tried to smooth matters. "I believe," she said, "that it would be a comfort to your father, especially under the present conditions, if you could prevail upon yourself to do it." "Don't make it so damned hard for me," growled Martin morosely. "Must you all make it so hard for me? Those curs, those mean, low curs!" he shouted suddenly.

Berthold had never before heard his father shout. Startled, he jumped up and looked into the other's eyes, which were wide open, sullen, and blood-shot. Liselotte, too, was very pale. "I think you should do it, Berthold," she said very gently. "Should, should," scoffed Martin. "He *must* do it. I, also, must do a great many things which I do not like," he repeated obstinately, viciously.

"We won't make any decision now," pleaded Liselotte. "Let us sleep on it. No one is going to coerce you," she encouraged Berthold. "You need do nothing, my boy, which you do not do of your own free will."

Martin, after his outburst, had sat down again. He pressed his lips firmly together. "Sackcloth and ashes," ran his thoughts, "Canossa, Job. I should not have talked to him until tomorrow." He stared at his son and his wife vacantly. "It has taken me forty-eight years," he said finally, "to find out that dignity can sometimes be overestimated. You are seventeen, Berthold. I tell you it is so. But I do not expect you to believe me." He spoke soberly, but it sounded like a monotonous lament. The words sounded far-off; the whole man in all his heaviness was so exhausted that Berthold and Liselotte were even more shocked by his weariness than they had been by his outburst.

13

Next day, at five minutes to eleven, Martin Oppermann sat on a chair on the third floor of the furniture shop of Heinrich Wels and Son.

Wels had made an appointment with him for eleven o'clock. Wels had not spoken to him personally on the telephone. He had sent an employee to tell Martin he might come at eleven o'clock. Martin came at five minutes to eleven.

He was not conducted to a private ante-room. They let him wait in the sales department. This floor was large, airy, and scrupulously clean. The firm of Heinrich Wels and Son believed in cleanliness. Martin Oppermann had ample time to take note of this, for he was kept waiting a long time.

He was sitting on a chair, really too small for his heavy person. He sat upright, in an uncomfortable position, forcing himself to look straight ahead, glancing neither to the right nor to the left. Business was quiet, yet there was much activity in Martin Oppermann's vicinity. The employees rushed back and forth on fictitious errands, eager to look at the head of Oppermann's Furniture Stores as he crouched there, waiting until it should please Herr Wels to receive him.

Martin Oppermann saw them looking at him but pretended not to see them. He sat motionless.

He glanced at his watch. He thought it must be twenty past eleven but it was only eleven-sixteen. His watch was a fine, heavy, gold one. He had received it from Grandfather Immanuel the first time he had been called upon, at the age of thirteen, to give a reading from the Torah. The German Furniture Company had, of course, a new trade-mark. The picture of old Immanuel had vanished from the firm's letterheads. The new emblem was a very fine one. Klaus Frischlin had had it designed by a first-class artist. But many firms had fine emblems on their stationery.

It must be eleven-twenty-five now. It was eleven-twenty-one. All he had to do was to sit straight and keep his head up. Berthold would be worse off. All that he, Martin, had to do was to go on sitting there. The boy would have to act. The boy would have to step before all his companions and say: "The truth I uttered was a lie. I have lied." It was eleven-thirty. Martin turned to an employee and asked him to remind Herr Wels that he was waiting to see him.

At eleven-forty Heinrich Wels called him in. He was sitting in the uniform of a storm troop officer: starred, braided, buckled. "I let you wait a long time, Oppermann," he said. "A matter of politics. As you know, Oppermann, politics are now

the first consideration." There was a thin, sharp smile on his
hard, deeply wrinkled face. He spoke in the tones of a superior
to a subordinate. He was determined to enjoy his triumph to
the full, Martin saw that at once. He had called him "Oppermann." That had given Martin Oppermann a shock. But this
very shock had produced a second result: it had aroused in
Martin all his trader's instinct, every instinct for shrewd business dealing. That fellow there, that conceited rascal, wanted to
humble him. He must permit that, he must disregard his dignity, that dignity which he had preserved for forty-eight years.
That was how things stood in Germany during this February.
Right, he would do it. But he would exact payment for it.
"Oppermann" the swine had called him. Well, he would swallow that, he would not be Herr Oppermann any longer. He
would swallow even more. But you'll find it on the bill, Herr
Wels.

"Yes, of course, Herr Wels," he replied courteously.

He was still standing. "Your Herr Brieger has spoken to me
about your offer," said Heinrich to his standing visitor. "Negotiations are more easily carried on with your Herr Brieger than
with yourself, Oppermann. But it has been my experience that
later on 'misunderstandings' come up. I wanted to avoid that.
That was why I sent for you. Sit down, please."

Martin sat down obediently. "It is quite clear to you, I suppose," Wels went on, "that the name of Oppermann and everything that recalls it must disappear. There can be no more
Oppermann furniture in New Germany. You understand
that?"

"Of course, Herr Wels," said Martin Oppermann.

Martin Oppermann understood everything Herr Wels
wished him to understand. "Yes, Herr Wels. Of course, Herr
Wels," came constantly from his lips. And when Herr Wels
made grim jests in his hollow voice, Martin smiled. Only once
he made a determined stand of opposition. That was when

Herr Wels demanded that the original shop in Gertraudten Strasse be closed up and that the main office of the German Furniture Company be established here in his, Heinrich Wels's, main store. Martin entreated him courteously to make an exception in the case of the original shop. This little place, which he wished to run personally under his own name would hardly be a serious competitor to the vast business conducted by the United German Furniture Company. "The arrogant crew," thought Wels. It was clear that Oppermann was right, that the retention of the shop in Gertraudten Strasse was really nothing more than an expensive luxury which Martin Oppermann wanted to indulge in personally. But Wels did not mean to leave him even that. He insisted, haughtily, and Martin, courteously, refused to give way. With due modesty he presented an argument which was bound to impress Wels. If one Oppermann establishment were still maintained, he explained to him, the entire transaction would not have the appearance of a get-away, a compulsory measure. After much discussion, an agreement was reached whereby the original shop could continue to be run as a private enterprise by Gustav and Martin Oppermann until the first of January, but should then be liquidated or else transferred to the control of the German Furniture Company. "Is that quite clear to you, Oppermann?" asked Herr Wels. "Of course, Herr Wels," answered Martin.

They went into details. Discussed the complicated adjustment of such questions as to what extent the Oppermanns should share in the management and in the profits of the new business. And now Martin realized with the greatest satisfaction that he was in excellent form. He constantly found new and successful solutions of specific problems, solutions more adroit even than the cleverly contrived general directions of Professor Mühlheim. Heinrich Wels's demands were enormous. But he had exhausted his energies in despotic requests for external, humiliating things and was no longer capable of suspecting the snares and pitfalls in Martin's nimble and complicated proposals. He made concessions with foolish disregard of apparently minor points.

When the administrative and financial details had been settled, he again mounted his high horse. That Martin Oppermann had given him such bitter pills of every kind to swallow for so many years. Now he was going to feel that it was Heinrich Wels who was top dog and the other quite at his mercy. "'Oppermann customers buy good goods cheaply,'" he quoted scornfully. "That word 'cheap' was right. But the German Furniture Company will put the emphasis on 'good.' Your cheap rubbish," he declared in a harsh, boorish, haughty tone, "will disappear once and for all in the new concern. New Germany is not going to stand for shoddy truck. Our goods will be more expensive but they will have quality." "Fool, idiot, dunderhead, rotten apple, brown-uniformed ass," thought Martin Oppermann. "Of course, Herr Wels," he said aloud.

When Martin Oppermann had gone, Heinrich Wels remained seated a while longer. He fingered the stars and the braid on his brown uniform mechanically. He was pleased with himself. He had given it to that arrogant crew. It had been good to have his adversary here on the ground and to watch him writhing under his heel. He had had to wait a long time, he had had to wait until he reached the threshold of old age. But he was still strong enough to enjoy the experience to the full. They had reached the issue now. Things were straightening themselves out in the world. Now there was some sense in the stars and in the braid on his brown uniform. The masters, the rightful masters, were now sitting where they belonged and the upstarts were kneeling before them and listening to the laws that were dictated to them. How polite that Martin Oppermann could be. "Yes, Herr Wels. Of course, Herr Wels." The subdued, courteous, modest ring of those words would be a comfort to him even on his death-bed. He thought of the time when Martin Oppermann had humiliated him that day in Gertraudten Strasse. "Those gentlemen are going to burn their fingers some day," he had thought then, in the lift. He still remembered what the elevator looked like and how amazed the elevator-boy had been at his scowling face. The gentlemen had burnt their fingers now and the scowl was no longer on his face.

Martin did not feel as tired as he had expected after the tremendous strain he had undergone. He sat in his car, driving to Gertraudten Strasse; before him were the broad shoulders of Franzke the chauffeur. Perhaps he was not sitting quite as erectly as usual but he was sitting erectly and there was a calm, complacent smile about his mouth. Yes, he was satisfied. He had been managing things badly for a long time now, for a year, perhaps for several years. If Immanuel Oppermann had been in his place, he would long ago have made sure of the safety of his people as well as that of his money and would have liquidated the business. But Grandfather Immanuel would have been pleased with the way he had managed things today. There was no doubt that Heinrich Wels, that dunderhead, believed he had won a tremendous victory. It was a victory like that of the Germans in the World War. They had been victorious but the others had won. "Of course, Herr Wels!" He smiled.

Without delay he sat down and wrote out the agreement he had made with Wels. He sent for Mühlheim. The suggestions he had made on the spur of the moment, during the interview with Wels, were so shrewdly calculated that it took even Mühlheim some time fully to appreciate their significance. That was a great satisfaction to Martin. He signed the agreement he had made with Wels and also had it countersigned.

It was not easy to realize that the Oppermann pictures were about to disappear, that the name of Oppermann was to dis-

appear. Yet, that very day, he began to arrange for their dis-
appearance. For that purpose he summoned Herr Brieger and
Herr Hintze into his office and arranged the necessary details
with them. Herr Hintze, very depressed and sitting very
straight, proposed that in place of Immanuel Oppermann's
portrait, a large photograph of Ludwig Oppermann—the
brother who had been killed in France during 1917—be hung
up. "That gang still has a little respect for such things," he
said in a grating voice. Martin, as both gentlemen had noticed,
had dropped the armour of his dignity and had become much
more accessible. But now, suddenly, he reverted to his former
manner. He gave Herr Hintze a sharp sidelong glance. "No,
Hintze," he said coolly in a tone that brooked no argument,
"I do not purchase concessions on the reputation of my brother
Ludwig."

That evening, although this was not necessary, he personally
took down the framed letter from Field Marshal von Moltke,
wrapped it up carefully, tied it neatly, and took it away with
him. As he left the building the surly old doorman Leschinsky
spoke, a thing which had never happened before, and said:
"Good night, Herr Oppermann."

At home, Martin's satisfaction with the commercial success
which he had bought so dearly melted swiftly away. Hitherto,
it had always required a great deal of effort on his part to
make any unpleasant communications to his family. Face to
face with the importance and the harshness of the blow which
was now about to fall upon them, all his thoughts of restraint
and dignity vanished. Sorrow of such magnitude did not have
to remain hidden. It could be displayed without shame, it could
show itself in all its starkness. He asked the family to visit
him the following evening and they came.

He gave them an account of the agreement he had come to
with Wels. He did not mention the humiliations with which
he had purchased his success. The others did not even seem

to realize that he had won a success. All they could grasp was that the Oppermann Furniture Stores were done for. Jaques Lavendel was the only one who understood him. "Good work," he said with a friendly look, full of cordial approbation. "You did that magnificently, Martin. What more could you want? At first it looked as though you were all washed up and now you're on velvet again. Or at any rate, on velveteen."

But the others did not enter into this spirit. Martin made a feeble attempt at a rather bitter joke. He told Gustav that, since he owned the original portrait of Immanuel, he, Martin, had made sure of the original Moltke letter for his home. But soon, in the midst of the general dejection, Martin realized that the last trace of his pleasure in his own commercial success had faded away.

There they sat together, all the Oppermanns, at a great round table that went back to the time of Immanuel Oppermann. It was a solid old table of walnut, which had been made long ago under the personal supervision of Heinrich Wels senior. The portrait of old Oppermann hung above their heads. They had not been together since that evening in Max Reger Strasse on Gustav's birthday. They belonged together, that was obvious. And the picture also was part of them. This inseparability had now become their most precious possession, the only thing that still remained securely their own. Everything else around them was passing away, slipping from under their feet.

Jaques Lavendel again tried to console them by assuming an air of sceptical superiority, but it was a failure and he soon gave it up.

For some minutes they sat on in silence, those heavily built men. Gustav was not smiling. Martin had shed his poise and dignity, Edgar the impregnable self-confidence of the successful scientist, Jaques Lavendel his optimistic scepticism. Their heavy heads were bowed, their deep-set eyes stared into space. They were strong men, each one was a power in his own particular sphere, well equipped to withstand an enemy or a cruel blow of Fate. But their confidence had vanished, they brooded in heavy-hearted distress; for what they had to face, they felt it in their bones, was neither the attack of a single enemy nor a single stroke of Fate. It was an earthquake, one of those great upheavals of concentrated, fathomless, world-wide stupidity. Pitted against such an elemental force, the strength and wisdom of the individual was useless.

14

After some discussion the boys in the football club had decided to drop Berthold. They did so reluctantly. Not only because their match with the Fichte School had now no chance of success—on account of Heinrich's resignation—but because they considered Berthold a good fellow. They were not quite sure themselves why they were punishing him.

Heinrich Lavendel was furiously angry. He considered Berthold's attitude a bit foolish—in his place he would have recanted—but it was highly honourable. If he had been asked to give an example of heroism, he would have cited Berthold's action. Here a fellow was asked to write essays on the scruples of conscience of Wallenstein and Torquato Tasso. That was all rot, gentlemen. Here was a real problem: what attitude should one take in life, a safe one or a decent one? One of the classic French authors had somewhere written: "If anyone accused me of having stolen Notre Dame and of having hidden it in my pocket, I would leave town with all haste." The attitude recommended by that French writer was certainly an example of the safe one. He, Heinrich, also inclined to safety. That was why he had dropped all idea of showing-up that cheeky young ass, that damned fool, Long Lummox. Berthold, on the other hand, stuck to the decent attitude. He did not recant. In the twentieth century, no doubt one got along better with common sense than with decency. However, he was deeply impressed by Berthold's behaviour and he was very fond of him.

He noticed with bitterness the growing isolation of his friend and relative. For, once Berthold was dropped from the football club, other slights followed. The Young Eagles had snubbed him from the start as a matter of principle, now the rest of the boys gradually followed suit.

Berthold went about impassively, in silence. He began to sleep badly. One evening after dinner Liselotte said to him: "I see you keep the light on very late, Berthold. I think, in exceptional circumstances, you might take a sleeping powder. Take a powder from the medicine-closet any night when you can't sleep." "Thank you very much, Mother," said Berthold, "but I can manage to get along without."

Defiantly he tried to persuade himself that it didn't matter how the Lower Sixth behaved toward him. He had his uncle Joachim Ranzow, his cousin Ruth, Heinrich Lavendel, Kurt Baumann. Kurt, he must say, had been marvellous. He did not think of taking part in the silly hero-worship which the other boys accorded to Long Lummox. That meant a whole lot.

About this time Berthold was once more allowed to have the car. In his manly way, casually, as if it amounted to nothing and was no special treat, he said to Kurt Baumann: "Tomorrow evening, at six, after the English lesson, I can have the car. So I'll meet you at six-five in Meierotto Strasse." Kurt Baumann hesitated for the fraction of a second. Then he said: "All right. That'll be great."

The next day, at six-five, Berthold said to Franzke the chauffeur, who was waiting in Meierotto Strasse: "Just a minute, I'm expecting Kurt Baumann." "All right," said Franzke. At six-eight Berthold said: "Just another minute. He'll be here directly." "Certainly, Herr Berthold," said Franzke. At six-fifteen Berthold said: "We'd better start now, Franzke." "We can easily allow him another five minutes, Herr Berthold," said Franzke the chauffeur. "No, Franzke," said Berthold. "Let's start." He was doing his best to speak casually.

"Would you like to drive, Herr Berthold?" asked Franzke after a time, when they were near the Memorial Church. He, too, was doing his best to speak casually, as if it were no special concession for him to allow Berthold to drive in the thick of the traffic. "Thanks, Franzke," said Berthold. "It's nice of you, Franzke, but not today."

15

Rector François was sitting in the old-fashioned, cosy, smoke-scented, book-lined study of his home. The manuscript *The Influence of the Ancient Hexameter on Klopstock's Vocabulary* lay before him. It was not a simple matter to concentrate. But there was still a good half-hour before dinner, so it was worth while trying. He let himself be carried away by the hexameters as if they were waves of the ocean. Their even flow soothed his depressed spirits.

Suddenly the door was thrown open. Little Thundercloud burst noisily into the room. She rushed up to the slender François, her dressing-gown billowing about her. She was so full of what she had to say that she was unable to speak. Without a word, she slammed an open sheet of newspaper on the desk, so that it completely covered the manuscript and the volumes of the old classicist Klopstock. It was that day's issue of the Berlin Nationalist paper. "There!" Frau François managed to exclaim. Nothing more. She stood before him, the very incarnation of doom.

François read. It was an article on conditions at Queen Louise School. This school, which had long been a breeding-place for traitors, said the paper, was now in a state of complete corruption. A Jewish boy, a hopeful scion of the notorious Oppermann family, had, during a lecture before his entire class, most wickedly slandered Arminius the Liberator, and the boy's Nationalist class-teacher had so far been unsuccessful in his efforts to bring the young scamp to account. Protected by the director of the school, a man completely under foreign influence and a typical representative of their system, the impudent Jew boy still gloried in his treason. When would the Nationalist government at last put an end to these intolerable conditions?

François took off his glasses and blinked. He felt wretched. "Well?" asked Little Thundercloud in a threatening tone.

François did not know what to answer. "What shocking German," he said after a short pause.

It would have been better if he had not said that, for those words loosened Little Thundercloud's tongue at last. What? The man had ruined himself and his family with his eternal phlegmatic indecision and now he had nothing more to say against his enemies than that they spoke bad German? Was he mad? The porter's wife had given her the article. Tomorrow ten of her own friends would bring it to her. Didn't he see that everything was finished now? He would be driven from his position in shame and disgrace. It was doubtful whether he would even be granted a pension. What would happen then? They had 12,700 marks in the bank. Securities had fallen below par. That meant that their savings were worth about 10,200 marks now. How were they going to live? He, she, and the children? "On this thing here?" she demanded, aiming a blow at his manuscript but it was only the newspaper that she struck.

Rector François was stupefied by the uproar. Surely Little Thundercloud was exaggerating grossly, but he would have some dark hours to face, many very dark ones. That poor boy Oppermann. Oppermann was a dactyl, a useful thing in hexameter verse. François was also a dactyl but not a perfect one, not as ready for use. "Bear this grief also, my heart, that so many sorrows has suffered." From afar he heard the cadence of such hexameters. If only he could surrender himself to them!

Frau Emilie interpreted his silence as mulishness. Her exasperation increased. In wild, unending speeches—"far-resounding," said the crushed François to himself—she gave vent to her indignation. Tomorrow, she raged, he would have to put two alternatives before that young scoundrel. Either a full apology or else expulsion, in disgrace, from the school. She would like to go to the young rascal's father herself or to his uncle, that charming friend of his, Gustav. Where had her five senses been when she married him, dishrag and milksop that he was! François bowed his head. There was no use in standing up against such a storm. The only thing to do was to wait until Little Thundercloud had finished. Even her lungs must give out sometime. He only wished he could go without dinner and get straight to bed.

Frau Emilie had upset him so much that the shocks of the next day were mild in comparison. Mellenthin the porter had the paper conspicuously sticking from his pocket, all the teachers and the boys he met had a copy, and there were several lying on his desk. There he sat between Voltaire and Frederick the Great. A wave of muck had spread over his school, over the entire country. He was already so smeared with dirt that he scarcely noticed it any longer.

It was not very long, either, before Senior Master Vogelsang appeared in the rectorial office. He had changed. His face was set like a mask, the wryly amiable smile was gone. He entered the room with the air of a victor in the presence of a vanquished enemy, a stern avenger with an invisible sabre rattling at his side. So, thought François, might Brennus, the barbarian, have stood before the Roman senators, unfairly making the scales topheavy by throwing in his victorious sword.

Yes, Senior Master Vogelsang could now enjoy his triumph to his heart's content. He had learned that the elections were decided even before they had taken place. The Nationalist leaders—he had been informed secretly but from absolutely trustworthy sources—had determined upon a deed, a flaming deed which must turn the elections into a victory for the Nationalist policy under any circumstances. Senior Master Vogelsang had no need for further precautions either in the Rittersteg or in the Oppermann case. It was through them that he had achieved publicity and accordingly he now entered the presence of Rector François like a triumphant conqueror.

He had long denied himself this triumph but now he enjoyed it to the full. He did not spare the other an iota of humiliation. For two months, he sternly declared to little François, who sat before him, for more than two months the school had languished under this insult. It had lasted long enough. Unless the boy Oppermann made his apology before the month was out, he, Vogelsang, would make sure that every Prussian school would be closed to the boy. He could not understand how Rector François, after so many serious warnings, had hesitated so long. Now the ulcer had broken, and the entire school was polluted.

The triumphant senior master stood arrogantly between the busts of Voltaire and Frederick the Great. "Before the month is out," thought Rector François. "February has only twenty-eight days. How he squeaks! Little Thundercloud's uproar was a Mozart opera by comparison. *Brekekekex koax koax.* His collar is another half centimetre lower. He's adapting himself. The barbarians adapted themselves, too, when they were in Rome." "Won't you sit down, my dear colleague?" he asked.

But Vogelsang would not sit down. "I must ask you for a clear and unequivocal reply, Herr Rector," he demanded harshly. "Will you call the boy Oppermann's attention to the fact that before the first of March he must recant the impudent assertions he made in that lecture, otherwise he will be expelled?"

"I am not quite clear myself," said François with mild irony, "exactly what you want, my dear colleague. Sometimes you speak of apology and sometimes of recantation. And what is your idea of the matter from a technical point of view? Should Oppermann make his apology here in the rectorial office or before the assembled class?"

Bernd Vogelsang moved back a step. "Apology? Recantation?" he said in astonishment. He assumed a dramatic pose as though he were his own monument. "Both, naturally," he said. "I think, Herr Rector, the best thing for you, under the circumstances, is to leave the choice of atonement entirely to me." "The avenger of Arminius the German," thought François. "The poor Cheruscan did not deserve this!"

"Very well, my dear colleague," he said. "I'll talk to the boy Oppermann. He will make an apology and he will recant. I will only insist upon one detail being left to my own regulation: the style of the statement he is to make. The boy Oppermann may have his faults but he certainly is not a poor stylist. I'm sure you, too, have observed that, my dear colleague?"

Was that said in scorn? Bernd Vogelsang remembered the impudent criticisms which François had permitted himself in regard to the Leader's German when he had first approached him about the Oppermann affair. Style. *Habeat sibi*. There he sat, deprived of everything but his bit of irony. Poor stuff, Herr Rector. He, Bernd Vogelsang, would know how to stage the humiliation of this refractory schoolboy as an imposing spectacle. They should all see how he would drive the spirit of corruption out of the place. Rector François could console himself with his paltry irony. He, Bernd Vogelsang, would act.

16

Alfred François had been obliged to see much that was new and much that was evil during these past weeks. "The fist of Fate had opened his eyes," as the Leader was wont to say. But during the last hours so much trouble had descended upon him that he believed nothing could affect him any more. Yet, as he sat waiting for the boy Oppermann, he realized he was wrong. The worst was still before him.

"Sit down, Oppermann," he said as Berthold came in. "Did you read the passage in Döblin which I suggested to you?" "I did, Herr Rector," said Berthold. "It's good prose, isn't it?" François asked. "Wonderful," answered Berthold.

"Yes," continued François, endeavouring to avoid the lad's keen grey eyes. "This is not easy for me, Oppermann; it's deuced difficult in fact. But you yourself must realize to what proportions this thing has grown. I am unfortunately compelled to put two alternatives before you—" He sniffed slightly, did not finish the sentence.

Berthold, of course, knew what he alluded to. If he had been standing there as a fair-minded outsider, he would have seen the pain in the man's face. But as it was, with his heart brimful of bitterness, he did not think of sparing the other. "What alternatives, Herr Rector?" he asked, compelling François to look at him. "I must ask you," said François, still controlling his breathing with difficulty, "to apologize for and recant the statement you made in your lecture. Otherwise," he was trying now to make his voice sound official and matter-of-fact, "I shall, unfortunately, have to expel you from the school." He looked at the sad, bitter face of the boy. He must justify himself in the lad's eyes, that was the most important thing of all. "I tell you candidly, Oppermann," he continued hurriedly, "I should like you to recant. It would be horrible if I had to expel one of my favourite boys. My favourite boy, in fact," he corrected himself.

He rose. Berthold also started to get up but the other motioned to him to remain seated. "Stay where you are, Oppermann, stay where you are." He paced to and fro between the busts of Voltaire and Frederick. Then, suddenly, he stood still in front of Berthold, changed his tone completely, spoke to him as one man to another. "My own position is in danger. Realize this, Oppermann. I have a wife and children."

Berthold, despite his own bitterness, could not help but see the distress of the other. But he had no time for pity now. "I also have to do a great many things I don't like." His father's voice, unfamiliar, vicious, snarling, rang in his ears. "We are all turning into swine," he thought. "These times are turning us all into swine and ruffians."

"When we were reading Hebbel," he finally began, slowly and deliberately, *"Gyges and His Ring,* Dr. Heinzius told us that throughout Hebbel there was only one theme: the wounded dignity of man. *Laesa humanitas.* Afterwards I read *Herodes and Mariamne.* I did not read it in class but on my own account. Mariamne could have saved her life if she had spoken. She did not speak, she did not defend herself. She would have preferred to bite off her tongue. She died but she did not speak. Dr. Heinzius explained to us very clearly just what *laesa humanitas* meant. Did only the old kings have *humanitas?* Am I a piece of mud? Do you think you can all come and trample on me because I am seventeen and you fifty or sixty? After all, Mariamne was a Jewess, Herr Rector. Read my manuscript, Herr Rector. It was a good lecture. Dr. Heinzius would have been pleased with it. Am I a bad German because Dr. Heinzius happened to get run over? He never used to interrupt our lectures. He let us speak to the end. I am not sure, now, of my exact words, Herr Rector, but they were true. I read Mommsen, Dessau, Seeck. I did not misinterpret what they wrote. Why are you so unjust to me, Herr Rector?"

François listened attentively. What a clever, decent lad he was. He really was his favourite boy. What he must have suffered during the past weeks! What he must have felt all this time, sitting there in front of that mad bull, that Vogelsang, among his companions, cruel, thoughtless young people! What answer should he make to the lad? He would like to endorse every word he had spoken, endorse it with his whole heart. If he were to be honest, he could only say: "Yes, yes. You are right, Oppermann. Don't do it. Don't recant. Leave my school. It has become a bad, stupid school and you can now learn only nonsense and lies in it."

He opened his lips, then noticed he was standing below the bust of Voltaire. He felt ashamed, walked back to his desk. He sat down looking small and old. "When you gave your lecture, Oppermann," he said at last, "you were right. But since then, unfortunately, there have been many changes. Much that was then true I now have to brand as false." He tried to smile. "We shall have much to unlearn. You are young, Oppermann. I find unlearning things is deuced hard." He rose, went close to Berthold, put his hand on his shoulder. He said shyly, so that the words almost sounded like a humble entreaty: "Won't you apologize, Oppermann?" But directly after, filled with dread of what the answer might be, he added: "Don't answer me now. Think it over. Don't say anything. It will be time enough if you give me your answer on Monday. Write to me. Or telephone. Just as you like."

Berthold rose. François could see that the interview had been a great strain on the boy. "Don't take it *too* hard, Oppermann," he said. And then, not without weariness: "And forget what I said just now. It was"—he hesitated for the best word— "it was influenced by the object it had in view. You have one great advantage, Oppermann. In either case, whether you do what is proposed or not, you will be right."

17

The interview with François had been a great strain for Berthold. He had been quite prepared for something of the sort but now he had been given to understand quasi-officially that he had done something un-German and harmful to his country. He could not understand that. Was it un-German to tell the truth? A few months ago no one had had any doubt about his patriotism. He himself felt that he was German in a profounder sense than most of his companions. His head was full of German music, German words, German thought, German scenery. He had never seen, heard, or observed anything else during the seventeen years of his life. And now, suddenly, he was to have no further kinship to these things, he was supposed to be alien to them by nature. How could that be? And why? Who was a German, then, if he was not?

But there was no sense in racking one's brains over general considerations. It was now half-past three on Saturday afternoon. He would have to decide between now and tomorrow evening. Should he recant?

If only he had someone to help him. Surely there must be some salient point, some argument to dissipate all his doubts. He could not go to his father. His father also had a bitter fight on his hands. He could not expect him to advise his son to do something contrary to his own interests. And could he expect his mother to advise him contrary to the interests of his father?

He paced the streets of the great city of Berlin. It was dry weather, not cold, pleasant for walking. He was tall and slender, his face had grown thin, his grey, almond-shaped eyes had a gloomy, preoccupied look, he was absorbed in his bitter meditations. Many people glanced at him, many women especially. He was a handsome lad. But he took no notice of the people.

Suddenly he had an idea. Why hadn't he thought of it before? He rode out to Uncle Ranzow's.

"Hallo, Berthold," said Commissioner Ranzow in some astonishment. Berthold, whose understanding of human nature had increased tremendously recently, saw at once that Uncle Joachim connected his visit with the article in the Nationalist newspaper and quickly, anxiously, considered what was best to say.

Uncle Joachim, as usual, poured out a strong schnaps for him. Berthold explained his case simply, without sentimentality. "I should like to get some sensible advice," he begged. "What would you do in my place, Uncle Joachim?"

At any other time the Commissioner would probably have divined the distress of the lad underneath his matter-of-fact manner. He would also have taken the trouble of putting himself in the boy's place. But, unfortunately, at that time he was scarcely less preoccupied with his own affairs than the Oppermanns were. Influential friends were urgently advising him, since his own political views favoured the German Nationalists, to drop those who stood nearer to the Left than he did and whose days were numbered. But Joachim Ranzow did not want to insult people whom, during years of common effort, he had learned to regard as capable and reliable, even if these men were down on the proscription list. His friends remonstrated with him, besieged him. What they found most difficult to understand was how he could keep up a personal friendship with Councillor Freese, a man who was hated by the new government and who was a registered member of the Social-Democratic party. It was, in itself, no recommendation for a high official to be related by marriage to a Jewish family which was receiving as much publicity as the Oppermanns. Why, for instance, did he not relieve that offensive councillor of his duties? Every official of higher rank who wished to keep his post was doing that sort of thing in order to recommend himself to the new government. But Joachim Ranzow drew the line at unscrupulousness. It galled him that nowadays it was so difficult to be a Prussian official and still to remain a decent human being.

Such was the state of mind in which Berthold found his uncle Joachim. The lad's case was a ticklish one. The sooner it was cleared up, the better it would be for everyone concerned. It was a good thing that the boy himself seemed to be taking a reasonable view of the matter. "I believe," said Ranzow, "that you should make the desired explanation." He spoke calmly, clearly, concisely. The lad gazed at him, a bit nonplussed. He was surprised that anyone should be able to make so fast a decision in such a complicated case as his. Ranzow noticed his astonishment. He really had been rather too hasty. "After all," he said, endeavouring to substantiate his opinion, "you were wrong as far as appearances go."

Berthold recalled the eloquent, if somewhat ambiguous words Uncle Joachim had uttered some time ago on the subject of Arminius the German. These were only very commonplace words he was uttering now on his, Berthold's, behalf. He realized that Uncle Joachim was unwilling to see how important the matter was to him. "They twisted my statements malignantly," he said. "I am to take back something I never said at all. As far as the fame of Arminius, the Arminius legend, goes, I remember exactly everything you once told me, Uncle Joachim. It was by far the cleverest thing I ever heard about Arminius and I made a special note of it. And that was just what I wanted to bring out in the end. But in order to arrive at that point I naturally first had to make the facts, the historical facts, as clear as possible. I said nothing more than anyone can read in Mommsen and Dessau. Must I now go and confess that I am a bad German because I spoke the truth?"

Joachim Ranzow felt nervous and impatient. The lad had appeared so reasonable at first and now he, too, was making difficulties. Liselotte had enough to worry about, God knew. They all had enough to worry about. And now this too. All on account of Arminius the Cheruscan. "Good heavens, boy," he said with unwonted levity, "is that all you have to worry about? After all, what is Arminius the Cheruscan to you?"

No sooner had he spoken than he wished the words unsaid. For Berthold had grown still paler, reached for the glass of schnaps, grasped it clumsily, put it down again. Grasped it again, there was a tiny bit left, he drained it. Ranzow noticed for the first time how ill and worn the boy looked. "But Arminius is something to you, Uncle," he said. His lips were pursed, he looked at his uncle defiantly, accusingly. Joachim Ranzow made a slight gesture with one slim hand, as though he were striking out a sentence. He wanted to say something. But, good Lord, he didn't have to account for himself to that boy!

Before he could answer, Berthold continued. "You mean," he said, "that because I have Jewish blood in me Arminius is nothing to me. You do mean that, don't you?" "Don't talk such nonsense," exclaimed Ranzow, now really angry. "Have another schnaps instead." "No, thanks," Berthold said. "I don't see what else you could have meant," he insisted. "I meant exactly what I said," rejoined Ranzow sharply. "No more and no less. I must forbid you, Berthold, to imply such nonsense to my words." Berthold shrugged his shoulders. "You're right, of course, Uncle. You don't have to account to me for what you say."

The words sounded so bitter and so vindictively resigned that Joachim Ranzow, now thoroughly distracted from his own interests, earnestly tried to get the boy, of whom he was fond, back on the right track. "Your mother would not understand you, Berthold," he said. "Perhaps what I said was not particularly well expressed. We have all got our heads full of worries now. But I still cannot understand how you could interpret my words as you did." Berthold nodded his big head several times, a mannerism of his father. He was looking careworn and grown-up. Ranzow was sorry for the lad. "Be reasonable, Berthold," he urged. It was an entreaty and an apology. "Take my advice. It is not easy for a man nearly fifty to say how he would act today if he were a boy. When I was your age, times were different. Frankly, if I had been in your place then, I would not have recanted. If I were in your place today, I know or, to be honest let us say, I believe that I would recant. You will help yourself and all of us if you do it."

Berthold had hardly gone when Ranzow at once rang up his sister. He gave her a short account of his interview with Berthold and added with perfect frankness that he had not been in very good form when the boy had come. He believed that Berthold was taking the affair much more tragically than it deserved. Liselotte might try to get him out of this frame of mind.

But Joachim was not talking to the Liselotte he knew. She was completely changed. She begged him urgently to come

and help her. In front of her husband and son she had to sim-
ulate confidence all day long. She could bear it no longer. In
the presence of those two, she was so desperately ashamed of
being a German. She needed help herself, she wailed; she
must have someone to whom she could unburden herself.

Ranzow pulled himself together and did his best to comfort
her. He found phrases which, even to him, sounded almost
genuine. He passionately regretted having let himself go for a
moment in the boy's presence. One should never do that. Liselotte, poor girl, had to play dance music all day long on a sink-
ing ship. He had only been asked to control himself for twenty
minutes and he had failed.

He compressed his lips. He rang up Councillor Freese, the
unpopular, the proscribed; asked him to dine with him that
evening at Kempinski's, where they would be certain to be
seen together.

18

Berthold, meanwhile, paced once more through the streets
of the great city of Berlin. It was evening now and colder.
A few shop windows, a few electric signs, the headlights of a
few autos were lit, but the street lights were not yet turned on.
Berthold, himself, did not know why he had not taken a street-
car or the subway. He walked on and on, very quickly, as
though bent on an important errand. Sunday, week, would be
election day. The streets were full of people. Everywhere he saw
posters hostile to the Jews, and the brown shirts of the Nationalists. Berthold, for all his haste, observed the passers-by nar-
rowly. He looked into hundreds of faces, analysed them
quickly and accurately. Suddenly, when someone returned his
quick glance sharply, it flashed upon him that thousands of

the people, there in the streets, must have read the article about
him. An unreasoning fear gripped him, he might be assaulted,
struck dead, just as Karper the editor had been murdered by
Long Lummox.

However, he did not rush home. He raced on mechanically,
aimlessly, through the streets. What was Germany to him, the
Jew boy? Uncle Joachim could not have meant anything else,
not if words make sense. But if such a fundamentally decent,
clever man as Uncle Joachim thought he was not a German,
then Vogelsang, after all, must be more than an ill-natured
idiot.

He got home very late. They were already waiting dinner
for him. Liselotte told him that Ruth and Uncle Edgar had
called that afternoon and that his cousin had been very disappointed not to have found him in. Otherwise it was a silent, uneasy dinner. Liselotte did most of the talking. She spoke about
music, about the concerts given by the Philharmonic Orchestra. Berthold usually went to the final rehearsals on Sunday
morning, she and Martin to the performances on Monday evening. Tomorrow morning there would be a final rehearsal of
Brahms's Fourth, as well as the violin concerto. Furtwängler
was conducting, Karl Flesch was playing. It was doubtful
whether Berthold could go tomorrow morning. He had very
much to do. Nor could Martin say as yet whether he would
have the time to go on Monday evening.

Berthold told himself that his father was really demanding a
big thing of him. He could at least open his mouth to discuss
the matter again. In the beginning his father had been furious
and had lost his temper, now he sat there and did not say a
word. "The Fourth," said Liselotte. "That is the one in E
minor. The violin concerto has a lovely first movement."
Berthold sat and waited for his father to speak. But he remained silent and Berthold was indignant.

He gave a sigh of relief when dinner was over. He liked

order. But that evening, in the quiet of his bedroom, he did not put his clothes away as tidily as usual. He fell into bed, heard the sharp grinding of brakes in the street below, and went off into a deep, sound sleep.

He slept very late. It was half-past eight when he woke. He roused himself slowly. He had not slept so late for a long time. It was Sunday, it did not matter. What did he have to do to-day? He suddenly remembered: the letter to François.

He had enjoyed the sleep, he felt refreshed. He took a shower—cold, so ice-cold that it took his breath away for an instant. As he was drying his flushed skin he knew what he was going to write Rector François: that after thoughtful consideration of the matter he did not have the slightest intention of recanting.

He breakfasted with good appetite. Should he go to the Philharmonic concert now? He did not know much Brahms. What he had heard he remembered. . . . He tried to recall a certain melody, found that he could. That pleased him.

First of all, he must ring up Ruth. He was sorry he had missed her yesterday. He would ask her to come for a walk with him that afternoon. He could not spare the time for both Ruth and the Philharmonic. He still had some mathematics to do. He would have to deny himself the concert. He rang up Ruth and made the appointment with her.

While he was doing his mathematics, Heinrich arrived. He beat about the bush for a time, then out it came. Yes, he really must have another talk with Berthold about that silly Vogelsang business. "Certainly," said Berthold politely and gave Heinrich an attentive glance. The latter looked about for an unusual place to sit but could find only the table. He seated himself on it and swung his legs rapidly backwards and forwards. "If the historian Dessau were to declare today," he said, "that he had arrived at the conviction, contrary to his earlier opinion, that the battle in the Teutoburg Forest was the actual cause of the decline of Rome, that would be something to go on. But if you or I or Herr Vogelsang or my father were to make such a statement, it would be merely funny." He pointed to Berthold's open mathematics book. "If Rector François were to ask me today to write a solemn letter to the newspapers and say that the equation, $(a+b)^2 = a+2ab+b$, was wrong and antagonistic to the integrity of Germany, otherwise he would expel me, I tell you, Berthold, I would go straight off and put it in the newspaper. With the greatest of pleasure."

Berthold listened thoughtfully. Then he answered slowly and deliberately: "I'm sure you're right, Heinrich. The true facts would not change whether I recant or not. It is very good of you to come here again and talk to me on the subject. But you see, the issue no longer concerns the Teutoburg Forest or Arminius or even Vogelsang or my father; it only concerns me. I can't quite explain why, but it is so." Heinrich had a vague idea of what the other meant. He knew that his own arguments were wiser but, all the same, Berthold was right. He felt a passionate anger against the idiots who had put Berthold in this position and at the same time a great affection for Berthold. "Don't talk rot, Berthold," he said rather gruffly, for he was furious at not being able to help his friend.

When he got home, his fresh, boyish face was still dark with rage. He cursed himself mightily in English and in German for not being capable of bringing Berthold to reason. And yet, at bottom, he did not wish to do so. Berthold was made of different stuff and was right from his point of view. The usually sensible Heinrich was filled with wild, blind indignation. He sat down and wrote to the public prosecutor, notified him clearly and circumstantially of what Werner Rittersteg had said to him before he stuck that knife into the editor Karper's guts. Having written the letter, he grew calmer. He felt as though he had fulfilled a duty towards Berthold.

That afternoon Berthold went for a walk with Ruth. They

walked through a slush of rain and snow, but they did not notice it, they were arguing so earnestly. Ruth Oppermann saw what everyone else had noticed, how much more serious and grown-up Berthold had become during the past weeks, how lean his formerly chubby face with the keen grey eyes had become. She tackled him with double eagerness. "What are you wasting your time in Germany for? It's a pity. You don't belong here."

Later, when the weather got really too bad for walking, they sat down in a little café. There they sat, in their damp clothes, among the small tradespeople in their Sunday best. Berthold asked her whether she had noticed how much older his father had grown during the last few weeks on account of the recent happenings. But Ruth, in a subdued tone, yet as earnestly as ever, flared up against fathers in general. "Our fathers are a worn-out race. They are no concern of ours, they have no claims on us. Whose fault is it all? Only theirs. They made the war. That was all they could think of doing. They have chosen the most comfortable instead of their true homeland. My father is personally a very decent man and a good scientist. Your old man, too, is relatively fine. But one shouldn't be hampered by personal sympathies. Chuck up what you are doing here altogether. Call yourself by your real name: Baruch. That was Spinoza's name. Don't call yourself by that silly name Berthold, the name of the inventor of gunpowder. That's the real difference, don't you see? The one discovered gunpowder and the other discovered the social law. Go to Palestine, that's where we belong."

There was a smell of cheap food and damp clothes in the crowded room; the air was filled with noise and smoke. Neither of them paid any attention to their surroundings. The girl's passion, her determination and her single-mindedness, pleased Berthold. He thought her beautiful. It suddenly occurred to him that there was some sense in what she was say-

ing. Was not Palestine just as close to him as Germany? If
Germany expelled him, that other country would not refuse to
give him a home.

But when she had gone and he was walking home alone, her
arguments began to lose their force. He thought of his Uncle
Joachim, of his mother's light skin and fair complexion, of her
grey, almond-shaped eyes, which he had inherited. No, that
mother's son, that uncle's nephew, did not belong in Palestine.
He belonged here, to this country, to its pines, its winds, its
slush of rain and snow; to its slow, thoughtful, steady people,
to its wisdom and its folly, to its Brahms and Goethe and
Beethoven; yes, even to its Leader.

Yes, he belonged to this country. And yet this foolish country wanted him to purchase his nationality at the price of
something thoroughly un-German and silly. No, he would
not dream of it.

It was now half-past six. Early tomorrow morning, by the
first mail, François would be expecting his letter declaring that
he was prepared to recant. If he did not write, his silence
would be a sufficient answer. He had reached the last mail-box
he would come to before he was home. When would the last
clearance be? At nine-forty. So, if he didn't put the letter in the
box before nine-forty, he would be a good German but would
be declared a bad German. Whereas, if he did put the letter
into the box, he would not be declared a bad German but he
really would be a bad German.

He reached home. Another of those awful, silent dinners. It
would not be over before nine o'clock. This evening, too, Berthold waited for his father to say something. In vain. He
glanced at his mother's face. It was self-possessed but less calm
than usual. There was no way out for him. He could not leave
this country. If the country required him to do something de-
grading, he would be obliged to do it.

It was past nine when dinner was over. Silent and uneasy as

it had been, the three still sat around the cleared table. Berthold wanted to rise but he felt as though he were paralysed. He waited. At last his father did speak. "By the way, Berthold," he said, apparently casually, "did you do anything about that business with Senior Master Vogelsang?" "I was supposed to inform Rector François by tomorrow morning if I decided to recant. I have not written to him. I suppose it's too late now, the box won't be emptied again tonight." Martin glanced at him thoughtfully, affectionately, sadly, with his dull eyes. "You might send a special delivery letter," he said after a pause. Berthold reflected. It seemed as though he were only considering the technical question of how the letter could be delivered in time. "Yes, I could do that," he answered.

He said good-night to his parents and went up to his room. He wrote a letter to Rector François, to be sent special delivery, to the effect that he was ready to recant. He took the letter to the box himself and mailed it.

The boys had made bets as to whether Berthold would recant or not. The odds stood five to one that he would. They were eager to know what he had decided to do but they did not dare to ask him. On Monday morning, during the first recess, Berthold sat alone at his desk. Some of them might have enjoyed making a sarcastic remark but, under Heinrich's threatening eyes, they chattered with deliberate cheerfulness on indifferent subjects. Suddenly Kurt Baumann went up to Berthold. His chubby, round face was flushed, his voice not altogether firm. "I believe," he said, "we had an appointment the other day, Berthold. But I made a mistake in the day. I thought it was for Friday." It required courage just then, under the watchful eyes of the rest, to speak to Berthold. "It was for Tuesday, Kurt," he said. "But it doesn't matter." He was pleased with Kurt Baumann. "It was a silly misunderstanding," Kurt Baumann continued eagerly. Then Heinrich La-

vendel joined them. The three boys stayed together all through
recess and enjoyed themselves, talking about cars.

19

No, thank you, Schlüter," said Gustav, "leave it as it is."
He was sitting in the dusk, the newspaper he had just
been reading was on his knees. Only the small floor lamp was
turned on. As soon as Schlüter had gone, he got up, pushed
back the heavy chair impatiently, and began pacing up and
down. His face darkened and he ground his teeth slightly.

These newspaper articles against him, silly as they were,
were producing results. Many of his acquaintances in the Golf
Club and the Theatre Club answered perfunctorily whenever
he spoke to them and tried to break off the conversation as
quickly as possible. Even the polite Dr. Dorpmann of the Minerva Press, when Gustav had telephoned him the day before,
had been damned cool to him. Gustav was sure that he would
not get the contract for the Lessing biography now. He sometimes itched to give up Berlin altogether, to pack up.

"The thermometer never drops under twenty below in
this locality," he had said to his nephew Berthold. That had
been a poor, superficial sort of consolation. Now that this city
of his, Berlin, had unexpectedly turned so cold and gloomy and
had, overnight, contorted its friendly, familiar face into a malevolent grimace, he realized how little such a phrase meant.
Friends who had seemed devoted were slipping away. Everyday more and more of them; things which had seemed secure
to him for all time collapsed before he could properly grasp it.
God knew he was no coward, he had shown that during the

war and on many other occasions. But now he sometimes felt as though the whole great city were preparing to rush upon him and crush him under its gigantic weight, and an actual physical fear seized him.

It was horrible to stay at home alone these days, with disappointment and helpless anger in one's heart. It was nearly three weeks now since he had seen Mühlheim. Mühlheim had been right to go off angry that day. They had all been right, unfortunately; they had scented betimes the hatred around them. It was only he who had gone about in the midst of his enemies, as blind, stupid, and innocent as Siegfried. What fine, genuinely German rubbish he had talked to François when he had come to see him about the lad. The others must really have thought him crazy. Was the boy to let himself be expelled so that he, Gustav, might have the pleasure of telling himself that at least one member of the family resembled a story-book hero?

No. Mühlheim was right to feel annoyed. Mühlheim had given him good advice and had worn himself out trying to make him see reason, and he, instead of thanking him, had replied with a lot of vague, maudlin rubbish and had snubbed him. It was madness to have let the thing go on so long. He ought to have put it to rights long ago.

He took up the telephone receiver and asked for Mühlheim's number. His manservant answered. No, the Professor was not at home, nor was he at his office, nor would he be home for dinner, nor had he left any message as to where he could be found. Yes, of course, he would tell him Herr Doctor had called up.

Gustav hung up the receiver. His anger vanished and turned to brooding melancholy. Now that he had been unable to find Mühlheim there was no one left to whom he could tell his distress. Sybil, of course, sympathized with him and did her best to grasp the great, frightful changes that had come into his life. But she herself was scarcely affected by those changes and the well-fed cannot understand the hungry. Once more he felt, with a pang, that Sybil would always remain on the outer fringes of his life. And Gutwetter. Good lord, he meant to be sincere but his outlook was such an abstract one, he looked at things on such a grand scale, that he could not be of any help to a mere individual.

Anna. She would understand him. He should really go to Stuttgart and talk things over with her thoroughly. Yes, that was the best thing to do, that was what he would do. He would write at once, tell her he was coming and why.

He switched the lights on and began to write. But in the brightness, everything seemed quite different. Anna would surely think him sentimental and boyish to come to Stuttgart just to exchange general ideas with her. He really thought it sentimental himself. But he had determined to do it. He went on writing. He read the first page. The words were full of irony and strained humour. No, he couldn't write to Anna like that. He tore up the letter.

He tried to work. He could not. He took up a book and put it away again. A long and dreary evening lay before him. Finally he went to the Theatre Club.

He was treated with courtesy but his sensitiveness suspected rebuffs everywhere. He dined alone. He was about to go home when Professor Erkner, a well-known producer, challenged him to a game of écarté. Gustav, glad of the diversion, played with careful attention at first. But soon his interest waned. Mühlheim, the Lessing biography, Anna, all came forcibly between him and the cards. He blinked nervously and began playing carelessly. But his opponent, Professor Erkner, was also playing carelessly. The Berlin theatre, which two years before had been the best in Europe, had deteriorated rapidly as a result of the Nationalist movement. If the Nationalists really came into power, the German stage would be ruined for good.

The producer was no less worried than Gustav. Gustav was surprised to find, when they stopped playing, that he had won a considerable sum.

He pocketed his winnings absently. Told Professor Erkner he would give him a chance at revenge some evening soon. He looked across to where Herr von Rochlitz was talking to some acquaintances and wondered whether Rochlitz would stop him as he passed and have a chat with him, as he often did. Herr von Rochlitz waved to him with a "Hallo, Oppermann," but went on with his conversation and let him pass. Gustav looked straight ahead, walked on with precise, not too rapid, stride, his entire sole firmly pressing the ground. Others, too, waved politely to him but were obviously not very anxious to speak to him.

Gustav walked on, staring straight ahead. The old club servant Jean was standing near the entrance of the card-room. He was waiting for his usual five-mark piece. Gustav passed him absentmindedly, without even nodding to him. The old man's face grew blank with bewilderment. It was nearly half a minute before he regained his air of reserved dignity.

20

That night between Monday and Tuesday, shortly after three o'clock in the morning, Gustav was awakened by the ringing of the telephone on his night-table. Mühlheim's voice came over the wire. He said he must talk to Gustav at once. He could not tell him what it was about over the telephone. He would be with him in twenty minutes.

Gustav, startled, heavy with sleep, put on his black dressing-

gown and rinsed his parched mouth. What was wrong? Mühlheim's voice had sounded quite altered. Gustav blinked nervously, was conscious of a slight headache and of nausea.

At last Mühlheim arrived. He told the cabman to wait. Even
before he was inside of the house, while Gustav was greeting
him, he said: "The Reichstag is burning." "What?" Gustav
returned. "The Reichstag is burning?" He couldn't make it
out at all. Was that why Mühlheim had awakened him? In
anxious suspense he awaited Mühlheim's explanation.

It seemed an eternity before Mühlheim had taken off his
overcoat and was seated in Gustav's study. At last they were
sitting opposite one another. Gustav had switched on the bulbs
on the ceiling, the room was much too bright. The strong
lights showed Gustav that Mühlheim was badly shaved and
that his face looked dreadfully strained. At other times, his
many little wrinkles produced the effect of a mask, today they
merely made his face look old and exhausted.

"You must leave here," said Mühlheim. "You must get
across the frontier. At once. Tomorrow." Gustav started, his
eyes and mouth as wide open as a fool's. A tassel of his hastily
tied dressing-gown was trailing on the floor. "What?" he
asked.

"The Reichstag is on fire," Mühlheim repeated. "A bulletin
has been issued stating that the Communists started it. That's
nonsense, of course. They started it themselves. They want a
pretext to suppress the Communists so that they alone, without even the help of the German Nationalist party, can obtain
an absolute majority. So much is certain. They can't go back
now. After this act of violence they can only proceed to more
and more ferocious terrorization. It is perfectly clear that they
are already carrying out now the programme they had arranged for the night of the Hindenburg elections. They hate
you. They have turned their searchlights on you during these

past days. They will want to make an example of you. You must get away over the frontier at once, Oppermann."

Gustav tried to follow what he was saying. It was impossible. The words rained down like blows upon his head. What was all this rot Mühlheim was trying to make him understand? That was perhaps the way bandit gangs waged war upon each other somewhere in Central America. But political parties? In Berlin? In 1933? Mühlheim must be suffering from a nervous breakdown.

"It's cold here," said Mühlheim suddenly and shivered slightly. Gustav, barely awake, was chilly also. "I'll turn up the heat in the hall," he said, getting up. "Never mind," said Mühlheim, "but you can give me a cognac." He was overtired, his voice was rasping. Gustav poured out the cognac for him.

"It is evident," thought Gustav while Mühlheim gulped down the cognac, "that the panic around us has driven him crazy. Setting the Reichstag on fire! They would have to be mad. How could they expect to get away with such a monstrous, clumsy lie? Nero might have put over such dime-novel stuff in burning Rome. But things like that were impossible today, in the era of the telephone and printing press." He glanced at Mühlheim, who was pouring himself a second glass of cognac. The God's Eye was moving back and forth, Immanuel Oppermann's portrait was staring into space, stiff and lifeless in the glaring light. It was nine minutes past four. "And yet, perhaps, he is right. Four weeks ago one would have thought much impossible that has happened since then. He is not a visionary. Monstrous things are happening now. Whatever happens, I must not irritate him or contradict him too sharply. I don't want to lose him again." He mentioned his doubts to him very cautiously.

Mühlheim waved them aside. "Certainly this arson has been managed clumsily and stupidly," he said. "But everything they have done has been clumsy and stupid; nevertheless, so far, they haven't made a single miscalculation. They have gambled on the stupidity of the masses with alarming accuracy. The Leader himself frankly stated that such gambles were the fundamental principle of his political actions: why shouldn't they continue along these lines? With dreadful single-mindedness of purpose, they continued the lies which General Headquarters had to drop at the end of the war. And the peasants and small tradespeople believed every lie they uttered. Why shouldn't they have been taken in by those lies? The principle of those fellows was really appallingly simple: let your *yes* mean *no* and let your *no* mean *yes*. They don't bother about unnecessary niceties. They are gigantic, shockingly coarsened, provincial Machiavellis. Their success is chiefly due to this primitive peasant craftiness. The fact is, the others inevitably persist in believing that no one could be taken in by such crudeness. And then, equally inevitably, everyone is taken in."

Gustav tried to listen. What Mühlheim was saying sounded as though it made sense. But Gustav did not want to believe it, his whole being revolted against it.

Mühlheim went on: "This consistent profession that the lie is the most fundamental principle in politics is certainly enormously interesting! If we were not in such a hurry, I should be glad to prove its efficacy to you. But things being as they are, I can only do one thing: I most earnestly entreat you, leave here, cross the frontier, tomorrow, at once."

There it was again. That was what Mühlheim had said at first, at the very beginning. Gustav had not wanted to hear it but long ago he had known that Mühlheim would come back to it. What nonsense! Because the Reichstag was on fire, he, Gustav, would have to leave Berlin. He suddenly noticed that a tassel of his dressing-gown was trailing on the floor, evened the cord, and tied it properly. He had no idea of going away. That would be absurd. Everything would, of course, remain perfectly quiet in Germany and then how silly one would feel sitting on the other side of the frontier. But he couldn't tell Mühlheim that. He couldn't afford to offend him again. He couldn't do without him, he was lost without him, he needed him as much as he needed bread and water. Cautiously he endeavoured to explain to Mühlheim why he could not leave Berlin just now. He was getting on so well with the Lessing. Frischlin was now familiar with the routine, they were going ahead famously. He couldn't leave things half done. Wasn't Mühlheim's view perhaps too pessimistic? He became eloquent. Tried to give himself confidence by his own arguments. But he had scarcely begun to speak before he realized that Mühlheim was right, Mühlheim had always been right so far. What he was saying was sentimental rubbish, what Mühlheim was saying was the real thing. Yet he went on talking, though without conviction.

Mühlheim noticed his half-heartedness. He had expected Gustav to be much more difficult. He was relieved that Gustav was showing such slight resistance. If Gustav had made serious objections, he would not have had the strength to oppose him on that dreadful night.

Gustav saw how worn out Mühlheim was. What horrible, glaring lights he had turned on. He switched off the ceiling lamp. Mühlheim already had himself in hand again. "Don't waste your breath, Oppermann," he said. "Don't deceive yourself. Those fellows are carrying out a deliberate programme. They intend to make mince-meat of every antagonist who crops up. They're scoundrels and they believe you are a dangerous enemy. I can only say to you: Pack up. Go to Denmark. Or Switzerland. The weather-reports are not favourable but they will have to do. Don't keep me here"—he suddenly became irritable—"making pretty speeches to you for hours. I have all sorts of things to attend to. I shall have a busy day tomorrow. I should very much like to get three or four hours' sleep. You won't get rid of me until you have said yes. Say yes, Oppermann."

Gustav saw the other's earnestness and excitement. He believed him, though, as yet, he had not quite grasped the details. "But you're coming along?" he asked helplessly, like a little boy.

"You must realize I can't do that," Mühlheim answered impatiently, almost rudely. "I am in no danger here, at least not for the time being. I have never exposed myself in the way that you have. And I am more important here than you are, with all due respect to your Lessing. There will be fifteen or twenty people waiting in my office tomorrow morning, for whom I represent the last drop in the water-bottle. I can't recite the entire statute book to you here, man—" He stopped brusquely and stood up. "I tell you for the last time: if you don't want to be locked up in the pen or something worse, then vamoose."

Gustav suddenly was amazingly calm. He always liked Mühlheim particularly when he spoke in idiomatic jargon. He was always right then. He answered casually, in the manner of his friend: "You're due for a surprise. I'll do it. I'll leave tomorrow. That's that. And now we'll have one more cognac and then off you go: home and to bed. Or, if you like, stay and sleep here. I'll grant you a further two or three days to finish up your business but then you must join me."

Mühlheim heaved an audible sigh of relief. "You have certainly detained me on your 'busy line' a long time. That taxi must have been waiting a good two marks' worth. I'll add that to your bill, my boy." Gustav escorted him to the taxi. "Thanks, Mühlheim," he said. "I was an idiot to let things drag on for three weeks." "Don't talk rot," said Mühlheim. He climbed into the taxi, gave the address, and went to sleep.

2 1

Gustav went back to the house and took a cold shower. He felt refreshed and excited. He had to tell someone what had happened. He rang up Sybil.

Sybil, only half awake, answered sulkily, peevishly, like a child. She had been at the opera. He knew that but he did not know that she had been there with Friedrich Wilhelm Gutwetter and had later brought him along to her pretty little flat and done some work with him. Yes, the great essayist had taken more and more pleasure during these last weeks in the company of the girl Sybil Rauch, in her intelligent docility, in her charming aloofness. Not only did his famous volume of essays, *The Prospects of Western Civilization,* with a flattering inscription, lie on her bedside table, but Friedrich Wilhelm Gutwetter made it a point to inquire personally every day as to how her work was progressing. In his old-fashioned garb, he sat quietly in her pretty room, watched her with bright childlike eyes, and assisted her with patient advice. All this flattered Sybil tremendously. If Gustav had asked her about it, she would not have hesitated to tell him of these meetings. But he was very busy with his own affairs just now and did not ask her.

She had been up late and she was very provoked at his waking her now. He told her he would have to leave Berlin the next day. The matter was most urgent. Would she like to come with him? It would mean so much to him if she did. He wanted to discuss everything with her at once and asked whether he might come directly. He was disappointed and extremely annoyed when she refused his request point-blank. She wanted to sleep now, she declared, she could not dream of making decisions when she was only half awake. Finally, she promised to come and see him early in the morning.

Gustav himself tried to get a little sleep but it was fitful and hardly invigorating. He was glad when the time for his morning ride had come. At first it was rather foggy, then it cleared up. The first slight hint of spring was in the air, a greyish-green, scarcely perceptible fluff was on the bushes. Sudden fury seized him because they were compelling him to leave his home, his work, his people, his country—ten times more his country than that of the people who were driving him out. Grunewald was at its best at this time of the year. It was a pity to be obliged to leave it just now.

"I am going abroad today, Schlüter," he said as he dismounted. "How long will you be away, Herr Doctor?" asked Schlüter. Gustav, after a slight nervous twitching of his eyelids, replied: "For about ten days or two weeks." "Then I'll pack your dress clothes and some sports things," suggested Schlüter. "Yes, do, please, Schlüter," said Gustav. "I'll take the skis too." "Very good, Herr Doctor," said Schlüter.

Now that he had declared that he was going away for only a fortnight, Gustav felt easier about the whole trip. Only one point remained unsettled, whether Sybil would come with him or not. It seemed of paramount importance. He nervously awaited her decision.

Meanwhile Sybil was talking to Friedrich Wilhelm Gutwetter on the telephone. She told him that Gustav, possibly in consequence of the burning of the Reichstag, was going abroad and had asked her to come with him. Gutwetter had not heard the news. "Indeed?" his calm, childlike voice asked over the wire in astonishment. "You say the Reichstag has been burning. How did that happen? Surely that concerns the fire department more than our friend Gustav." Sybil had to explain at length. She herself could only guess at the reasons but she was as quick to understand logical connexions between things as Gutwetter was slow. Gutwetter finally gave up hope of grasping the connexion between the two events and contented himself with the fact that Gustav was running away on account of impending political events. "I don't understand our friend Gustav, my dear Sybil," he said. "This country is about to give birth to a great new type of humanity. We have the enormous luck to be present at the birth of this gigantic embryo and to hear the first babblings of the noble monster. And our friend Gustav goes and runs away because one of the outcries of this nation in travail is offensive to his ears? No, I don't understand our friend. I am no longer young. I am on the downgrade. But in spite of the increasing numbness of my years, I would rush here from afar to see, at first range, the development of this type. No one could rob me of that privilege. I envy you, my dear friend, for being able to experience this great drama in the first freshness of your eager and vital youth." Such were the childlike and lovable words of the great essayist.

Sybil, also, thought Gustav's caution rather exaggerated. Middle-aged men become suspicious of everything and want their comforts, that was their privilege. She, however, was not so old and would willingly give up a little comfort for the sake of a thrill. Even after she had discounted the ecstasy in Gutwetter's words, the fact remained that an enormously interesting drama was going on: the unforeseen swamping of a civilized country by the barbarians. She awaited the outcome of this drama with the intense excitement of a child awaiting the scheduled feeding-time in front of a cage of wild beasts. She must not miss that drama. When she arrived at Gustav's, she felt little inclination to leave Germany at just this time.

But when Gustav told her what he had heard from Mühlheim about the burning of the Reichstag, when he soberly informed her that Mühlheim expected, with good reason, that a few weeks of violence, injustice, and lawlessness would ensue, she, too, began to see things in a different light. Sitting in her comfortable armchair and looking like a slender and lovable child, she watched his lips. What was happening? Her friend Gustav had suddenly become a man of destiny. His face seemed larger, more authoritative. He was now not only a kindly, middle-aged gentleman, he was—first of all—a man. After Gustav had finished speaking, she went over to him and sat on the arm of his chair. She hesitated as to what answer she should give.

However, soon after Gustav had finished speaking, the idea of work, her work, again obsessed her. Perhaps it was not such a very important thing but it was her life-work. She now had the opportunity to work with Gutwetter. She worked very well with him. Her words, her vision were gaining fresh power. She should not allow that fortunate collaboration to be interrupted. She owed that to herself.

She would very much like to go with him, she told Gustav. She, too, had the feeling that she belonged to him and that she needed his company now. But he would not want her to jeopardize her work at this critical stage. She could not interrupt it just now, she could not risk any set-back now, nothing would turn out right away from Berlin. She must have the next eight or ten days free for her work. If he were really only going to be away two weeks, she hoped that she would be able to surprise him, on his return, with some particularly successful achievement. But if his return should be delayed, she could then go to join him and, having overcome the difficulties of her work, she would be free to devote herself to him entirely. For the time being, she would consult with Schlüter to see that he was taking the proper things along and then he must have lunch with her and tell her exactly what train he was going on so she could get him to the station in good time. Gustav gave her evasive answers. Nor did he have the slightest intention of telling her when he was leaving. He was deeply offended.

Mühlheim looked in for a moment, hurriedly, with nervous briskness. Gustav's train left at eight o'clock, from the Anhalter Station. Mühlheim had reserved a sleeping compartment for him. He asked Gustav for a general power-of-attorney. All sorts of things might happen in Germany which would require immediate action. Gustav, obstinate again, declared with a frown that he did not intend leaving Germany for any length of time and did not wish to plan for such a contingency. Mühlheim dryly rejoined that he, too, hoped Gustav's absence would only last a short time but he was not a clairvoyant and it was always better to be on the safe side. "Moreover," he added, "whether you are away three months or three years, since you're a good German, Germany will be wherever you are." This unwonted sentimentality from the lips of Arthur Mühlheim astonished Gustav and he said no more.

When Mühlheim had gone he wandered about the fine house he loved so much. All excitement regarding his impending trip vanished; he felt, instead, only melancholy and was grieved. He persisted in telling himself that it was only a question of a few days' holiday. But, already he had the conviction that his exile would be a very long one. He had at first thought of asking Sybil to help Schlüter to look after the house during his absence. But now Sybil no longer seemed to be the right person to ask. He would telephone her again but he did not feel it necessary to see her a second time. He could entrust the house to François, he would understand perfectly what was essential. But Francois, too, had forsaken him. Mühlheim had enough to do already; Gustav could not expect him to concern himself with every little detail that meant so much to him. Martin was in the same position.

He rang up Martin to say good-bye to him. Martin felt Gustav was doing the right thing by going away. He would like to do the same, but Wels was too dangerous and he could not leave the business at this stage. Both brothers regretted not being able to be together during these weeks. Yet they had no real similarity of outlook, they were both too absorbed in their own troubles.

When Gustav had hung up the receiver, he considered the question further It was not a pleasant subject for reflection. His intimates were very few. Gutwetter? He rang him up. Friedrich Wilhelm Gutwetter was as calm, cordial, and childlike as ever. If anyone was sorry Gustav was going away it was he. He had no very clear idea of the reason for it. "But I'm sure our mutual friend Mühlheim knows what is best," he remarked peacefully. It did Gustav's heart good to hear Gutwetter speak. But there was no sense in troubling him with the house. He was too unreliable in all practical matters.

He sat on idly, reviewing mentally the faces of his friends. He was tormented by the thought, as though it were a thorn in the flesh, that he had forgotten or neglected to do something. Already several times during the day this thought had tormented him. But he could not find the solution. He must leave it to chance, one could not force such things.

Dr. Klaus Frischlin then arrived for the day's work. Curiously enough the work went well. At midday the manuscript was put away. Frischlin prepared to take his leave. He stood there, slender, his complexion poor, his hair thin. And suddenly Gustav was convinced that this man was more tenacious, more loyal, more reliable than the rest; this made him say: "I am going abroad, Dr. Frischlin. I hope it will only be for a short time. But if it should be for a longer period, please look after my house, my books, and the things I am fond of. You know about everything here." Frischlin answered quietly and sincerely, "You may rely on me, Dr. Oppermann."

Together with Frischlin, Gustav selected the books he wanted to take with him. He would have liked to take all his books and not only his books: he would have liked to cut the paintings of Immanuel Oppermann and Sybil out of their frames, would have liked to trail the God's Eye about with him as well as his typewriter, his work-table, and the whole house. He felt he was being ridiculous. In the end he did not take anything with him. Not even his manuscript. For it would be no use trying to work away from his library. He was only going to be away a fortnight, no longer. He would not, by taking his favourite things with him, conjure up evil powers which might turn his short absence into a long one.

After lunch he went into his garden. He descended the steps of the first terrace to the second, and of the second to the third. Woods and hills rose about him. It was only the twenty-eighth of February, but spring was actually beginning. Was it imagination or had the soft green tint of the foliage, which had been barely perceptible early that morning, already become more definite? Gustav took in the details of the familiar landscape, drew deep breaths of the familiar perfume, and grieved.

And suddenly, unexpectedly, the thing that had been tormenting him all day came to him. Yes, he really would have to settle that. He could not go away and leave a disappointment like that behind him in Berlin. But, if he did that, he would not be able to leave at eight. Never mind. There were later trains to Switzerland.

He telephoned Mühlheim at once and told him he would have to defer the hour of his departure. Mühlheim asked why. Gustav did not give him any reason but he insisted on going by a later train. Mühlheim was annoyed. The trains were overcrowded. Gustav would not be able to get a sleeping-compartment. And apart from that, the sooner he went the better. But "I have my reasons, Mühlheim," said Gustav smiling and let him talk on. He made the necessary arrangements. He would go, then, by the half-past ten train.

At nine he was at the Theatre Club and dined there. Then

he went into the card-room as though he were looking for someone. The room was completely empty, only Jean, the old club servant, was standing near the entrance. Gustav went up to him, put a five-mark piece into his hand. "I was a little pre-occupied yesterday," he said. "Forgive me, Jean." The old man thanked him in his dignified way, unobtrusively yet sincerely. Gustav could now start on his journey in peace.

At the Anhalter Station it turned out that the wily Mühl-heim, by bribing a guard, had managed to secure another sleeping-compartment for Gustav. There were many people he knew in the train. But many of them pretended not to recognize one another. Nobody wanted to be seen. "Come and join me as soon as you can, Mühlheim," Gustav requested. "Don't do more silly things on the way than you can help," Mühl-heim said. Then the train started. The last that Gustav saw of Berlin was Schlüter, standing very straight, looking after the train with his imperturbable, stubborn face.

22

About the same time Berthold was saying good-night to his parents. Tomorrow, Wednesday, he was to take up his case and make his explanation in the assembly hall before all the masters and the boys of Queen Louise School. Liselotte wanted to speak to him; she was about to begin but she knew how difficult it sometimes was for him to discuss things, so she gave up her intention and only said: "Good night, my boy."

Berthold went up to his room, undressed with great care, hung up his clothes neatly and, as usual, got his school things ready for the next morning. Tomorrow his role would really be very simple. His explanation was very brief. It would not be as simple for François and Vogelsang. They would have to talk a tremendous lot of rot. During that entire time, he would have nothing to do but stand still. Stand in the pillory. If it depended on Dr. Vogelsang the—what was the best way to put it?—the ceremony would take place at the foot of the Germania monument at Niederwald.

He would go to bed now. With a book. Kleist's *Arminius's Fight,* for instance. But it happened that he took up the fourth volume of his Kleist instead of the third. It contained the *Tales.* He read the story of Michael Kohlhaas, the son of a schoolmaster, at once one of the most upright and most wicked human beings of his day who, obsessed by a sense of justice, becomes a thief and murderer. For the sake of two horses he loses his integrity, starts a rebellion, and finally comes to a gruesome end. But as he mounts the scaffold, he has the satisfaction of knowing that the two fine horses, which had unjustly been worked into sorry nags, were again sleek and well-fed and that they belonged to him. Berthold knew the story well and yet he read it with fresh and keen excitement. He read several passages over two or three times. For example, the answer which the horse-dealer gives his wife when she anxiously asks him why he is selling his property. "Because," he replies, "I don't wish to remain in a country where my rights are not protected. Better to be a dog, if I am to be trampled on, than a man." Berthold read the passage through, nodding his head several times in assent.

He put the book aside. He realized now that he had not slept the night before and that the days that lay behind him had been strenuous ones. He did not want the dark to come yet. He was afraid of the darkness. He turned off the lights on the ceiling and switched on the shaded lamp by the bed. He lay on his side, his eyes half-closed. He saw the fantastic bird on the wallpaper sitting on the drooping twig. Again the face of Arminius stood out from the ornamental design, the broad forehead, the flat nose, the wide mouth, the short, strong chin. Would he have any prospect of rising high in the Germany of today? He smiled. Unexpectedly verses came to him.

> Who now in Germany strives to lead
> What traits must this lad possess?
> A lantern jaw, a low, mean brow—

It was very seldom that he thought of verses. He had a sense of style and knew what good prose was; Dr. Heinzius had always said so. The present era was no time for poetry.

Ruth and that fellow Arminius would probably have understood one another. He saw her again as one of the German women in the wagon camp. She would indignantly protest against such an idea. But it was right just the same.

Ruth had an easy time of it. She would know exactly what to do if she were in his position. Many people in Germany had an easy time of it, millions of them did. But many too, still more millions of them, had a bad time of it, just because they did not know what they should do. He had heard the story of the brother—or was it the brother-in-law?—of the servant Schlüter, who had testified against the Nationalists and had been killed for it. Millions had declared themselves against the Nationalists and thousands had suffered death by their declaration. The facts were known in some cases, in thousands of cases, but in hundreds of thousands, in millions of cases the facts were not known. Who was Germany? Those people in brown uniforms who roamed about the streets, shouting, with weapons in their hands which they had kept in defiance of the law, or those millions of others who were such fools as to believe in law and who had given up their weapons and who now got knocked on the head if they opened their mouths? No, he was not alone, he had comrades, hundreds of thousands, millions of them. A monument had been erected to the Unknown Soldier but no one ever spoke of the Unknown German, or of his Unknown Comrade. "My Unknown Comrade," he thought. And then:

> Now everyone is hounding you,
> They beat you up, imprison you.

And again:

> The destiny of countless men
> Your tortured form exemplifies.

And then:

> Comrade Unknown, the dawn must come,
> And when it comes, Thou shalt arise.

All that wasn't worth anything. He couldn't write verses. But one day someone would come and write a poem about the Unknown German, the Unknown Comrade.

Someone might write it, perhaps, but it would not be printed or sung and no one would listen to it. And even if he, Berthold, could write the poem, he would not recite it. He would recite something else. He would go up there into the assembly hall before his grinning comrades, his well-known comrades, and say: "I have spoken a truth. I now declare that truth to be a lie."

No. He would not say it.

Of course he would say it. He had not wanted to write that letter to François either, he had not written it, he let the time expire. Then his father had said: "You could send a special delivery letter," and then he had written it.

He might stay away from school tomorrow, simply not go. They would all stand in the hall and wait and he would not

be there. He smiled. He could visualize everything with the ut-
most clearness, the faces of Vogelsang and Werner Rittersteg
and Mellenthin the porter at the entrance. "We will sing the
Horst-Wessel song," Dr. Vogelsang would finally say. But that
would not be much of a consolation. There would have been
no need to assemble the whole school in the assembly hall to
sing the Horst-Wessel song. Rector François, perhaps, might
even be glad if he did not come. Heinrich would certainly be
glad, though he had advised him to come. Kurt Baumann, too,
would be glad. Yes, that would certainly be a satisfaction, a
heartfelt relief, for an hour or a day or perhaps a week. But
afterwards, what should he do then? He would be expelled.
He would have to leave Germany. It might be an eternity perhaps before he could get back to Germany. And would it still
be his Germany then?

There was nothing else for it. It would have been fine to
make them wait. But it wouldn't do.

Yes, it would.

He got out of bed. He took out the manuscript of the Arminius lecture. He had put it away carefully, he had to turn
on the ceiling light to get it out, that took some time. It was
a very neatly written manuscript, on ruled paper, with a margin and few corrections. He took a scrap of paper, wrote on it:
"There is nothing to explain, nothing to add, nothing to leave
out. Let your *yes* mean *yes* and your *no* mean *no*. Berthold
Oppermann." He laid down the pen, then took it up again
and added: "Berlin, 1st March, 1933."

He would really have liked to write out the verses which had
previously occurred to him about the "Unknown Comrade."
But no. Prose was better. He wrote: "Better to be a dog, if I
am to be trampled on, than a man. (Kleist. Insel Edition. Vol.
IV, p. 30.)"

He went into the next room, not especially quietly, and
opened the medicine cupboard. There were three little tubes in

it containing sleeping tablets. He took the one he thought was the strongest. It had hardly been touched. He was sure it would be enough. Then they'd have to wait, tomorrow, in assembly.

He got a glass of water, set it carefully on a plate, so that it would not leave a rim on the table, dissolved the tablets, and placed the glass on the night-table. He glanced at the manuscript. The scrap of paper was lying loosely on the top of it. It would be better to fasten it. He wound up his watch and laid it beside the glass. He switched off the ceiling light again, turned on the lamp by the bed, and lay down.

It was one-thirty-eight. He drank the water with the dissolved tablets in it. The stuff didn't taste good, it took some determination to swallow it. But there were worse things.

He lay and waited. His watch ticked on the night-table. He heard the sound of a motor-horn below in the street, hooting long and loud, in defiance of the regulations. How long would it be before he went to sleep? He had been lying there two minutes and forty seconds now. It would surely not be longer than six or eight minutes. If no one found him during the next half-hour, no one could ever wake him up again. That was certain. Fortunately, it was extremely improbable that anyone would come into his room now. If he switched off the lamp by the bed, it would be out of the question. He switched it off. He felt heavy and tired already, not so pleasantly tired, to be sure, as he had hoped. It was a leaden, oppressive feeling.

There was another car again. But this time it did not hoot as long. He had made a good job of that manuscript. Dr. Heinzius had told them that one of the intrinsic differences between the present age and antiquity was the estimation in which suicide was held. The Romans taught their children at a very early age that man was superior to the gods in one respect: he could always have recourse to the expedient of voluntary death. The gods did not possess that privilege. It was a very honourable death. He had put everything to rights, too, in a perfectly orderly manner, before he swallowed the stuff. There was the manuscript. Anyone who wanted to could see it, and anyone who did not want to, would have to see it. A few days before he had read of a woman who, before she went her way, had not only put on the dress in which she wished to be buried, but had also sewn a piece of crape on her husband's sleeve. We Germans are an orderly people. He smiled slightly. He could permit himself that now. He could now permit himself to say: "We Germans."

There was another car again. He found himself, suddenly, sitting in it. They were on the Avus track, it was a race. Franzke was sitting at the back, it was funny he was not sitting beside him. Franzke kept shouting instructions to him but he could not hear them. He did his very best but there was a fearful noise all about, the wind was so high. And who was that sitting next to Franzke? There was someone sitting there. It was Dr. Heinzius. That was good. He was better able to make himself understood than Franzke. Now the curve was coming. He rounded the curve splendidly, hunky dory. He had broken himself of the habit of saying "hunky dory," it was an ugly expression. There was a car in front of him. Who was that at the wheel? Yes, it was Dr. Vogelsang. He was going to drive into him, that would be hunky dory. Did Franzke understand what he was going to do? But it was no good. Funny thing. He simply couldn't get near him. Step on the gas, step on the gas, don't slow down, he can't make it, a suffocating heat was coming up from below, the gear shift was red hot, the car was skidding, the gear shift was pressing against his stomach, no, the car was not skidding, it was swimming, it reminded him of that time in Bavaria on the icy road, all of a sudden the car slid away, he didn't know how, everything was getting black, it was stifling, he must scream, whether he wanted to or not, but he can't scream, he is lifted up, the car was being lifted up, but it isn't the car, that has slipped away, he is on the scenic railway in Luna Park, no, on the swings, no, it couldn't be, this was in Munich during the October harvest festival, those swings were very high, Vogelsang is still near him, now he has overtaken him, he really is on the Avus track, but without the car, he is swimming, swimming without a car, how high the swing flies, it tickles him in the pit of his stomach, it's pulling his stomach out of him but he mustn't let on, he must keep smiling, it was a real ship, it was swimming away from him, the waves are even and flat, they were crushing him, it is no joke, they were crushing him horribly, he shouldn't have gone swimming at night, they keep on breaking over his head, he couldn't float, he could never get his breath again, everything was vanishing, everything but the face of Vogelsang, but it was no longer the face of Vogelsang, it was the face of Arminius with his flat nose and determined chin, he was standing on the shaft of the Niederwald monument, no, the statue of Germania stood there and that was well, but Arminius was standing there anyway but now the whole shaft was gliding away—now a very big wave was coming, a very big one and he would have to duck it——I can't give you my hand, my Unknown Comrade, the wave is coming, it is much larger than I thought, perhaps I can ride it——now it is here.

23

About the same time Gustav, in his sleeping-compartment, was already a good distance to the south-west of Berlin. He had been sleeping soundly and deeply but a violent jolt of the train woke him. He came slowly to himself. And then it suddenly occurred to him with a pang that he had, to be sure, thought of Jean, but the one he had not thought of had been his nephew Berthold. He might at least have asked Martin what had been the end of that silly affair of Arminius the Cheruscan. This negligence worried him for nearly half an hour. After that, he dozed off again but did not sleep as soundly the balance of the night as he had before.

Book Three: Tomorrow

"*It is upon us to begin the work,*
It is not upon us to complete it."
—TALMUD.

TOMORROW

Iᴛ ᴡᴀs not until after Berthold's burial that Gustav received the news of his death. Mühlheim, who was the only person who knew his address, had delayed notifying him in order that Gustav might not run any risks by returning.

During these days he had been wandering about the beautiful and delightful city of Berne. It was spring, the air was clear, the towering peaks of the Oberland stood out in infinitely delicate and pure contours against the horizon. But Gustav took no pleasure in the view, his mind was stunned by the events which had taken place in Berlin. When he got the news, he felt as though he had received a shock which he had long been expecting.

He could not bear anyone near him now, he went off into the mountains, he had to be alone. He could not understand the things which were happening, he had to think things out for himself. The place where he finally stopped was situated at the base of the Jungfrau. But there was no more snow and he was the only guest at his small hotel. He avoided the crowded mountain railway and carried his skis himself as far as the snow-line. With some difficulty he ascended a slope that lay apart from the main route. He lay down in the snow and the sunlight. The outlines of the mountains rose high and smooth into the marvellously pure air. He was alone.

He began a searching self-examination. He had remembered old Jean, but not Berthold. He was largely to blame for what had happened. He had always done the wrong thing. He had led a useless, indolent, self-absorbed existence. He had gone to

Sybil instead of to Anna. If he had only interested himself in politics, in political economy, in some branch of the business, it would have had more purpose than the things he had done. He had proved that Lessing had written a certain letter on the 23rd of December, not on the 21st. What of it? That phrase might be an appropriate caption for his entire life.

Perspiring in the heat of the sun, he squatted in the snow and took stock of himself. The result was not gratifying.

He spent four days in this manner, in the quiet of his mountain retreat. The narrow road up which, day by day, he trailed his snow-shoes, ran the length of the valley, overlooking it from a great height. Tiny villages lay on the slopes opposite. The towering peaks of the Jungfrau spread before him in sunlit whiteness. He would sit for hours on his secluded lofty peak. There was a clean fresh warmth in the air. The roar of the avalanches, deadened by distance, came to his ears. He saw what lay before him and around him but he appeared conscious of neither the air nor the view. His senses were benumbed. The same thoughts continually occupied his mind, revolved and pierced ever deeper and deeper into his consciousness. The wisest thing for him to do was to overtax his body until he would be too exhausted to think. He sometimes managed this on the way home. Then he would sit by the roadside, actually glad of his utter fatigue, his mind a blank, nodding his head mechanically and laughing like a half-wit. Sometimes the road would be empty for hours. Once a young boy with a cart passed. He stared at him in astonishment and turned his head to look back at him for a long time.

This stupor lasted for four days, paralysing him; his head felt as though it were wrapped in cotton-wool. Suddenly, on the morning of the fifth day, after a long night's sleep, the mists about him lifted. Gustav raised his head, looked about him, emerged completely from the shadows. Five days had actually passed since he had had news from Germany, since he had seen a newspaper. There could be few Germans, just now, who were so devoid of curiosity. He obtained whatever papers he could: German, Swiss, English, French. With the big bundle under his arm, he climbed his usual beautiful road. He felt a sudden mad anxiety which he could scarcely control. Although the ground was still damp, he sat down by the roadside and began to read.

As he read, all the blood seemed to rush to his head. Keep quiet, don't lose control, keep steady, think quietly. In days like these it is impossible to stop all sorts of absurd rumours from getting about. All his life he had been interested in compiling accurate source materials, he was not going to be taken in now by the ravings of a few over-imaginative reporters. What papers were these? They were the *Times,* the *Frankfurter Zeitung,* the *Neue Zürcher Zeitung,* the *Temps.* And the reporters were not just anybody, they were people with reputations. The statements were concise, businesslike. Correspondents of high standing could not afford to publish such monstrous things in such minute detail unless they were sure of their ground. There was no question but that the Nationalists had carried out their programme point by point, that programme at whose primitive barbarism people had so often smiled; he himself had been among the most incredulous. They had arrested, kidnapped, ill-treated, killed all those who were in disfavour with them, destroyed or confiscated their property, simply because these persons were their adversaries and for that reason had to be annihilated. Gustav read names, dates. Many of the names were known to him. Many of these men were his close friends.

His quiet, animal-like despair was over. A violent rage against himself and against the Nationalist party overcame him. He read the insane speeches of the Leader. The aged President had handed the Reich over to them in good order. They had ruthlessly broken their solemn pledges, trampled

law underfoot, and substituted caprice, disorder, and brutality
for civilization and order. Germany had become a madhouse
in which the patients had overpowered their warders. Did the
world realize this? What was it doing about all this?

He travelled back to Berne that same day. Had he been mad
to hide away in that lonely place without even giving his address? Did he imagine this horror would have less effect upon
him if he wrapped his head up in cotton-wool? He was determined to know, he must know, more, everything, every detail.

In Berne he found telegrams, letters, and newspapers. The
mercenaries had entered his house, too, and searched it, destroying much and pilfering more. There was a telegram from
Frischlin, asking Gustav to ring him up. He did so.

It gave him a peculiar sensation to hear Frischlin's voice. It
was the voice he knew so well and yet it was altered, it was
tense, anxious, full of energy. Gustav wanted to ask questions
but Frischlin interrupted him at once. He stated that he had
made a good deal of progress with the Lessing but he considered it would be best if he came to Berne and made his report
personally. Moreover, that was also Mühlheim's opinion.

He arrived the very next day. "I should prefer to stay at a
different hotel from yours," he said, almost before he had left
the train. "It would be a better policy if our names were not reported as being on the same register. I suggest that we then
take a walk. I can give you a better report if I am sure we
cannot be overheard." He spoke with modesty, yet with assurance. Gustav noticed with amazement how much the man
had changed. In Berlin, with his long thin legs and his long
thin hands protruding from sleeves which were always too
short, with his shy, awkward manner, he had always impressed Gustav as a student whose inner and outer qualifica-
tions had been inadequate. Now, for all his simplicity, he had

acquired the firmness of manner of a man who knew exactly what he wanted.

They drove out to the Gurten. It was a dazzling day of early spring, the white outline of the mountain ranges gave an effect of extreme delicacy and clarity. It was still too cold to sit for any length of time on the natural platform overlooking the view. They walked up the wooded heights. Gustav slackened his rapid, firm stride and Klaus Frischlin made his report.

The mercenaries had appeared in Max Reger Strasse during one of the first nights after his departure; it had been towards morning, there had been eight of them. Fortunately, the day before, Frischlin had deposited the manuscript, the most important of the Lessing literature, and the card index of notes with persons above suspicion. All the documents that remained had been pilfered or damaged. They had spared many of the books; at any rate their devastations had been a good deal worse in some other houses. They were very erratic in the choice of the books which they tore up or took away with them. They seemed especially enraged by the many editions of Dante's *Divine Comedy,* which they took for propaganda literature in behalf of the "godless movement"; probably they had been misled by the word "Comedy." They had confiscated the car and the typewriter. The portrait of Fräulein Rauch had shared the same fate. The portrait of Immanuel Oppermann, on the other hand, was untouched. Frischlin had now placed it in safekeeping. They had also overlooked a stack of private correspondence. This Frischlin had sent on to Gustav's present address by a circuitous route. It should arrive during the next few days. The servant Schlüter had proved himself very reliable. They had beaten him severely on the first occasion. Nevertheless, immediately after the looting, he had rescued the remaining property with the aid of his brother-in-law's widow. It was a good thing he had done so, for the very

next night they had come again and got their talons into what
was left. Frischlin had put the things which he believed Gustav
especially valued in Fräulein Rauch's house.

"Was Fräulein Rauch able to help you?" Gustav asked.
"Not much," returned Frischlin. She had been very willing to
help but, somehow, very little had come of it. Fräulein Rauch
was very busy with her own affairs, he added with marked
reserve. However, he spoke with enthusiasm of Mühlheim,
with whom he had apparently come to an excellent understanding. Mühlheim wanted Gustav to telephone him, if possible, between six and seven that evening, at the Hotel Bristol.

It was nearly six o'clock when Gustav returned to his hotel.
He must telephone Mühlheim at once but he did not want to
hear anything of business or anything of the sly schemes
which, to be sure, was the only sensible method to employ
against the Nationalists. All the same, his house, of which he
was very fond, was at stake. It was horrible to think that Nationalist troops might soon be wallowing in those beautiful
rooms. He must really speak to Mühlheim. But when the hotel
operator answered, he gave her, at the last moment, not Mühlheim's number but Sybil's.

He soon heard Sybil's voice. She was surprised, and her surprise had an element of fear in it, as he noted with quickly
aroused suspicion. Perhaps it was imprudent to telephone anyone from abroad just now. But as far as Sybil was concerned,
the risk was exceedingly slight and she need not have been so
aloof. He remembered how briefly and coolly Frischlin had
spoken of her. Yet he longed to see her, he longed for the
fragrance of her childlike body. Very earnestly he begged her
to come, told her how much he needed her now. She readily
assented. But when he wanted to set a definite date, she hesitated. She would wire tomorrow or, at the latest, the day after.
Gustav did not know she was thinking of Friedrich Wilhelm

Gutwetter. But he realized that she was hiding something from him and was much distressed.

Frischlin's report, too, clear and detailed as it was, now seemed insufficient to him. The fact of the matter was that public events in Germany were beginning to interest him more intensely than his house and his manuscript. He had always hoped Frischlin might begin to tell about them of his own accord. But Frischlin had not done so and he hesitated to rush the deliberate, level-headed fellow.

At last, that evening, in a very pretty little restaurant which Gustav had discovered, Frischlin gave him some account of conditions in general. It was not easy, he began, to secure authentic details in Germany today, the authorities successfully tried to shroud everything in uncertainty. His account would, therefore, be very incomplete. But Gustav soon found that the names, dates, and places which Frischlin was sure of were alarmingly numerous.

Of all the detachments of mercenaries stationed in Berlin the most notorious were the shock battalions 17 and 33, the so-called Murder Battalions. The places which were spoken of with the greatest horror were the cellars of the Nationalist quarters in Hedemann Strasse, in General Pape Strasse, and several in Köpenik and Spandau. In these spots, Frischlin observed, and this comment sounded disconcerting in the midst of his otherwise extremely sober narrative, there may well be erected—when the power of the Nationalists is finally broken —memorial tablets to the deepest blot on the reputation of the German people. The most dreadful thing about the activities of the secret police and the mercenaries, he continued, was the system, worked out to the smallest detail, the thorough organization, the half-military, half-bureaucratic regulations in accordance with which the ill-usage and the slaughter proceeded. All was duly registered, signed, and recorded. After each case of ill-treatment the victim had to state in writing that he had not been ill-treated. In the case of killings, the doctor certified that the man who had been killed had died of heart failure. The body was delivered to the relatives in a sealed casket, the opening of which was forbidden under the severest penalties. Those who were dismissed after mistreatment were supplied with fresh suits and underclothing, so that their blood-bespattered garments would not be too conspicuous. They had to guarantee in writing to return the fresh clothing within twenty-four hours properly cleaned. Furthermore, payment had to be made for board and the services rendered in the Nationalist barracks. Not much, to be sure: one mark a day for lodging and one mark for board and services. The board and services of those who had been killed, that is to say those who had "died of heart failure" or who had been "shot while trying to escape," had to be paid for by the surviving relatives. Services rendered also comprised spiritual things and were not devoid of a certain grim humour. The prisoners, for instance, had Nationalist songs played to them on a phonograph while they were undergoing treatment. They had to join in the songs, the rhythm was impressed upon them with steel rods and rubber truncheons.

The Nationalists apparently intended to carry out their system on a grand scale. They established enormous concentration camps in which the prisoners were taught "the qualities of mind required by the spirit of the new age." For this educational process, psychological methods were also employed. For example, they drove the prisoners through the streets in long, ridiculous processions and forced them to make grotesque utterances in chorus such as: "We're Marxist swine, we're Jewish swindlers," and so on. Or they forced individuals to mount on boxes and make genuflections and after each genuflection to call out: "I am a Jewish swine, I have betrayed my country, I have seduced Aryan girls, I have stolen public funds," and so

on. Occasionally prisoners had to climb trees, poplars for instance, and proclaim similar traits from aloft for hours.

In addition to this, the prisoners in the cellars of the mercenaries' barracks, as well as those in the concentration camps,
had the opportunity of thoroughly familiarizing themselves in
a very short time with the programme of the National-Socialist
party and the Leader's book. The method of instruction was
rigorous. Harsh penalties awaited those who made mistakes or
were careless; the era of liberalism and humanistic drivel was
past. Many, as already stated, did not survive the instructions.
In Berlin alone he knew of seventeen cases, attested by documentary evidence, which had ended fatally.

Such then was the information imparted by Dr. Klaus
Frischlin to Dr. Gustav Oppermann in the little wineshop in
Berne, the capital of the Swiss confederation. He spoke in a
low monotonous voice, for there were people sitting at the next
table. From time to time, to moisten his throat, he took a sip
of the light sparkling wine and when he did this his hands
looked remarkably long and thin as they emerged from his
sleeves. Gustav ate little that evening, nor did he speak much.
There were not many questions he could ask. Klaus Frischlin
told his story accurately and precisely. The only occasions
when his German was not precise were when he quoted the
words of the Leader which the ill-treated had to learn by heart.

When Frischlin had finished, the two men sat together in silence for some time. Frischlin slowly drank up his wine and
ceremoniously poured himself out a fresh glass. There were
only three other occupied tables in the room. Gustav had lowered his heavy eyelids and looked as though he were dozing.

"There's just one thing more, Frischlin," he finally said with
an effort. "You have not yet told me anything about my
nephew Berthold's death."

"Your nephew Berthold? His death?" Frischlin asked. It
developed that he knew nothing whatever of the whole affair.

"How can that be?" Gustav grew indignant. But Frischlin was not surprised. Steps were taken in Germany nowadays to prevent people from hearing what had happened to those closest to them if such events did not please the Government. Obviously the newspapers had been obliged to suppress the report. One heard nothing without making diligent inquiries. No one went out in Germany nowadays without a mask. People told with noisy, hysterical enthusiasm how well they were getting on and only after carefully looking round did they dare to tell one another, in whispers, what the true facts were. In a large city, even neighbours knew nothing about one another, they got their information about what was happening in the flat next door from the newspapers. But the papers were not allowed to report unpleasant matters. In a country of sixty-five million people, it had become possible to slaughter three thousand people, to cripple thirty thousand, and to imprison one hundred thousand without trial and without reason, and yet preserve an outward aspect of peace and order. The one thing necessary was not to allow the radio or the press to report these events.

Gustav asked Frischlin to let him go home alone. It was a clear night, it was late, the streets were empty. His firm, brisk steps re-echoed under the archways. He walked quickly, as usual, yet he felt weighed down. Frischlin had put a new idea into his mind, a new, unfamiliar, difficult idea.

Frischlin left during the next day. Gustav stood at the station. He was really glad that the disturbing fellow was going now. But as the train left, he felt as though the tracks were not separating them but as if they were threads connecting them, and no matter how far they would unwind, they could never break off. And it seemed to him that solitude was now much worse than Frischlin's company.

2

Edgar went off to the municipal clinic as usual. Gina had implored him not to go today; Ruth, too, contrary to his expectations, had urgently advised him against it. For the Nationalists had directed that on this Saturday, in addition to all other propaganda against the five hundred thousand Jews in the country, a boycott was to be carried out. The Nationalists explained that they were forced to give the lie to the statement, endorsed by thousands of documents, that they had employed sinister violence against the Jews. They were giving it the lie by inflicting economic annihilation on the Jews! Many Jews remained at home that day, many others had already left the country. It might be foolish, but Edgar Oppermann could not do otherwise: he went to his clinic.

He had no ulterior motives. He knew that his activities in Germany were over. He could leave Berlin today if he wished. He had received flattering offers from London and Paris. Most of the medical institutions of the civilized world took an interest in the inventor of the Oppermann treatment. He intended to accept one of these offers. It was true that his work here would be, to a large extent, destroyed. For little Dr. Jacoby was, naturally, leaving also and he would have been the man most capable of carrying on his experiments. He was actually going to Palestine, as Edgar had once imagined in an ironical mood. He was going on the same boat as Ruth. Yes, Edgar would have to make a fresh start in London, Paris, or Milan. It would take five or ten years before he could attain his previous eminence. He would have large funds put at his disposal but these funds would not suffice to remove all the obstacles which he would have to contend with in order to build up his

Institute. Difficulties of all kinds would arise, and he was no longer a young man.

It would not be easy to leave his Institute here, his laboratory, his operating-room, Jacoby, Reimers, Nurse Helene, and old Lorenz. He could not imagine how he could get on when he was far away from Germany. He did not think only of his professional establishment but also of his everyday life, his home. It would be an eternity before they could get used to the change. Gina took little things so damned seriously. He also would have to part from Ruth. He could not blame her for going to Palestine.

The city looked as though it were a public holiday. People were jostling one another in the streets in order to watch the boycott in operation. He passed innumerable placards: "Jew." "Don't buy from Jews." "Death to Judah." The Nationalist mercenaries stood about overbearingly, their legs encased in high boots, and bawled in unison, their silly young mouths wide open:

> "Until the last of the Jews is dead
> There'll be no work and there'll be no bread."

Perhaps Gina and Ruth were right and it was foolish to go to the clinic today. But he could not desert the case of Peter Deicke. Peter Deicke, Case 978, eighteen years of age, third-class patient, had been given up as beyond hope before being sent to his hospital. One operation had not sufficed. Perhaps a second would not achieve the desired result either. But at all events it was the only expedient that held out any hope of saving Peter Deicke. He could have left the second operation in Reimers's hands. But no. He could not increase the risk of a fatal outcome just because those gentlemen had decided to hold their silly boycott today.

He sailed through the long corridors of the clinic. Everything was going on as usual. There were twenty-four Jewish doctors attached to the clinic. They were all there, even little Jacoby. Everyone was in a hurry, as usual. No one mentioned the boycott. But Edgar could see the suppressed excitement on the apparently indifferent faces. Little Jacoby was pale. In spite of all the measures he had taken to prevent it, his hands that day were perspiring slightly.

"Get Case 978 ready," Edgar instructed Nurse Helene. Dr. Reimers suddenly put in an appearance. In a low voice, in his good-natured, rather blunt way, he made his request to Edgar. "Better pack up and go, Professor. There's absolutely no sense in your staying here. No one knows what the mob may do if they get out of hand. If you go, perhaps I shall be able to get little Jacoby away too. It's simply suicidal of that fellow to have shown up here." "All right, my dear Reimers," replied Edgar. "Now you have spoken your piece, we can get on with Case 978."

He began the operation.

Scarcely had the patient been wheeled back into his ward when they arrived. They had a list of the twenty-four physicians who officiated at the municipal clinic. They asked for them. But the staff resorted to passive resistance and refused to disclose their identity. A search was conducted under the guidance of a few Nationalist students. Whenever they found one of the Jewish doctors, they seized him and took him outside of the building. They did not allow the doctors to take off their white smocks. In fact, if they caught one without his smock, they forced him to put it on. Outside, before the main entrance, an enormous crowd was gathered. Whenever another white-smocked figure appeared, it was greeted with catcalls, whistling, and lewd insults.

Presently they found Edgar. "Are you Professor Opper-mann?" he was asked by one who had two stars on his collar. "Yes," said Oppermann. "He's number fourteen," said another with satisfaction, striking the name off his list. "You are to leave this hospital at once," said he of the two stars. "Come along." "Professor Oppermann has just finished an operation," interrupted Nurse Helene. Her voice was not as low as usual, her brown eyes were wide with anger. "It is important," she added quietly, "that the patient remain under his observation for some time yet." "We have orders to drive the man into the street," said the two-starred man. "Our business is to evict these twenty-four Jewish doctors and thus help purify Germany," he went on solemnly as though reading from a document and avoiding the use of dialect as well as he could. "That is final," he said.

Meanwhile one of the sisters had informed Privy Councillor Lorenz of what was happening. He loomed large before the intruders, his white coat billowing about him, his red face thrust forward, he looked like a moving mountain. "What's the matter here?" burst from his gold-toothed mouth, the words sounding like a small avalanche. "How dare you take such liberties? I am the master here, remember that." Privy Councillor Lorenz was one of the most popular doctors in the country, perhaps the most popular. Even some of the Nationalists recognized him from his pictures in the illustrated papers. The two-starred man had greeted him with the ancient Roman salute. "There is a national revolution, Herr Professor," he explained. "The Jews are to be kicked out. We have orders to clear twenty-four Jews out of here." "Then you'll have to clear out twenty-five men, gentlemen, for old Lorenz will go with 'em, see?" "You can do as you like about that, Herr Professor," said the two-starred man. "We have our orders."

Old Fear-God was helpless; for the first time in his life he was completely helpless. He realized that Professor Oppermann had been right: it was not an acute disease the nation was suffering from, it was a chronic one. He tried to compromise. "At least let the Professor here go free," he said. "I'll guarantee that he will leave the building." The two-starred man was undecided for a moment. "Very well, then," he said at last. "I'll take the responsibility. You guarantee, Herr Professor, that the man will not touch another Aryan and that he will be out of the building in twenty minutes. We'll wait until he is." His followers released Edgar and went off.

But twenty minutes later they were back again. "Who," they wanted to know, "who was shameless enough to allow himself to be operated on by a Jew today?" Old Lorenz had gone. "Now listen to me, please, gentlemen," Dr. Reimers demanded in his place; he was not quite able to control his voice, there was a snarl in it. "Hold your tongue until you are spoken to," the two-starred man warned him. One of the students led them to the man who had been operated on. They entered the ward. Reimers followed. Edgar, a bit dazed, brought up the rear with heavy, mechanical step.

The administration of an anæsthetic for an operation on the air passages is difficult. Oppermann had developed his own method for such cases. The patient, Peter Deicke, was conscious but he was full of morphia. His head looked like one huge white bandage and from this his glazed, dull eyes peered forth at the intruders. Terrified, her arms spread out protectingly, the attendant nurse stood before the bed. The mercenaries marched up to her with a firm tread and thrust the trembling, speechless woman to one side. The Nationalists are people who know how to organize to the smallest detail; they had prepared everything, they even had their rubber stamps with them. "You swine!" they said to Peter Deicke and on his bandage stamped the words: "I have been shameless enough to allow myself to be treated by a Jew." Then they shouted: "Heil Hitler!" and tramped down the stairs.

Edgar, as though hypnotized, as though he were being manipulated by wires, continued to follow them mechanically, his gaze vacant, confused. Nurse Helene caught him by the arm and drew him into the directors' room. She fetched old Lorenz. The two men stood opposite each other. They were both very pale. "Forgive this, Oppermann," said Lorenz. "You are not to blame, colleague," replied Oppermann with an effort, in a dry hoarse voice and shrugging his shoulders several times, heavily, automatically. "Well, I suppose I'd better go now," he added. "Won't you take off your smock?" Lorenz suggested. "No," returned Edgar. "No, thank you, colleague, I'll take that with me, at any rate."

3

"Please do me a favour, Martin," Liselotte had requested, the evening before the boycott. "Don't go to business tomorrow." She was thinking of the Jews who had been killed or had died as a result of the injuries they had received. She was thinking of those who had been ill-treated and who filled the hospitals all over the country. "Don't go to business," she urged and went quite close up to him. "Promise me you won't."

Martin took out his eyeglasses and polished them. His hair had turned grey and was thinner. His back was bent, his cheeks flabby. "Don't be angry at me, Liselotte," he said. "I intend to go to business. Don't worry." He patted her shoulder with his heavy, hairy hand, a thing he had never done before. "Nothing will happen to me," he went on. "I know exactly how far I can go. I've grown wise, Liselotte." He moved his head to and fro in a curious way. He had given up all pretence of poise and dignity; he was more talkative than formerly and sometimes he winked in a sly and confidential manner. He somehow began to resemble old Immanuel and even his brother-in-law Jaques Lavendel; Liselotte noticed it with surprise. Martin had become an old man and yet to her he seemed more virile, tougher, full of a deep understanding of the world and mankind. She loved him devotedly.

She did not urge him any further. They sat together in silence. She thought again of the dreadful incidents of the disaster. Not an hour passed without her thinking of them. Again and again, she stood before the door, as she had stood there that dreadful first time, hearing the rattling in the boy's throat. She saw him lying there, at full length, on his back. She raised his arm, it fell back dead; his leg, it fell back like a piece of wood. And yet that rattling continued, he breathed, his pulse was going, he was alive. Nevertheless, he was dead, his skin was cold and white, and there was no way of rousing him to consciousness. The doctors applied the stomach-pump over and over again, warmed his body, gave him nourishment by artificial means: mixtures of tea and cognac, milk. They administered heart stimulants, she remembered their many strange names: cardiazol, digitalis, strophantin, eutonon. He lay like that for three days, living and yet dead; for everyone knew there was no hope of saving him. The oxygen tank was of no use nor was the stomach-pump. He lay still, his skin was white and cold, the death-rattle was in his throat, he could not swallow the phlegm that filled his mouth. His pulse was very slow, at last it stopped altogether. But Berthold had already been dead when she had heard the rattle the very first time. She had known that. It was Martin who had kept on saying to the doctors: "Do something. Help him." She had known that no one could help him. It was she alone who might have helped him but she had not done so. She blamed herself entirely. Martin had his own worries, it had been her duty to watch over her boy.

In all this, the reckless abandonment of Martin's grief had been a consolation to her. He had shouted, wept, had attacks of delirious frenzy. He had read Berthold's manuscript over and over again, had it copied, and had then, like a madman, placed the manuscript together with Field-Marshal von Moltke's testimonial, in Berthold's coffin. Then he had mourned in the ancient Jewish manner, crouching on the ground, had torn his clothes, and said the prayer for the dead in the presence of nine orthodox Jews.

He had emerged from this seven days' mourning for his son a changed man. But she, Liselotte, had detected in the new Martin, the Martin she had surmised from the beginning. She discovered qualities in him that she admired in her brother-in-law Jaques, a display of cunning while fighting for what one believes to be right, the rejection of all superficialities, a tough elasticity when an actual issue was at stake. Martin and she were now, without expressing it, much nearer to one another than ever before.

They never spoke of Berthold.

On the other hand, Martin now often discussed business with Liselotte. He accepted every humiliation placed upon him by Wels without resistance, but fought for what was important to him with all the more tenacity and cunning. His activities in Gertraudten Strasse were to cease in less than a year but he worked as though that did not worry him. He engaged the Jewish employees whom Wels had dismissed from the German Furniture Company.

On the Saturday appointed for the boycott, therefore, he went to business as usual. He observed the crowds which were greedily and excitedly watching the boycott in operation. He saw the placards in the shop windows and heard the choral utterances of the Nationalist mercenaries. He nodded his head. This boycott, like most of the measures of the Nationalists, was a senseless comedy. The official pretext, that this method was to silence the indignation of the civilized world at the pogroms, was absurd. Even the Nationalist ministers would have to admit that complaints of ill-treatment are not refuted by continuing to assault the mistreated one. The real reasons for the boycott were different. The Nationalist leaders had been promising their adherents for fourteen years that they would be allowed to slaughter the Jews and plunder their homes and business premises. But scarcely had this process begun before the leaders found themselves compelled, on account of the indignation throughout the world, to call off their followers. By means of this ostentatious boycott they now wished to mollify their disappointed partisans.

Martin got Franzke to pull up at the corner of Gertraudten Strasse. He wanted to observe, at leisure, how things stood in the neighbourhood of his shop. They had not forgotten the name of Oppermann now that they were in power. They had stationed more than a dozen mercenaries in front of his not particularly large shop, and a man with two stars was in command. All the show-windows were thickly plastered with notices: "Don't buy from Jews," and "Death to Judah." They had found a picture of old Immanuel Oppermann and, in humorous vein, had pasted a sign "Death to Judah," in such a way that the words seemed to come from his mouth like a slogan. "The Jews bring you bad luck," Martin heard the young mercenaries shouting in chorus. He noticed that there was a large sign in the end window inscribed: "May the hands of this Jew rot off." Martin looked at his hands. They were reddish and hairy, presumably they would take a long time to rot off.

He arrived at the main entrance. The old porter Leschinsky was standing there with his set face and his grey moustache. But he did not swing the door open for him. He, too, had a placard hung round his neck with the words: "Death to Judah." He looked at his master humbly, helplessly, angrily, and hopefully. Martin did not salute him by putting one finger to the brim of his hat as he used to. He took off his hat to him and said: "Morning, Leschinsky." But he did not attempt anything more. He was too wise. As he was about to swing the door open the leader of the detachment stepped up to him. "Don't you know, sir," he said, "that there is a boycott of the Jews today?" "I am the head here, if you will allow me to say so," said Martin. The other Nationalists in uniform were standing around them, other people were listening too, silent and interested. "Really?" said the leader. "You're a devil of a chap then." And Martin, while they all stared at him, entered his premises.

All the employees were at their posts but there were no customers. In the private office Martin found Brieger and Hintze. Herr Hintze had finally hung up the photograph of Ludwig Oppermann; it showed him in uniform with the Iron Cross of the First Class. Hintze had written beneath it in very large and clear letters: "Killed for the Fatherland, 22nd July, 1917." "You should not have done that, Hintze," said Martin morosely. "You should not have come here at all; you only harm yourself and you are no help to us.

"Any news?" He turned to Brieger.

"People have been quiet so far," the latter informed him. "On my way here I saw a Nationalist guard standing outside the little Jewish cigar-shop in the Burg Strasse. The man was looking at his watch. It was not yet ten o'clock, which was the official hour set for the boycott to begin. He took down his placard, went into the shop, bought himself some cigarettes, and hung his placard up again. Our own fellows, too, inspected some of the things in the windows with great interest and asked what the prices were. I am convinced that they will be hooked later, if their leaders don't incite them to help themselves without payment. The receipts will certainly be on the lean side today. Six customers have been in, so far, of whom one was certainly a *goi*. The *goi* was a foreigner, he was brandishing his passport. He came in for a lark and bought a

chair button for sixty pfennig. After that old Frau Lietzen-
meier came. They would not let her in but she declared that
her mother had always traded with us and that she just had
to pick out a new bed for her maid today. They cut her hair
off and stamped her with the words: 'I, shameless one, have
traded in a Jewish shop.' "

"What was the matter with Leschinsky?" Martin asked.
"The old chap got a bit above himself," Brieger informed him.
"He called out something at them, 'Pack of swine,' or something like that. They're easy-going fellows, those brown-shirts
in this neighbourhood. They didn't carry him off to their barracks, they merely hung that placard around his neck."

Time was passing very slowly. "You see, Herr Oppermann,"
said Brieger, "we are finally keeping the Sabbath here in Gertraudten Strasse. I always told you we should."

A little later two of the mercenaries came into the office.
They brought the bill for pasting on the boycott placards.
There had been eighteen placards pasted on altogether and
the one they had hung round the doorman's neck. They
charged two marks per placard for the pasting. Accordingly,
the full amount due was thirty-eight marks. "Have you gone
mad?" Hintze burst out. "Have we got to pay because
you—?" "Be quiet, Hintze," commanded Martin. "Those
are our instructions," said one of the two mercenaries in a
matter-of-fact tone. "That is what is being done all over the
Reich." Hintze wrote out the order on the cashier with a sullen expression. "Two marks a placard," Brieger shook his
head and whistled through his teeth. "Your prices are somewhat steep, gentlemen. Our painters could have done the job
for thirty pfennig a placard. Couldn't you reduce it to one-
mark-fifty?" The mercenaries stood by without smiling.
"Heil Hitler!" they exclaimed and went off.

That day placards of this sort were pasted on the premises
of altogether 87,204 Jewish shopkeepers, doctors, and lawyers.

A Jewish lawyer in Kiel, who offered resistance after an argument arising from the mercenaries' demand for payment for pasting up the placards, was lynched in a police-cell. Forty-seven Jews committed suicide that Saturday.

At two o'clock in the afternoon Liselotte came to Gertraudten Strasse to fetch Martin. The troop-leader went up to her and called her attention to the fact that there was a boycott of the Jews that day. "I am the wife of the owner," said Liselotte loudly. The mercenaries stared at the tall, fair gentlewoman. "You ought to be ashamed of yourself," said the troop-leader and spat. Ten minutes later Liselotte left the building through the front entrance with Martin.

4

Markus Wolfsohn came into the private office in Gertraudten Strasse. He had been dismissed from the German Furniture Company. "All right, Wolfsohn," said Martin. "You can come in with me."

That very afternoon the packer Hinkel, the leader of the Nationalist nucleus in Oppermann's Furniture Store, appeared in Martin's office. In a state of great excitement he demanded that Martin should cancel the appointment of Herr Wolfsohn as well as that of three other Jewish salesmen and appoint "Aryans" in their place. "I believe," said Martin amiably, "that you labour under a delusion as to the extent of your authority, Hinkel." He showed him a newspaper paragraph; only those holding official positions, said the paper, not the leaders of the individual Nationalist organizations, were to be allowed to interfere with business. Hinkel the packer looked at his boss vindictively. "In the first place," he replied, "you are to call me

'Herr' Hinkel when I am in uniform. In the second place, that decree has only been printed for the benefit of foreigners and does not concern me. In the third place, I shall know how to report your behaviour to the proper quarter." "Very well," said Martin. "But for the present just see to it, Herr Hinkel, that the consignment for Seligmann & Co. is ready at once. Herr Brieger tells me that it was entirely your fault that this shipment did not go off yesterday." "The work for the National awakening always comes first," returned Hinkel the packer.

The same afternoon, Franz Pinkus, a business acquaintance of Martin's, showed him a letter which contained the following passage: "Although you have disregarded the various statements we have sent you and have not made payment as yet, we shall give you one more opportunity. Unless the sum in question is in our possession within three days we, being members of the National-Socialist party, shall hand your case over to the proper authorities. They will wind up your business and place you in a concentration camp, as you are guilty of shifting the detrimental results of the boycott upon the shoulders of your wholesalers. New Germany will then show you the right way to behave. Respectfully yours, Weber Bros." "What will you do?" asked Martin. Herr Pinkus looked at Martin thoughtfully. "There is a doubtful item of 7343 marks on the bill," he said. "I told their representative that, if he would get me a foreign visa for my passport, I would pay."

During the night, towards dawn, they arrived at Martin Oppermann's house in Cornelius Strasse. Thrusting the bewildered maid to one side, one of them entered Martin's and Liselotte's bedroom armed with revolver and truncheon; he was followed by four or five more, all very young lads. "Herr Oppermann?" inquired the leader in a courteous tone. "Yes," said Martin. It was neither fright nor a desire to be disagreeable that made his voice sound gruff, it was merely that he was still half asleep. Liselotte had started up. She stared with wide, terrified eyes at the lads. It was said all over the country that those who fell into the hands of the state police were lucky, but woe to those who fell into the hands of the Nationalists. And these fellows were Nationalists. "What do you want from us?" asked Liselotte anxiously. "We want nothing from you, madam," said the young man. "You are to dress and come with us," he said to Martin. "Very well," returned Martin. He tried to figure out the lad's rank in the mercenary army. It was indicated by the metal ornament on the collar, the "mirror," as it was called. Wels had four stars. The man here had two, but Martin did not know what the title of his rank was. He would have liked to inquire but the young man might take the question as a sign of contempt. Martin was very calm. It was known that many were done to death in the cellars of the mercenaries' barracks, their names were known. There were only very few who came out of these cellars entirely without injuries. But, strangely enough, he was not afraid. "Don't worry, Liselotte," he said. "I shall soon be back again." "That won't be altogether left to your decision, sir," said he of the two stars.

They put him into a taxi. He sat limply, his eyes half closed. There was not much more that could happen to him. His affairs in Berlin were all·settled. In the fight against Wels, Mühlheim had combined Jewish shrewdness with the Nordic craftiness of a lawyer who was popular with the Nationalists. Whatever might happen to him, Liselotte would be provided for.

His guards were carrying on a conversation in low tones. "Will we be allowed to stick him against the wall right away? I hope they let us and not the Thirty-Eighth examine him." Martin rocked his head back and forth. What a childish way of carrying on. They wanted him to dismiss his Jewish employees. Perhaps they would attempt to bully him into it by ill-treatment. Merchants of high standing and directors of industries had been dragged off to Nationalist barracks and concentration camps in order to extort voluntary resignations from them or the renunciation of some legal right. The Nationalists wanted to get possession of the industries which had been built up by the five hundred thousand Jews. They coveted their businesses, their positions, their money. They considered all means towards this end justified. In spite of all that, Martin instinctively felt that he, personally, was safe. He did not believe that he would be detained long. Liselotte would get busy on the telephone, so would Mühlheim.

He was taken into a dreary room on an upper floor. A man was sitting there with four stars on the collar of his uniform and there was another seated at a typewriter. The two-starred man reported: "Troop-Leader Kersing with a prisoner." That was it, the two-starred men were called troop-leaders. Martin was questioned as to his identity. Then a personage appeared in a more ornate uniform of brown. He had no stars on his collar but a simple leaf. He sat down at the table. It was a fairly large table, a candelabra with lighted candles upon it, as well as a bottle of beer and some books which seemed to be treatises on jurisprudence. The man thrust the books aside. Martin gazed at the candelabra. What a silly setting, he thought, and in the age of Reinhardt too. The chap had a leaf on his collar, had he? As a matter of fact, it wasn't a leaf but an oak twig. They were very exact in such details.

"Your name is Martin Oppermann?" asked the man with the oak twig. It's about time they knew that, thought Martin. It occurred to him that the thing was called a standard. Those with twigs on their collars were called standard-bearers. That man was quite a big shot, a robber chieftain. "Yes," he said. "You have resisted official regulations?" came the question from behind the candelabra. "Not that I know of," said Martin. "In these times," the man with the oak twig said sternly, "resistance to the regulations of the Leader is a treasonable act." Martin shrugged his shoulders. "I resisted the regulations of my packer Hinkel," he said. "I am not aware that he has been appointed to discharge any official function." "Write that down," said the man with the oak twig. "The accused denies his guilt and makes evasive answers. Take the man away," he commanded the guard.

The two-starred man and three others took Martin down the stairs again and then lower still, down badly lit steps. This is the cellar then, thought Martin. They were now in complete darkness. The way led through a long passage. Martin was seized firmly by the arms. "Walk in step, man," said a voice. The corridor was a long one. They turned a corner, then another. Someone flashed an electric torch into his face. Then they ascended a few steps. "Keep in step, you," one of them said to him and gave him a push in the back. What a childish way of carrying on, thought Martin.

After he had been marched about in different directions for about ten minutes, he was thrust into a fairly large, dimly lit room. Here things looked a bit more serious. Men were lying about on boards and on heaps of rags. There were between twenty and thirty of them, half naked, bleeding, groaning, hideous to look at. "Say, 'Heil Hitler,' when you enter anywhere," commanded one of his guards, giving him a blow in the ribs. "Heil Hitler," said Martin obediently. They pushed through the rows of hideous-looking, groaning people. There was a smell of sweat, excrement, and blood in the room. "There's no more room in waiting-room Number 4," said the man with the two stars.

Martin was taken into another room, which was smaller and crudely lit. A few people were standing in it, their faces to the wall. "Stand over there, Jew-pig," said someone to Martin. He stood beside the others; a phonograph was playing the Horst-Wessel song:

"Make way for the boys of the Brown Battalions,
Make way for the boys of the Shock Brigades,
The swastika blazons the hope of millions,
The era of Freedom and Plenty begins."

"Join in the song," came the order. The truncheons began to swing and the people with their faces to the wall sang. Then a record of one of the Leader's speeches was played and after that the Horst-Wessel song again. "Salute," came the order. Those who did not hold their arms or fingers stiff enough in the ancient Roman salute were struck on the offending arms or fingers. Then "Join in the song," came the order again. Then the phonograph was shut off and perfect silence reigned in the room.

That lasted, perhaps, half an hour. Martin grew very weary. He turned his head cautiously. "Stand still, will you, man," said someone and struck him across the shoulders. The blow hurt him but not severely. Then the phonograph started again. The needle's worn out, thought Martin. And I'm dog-tired. Even they will eventually get bored looking at my back. "We're going to say 'Our Father' now," commanded the voice. They recited 'Our Father' obediently. Martin had not heard it for a long time, he had only a vague idea of it. He took careful note of the words, they were really splendid words. The phonograph proclaimed the twenty-five points of the Party's programme. I'm getting training exercises of a sort now, thought Martin. Liselotte is surely telephoning by now. So is Mühlheim. Liselotte—she is the one I am worrying about most.

To stand for two hours sounds a mere nothing. But it is not easy for a man verging on fifty and unused to any form of bodily exertion. The glaring light and its reflection on the wall tortured Martin's eyes, the squeaking of the phonograph tortured his ears. But finally, after what seemed to him an eternity, though it was actually only two hours, the thing really did get too boring for them. They released him from the wall, drove him once more up and down steps and through dark passages and finally into a small room, which was rather dark. This time it was a man with three stars who sat at a table with a candlestick on it. "Is there anything else you want, or is there any message you wish to send to anyone?" he asked Martin. Martin reflected. "Give Herr Wels my compliments," he said finally in a noncommittal tone. The other gave him a puzzled glance.

The young men again took charge of him. Martin would have liked to talk to them but he was too tired. The next man who spoke to him was Hinkel the packer. He was not in uniform. "I have interceded for you, Herr Oppermann," he said, scrutinizing him with his mean eyes. "After all, we have been associated for a number of years. I think you would be wiser to give in. Sign a paper to the effect that you will comply with the regulations of the business committee, dismiss those four people and you are free." "I have no doubt that you mean well, Herr Hinkel," said Martin peacefully. "But I cannot discuss the matter with you here. I can only deal with business matters in Gertraudten Strasse." Hinkel the packer shrugged his shoulders.

Martin had a rough pallet in a small room allotted to him. He had a headache. Also the spot on his back, where he had been struck, was beginning to hurt. He tried to recall the words of "Our Father." But the Hebrew words of the prayer for the dead, which he had so recently spoken, substituted themselves. He was glad to be alone. He was exhausted. But the light had not been switched off and that prevented him from going to sleep.

Before the night was over, he was again taken to the room to which he had first been brought. Behind the table with the candelabra on it there now sat a man who had no twig on his collar, but only two stars. "You can go now, Herr Oppermann," he said. "There are only a few formalities for you to comply with. Kindly sign this paper." It was a statement that he had been well treated. Martin read it through, nodding his head. "If, for instance, I treated my employees in such a way," he said, "I doubt whether they would make such an affidavit for me." "You don't mean to tell me, sir, do you," snarled the man, "that you have been badly treated here?" "Don't I mean to tell you?" Martin asked in turn. "Very well," he added, "I won't tell you." He signed the paper. "Then there's this, too," said the man. It was an order to pay two marks, one mark for lodging and one mark for board and services rendered. The music was free, thought Martin. He paid and got a receipt. "Good morning," he said. "Heil Hitler," said the two-starred man.

Martin, when he got out into the air, suddenly felt utterly miserable. It was raining. The street was empty. It was long before daybreak. Twenty-four hours had not yet passed since his arrest. If only he could get home. His legs felt too weak, they were giving way under him. His kingdom for a taxi. There was a policeman; the policeman was watching him closely. Perhaps he thought he was drunk or perhaps he realized from his appearance that he had just come from the barracks of the mercenaries. The state police hated the Nationalist mercenaries. They called them the "Brown Pest," they loathed them. At any rate, the policeman stood still and inquired of Martin in a friendly tone: "What's the matter, sir? Aren't you well?" "Perhaps you could get me a taxi, officer," said Martin. "I'm not feeling well." "Very well, sir," said the policeman.

Martin sat down on some steps leading to a house. He kept his eyes closed. The shoulder where he had been given that blow was now extremely painful. It was a strange sight to see the head of Oppermann's Furniture Store crouching there in the street, badly bruised, down and out. At least he did not have to stand now, he could sit and keep his eyes shut. He really felt all right otherwise, though he was in such a state. How refreshing the light rain was. The taxi arrived, the policeman helped him into it, he just had enough strength left to give the address. Then he slumped in the taxi, leaning or rather lying on one side like a dead man. He slept and snored, contrary to his usual habit; the sound was a mixture of a snore and a rattle in the throat.

When the driver arrived at the house in Cornelius Strasse, he rang the bell. Liselotte herself open the door. The porter, half dressed, followed her; he looked astonished and delighted when he saw Martin. With his assistance Liselotte helped Martin up the steps. When they reached the morning-room, they could not take him any further. He sat there in an armchair, his eyes again closed, he slept and snored.

The maid, too, had meanwhile been awakened. She entered, saw Martin, and gave a half terrified, half delighted exclamation. Liselotte had, in fact, been telephoning the entire day as Martin had supposed. She was a plucky woman but she had been through a great deal during the past few weeks. One heard gruesome stories of what the Nationalists did to their prisoners. When they brought the lawyer Josephi home, they found he had been fatally injured. His kidneys had been ruptured. Every doctor had stories to tell of the Nationalists' prisoners who had been brought to them in pitiable conditions. Liselotte had imagined the most ghastly things. Standing there in front of Martin and looking at him as he slept and snored in his armchair, one of the rather uncomfortable Oppermann armchairs they had in the morning-room, she could not control herself. She screamed in spite of the maid's presence. Her serene face had become blotched and haggard; large tears were running down her cheeks. She uttered hysterical shrieks at the top of her voice, she threw herself upon the sleeping man and felt his limbs to see if he were hurt. He woke, blinking sleepily, and gave a faint smile. "Liselotte," he said. "There, there,

Liselotte. Gently, gently." Then he closed his eyes again and snored. She managed, with the maid's assistance, to get him into bed.

5

Gustav was crossing Lake Lugano on one of the pretty little local steamers. He was returning from the village of Pietra, where he had been looking over a house with the intention of renting or purchasing it. The Nationalists had confiscated his house in Berlin; it was now certain that he would not be returning to Berlin for some time.

If he rented the house up there in Pietra, he might not have to stay there alone. Perhaps Johannes Cohen would be with him for some time, perhaps he could persuade him to stay for a few months.

Yes, tomorrow Johannes Cohen, the friend of his boyhood, would arrive in Lugano. Gustav had received the telegram two days before. He was very excited. He did not quite know whether to dread or welcome the approaching reunion. He was restless and impatient. Whatever happened, there would be quarrels ahead.

There was no getting on with that fellow Johannes and yet there was no getting away from him either. Gustav had spent years, decades, quarrelling with him. He had said to himself a hundred times: I'm really not going to stand this any longer. But he went on standing it. That Johannes Cohen was a fellow who irritated and infuriated one. He upset a man, forced new theories upon him. But once you properly understood him, you kept going back to him for ever.

It was fourteen months now since Johannes had been heard from. He had not even congratulated him on his fiftieth birth-

day. Yet what Gustav had done should not have offended the
most sensitive of men. The winter before, just at the time when
the students' riots were at their height, Gustav had advised
him, in a strongly worded letter, to resign his professorship at
Leipzig. Had not Johannes now reached the goal of his ambitions? After the world-wide success of his book, *On the Astute-
ness of the Mind, or the Significance of Universal History,*
after so many foreign universities had endeavoured to secure
him for their faculties, the hostile senate had finally appointed
him to the chair of philosophy. Could he not be satisfied with
that? The Leipzig students simply had no use for him.
Weren't there riots every second day? Couldn't he live more
comfortably and calmly on the proceeds of his books? Must
he, who hated the Saxon dialect so, deliberately stay at that
difficult post in Leipzig, in the midst of students who subjected
him to vulgar abuse and in the Saxon dialect into the bargain? Was it really necessary for him to sit in his classroom
and wait until the police enforced silence to enable him to begin his lecture? Why must he teach students who absolutely
refused to be taught? His books could always reach those who
were worth reaching.

That was what Gustav had written to his friend Johannes
Cohen fourteen months ago. But Johannes had not replied.
Since then he had given no sign of life whatsoever. Gustav
did not want to admit it, but his friend's silence had hurt him
deeply throughout the year. Johannes, himself, had always assumed the prerogative of finding fault, often in a scornful and
bitter way, with everyone else. How often, when they had
been students together, had Johannes borrowed money of him
and in the same breath scoffed at him in the crudest manner?
Yet if one tried to give him a piece of advice in a decent and
friendly way, he hit back in the most ill-natured manner or
else, what was still worse, maintained a haughty silence for
more than a year. However, now it had turned out that Gus-

tav had been right when he wrote his letter: Johannes had been driven from his post in derision. But that, God knew, was no satisfaction to Gustav. Of course, the obstinate grimness with which his friend had stuck to his job had annoyed him greatly, but at bottom he respected that grimness, unreasonable as it was, and envied Johannes for it. Indeed, to be quite honest, such tenacity was a silent and permanent reproach to himself.

He had heaved a great sigh of relief when he had received the letter from Johannes a few days ago. That Johannes, when he was in need of a friend, should have turned to him, made Gustav proud. He had wired him at once, inviting him to come. Johannes would arrive, then, tomorrow. Gustav paced up and down on the deck of the little steamer with his precise, rapid stride, his entire sole firmly pressing the planks. He had an alluring vision of the yellowish-brown, sharp-nosed, haughty, animated face of his friend; he looked forward to the intellectual massage that awaited him.

This spring at Lake Lugano was the loveliest in years. It was very warm and there was a fragrant and brilliant blossoming all around. It would be splendid if he could persuade Johannes to stay with him up there for a few months. His enforced exile from Berlin suddenly appeared to Gustav almost as a boon. It was a boon when a man of fifty had the prospect of thoroughly making himself over again. With the assistance of Johannes he might make a success of it.

The steamer docked. Gustav walked along the beach promenade. He had to acknowledge many greetings. He wanted to be alone. He walked to the extreme end of the promenade and sat down on a bench.

Very many people had left Germany but very many more had remained. The Nationalists could not kill or imprison all their adversaries, for their adversaries comprised two-thirds of the population. People tried to establish a *modus vivendi*. The strangest relations, social and commercial, existed during this period of change between the Nationalists and their enemies. Hundreds of thousands rose in the world and hundreds of thousands fell, that was obvious.

> We rise and fall, are pulled hither and yon.
> We are like pails on the pulleys of a well:
> Fate fills the one, empties the other,
> It lifts us up, then casts us down;
> Links us to hostile, foreign things;
> Acts like a capricious child at play.

Yes, those who rose and those who fell were bound to one another and they knew that they were. Everywhere persecutors were making offers to the persecuted to save their positions or their wealth, provided that they might share in the profits. When one came to look at it closely, the entire Nationalist revolution resolved itself into millions of small commercial transactions, conducted on reciprocal terms.

On this glorious afternoon Gustav felt clear-headed and full of happy excitement at the imminent arrival of his friend. He thought, with tolerant amusement, of the curious anecdotes he had been told.

Holsten the painter had been an artist of the second rank, a good-natured, bluff sort of man. He had come down in the world. But in the days of his prosperity he had treated his manservant with generosity and friendliness and the latter was now in the service of a Nationalist minister. The manservant had *savoir vivre,* he knew how to show his gratitude. The painter, today, was the man who decided who should succeed to the presidencies of the leading societies of artists and to whom the state should entrust its commissions.

A Nationalist lawyer, one of the noisiest champions in the struggle to evict Jews from legal practice, helped a Jewish lawyer to arrange his flight across the frontier. "I am counting on you, colleague," he said, on taking leave of the other, "to do as much for me if ever the necessity should arise." Many of the new masters were insuring their own safety in case the new regime broke down, through the very men they were now persecuting.

Gustav thought of his friend Friedrich Wilhelm Gutwetter with some uneasiness. He had read an essay by him which proclaimed the "New Humanity" in terms of noble solemnity. It was received in Nationalist circles with great rejoicing and in those of their adversaries with regret, attacks, and ridicule. Gustav, who was convinced of the perfect sincerity of his friend, wished that the article had never been written. He had had a letter from Gutwetter yesterday. Gutwetter, in view of the fact that Gustav's sojourn abroad was being prolonged, requested permission to use the library in Max Reger Strasse during his absence and to be allowed to work there.

While Gustav was thinking of these matters, judging them tolerantly, a young man passed him. He was in his early thirties and sturdily built, with a strong, lean face. Gustav recognized him. He was a certain Dr. Bilfinger, a wealthy young South German. Gustav had already noticed him during the last two days. The young fellow made a striking figure as he went about in his light grey spring overcoat, always alone, very correctly dressed, with a stiff collar, always with his hat in his hand and a preoccupied air, staring into space. On seeing Gustav, he hesitated, finally approached, and inquired whether he might sit down beside him. He obviously had something on his mind. Gustav in his frank, friendly way encouraged the reticent man to talk. Yes, he said finally, he had an extraordinary story to tell and he would like Gustav to hear it. He had heard something about Gustav through his friend Frischlin. Gustav was, as a matter of fact, an interested party and in a way he felt he owed him an apology. The reference to Frischlin startled Gustav. The coincidence was not particularly remarkable, indeed he remembered now that he had sometimes heard Frischlin mention Bilfinger's name. But it seemed to him as though he had lately, almost on purpose, forgotten Frischlin. He remembered the tracks at the railway station at Berne and how he had compared them to threads. Young Bilfinger appeared to him in the light of a messenger from Frischlin. He looked at him. Dr. Bilfinger, in his light grey spring overcoat, looked very conservative. His strong face, his hair—neatly brushed up on end—all inspired confidence, though his facial expression showed he was a man obsessed by a single idea. "Please talk quite freely, Dr. Bilfinger," he requested. But Bilfinger answered that he had gone through some unpleasant experiences. He would only like to tell his story in a place where they could be sure of not being overheard by spies. He suggested that they might drive out together somewhere after lunch. In the open air a man could talk and listen without fear of interruption.

Later that afternoon, then, they sat in the sun on a sloping, grassy bank by the shore of the lake and Dr. Bilfinger told his story. He had been in Swabia, on an estate to which he was heir, near Künzlingen, at the house of his uncle, Herr von Daffner, who was President of the Senate. Well, on the 25th of March he had gone to Künzlingen to get some money from the bank. He had been a spectator of the occupation of the place by Nationalist troops under the command of Standard-Bearer Klein of Heilbronn. He had seen them surround the synagogue—it was a Saturday—and interrupt the service. They drove the men out of the synagogue and locked the women in without telling them what they were going to do with the men. They took them to the town hall and searched them for "weapons." Why the men should have taken weapons with them to the usual Saturday service at the synagogue remained a mystery. As invariably happened, each one of them was beaten with steel rods and rubber truncheons, so that, when they left the town hall, most of them were a piteous sight. A seventy-year-old man by the name of Berg died the same day; as a result of heart failure it was stated later. The mayor advised the Jews, who were generally very popular, to leave Künzlingen at once, as he could not guarantee their safety. But there were only a few who could follow his advice, most of them had to keep to their beds.

This episode had disturbed him, Bilfinger, very much, and he had gone, accompanied by his uncle, Herr von Daffner, to Stuttgart, the provincial capital, and presented a petition there to the deputy minister of police. The latter, a certain Dr. Dill, immediately telephoned the mayor of Künzlingen. The mayor kept shifting his ground; sometimes he acknowledged what had happened and sometimes he disputed it. The fact was that the Nationalists had threatened that, if anyone revealed a single detail of the maltreatment, he could consider himself doomed. The minister, in order to get to the bottom of the affair, sent the Stuttgart murder-squad, in charge of the police commissioners Weizenäcker and Geissler, to Künzlingen. The squad reported that Bilfinger's account of the affair was considerably short of the truth. But the only consequence of the investigation was that one of the Nationalists was remanded for four days for inquiries and that Standard-Bearer Klein of Heilbronn was, by way of punishment, shifted to another standard-unit. The account of the incident in the leading newspaper of Stuttgart was as follows: "In the neighbourhood of Mergentheim a number of the population were searched for weapons. During the search several cases of illtreatment appear to have occurred, consequently one of those conducting the search was arrested."

He, himself, Bilfinger continued, was a jurist; he had made a profound and earnest study of the law, and it was a sore point to him that actions which so openly flouted sections of the country's Criminal Code were allowed to go unpunished.

He had made further investigations in the neighbourhood between Mergentheim, Rothenburg, and Crailsheim. It was not easy to gather authentic material. For those who had been ill-treated were subjected to the direst intimidation; some had been driven to the borders of insanity by terror. Threats had been uttered to them, to their wives and children as well, that, if they uttered a single syllable of complaint, it would be followed by vengeance. The people would not let anyone come near them now. They refused, with distracted looks, to make any sort of statement whatever. Nevertheless, he had managed to see and even to interview injured persons. He had spoken with reliable eye-witnesses, members of the state police force, doctors who had attended the victims, and he had seen photographs. So much was certain: disturbances of the peace had occurred in this neighbourhood, there had been organized pogroms. The evidences of the breach of peace in the province were beyond dispute.

For instance, in the market town of Bünzelsee, thirteen Jewish men, the first carrying a flag, had to parade through the streets. They were beaten as they went along and had to call out in chorus: "We have lied, we have cheated, we have betrayed our Fatherland." Hair was plucked from the heads and beards of these men, they were severely beaten with steel rods and rubber truncheons. In a place called Reidelsheim the Nationalists had beaten, among other Jews, a certain teacher, from whom they had demanded with the words: "Isidor, where is your list?" a memorandum, which did not exist, of firms to be boycotted by the Jews. The teacher was so roughly handled that a relative of his by the name of Binswanger, who came to visit him later that evening, had a heart attack at the sight of his wounds. The Christian doctor who treated the case, Dr. Staupp, begged the patient to release him from his doctor's bond of secrecy. He did not wish to live in a Germany such as this any longer but intended to leave and proclaim what he had seen.

In Weissach the nine most prominent Jews in the place were put with their faces to the wall, in the town hall. They were "examined." If any of them, in making a reply, turned his head automatically away from the wall towards his inquisitor, he received a box on the ear. Two of those so "examined" had served in the war as officers at the front. One of them had lost his hand during the war. Many of the Christian inhabitants of the place had loudly voiced their grief and indignation at these proceedings.

In Oberstetten an old Jewish woman lay dying. The Nationalists drove her two sons away from her death-bed and searched the house "for weapons." The representative of the state police who was present declared that he would not stay to witness such things. The woman died without having her dearest relatives near to comfort her. The police official lost his position.

As the authorities of Württemberg, continued Bilfinger, obviously intended to take no measures—apart from the four days' detention of a single mercenary for investigation—to punish the pogroms, he and his uncle, the President of the Senate, went to Berlin to make their protests to the chiefs of the new government. But wherever they went people merely shrugged their shoulders, and they were informed that a revolution was not a tea-party. When they persisted, they were met with disagreeable receptions. They were given to understand that it was extremely objectionable for private individuals to concern themselves with questions of public administration. A young lawyer had been sentenced to ten months' imprisonment simply because he had drawn up some lists of those who, according to official reports, had been injured in political disturbances. Finally, some well-disposed persons warned them to get across the frontier as quickly as they could. Otherwise they would run the risk of arrest for their own protection. A "protective" arrest was an administrative measure. It was a measure to protect the public against the person who was arrested, as well as to protect the latter against the public. "To protect him from the righteous anger of the people," was the phrase used by the new authorities. It was within the rights of the leaders of the mercenaries and the secret police to inflict such an arrest. The prisoner was not brought before any magistrate nor was he informed of the reason for his detention. No complaint was lodged and no trial was arranged for, nor was the prisoner allowed to see a lawyer. The period of these protective arrests was spent in the concentration camps, which corresponded to some extent to such reformatories as were provided for by section 362 of the Criminal Code. The concentration camps were under the jurisdiction of the mercenary army, and the intervention of any other authority was strictly prohibited. The mercenaries were for the most part recruited from very young men of the unemployed class. To them, therefore, was entrusted the instruction of the inmates: professors, authors, judges, ministers, and political leaders, in "the qualities required by the spirit of the New Age."

Such was Dr. Bilfinger's story, which he told sitting on a grassy bank by the shore of Lake Lugano. He made his report in precise, official language, with much circumstantial detail. He was not a good story-teller. His drawling Swabian inflection was a strange contrast to what he had to relate. He sat quietly in his light grey overcoat, without omitting a single detail of his report, which lasted nearly an hour. Gustav listened. He was sitting in a rather uncomfortable position, so that his legs kept going to sleep, but it was only rarely that he moved. At first he occasionally blinked nervously but soon his eyes, as well as his body, became motionless. He did not interrupt Bilfinger once. He had heard many things and worse things, but the legal, businesslike manner of this young man made the scenes of filth and blood, which he described, more vital than all the previous reports. He listened attentively, avidly. He greedily absorbed the other's words, sank them into his consciousness, so that they became not only knowledge, but also feeling, a part of himself.

Bilfinger had been talking slowly, in a monotonous voice, without pausing. Up to now, he said, he had only reported what had taken place in isolated cases. This was the first time he had found himself in a position to tell of a series of connected events, without any kind of circumlocution, objectively, as became a decent jurist. Gustav must please understand him, he urged. It was not the individual crimes which had so deeply disturbed him, it was the fact that they remained unpunished. He was a German to the core, he was a member of the Steel Helmet Association, but he was also a jurist to the core. That there were brutal persons of infirm understanding to be found in a nation comprising sixty-five millions of human beings, he could very easily understand. But that the barbarism and criminality of the cave-man should be proclaimed as the normal temper of the nation and should be written into the laws of the country, that was what made him ashamed to be a German. The cold-blooded pogroms which were undertaken against workers and Jews, the anthropological and zoölogical nonsense which now inspired legislation, the legalized sadism—it was all this which excited him so tremendously. He came, personally, of an old-established family of lawyers and it was his conviction that a lawless existence was not worth living. He could make nothing of this German code which those now in authority had substituted for the Roman code. It was not based on the assumption that all men were equal in the eyes of the law, but that the man of German ancestry was the rightful master and therefore superior to all others and consequently had to be judged on a different basis from that of people not of his nationality. With the best of intentions he was unable to recognize as legal the decrees of the Nationalist "law-givers." For some of the men who formulated them were deserving of punishment as criminals according to the legal regulations of all the other white nations, and the balance of them should, in the opinion of responsible physicians, be shut up in lunatic asylums. A man who, according to the legal verdict of Swedish judges, was not mentally normal and therefore was not competent to be the guardian of his own child, was certainly not competent to be the guardian of thirty-eight million Prussians. Germany had ceased to be a constitutional country. He, Bilfinger, was absolutely fed up with all this. He considered that the pure German air had, to put it bluntly, become foul and pestilential by what had happened, and the fact that such things went unpunished made the pollution far worse. He could not continue to live in such a country. He had thrown over all his opportunities in Germany and left it for good. He stared straight ahead through his big, gold-rimmed spectacles with an embittered expression on his angular features. "They have smashed the standards of the civilized world to pieces," he said sullenly in his Swabian accent, helpless fury in his tone.

Gustav said nothing. "They have smashed the standards of the civilized word to pieces." The words rang in his ears in the young man's Swabian intonation. "They have smashed the standards of the civilized world to pieces." He had a vision of a man taking measurements of some diminutive object with a yellow centimetre-rule. The object was perhaps fifteen centimetres high, twenty at most. The man measured it twice. Then he broke the centimetre-rule to pieces and wrote down: "Two metres." Then another man came along and wrote down: "Two and a half metres."

Gustav did not speak for more than a minute. "Why did you choose me to tell this to?" he asked finally. His voice was shaky, he had to clear his throat to steady it. Bilfinger gave him a troubled, embarrassed look out of his narrow eyes. "There were two reasons," he said, "why I believed you would be interested. First, because you signed a manifesto against the barbarization of public life, and secondly because my friend Frischlin once said of you that you were a man of 'contemplative' type. I am very well aware what he meant by that. I have a high opinion of my friend Frischlin." He had flushed slightly and spoke in an embarrassed tone.

The sun had gone down, it had grown cold. Gustav, still speaking with an effort, said: "I thank you, Dr. Bilfinger, for having talked to me." Then he continued very rapidly: "It's getting cold. We'd better go back."

On the way back he said: "We'll say no more at present, Dr. Bilfinger. There's no sense in discussing it." What, indeed, could anyone who loved Germany say regarding such a report. What did "love" mean? A scrap of verse came into his head; had he or someone else written it?

> And lov'st thou Germany? O senseless cry!
> Can I love that which is naught else but I?

Bilfinger said: "I have written down, in minute detail, what I have seen with my own eyes and what others have told me. I have had it drawn up in due form by a Zürich notary and have duly sworn to its truth. Others, who were able, as eye-witnesses or victims, to give similar information have likewise done so, that is, those who have been able to take refuge abroad. I can send you the document if you like. But it is very long and makes far from pleasant reading." "Please send it to me," said Gustav.

He could eat nothing that evening, nor could he sleep that night, and the idea he had been playing with, to rent or purchase the house up in Pietra, now seemed absurd to him.

Young Dr. Bilfinger had sacrificed his excellent prospects in Germany and had renounced the land he loved because these things had happened and had gone unpunished. Bilfinger was a German and a German only, one with the assailants. It was worse for him, Gustav. He was one with the assailants and one, also, with those who were assailed.

A man is ill-treated, punched in the kidneys, so that they become ruptured, his bones are laid bare. He had read of it and had been told of it. It had happened in East Prussia, in Silesia, in Franconia, and in the Palatinate. But the news had been mere words to him. Now for the first time, after the young Swabian's narrative, the words had become actual facts. He could see them and feel them now. The blows of which he had heard made jagged wounds in his own flesh.

No, he could not go and sit up there in Pietra, without doing anything in these times.

The wave dissolves, the feelings and thoughts of mankind dissolve like the wave. But it is given to man to make the impossible possible. No one can step into the same wave twice, yet man has made it possible. Man can say: "Stand still, wave." Man can hold on to the ephemeral, he can change it into a tangible thing; into the written word, cut it into stone, make it eternal.

Others beget children to continue their lives. It had sometimes been granted to him, Gustav, to transmit to others the beauty he had observed. Frischlin had said that he was a man of "contemplative" type. That entailed a great moral obligation. Was it not his duty to hand on to others the burning indignation which he had felt?

Events of such horror as the Occident had for centuries believed impossible ushered in the reign of the Nationalists. Moreover, they entirely cut off Germany from the rest of the world. Anyone who dared to tell the Germans themselves about what was happening in their country, even in whispers, was persecuted to the third generation. On the Kurfürsten-damm in Berlin, on the Jungfernstieg in Hamburg, on Hohe Strasse in Cologne, none of the horrors had been seen or heard of: which proved, said the Nationalists triumphantly, that they did not exist. Then should one not shout them into the deaf ears of the people on the Kurfürstendamm, on the Jungfern-stieg, and on Hohe Strasse? Should they not be displayed to their dull eyes until their senses were awakened at last? Was not his fury a good weapon to achieve such a purpose?

The next morning Gustav again sat on his bench at the end of the promenade by the shore of the lake, alone. Events are linked together in strange ways. If he had not signed that admittedly useless manifesto, he would not be sitting here now, Bilfinger would not have spoken to him, he would now —perhaps—be going about like one of those on the Kurfürsten-damm, the Jungfernstieg, or Hohe Strasse, blind and deaf, with his heart and mind sealed. Such a slight event had brought him into this maelstrom. It had been chance, yet not chance entirely.

It had not been chance. Frischlin had said he was a man of "contemplative" type. He knew what Frischlin had meant. "The man who acts is always unscrupulous; the contemplative observer alone has scruples." He was proud that Frischlin had called him a contemplative observer.

Young Bilfinger had written down and sworn to the events he had narrated. He was going to send him this document. Gustav was physically afraid of it. He was afraid that it might be lying in his room, on the inadequate little hotel desk. Down-stairs in the dining-room the musicians were playing, there was dancing in the hall, people were sitting in the bar, drinking and flirting, and the document would be lying in the drawer of the desk.

If only Johannes Cohen were here now. It was damned difficult to settle all this by oneself. Gustav pictured his friend's yellowish-brown, lean, shrewd, and scornful features. He would be sure to wax sarcastic if he suspected Gustav's ecstasy and his despair of the previous night. It was good that he was to arrive that evening.

He was so deep in his dreams that he gave a slight start when someone hailed him with a "hallo, Oppermann." It was Rudolph Weinberg, head of a large factory for hospital supplies. The stout, well-groomed gentleman inquired whether he might sit down beside him. He was obviously pleased at meeting Oppermann. As a rule he did not care, he explained, to walk longer than ten minutes. But one really had to go to the very end of the promenade before one's ears could escape the whining of all the refugees in this place. He sat down, out of breath. "One feels for them, of course; but they don't do themselves any good by spoiling one's short holiday with their lamentations. It's a bad business, of course, a very bad business. But if you give the Nationalists a chance to settle down, things will soon adjust themselves. People always improve as soon as they are safely established on top. Economically the outlook isn't too bad. Dreadful things have happened, of course. One can't sweep without a broom. But, honestly, aren't the atrocities the exception and not the rule? And aren't things improving already? When I walk through Berlin nowadays practically nothing seems changed. Still they're shouting blue murder. It's really foolish the way they're behaving. Their squawking merely irritates the authorities. You'd really think, from the foreign papers, that a man can't cross the street in Germany without being set upon. I don't consider that fair."

Herr Weinberg sat basking in the glorious sunshine and shook his head over the foolishness of the world. "M'm," Gustav said and the vertical furrows showed on his forehead. "You believe, then, that it's easy to get along with the Nationalists? That's interesting. Really interesting. By the way, Weinberg," he went on more cheerfully, "you have a branch in Munich, I think. What's the situation there? Have you been in Munich lately?" "Yes," said Weinberg. "I came through Munich on my way here." "Perhaps you can tell me, then," continued Gustav in an amiable tone, "how Michel the lawyer is getting on? They stripped him of his coat, cut up his trousers in a ridiculous way so that his underwear showed, and hung a placard round his neck reading: 'I will never complain of the good Nationalists any more.' They drove him through the busiest streets of the city in that array. He looked pretty well bruised; I've seen photographs. And do you know how the chief rabbi of Munich is getting on? They led him out of the city, beat him up, and finally left him, very scantily clothed, in a spot a good hour's walk from the city; it was a bitterly cold night. And did you hear anything about Alfred Wolf the lawyer? He had a dispute with a Christian colleague. He had collected all sorts of evidence against the colleague in question, who had now become Minister of Justice. The lawyer Wolf straightaway disappeared in a concentration camp. Did you ever hear of a concentration camp, Weinberg? Concentration camps do exist in Germany now, there are forty-three of them so far. You should go and have a look at one of them, Weinberg. How many miles is it to Oranienburg? About twenty, I believe. If you ever drive to the seaside, do stop at Oranienburg. You can see extraordinary things there without giving yourself much trouble. Wolf the lawyer, then, went to the concentration camp at Dachau. That's one of the worst of them. There is a prayer in Bavaria which runs: 'Dear God Almighty, make me dumb, so that I'll ne'er to Dachau come.' But lawyer Wolf did not become dumb and he did come to Dachau. He was rich and had powerful friends. These friends used their influence; there was a certain amount of discussion. The Leader himself spoke with the Minister of Justice. But the Minister of Justice insisted. 'That man belongs to me,' he said. At any rate, three days later a policeman came to Dr.

Wolf's mother and asked her whether her son had at any time suffered from heart disease. The woman jumped to the conclusion that her son had pleaded heart disease so as to obtain better treatment. 'Yes,' she said eagerly. 'He always had a weak heart.' 'That explains it then,' answered the policeman. 'The fact is, he just died.' The corpse was delivered in a sealed casket, and a solemn oath had to be given that the casket would not be opened. Didn't you hear anything about that in Munich, Weinberg?"

Weinberg the manufacturer stirred uncomfortably on the bench. Oppermann had not spoken in a low tone and practically everyone here understood German. Ah, of course, how was it he had forgotten? That fellow Oppermann had placed himself on record during the first critical weeks, the idiot. "Certainly, certainly," he said soothingly. "Terrible things have happened. No one denies it. I have said so myself. But that was just at first. The government has put the brakes on a long time ago, I assure you. And the entire Anti-Semitic movement would fizzle out if only the Jews abroad would make up their minds to stop chattering. I know that. I have talked to high officials. They would be glad to eliminate that plank from their platform altogether. But those abroad won't allow them to. They still keep the hunt going, instead of letting bygones be bygones. I tell you, Oppermann, it is to our interest, to yours too, to give the lie to exaggerations. All this weeping and wailing only injures the Jews who have remained behind. And anyhow you will want to return some time, I suppose."

Gustav was silent. Herr Weinberg assumed that his arguments had made an impression and tried to appease him completely. "Moreover," he added, "as far as that lawyer Wolf is concerned, the incident remains, of course, an exceedingly deplorable one. But, between ourselves, the fellow must have been a peculiarly difficult customer to deal with. I am told he was one of the last men in the world to elicit sympathy."

"Possibly," said Gustav. "But you know, Weinberg, it's a curious thing about sympathy. It's possible, for instance, that you, too, may not be quite the person to stir the sympathy of everyone. But you wouldn't approve of my, let us say, throwing you into the lake on that account, would you?"

Weinberg rose. "One has to make some allowance for your hysterical state of mind," he said with dignity. "But I solemnly assure you, Oppermann, that if one does not deliberately make oneself conspicuous, one runs very little risk. You may believe it or not, but I personally have seen practically nothing of the whole Anti-Semitic movement. You may take it from me, Oppermann, that you yourself will be allowed to return to Germany before long. You'll see that the sleeping-car porter will thank you as much as ever for your tip and that the traffic policeman will be just as courteous in giving your chauffeur information as he was a year ago." "You are quite right," said Gustav. "One really should not be too greedy."

After Herr Weinberg had disappeared, he stared at the peaceful landscape in front of him but the vertical furrows still showed on his forehead. The nervous blinking of his eyes had grown worse; he had taken little exercise lately. He held his heavy head down as though he were searching for something on the ground. Herr Weinberg's chatter had disturbed him more than he was willing to admit.

There were many who adopted Herr Weinberg's attitude. They drove along the broad streets in the West End of Berlin, resided in their great houses, and did not want to see what was going on in other places, not even in the cellars of their own buildings. They considered that peace and quiet reigned in Germany. They got very cross when people spoke of the one hundred thousand human beings in the concentration camps and of the forty million more who—in order to insure their good behaviour—were threatened with them. They were silent, they buried their knowledge so deeply within themselves that finally they no longer believed it themselves. They made common cause, all of them, actively and passively, in distorting the truth stupidly and shamelessly. "They have smashed the standards of the civilized world to pieces." He could hear Bilfinger's Swabian accents clearly; could see the man with the yellow centimetre-rule and see him writing: "Two and a half metres."

He sat on gloomily, with bent head, grinding his teeth a little. Perhaps it was useless, perhaps it was unreasonable, but one had to speak. They forced their prisoners to stand on boxes, make genuflections, and call out: "I am a Marxist swine and have betrayed my Fatherland." One could not go on living and keeping silence and looking on while they stupidly and shamelessly distorted the truth.

He continued to stare in front of him, lost in thought. A clock struck somewhere. He noticed the striking of the hour, at first automatically, then consciously. With an effort he emerged from his reverie. His usual lunch hour was long past. He suddenly realized that he was hungry and started back to the hotel. He hurried along the promenade with precise, rapid stride. He jeered at himself. What on earth was the matter with him? What was it he wanted? What was this mess he was in? He was a Berlin business man of 1933, with literary avocations, he was well-off. Because he had ill-advisedly, in a moment of vanity, put his signature to an utterly superfluous document, various unpleasant things had happened to him. And was it for this he proposed to take his place among the prophets? What business had wealthy people among the prophets? That must be the correct interpretation of "Saul among the Prophets": What business has a rich man among the prophets? But he was a man of "contemplative" type, Frischlin had said. It was because he was a "contemplative" type that Bilfinger had spoken to him. It was obvious they assumed that this bound a man to do something. Nonsense.

What a romantic, what an unmodern view that was. If you are absolutely determined to rise to further heights, Dr. Oppermann, the best thing you can do is to get on with your Lessing. Herr Doctor Frischlin would do better, too, to concern himself a little more with Lessing than with the administration of the world. To tell the truth, to shout, to wake up the world, such things were missions for others. How do you come into it, Herr Doctor Oppermann? Who gave you your commission?

He went in to lunch. He made an excellent meal and had a good appetite. His foolish, romantic whims went the way of his hunger. He lay down, went to sleep, and slept soundly, without dreams.

He was awakened by Bilfinger, who was bringing the documents. It all came back to him again, instantly. He wanted to plunge into the documents at once, without losing a moment. He must study them before Johannes Cohen came, so as not to let him confuse his sentiments.

But Bilfinger did not let him. Bilfinger did not go away again; Bilfinger remained. Dr. Oppermann had given him one hearing, he was in duty bound to hear him further; one was as much concerned as the other. He sat there, that impassioned jurist Bilfinger, looked at Gustav through his gold-rimmed spectacles, and spoke in precise, literary style. The Germans had always been inclined to substitute the authority of a single leader for written law. Even in the days of the Romans they had considered that a code of laws applicable equally to all men was contrary to the honour of individuals. If they hated the Romans, it was not because the latter wished to impose Roman law but because the Romans wished to impose any law upon them. They preferred to be judged by the decree of one superior person, in whom they trusted, rather than by definite laws, drawn up by the dictates of reason. Unfortunately, their Leader approved of murder. Their Leader had saluted certain Nationalists, who had been found guilty of the brutal murder of a workman, as his comrades. That was the kind of thing that convinced people that what counted was not a judicial sentence but merely the Leader's inspiration of the moment. This led to such experiences as he had lived through in Württemberg.

It had not been an easy matter for him, he continued, to leave Germany. It was not only Germany that he was leaving behind together with the prospects of an honourable career and the succession to a fine estate which had been the home of his family for more than a century. He was also leaving behind a girl to whom he was devoted. He had now given her a choice: either to come to him and renounce Germany, until it became a constitutional country again, or to release him from his promises. Bilfinger explained these things to Gustav, speaking anxiously and earnestly in Swabian accents.

While Bilfinger was speaking, Gustav stared at the documents. There they lay, just as he had imagined, large and heavy, on the pretty little hotel desk. Bilfinger had scarcely left the room before he made a dive at them. He seized them, read them. Yes, the same excitement emanated from them as from Bilfinger's narrative. Again, the businesslike words became alive. The organized sadism, the subtly thought out system of humiliations, the shattering of human dignity by bureaucratic regulation, all the episodes described in the sober, official language of the documents, were transformed into living pictures. They were reflected in the amber centre of the pupil of his eye. There were many documents, he read them through carefully; the reading lasted a distressingly long time; it was two hours before he had finished.

Then, moving heavily and mechanically, he opened the drawer to put them away. But the drawer was a small one and there was already a bundle of letters in it. He took it out. It was the packet of correspondence which Frischlin had for-

warded to him. On the top lay that admonitory postcard which
he had dictated on his fiftieth birthday:

"It is upon us to begin the work,
It is not upon us to complete it."

Gustav was struck by it as by an actual blow. The tracks at
the station at Berne, threads between himself and Frischlin,
unwinding themselves endlessly, never breaking off. Bilfinger,
the messenger. "Who gave you your commission?" he had
asked himself, in that easy-going way, a few hours ago. And
then he had eaten and taken a nap.

He stared at the card. Klaus Frischlin, as was his usual
custom, had typed the name under the message, leaving a
space for the personal signature. Gustav took a pen and signed
his name to the card, then he placed it on top of Bilfinger's
papers and put everything neatly away in the drawer.

He sat down, then, his arms lying upon the plate-glass of the
inadequate little desk, and blinked painfully and furiously.

That evening he stood on the station platform to meet
Johannes. It was still very early. The train was late. At last it
came in. Gustav looked for his friend's yellowish-brown, animated countenance, filled with expectation of the malicious
witticisms with which he would be greeted. Many people got
out of the train, some of whom he knew. It was night and the
station was not well lighted. Gustav searched for a long time
but in vain. Perplexed and deeply disappointed, he returned to
his hotel. Perhaps Johannes had missed him and driven
straight to the hotel. But he did not find him in the hotel
either. Johannes had not arrived.

He was not there the next morning either. Gustav sent a
telegram. He waited for the reply all day. It did not come. The
next day a telegram arrived: "Johannes unavoidably delayed

for the present Richard." Gustav was startled. Richard was
Johannes's brother. What could be unavoidably delaying
Johannes?

Two days later still, he received a letter, posted in Strasbourg
by a man unknown to him, informing him in the name of
Richard Cohen that Johannes had been arrested by Nationalist
mercenaries on Thursday and had apparently been taken to
the concentration camp at Herrenstein.

6

Gustav wrote in reply to Friedrich Wilhelm Gutwetter's
letter that Gutwetter could use his library, or rather
what was left of it, as much as he liked. The only point was
that, as far as he knew, other authorities now considered themselves entitled to grant or withhold such permission. If Gutwetter could manage to secure an entry to the house in Max
Reger Strasse, he would oblige him by making a careful examination of the library and seeing what was still there, what
was missing, and, especially, what volumes had been damaged
or defaced. Many book-collections in Germany were in the
same disabled state as their owners, unless the owners had
sought safety in flight. As soon as Gutwetter had finished de-
scribing in eloquent terms what the "New Man" was going to
look like, he might begin to describe the sufferings of those
old-fashioned men who, without being in the least responsible,
had to foot the bill for the creation of this "New Man."

Gutwetter, when he read this, shook his calm, kindly head.
"What does our friend want?" he said to Sybil in astonishment. "Whence this irritation? How can he ask me to describe
the petty experiences of individuals in terms which are only

suitable for cosmic events? Does he seriously demand that I should disregard this epoch-making experience, of which I should be proud to be the bard, simply because a few unpleasant things have happened to him?"

Friedrich Wilhelm Gutwetter had a new lease on popularity. He had gone on as he had begun. He had lauded the advent of the "New Man," that splendidly natural type that relies on his aboriginal, savage instincts, as he had previously lauded it. He had done nothing more. He was not surprised that history had now, at last, made his, the poet's, vision come true. The Nationalists, however, were surprised to find such a voice as his raised on their behalf. Almost all scholars, almost all artists of any standing, had turned their backs on the Nationalists. What a bit of luck it was that a great writer should now suddenly come forward to espouse their cause! What Gutwetter had innocently written out of the fullness of his cosmic feeling was unexpectedly given the status of a great political epic. The government gave instructions to exploit him for the sake of publicity. He was exploited: all the papers printed his remarks, he was highly honoured by the leaders, he became a popular favourite overnight. Far from petty ambitions, smiling indulgently, he rode the whirlwind of his success. He consented to be the guest of honour at many of the great banquets given by the Nationalist ministers. His serene, large-eyed face rose with distinguished effect above his outmoded clothing. He was a joy to the photographers. He submitted to everything, naïvely flattered; he informed his acquaintances that his pleasure was that of an adult taking part in children's games.

He tried to take Sybil with him on his belated, miraculous ascent to fame. She willingly adapted herself to him in her charming, confiding way. All the time she had been with Gustav, she had shared his liberal views; the Nationalists had seemed unspeakably stupid and clumsy to her then. However, that did not prevent the visions of Gutwetter from being true

if one took a large and dispassionate view of things. She did
not take much interest in politics, she was not very sure of
her ground on that subject. She was not a visionary like Gutwetter; what had already taken tangible shape for the poet
still remained a vague vision to her. In her lively, aloof, childlike way she joked about the innumerable grotesque follies the
Nationalists committed, and Friedrich Wilhelm Gutwetter
heartily joined in her laughter.

But after a short time Gutwetter's grandiloquent artlessness
lost its original fascination for her. She began to feel that his
high-sounding utterances were in bad taste and very vague;
his lyrical rhapsodies grew irksome. She had learned all the
literary lessons that he had to teach her. His never-ending
childlike admiration for her person became a bore. She longed
for Gustav, for his generosity, his worldly wisdom. He had
praised her good points with unobtrusive discernment and had
censured what he had disliked with equally unobtrusive re-
buke. After Gutwetter's undiscriminating admiration, she
needed this critical type of friendship more than ever. She regretted that she had taken so little interest in Gustav's affairs and had maintained such slight contacts with the loyal
Frischlin.

But Gustav was a good-natured man. There had often been
periods when she had been so busy with her own affairs that
very little time was left over for him. He had never held this
against her, nor would he do so now. After her long silence,
she wired him that her work would now permit her to visit
him.

This telegram reached Gustav at a time when she was fur-
thest from his thought. Bilfinger's papers were lying on his
desk and he had no one with whom he could discuss them. His
friend, Johannes Cohen, was in a concentration camp, in the
fortress of Herrenstein in Saxony. When he closed his eyes,
he could visualize him, in an emaciated condition, standing on

a box, making genuflections, grotesque, his noble head closely shaved, except where some hair cut in the design of the swastika was left upon it, calling out after each genuflection: "I am Johannes Cohen, the swine who betrayed his Fatherland like a dirty Jew." It was horrible. Johannes Cohen looked like a marionette in this vision. He looked like a famous dancer whom Gustav had once seen at a pantomime. He sprang high into the air, nimbly, as though jerked on an elastic; he rattled off his speech in a harsh, cawing tone like a parrot's. Gustav had to laugh and the laugh caused him great pain. Now, since the arrest of Johannes, Gustav was torn more than ever between sober reason and the passionate indignation of the accuser. Into the midst of all of this came Sybil's telegram. His slim little Sybil. No, he could not have her here now. He could not talk to her about these things, yet he could not talk about anything but these things. A little while ago he had needed her desperately but she had not come. There was nothing else for it now but to thrust her aside. He did so in as gentle and tender a manner as possible.

But Sybil gave no thought to the manner of his refusal, she only realized the fact that she had been refused. Pouting like a child, she screwed up her mouth and slowly, like a child, she began to weep. She wept without stopping, lying face down, until the pillow was quite wet. Gradually, however, her disappointment turned to anger. Gustav was proscribed in Germany, it was dangerous to be friends with him, to have dealings with him. She had been willing to take the risk, she had been willing to go to him, and he, with a careless, haughty gesture, had rejected her friendship. He had never seriously exerted himself to understand her feelings. It was just because she realized in her heart that she had lost the man through her own fault, that she was so indignant with him. She did not answer his letter.

She was no longer bored when Gutwetter paid court to her

in his quiet, old-fashioned way. Soon Gutwetter was never seen anywhere without her.

7

Senior Master Vogelsang, when the boy Berthold Oppermann had not appeared in assembly to make his apology, was profoundly angered. He had sent for a reporter from the Nationalist press, assembled the teaching staff and the pupils of the school, prepared an energetic and eloquent speech, and now that Jew boy had the cheek simply to stay away and do him out of the entire edifying ceremony. When a telephone message to the boy's house brought the information that Berthold Oppermann's life was in danger, Vogelsang only smiled scornfully. He was not to be taken in by such tricks. He declared in his squeaking voice that the impudent fellow would not succeed in evading the expiation of his crime by the pretext of this alleged illness. When, three days later, the alleged illness ended in the boy's death, the Lower Sixth form recalled Vogelsang's remark and resented it keenly. There arose, as he entered the classroom and began to speak, that muffled, humming sound, produced with motionless faces, which had once caused Senior Master Schultes of Kaiser Friedrich School to turn his tearful eyes to the wall. Vogelsang did not turn to the wall; his scar grew redder and redder. He resolved, inwardly, to trample this spirit of insubordination into the dust for ever.

He soon had the opportunity. The fact was that Senior Master Schultes's tears had not prevented him from becoming Minister of Education. Bernd Vogelsang, who had known Schultes well for some years, had become even more friendly with him since he had been in Berlin. Nothing now stood in the way of his promotion to the Ministry of Education.

But, first of all, he had to put things to rights here in Queen Louise School. This had been his original object when he came to Berlin. A German man does not leave a job half done.

The first point was the Werner Rittersteg affair. Of course, the case against him had been dropped. He was the recognized leader of his companions. Mellenthin the porter stood at attention, when he passed, for almost as long as when Vogelsang himself went by. However, there was no question but that Rittersteg's work in literature and mathematics was unsatisfactory. The existing rules of the school did not permit of his being promoted to the Upper Sixth. Vogelsang, for his part, considered that pedantic rules were out of place in this case. One could not inflict the ignominy of not being promoted upon such a hero as Rittersteg. He declared that mere knowledge of dead facts did not mean everything. Deficiencies in scholarship were in this case more than balanced by exceptional ethical qualities. However, Rector François looked on this point of view with icy amazement. A boy who did not give satisfaction in two separate departments of education could not possibly be promoted. The Rector, obstinately and pedantically, took his stand upon the letter of the rules.

Bernd Vogelsang only smiled haughtily at this stubborn behaviour. What was power for? Rules, which belonged to the era of German decadence and German humiliation, were—in face of the Nationalist revolution—no more than cobwebs before a machine gun. One sat at the very lever of the administrative machine. A brief turn of the hand and whole libraries of former rules became waste paper. Did they intend to entangle a young hero in the maze of stupid rules, to impede his career, his activity on behalf of New Germany, merely because his scholarship had not stood the hazards of an examination? That would be perfectly ridiculous. A clean sweep would have to be made of such malignant sabotage. Vogelsang instigated at the Ministry the passing of a decree whereby students, who

had rendered exceptionally meritorious service to the Nationalist cause, whether at high school or university, were to have
their academic tests made considerably easier. Certain old-
fashioned ministerial officials contended that such a decree
would ultimately result in patients being treated by doctors
who, to be sure, were Nationalists but who might not be reliable scientifically. Vogelsang's patriotic fervour made short
work of such considerations.

When the decree had been issued, he again presented himself before François. There was still another point that required
settling and that was his personal relation to the Rector. He
would emerge just as triumphantly from this undertaking as
from the other. While he was in Tilsit, he had been able to
visualize triumph only as confronting one's enemy clad in
steel and placing one's foot upon his neck. In Berlin he had
come to know a different species of triumph, a more gentle,
more elegant one. With a view to getting the most out of this
type of triumph he was now sitting in the rectorial office, in
an attitude more worldly than formal, one leg thrown over
the other, his arms folded, the invisible sabre laid aside. An
almost gracious smile lurked under his short, corn-coloured
moustache, his collar was actually two more millimetres lower.
"I am anxious, Herr Rector," he began, trying to make his
squeaking voice sound buoyant, "before I leave this establishment, to clear up just one more point. We could not agree, on
one occasion, whether the study of the book entitled *My Battle*
should be introduced in schools such as this. You remember,
Herr Rector?"

François nodded. His blue eyes were fixed upon Vogelsang
thoughtfully, not with hostility or even unkindly. The latter
was there to enjoy to the full his last and most important victory. For he was still goaded, deep down, by the recollection
that he had once been unable to find the right answer to the
slander against the revered book. With that anecdote about the

Emperor Sigismund, who was above grammarians, that other fellow had put him *hors de combat* on that occasion. Now Vogelsang had the answer; it was belated but very much to the point. "Permit me," he continued with an elegant air, "to relate to you in return for that anecdote of the Council of Constance—to which you then drew my attention and in which you ironically compared the Leader with the Emperor—another anecdote from Church history. At the Synod of Cyprus," he spoke slowly and pointedly, "a bishop quoted the Saviour's words to the man sick of palsy: 'Take up thy bed and walk.' But the learned prince of the Church, who was a stickler for refinement of style, considered the word 'krabbaton,' which appeared in the actual text, too vulgar and substituted the literary word 'skimpous.' At that, Saint Spiridion jumped up and shouted at him: 'Are you a better man than He who said krabbaton, to be ashamed of using the words He used?'"

François had been listening intently. He was a very just man. That was no bad answer. For a Nationalist, it was a remarkably good one. He sat and thought it over in silence.

Vogelsang misunderstood this silence. He had crushed the other. The senior master, in his good-humoured mood, was positively sorry to see the poor little man cowering before him, vanquished by his adversary with the very weapon to which he had attributed most importance: words. A Nationalist man, as soon as he has his knee upon the chest of his adversary, is magnanimous. You're going to make a discovery now, my boy. He would leave the man at his post—after all, what did it matter—for a few months longer, under strict supervision, of course, so that he could not poison the boys' minds any more. He would have to do penance first, to be sure. Bernd Vogelsang intended to witness his humiliation; he was not going to let him get away without that. The fellow would have to acknowledge his defeat, *expressis verbis.* "You know," he said, "that I am taking over the Staff Department at the Ministry of Education. I know you better than most of your colleagues do. But to help me to the decision which I shall soon, perhaps, have to make, I must know one thing. What is your present attitude to our former discussion? Do you now support my Saint Spiridion version or do you still believe that your boys should not be brought into contact with the ethical spirit of a book if you do not approve of its style?"

François did not think that Bernd Vogelsang was behaving badly. The man was offering him a few more months of grace, perhaps even longer. It was a temptation. But he knew the other would not be content with this one sacrifice. More and more would be demanded of him. He would constantly have to choose between dishonesty and poverty. And then, one day he would lose control of himself and they would thrust him aside. His fate was sealed. He would have to sink into poverty, into the gutter, his children would have a hard, wretched life of it, and he would have a hard, wretched old age.

Well, this man was offering him a brief respite. It would cost him one single little concession. He had made so many concessions already. The last one was in the case of the boy Oppermann. He would make no more. He was still this side of the dividing line, it still rested with him how he would cross it, upright or stumbling. Once he was across, his mind as well as his body, would go to ruin. He was old enough to know that the destitute have no chance of remaining decent. Well, he would at least take the decisive step with his head erect. "It is good of you, colleague," he said, "to allow me to decide to some degree whether I shall still remain here for a little longer." He rose. Involuntarily—his movement resembling a retreat—he went and stood under the bust of Voltaire. "The peace and security of this room," he went on, "is undoubtedly worth the small *sacrificium intellectus* that you ask of me. But you know, colleague"—his tone was more courteous than ever and there was the trace of a smile under his upturned moustache—"I am not adaptable enough, perhaps I have too little 'Nordic cunning' to make that small intellectual sacrifice. I am sorry, but I must insist on my point: we are here to impart a knowledge of decent German to the boys. There is so much of ethical value written in decent German that we can afford to dispense with the ethics voiced by your Leader. For whether this author be Chancellor or not, it is a torture to read his book. The study of that book corrupts the German of our young people."

There were those words again which Bernd Vogelsang had wanted to silence. The man was on the floor, the man had been counted out. But he would not be silent. Vogelsang was secretly impressed by this behaviour. It just showed you; even foreign families became acclimatized after they had lived among Germans for a hundred and fifty years. He concluded his last visit to this room by saying in a squeaking, cool, yet not ill-natured tone: "I sincerely regret that you persist in your false doctrine. It will hardly be possible for me, under these circumstances, to take you with me into the New Germany. But if my convictions will permit, I shall endeavour to make your departure an honourable and easy one." And such was his genuine intention.

François did not, naturally, say anything to Little Thundercloud about Vogelsang's offer and his reply. Moreover, these critical days of change turned out more pleasant for him than he had anticipated. The fact was that Little Thundercloud, having reached the conviction that the fate of her husband was finally sealed, had now changed her tune. It would, of course, have been cleverer of him to have been a time-server. But she had really known all along that he, in spite of his apparently slovenly habits of mind, was at bottom a determined person. It was because of his strongmindedness that she had married him. Naturally, one had to try to make him conform with the spirit of the times. But once that had failed and decisive steps had been taken, as was now the case, there was no sense in tormenting the man any longer. Accordingly, she became positively meek. She tried to console him. She remarked that he could now finish his manuscript, *The Influence of the Ancient Hexameter on Klopstock's Vocabulary,* in peace, as he was really now not capable of doing anything else. Meanwhile she would take steps to find him a position in some private school or abroad. It would be difficult. But they had three years to look about in, their available capital would last that long in any case, and perhaps he would get a pension after all, and, whatever happened, she would find a way out.

These comforting words did François good. He had always known that Socrates must have had some good reason for marrying Xanthippe.

8

Jaques Lavendel informed Friedrich Pfanz, the head of the Department of Economics, that he proposed to leave Germany and that he would liquidate his German business interests. Friedrich Pfanz was one of the men who pulled the strings which made the Nationalist leaders dance and Jaques Lavendel was an intimate business acquaintance of his. Jaques Lavendel could therefore very easily, especially as he was an American citizen, have remained in Germany without running any risks. But he did not wish to do so. "I am a just man, Pfanz," he said. "I know only a few of you have been doing these rotten things. I am willing to concede that the people are sound at heart. They have had to listen to the most wicked and cruel propaganda against the Jews for fourteen years— you know well enough how it was done, you also contributed your bit—and it is really extraordinary that nothing worse has happened. *Well*. But for the time being, the air around here is polluted for me. I am a capitalist; I understand your motives. I know that the only way you could save your rotten economic system was by calling in that lousy gang to help you. But you must remember that I am a Jew as well as a capitalist. When you tell me: 'It's true we are murdering the Jews, but we only mean to attack the trade unions,' that doesn't bring my Jews back to life again."

Pfanz the economist would have liked to keep Herr Lavendel in the country. He pointed out to him that the present situation was merely temporary, that the rabble would soon be got under control again, that the regular troops were holding themselves in readiness to cut down the mercenaries, that regular officers would then be in charge in place of sergeants, that he had himself resolved to enter the government service. And he proposed that Herr Lavendel should join him in the large insurance concern for the sake of which he was burdening himself with the uncongenial ministerial post.

But Jaques Lavendel did not bite. "I quite believe you, Pfanz," he said in his hoarse voice, "that the present leaders will feel the check-rein when you assume your official duties. But I'm no longer young, you know, I'm no longer rapacious, I'm no longer curious. When I am in some foreign country, I shall be quite satisfied to watch in the news-reels your big clean-up campaign over here. I prefer to join your ranks in the spirit only. So mind you make a good job of it, Pfanz, and I shall hope to see you again when you have finished your economic crusade."

He had long ago allowed for present conditions in his plans and had prepared for the liquidation of his business interests far in advance. The exact character of these interests was vague. He controlled a number of large real-estate companies, and now it developed that these companies were really insolvent. They would have to receive substantial official subsidies or the banks holding the mortgages would lose their money. As many of the banks had already received subsidies from the State or the country at large, the withdrawal of Jaques Lavendel from his German interests meant a serious loss to the State. Shaking his head with a slight, scarcely perceptible, smile Jaques Lavendel put up with that aspect of the matter.

He was really not a rapacious man. He and Klara had resolved to take a holiday for some years. They would, to begin with, retire to their fine estate at Lugano. They had invited the three Oppermann brothers to stay with them over Easter. Heinrich, too, would be there then. Jaques Lavendel had given his son the choice of completing his education in either Europe or America. Heinrich had preferred to remain in a German-speaking country; he intended to complete his studies in Zürich or Berne. This pleased Jaques Lavendel; he had always had a foolish devotion to Germany.

Heinrich still had a certain score to settle before they left the country. His notification to the public prosecutor had only resulted in the appearance of a detective at the Lavendels' house and in a clumsy and incomplete examination of Heinrich himself. His statement had produced no further results, either for Werner Rittersteg or for himself. It appeared that Werner had not even heard of it. Heinrich could not possibly leave matters in this state. He became more and more obsessed by the idea that it was Werner Rittersteg, with his Young Eagles and his spiteful motion in the football club, who had caused Berthold's death. While he was intently but unsuccessfully considering how he could bring the business to a satisfactory conclusion, Werner himself came to his assistance.

Long Lummox had not been unaffected by the death of Berthold. But he told himself, with primitive logic, that, as Heinrich had now lost his best friend, he would perhaps be more accessible to his own companionship. His father had kept

his promise and had installed an outboard motor on his row-
boat, which was lying in a boathouse at Lake Teupitz. Casually, as though nothing had happened, Werner invited Heinrich to come out with him on the lake and test the engine.
Lo and behold—Werner Rittersteg's heart stood still with surprise and delight—Heinrich, after a very few moments' reflection, accepted. He even volunteered to drive Werner out to
Teupitz himself.

He therefore surreptitiously borrowed his father's car and the
two boys drove to Teupitz. Heinrich was a skilful and steady
driver. They got into the boat and went rattling to and fro
across the pleasant waters of the lake. Werner was embarrassed
and ill at ease, but Heinrich's technical interest in the boat
helped him to get over his confusion. Heinrich was, on the
whole, rather monosyllabic but not unfriendly. Later on, they
sat in the big restaurant, which was quite empty at this season
of the year, and drank a mixture of light beer and raspberry
juice and ate sausages. It was rather late in the evening before
they started their return home.

Werner sat in the car with mingled feelings. They had
talked together as those taking part in the same sport are accustomed to do, but that was really all. Heinrich had by no
means been as friendly as he had hoped. It even looked now as
though he were repenting of having gone out at all. At any
rate, he was unusually silent.

"Where are you driving to?" asked Werner in a fresh access
of hope, as Heinrich turned off the main highway. "This road
is prettier," said Heinrich, "and only a little further." It was
already quite dark. The headlights showed a patch of pine
forest, there was a young crescent moon. Heinrich was driving
very slowly. Werner's uneasiness increased. "We might stop
and walk about for a bit," he suggested humbly. "All right,"
said Heinrich. He pulled up to the side of the road and
switched off the lights.

They walked off into the woods. The ground was damp and uneven. It was rather cold and very dark. There was a fine, strong scent of earth and pines. The silence was intense; their footsteps made no sound on the soft, wet ground; only now and then a piece of dead wood crackled under their shoes as they walked. There was a very light breeze in the air.

Werner stumbled several times in the darkness. Suddenly Heinrich grabbed him. Werner thought at first that he wanted to save him from a fall but Heinrich tripped him so that he fell to the ground. "What are you doing? Are you mad?" shouted Werner. Heinrich did not answer. He seized him by the back of the neck and held his face against the damp earth until he lost his breath. "You stuck a knife into Karper's guts, you swine. You did for Berthold. Now you know what it feels like to be done for." He spoke in a low tone, panting and furious. He thrust the other's face deeper and deeper into the ground. "Yes, man, you're being done for now," he continued to mutter, "and they'll say you were killed for being a Nationalist. No one will think of me. They'll say the Communists did for you. Perhaps you can get some consolation out of that right now. But when you're dead, you're dead, and all of Vogelsang's speeches won't do you much good." He pressed harder. The other kicked about wildly but could not get his arms free or his mouth open.

Suddenly Heinrich let him go and jumped off his back. "Stand up," he ordered. But Long Lummox lay where he was and did not stir. "Stand up," Heinrich commanded a second time and dragged him to his feet. "You sissy," he said. Werner stood before him, a pitiable sight, shaking with fright, his face scratched by twigs and bleeding from a deep gash across his forehead; his clothes were covered with damp earth. "Wipe yourself off and come along," Heinrich ordered.

He, himself, for all his gruffness, felt helpless and miserable. He had wanted to settle this business. But he had failed.

"Come on," he again called out to Long Lummox. He even helped him to tidy up a little. He half led, half carried him back to the car.

They drove home in silence. When they reached the first street-car, Heinrich dropped him.

9

Herr Markus Wolfsohn was sitting in his black wingchair in his flat in Karl Friedrich Strasse. The supper had been a scanty one, bread, butter, and a peculiar-looking meat-paste. Frau Wolfsohn jealously guarded every pfennig now and kept a very sharp eye on the cash-box.

This evening she was once more giving Herr Wolfsohn the benefit of her views. She often did that now. In a very distinct, but not loud voice; there was no need for the Zarnkes next door to hear. Herr Wolfsohn understood her, even when she spoke in a low tone; she had already said the same thing a thousand times before. They must get away, they must pack up and go, better today than tomorrow. The women who lived in the building, although their husbands nearly all wore the swastika, still talked to her but only surreptitiously. As soon as anyone approached, they stopped. Frau Hoppegart thought that the worst was yet to come. They all advised her to pack up and to get out. But how? And where to? They had 2674 marks in the bank. If Herr Wolfsohn had listened to her and had been more economical, if he had not always had such grandiose ideas about furniture, then they would have had their four or five thousand marks saved up. That armchair, for instance; it had been a bargain, a *metsiye*, she knew that. But if you were poor, you had to deny yourself even a *metsiye*.

Herr Wolfsohn let her talk. When a man has bad luck, the women start bawling and saying: "I told you so." That was an old story. But she shouldn't exaggerate so dreadfully, that was all. Four or five thousand marks! One could never have scraped together such a pile as that. The one luxury he had ever allowed himself in his life was the new frontage. But at that time things were looking much more hopeful. At that time they only threw people out of moving subways, not out of the country.

Herr Wolfsohn made a feeble attempt to be optimistic. It was true he had been thrown out of the German Furniture Company. But hadn't he got a comfortable berth, for the time being, at Herr Oppermann's? That, however, was as far as Herr Wolfsohn's optimism could possibly go. From that point on the clouds gathered. The Nationalist business committee were on the trail, Hinkel the packer was demanding that he should be dismissed. Herr Oppermann had been worried about it; Herr Oppermann had behaved very decently, but how much longer would he be able to keep him?

Even if he did keep him, life was not worth living nowadays. If the rest of his life were to go on as it was at present, one might just as well turn on the gas right away. It was only a question of time before they would bar him from the "Old Pickled Herrings." They liked him there but they would have to do it. And his lease here would not be renewed either. He was sitting on a landslide; the flat was crumbling away, so to speak, under his very feet. They would be certain to find ways and means to let Herr Zilchow, Herr Zarnke's brother-in-law, in even before the expiration of the lease.

There were really now only Herr Zarnkes left in the building. The original Zarnke did not even trouble himself now to utter threats. Whenever he saw Herr Wolfsohn, he simply stretched his arm out and shouted, "Heil Hitler." And Herr Wolfsohn had to reply, "Heil Hitler." Herr Zarnke often amused himself by asking: "What did you say?" And then Herr Wolfsohn had to repeat, "Heil Hitler."

Apart from that, one heard terrible things from one's business friends and from one's few Jewish acquaintances. Herr Wolfsohn simply refused to listen. If you repeated such things, even if you only listened to them, you were clapped into a concentration camp before you could turn around. Even Marie came home with stories like that, horrible stories, whispered to her by the East Jewish acquaintances of her brother Moritz Ehrenreich. But at this point Herr Wolfsohn lost his temper and told Marie to hold her tongue; he would not tolerate that sort of thing under any circumstances, that was the kind of bogy tales that got one into prison.

Were they bogy tales? Herr Wolfsohn told himself firmly that they were; he wanted to believe that they were. But once, at night, on his way home from taking inventory, he had seen a car standing in front of an old house in the centre of the city. It was one of those very large cars the Nationalists dashed about in. The headlights were on, so that the street was brightly illuminated for a considerable distance. Herr Wolfsohn's first intention was to make a detour, but he reflected that this would only render him conspicuous. So he continued down the street, past the gigantic car which, guarded by only two men, made a very unpleasant and warlike appearance, staring ahead with its powerful headlights. There was obviously a search going on in the house, a raid or something of that kind. Yes, just as Herr Wolfsohn was passing, they brought someone out. Herr Wolfsohn did not look; it was better to take no notice. But he could not help darting a sidelong glance of terrified curiosity across the street. He saw a man in a brown suit, similar to the one he himself was wearing. One mercenary held the victim by the collar, one held his right and another his left arm. The victim's head had fallen forward, he looked as though he had been beaten mercilessly.

For the fraction of a second Herr Wolfsohn saw his face. It was yellow, livid. There was a huge, bluish-black bruise over one eye.

Herr Wolfsohn had not told Marie anything about it. But he could not get the man's yellow, livid, and exhausted face out of his thoughts. Ever since then, when he turned into Friedrich Karl Strasse on his way home, he darted a timid glance down the street to make sure one of those big cars was not standing there. Night after night he was afraid that the powerful headlights of the car might suddenly shine into his windows, although that was impossible; his flat was much too high up. He imagined a ring at the bell in the middle of the night, they would be inside before one had time to open the door, one would get a whack over the eye with a truncheon, and there would be a bruise there as big as the spot above the picture, and one's face would be as yellow and livid as that man's.

Those nights he slept badly. He had not said a single word to Marie about his experience. It made all the more impression on him when once she suddenly moved over closer to him while he was lying sleepless and said: "I'm so afraid they will come tonight, Markus." He wanted to make an impatient retort and tell her what piffling rubbish that was, but he could not. She was really only giving expression to his own thoughts. He could not get to sleep again and he noticed that she could not either. His fear increased. He told himself it was all nonsense, he had nothing on his conscience. There were four million two hundred thousand people living in this city of Berlin, he had done no more and no less than any of them, why should he be the one among all of them to be afraid? But it was of no avail. He thought of Hinkel the packer, he thought of Herr Zarnke, and he was afraid; he became more and more afraid, he perspired, he had pains in his stomach, he wished the morning would come. Then he had another fit of anger because it was he who had to endure such terror. Why should it be he? Why shouldn't it be Herr Zarnke? At all events, he did not intend to go through another night like this. It was mere folly to go on living like this. He would just clear off across the frontier somewhere. Anywhere would be better than this. If only morning would come.

There were many in Berlin and in other cities in the Reich who were lying as Markus Wolfsohn and his wife lay. They were innocent, but there was a Hinkel the packer or a Herr Zarnke somewhere in the background, and they were afraid he would set the mercenaries on them. Their forefathers had lived in this country for centuries, in many cases longer than the forefathers of the mercenaries, and they found it hard to imagine themselves living elsewhere. And yet they would all have been glad to leave this country now, this their homeland. Ah, how gladly they would have left it! But how could they live elsewhere? If they had a business, they were compelled to give it up without compensation. If they had money, they were not allowed to take it with them, and other countries would not admit them unless they had money. There were others too, like Herr Weinberg, who stayed in Germany because they could not see how they were going to get along with less money than hitherto. They preferred to live a life of continual anxiety and danger but to remain near their money.

As for Herr Wolfsohn, he was a wreck the following morning. But as soon as he had taken a sponge bath and gone to business, he thought no more of getting out of Germany. Where could he go, anyway? To Palestine? They wouldn't let you in there unless you had money. And what was he to do there? Farm? Pick olives? Crush grapes? He was not quite sure how that was done. One trampled barefooted on the grapes and then they fermented. Anyhow, it wasn't a very pleasant job. And with 2674 marks the fermenting couldn't go on for any length of time, either. By the time one had got clear of everything here and come away, what with passports and fares, there wouldn't be more than two thousand left at most. To France? He might have a good French accent, but just the same he had forgotten a lot and though a man might be able to say *"Bon jour, monsieur,"* that would certainly not suffice for them to let you sell furniture in Paris.

Moreover, the following night was better and he slept soundly and well for two succeeding nights. But then he thought that Herr Hinkel was giving him such funny sidelong glances, so the next night he was afraid again and the night after that, too, was quite bad.

On the third night, Markus Wolfsohn and his wife had gone to bed early and were really asleep. Then they actually came.

Markus stood shaking and lanky in his crumpled pyjamas. Marie went to and fro cautiously, asking the men what Markus would be allowed to take with him. At intervals she whispered to him angrily: "I always told you we should have packed up and left." He was completely bewildered. She made him put on his best suit because it was the warmer and she packed up a few little things. The children stood about and were terrified. The policemen told her to put them to bed and let them go to sleep. They were polite, positively friendly, and did not hurry them; they were actual policemen, not mercenaries. When Frau Wolfsohn, at parting, began to weep, they said: "Don't worry, madam, you'll soon have your husband back again."

Frau Wolfsohn did her best to make this soothing speech come true. She immediately rushed to Gertraudten Strasse. There she met with most friendly solicitude and was assured that everything possible would be done. Then she rushed to the offices of the Jewish Community Centre. She was promised help here too. She rushed back to the shop. She saw Martin, himself, who told her that Nationalist lawyers had been engaged, who in such a case were the most suitable persons to handle the matter. As soon as they heard what Herr Wolfsohn was actually accused of, he would let her know. Frau Wolfsohn called again that afternoon, the next morning, and the next afternoon. Herr Oppermann was patient, Herr Brieger was patient, and so was Herr Hintze.

On the third day they were able to tell her something. It was something fantastic. Herr Wolfsohn was supposed to be implicated in the Reichstag fire. Marie Wolfsohn had been prepared for all sorts of things. Perhaps they had locked up her Markus because he had deducted three marks from the tailor's bill for his last suit. Perhaps one of the "Old Pickled Herrings" had given information that Markus had cheated at skat. It was a fact that today anyone who had a grudge against a Jew could get him locked up. But that Markus Wolfsohn, her Markus, should be charged with having set fire to the Reichstag, that thoroughly upset her. Didn't all the world know that the Premier of Prussia had planned the fire? Were they quite *meshugge* to go and fasten that crime on her Markus of Friedrich Karl Strasse? Even the youngest baby recruit in Hitler's Band of Youth would not believe such a thing. Beside herself, she screamed and shouted in the private office in Gertraudten Strasse. Martin Oppermann and Herr Brieger, in alarm, tried to pacify her. They explained to her that the monstrous absurdity of the charge was a certain consolation. For even officialdom would have to admit that the accusation of Markus Wolfsohn the salesman, of all people, could not be taken seriously, even during this Nationalist orgy.

The Markus Wolfsohn in question, meanwhile, sat in his cell. The cell was brightly lit and bare; it was just this dreary, empty brightness that made it so terrifying. He had no idea why he was sitting there and no one told him. Crouching, dumb, and solitary for three days in this tiny cell, always in bright light, for even at night the lamp in the corridor shone glaringly into the room, was a martyrdom which, as far as the sociable and talkative Herr Wolfsohn was concerned, could not have been more cruelly devised. Again and again he wondered what crime he could have committed. He could think of nothing. He had always kept as dumb as a fried fish whenever politics had been discussed. Whenever Nationalist mercenaries passed, he had promptly stretched out his arm, as far as he could, in the ancient Roman fashion and had shouted: "Heil Hitler." He was not musical. It took him a long time to distinguish the Horst-Wessel song from the many similar sailors' and harbour songs. Therefore, as a precautionary measure, he had instantly jumped to his feet and stood stiffly at attention whenever he had heard a tune of this type. What, in God's name, then, could they be charging him with?

They did not tell him. They let him sit by himself, without uttering a word, for three times twenty-four hours. A vast grey hopelessness completely overwhelmed him. Even if one day they did let him out again, he would be ruined for ever. Who nowadays could employ a Jewish salesman who had been locked up by the Nationalists? Poor Marie, he thought. How much better it would have been for her if she had remained Miriam Ehrenreich instead of becoming Marie Wolfsohn! Then probably she would now be attending some sporting event with her brother Moritz and would have enough to live on, in a setting of palms and camels. But, as it was, she was married to a traitor to his country, and the father of her children was a voracious wolf. If only he had not treated himself to that new frontage; then there would be fifty marks more in the bank. It was just a bit of luck that he had not paid the "Old Pickled Herring" Schulze the whole amount. It—but, hallo, perhaps he was the very one who had lodged the complaint against him because of this balance due, he had warned him twice already. Suddenly he heard August's tipsy voice again: "You're dreaming if you think we're going to take you

along at all this summer." What a mean business. He had paid
the biggest share into the treasury and now the others, at the
stag party on Ascension Day, would be making merry on his
money.

As long as Herr Wolfsohn's thoughts revolved about such
things, matters were not at their worst. But there were hours
during which he felt only fear, a dreadful, destructive fear.
They probably intended to do all sorts of frightful things to
him. If it had only been a trifling affair, they would have
brought him before a judge long ago. He remembered certain
speeches broadcast by the Leader to the effect that the execution of sentences was much too mild. The good old methods
should be introduced again. Criminals should be hanged in
public and be beheaded with an axe. Wolfsohn imagined himself driving in a tumbril to the place of execution. The man
with the axe would probably have a dress-suit on. He, Markus
Wolfsohn, would never get there alive. He would have died
ten times over of fright before reaching his destination.

He started humming, to give himself courage. As soon as
that awful silence stopped he felt better. He sang *"Moaus zur
yeshuosi"*—Rock and Refuge of my Redemption. He sang off
key but it pleased him. It was comforting to hear a voice, even
if it was only one's own. He sang louder. Someone shouted
into the room threateningly: "Hold your noise, Jew-pig!"
Once more the cell was bare, brightly lit, and silent.

He had been crouching there for three days now. He had
not shaved, he had not washed properly, he was wet with
perspiration, and his small moustache looked bedraggled. He
was far from smart now, in spite of the new frontage. He
cowered apathetically. His quick eyes had long since taken in
everything that could be seen in that cell.

Suddenly, on this third day, he was seized by a fit of reckless rage. He got up and stood, drawn to his full height, in the
tiny room, one foot advanced. The public prosecutor had fin-

ished speaking; he had shown that Markus Wolfsohn was a ravening wolf, that it was his fault the war had been lost, the currency inflated, and the entire German people made bankrupt, and he had demanded a sentence of death by the axe. But it now was his, Markus Wolfsohn's, turn to speak, and, as there was absolutely no hope for him, he told the judges just what he thought. "Gentlemen," he said, "all these accusations are vulgar lies. I am a good citizen and tax-payer. All I wanted was peace. During the day I had my customers; in the evenings I occasionally played a little skat, listened to the radio, and enjoyed my flat—the rent of which I paid promptly on the first of each month. Selling furniture is certainly not an occupation dangerous to the State. I am not the guilty party, most honourable court of justice, it's the swastika men who are guilty: Zarnke, Zilchow & Co. And, even if one is not allowed to say so, everything people whisper about them is true. They set the Reichstag on fire, they throw people out of moving subway trains, and then they appoint a man in a dress-suit to chop off the heads of decent people. That is carrying meanness too far, gentlemen." Thus did Herr Wolfsohn settle accounts with his adversaries—but, unfortunately, only in his imagination. The magistrate who seemed to sit above him, in a black gown with a judge's cap and ruff, had strong white teeth and reddish, fair hair and was, as a matter of fact, Herr Rüdiger Zarnke.

On the fourth day Markus Wolfsohn really was brought before a judge. The judge did not, to be sure, wear a black gown, but an ordinary business suit. "Bought straight off the rack," Herr Wolfsohn concluded. "Probably in a chain store, run by Jews, too. The chap won't be able to buy from them much longer. He'll have to pay more in future."

He was asked whether he had taken any interest in politics and what newspapers he read. The examination was really quite easy-going; in fact Herr Wolfsohn enjoyed being al-

lowed to talk again after such a long time. The magistrate
then asked where and how he spent his evenings, particularly
during the second half of February. At this period Herr Wolfsohn had already given up going to the "Old Pickled Herrings." He asserted with perfect truth that he had always
stayed at home. "Always?" asked the magistrate. He had a
thin voice, and at the end of a question it often rose a few
notes. Wolfsohn reflected. "Yes, always," he said. There was a
man there with a typewriter and the magistrate made him
take everything down. "You were at home, then, on the night
of the twenty-seventh to twenty-eighth of February as well?"
the magistrate asked. "I think so," said Wolfsohn with some
hesitation. "What were you doing that evening, then?" he
questioned further. Wolfsohn made an effort to remember. "I
can't exactly remember, now. We generally had supper and
then talked for a while. Then I probably read a little more of
the paper and listened to the radio for a bit." "You must have
done all that unusually quietly that evening," the magistrate
observed.

An association of circumstances dawned upon Wolfsohn.
Aha, Zarnke. It was Zarnke. Zarnke had been spying on him.
But they could only get at him if he had said anything, not if
he hadn't said anything. He made another effort to remember.
The night of the twenty-seventh to the twenty-eight. Hallo.
The twenty-eighth of February was the day Moritz Ehrenreich had left for Marseilles. That was a Tuesday and, the
night before, they had been at Moritz's farewell party. Of
course, he had not been home that evening. And, positively
beaming at his discovery, he said to the magistrate: "I beg
Your Honour's pardon. You were right. I was really not at
home that evening. I was at the farewell party of my brother-
in-law, a certain Herr Ehrenreich, who left from the Friedrich
Strasse station on the next day. I could not go to the station.
We were in the Dandelion, a tavern in Oranien Strasse. A

small place but very respectable. Excellent bockwurst, Your Honour. It was my brother-in-law's favourite haunt." "So you now assert that you were with your brother-in-law on the night in question?" the magistrate asked again. "Yes, that is so," declared Wolfsohn. Everything was duly recorded.

When he was back in his cell, he still did not know what they wanted him for. But he knew one thing. Neither Hinkel the packer nor Schulze the "Old Pickled Herring" was responsible. And the fact that it was neither of these but Herr Zarnke who was responsible, that Zarnke whom he had always suspected of being capable of any wickedness, was a certain satisfaction to him.

10

Frau Wolfsohn, who had not heard anyone coming, jumped when the bell suddenly rang loudly. Two men in brown uniforms, but they were only Herr Zarnke and another.

Herr Zarnke tramped in noisily. There was really no need for him to make an apology. But, being a man of orderly habits, he explained that he had been requested by the superintendent to look over the flat some time. Frau Wolfsohn made no reply except to say, "Please do so."

Accordingly Herr Zarnke and the other man, who was, of course, his brother-in-law, Herr Zilchow, inspected the flat. Frau Wolfsohn, silent and reserved, remained standing near the door. She knew well enough what the object of the visit was.

The flat was a small one, there was not much to look at. But the two men stayed a surprisingly long time. Herr Zarnke had imagined that everything in a Jewish home would be dirty and dilapidated. He was now astonished to find that on the whole there was little difference between this and his own flat. Indeed, he could not help noticing that the available space had been more cleverly turned to the best advantage. Moreover, he had always wanted a large armchair like the one here. Frau Wolfsohn herself, plump, with her fair, reddish hair and fresh complexion, did not look as untidy—though he had paid her a surprise visit—as Frau Zarnke often did, when someone surprised her. Herr Zarnke was a just man. "Your place is clean," he declared. "I must give you credit for that, even if your husband is a traitor to his country."

"A traitor to his country?" said Frau Wolfsohn. "You must be dreaming," she added. She could have said a great deal more, something pretty hot and pertinent. But she was not a fool, and since they had taken her husband away she had grown twice as clever. She knew that silence was always the wisest line to take. She saw that the flat and she herself had made a favourable impression on Herr Zarnke. Accordingly, however much he abused Markus, she would deny herself the pleasure of a suitable retort. Keep quiet, don't spoil the good impression you're making. Perhaps he wouldn't testify so unfavourably then.

The two men were, taking it all in all, very satisfied. There was only one thing that worried them. The brother-in-law announced it emphatically. It was the stain on the wall. They looked to see how far it reached behind the picture. "Allow me," said Herr Zarnke politely, and drew the picture entitled "The Waves at Play" a little to one side. "It's really a shame to have let it reach such a stage. That's a fine picture, by the way." The fact that he appreciated the picture induced Frau Wolfsohn to vindicate herself in regard to the stain. Herr Krause, she explained, had always promised her husband to have it repaired but then he got out of it because they were Jews. "Well," said Zarnke, "I can understand that. But when *we* come in here, that will, of course, be changed." Then he looked round once more, taking in everything with a pleased, comprehensive glance. Finally, "Good-bye for the present," he said, and off they went, not as noisily as they had come in.

The following day Frau Wolfsohn received another communication, not as important, perhaps, for her tangible affairs but full of significance for her inner life. That was, she received a notice bearing the blue seal of District Court No. 11, Berlin, S.W. This notice was a summons at the instance of the dentist, Schulze, to pay the sum of twenty-five marks, the balance due for dental treatment, together with the costs of collection.

Frau Wolfsohn stared at the printed form, into which only a few words and figures had been typed. Her husband Markus had deceived her, then, he had paid for the bridge out of his own pocket money and secretly kept back the money from her. Abysses opened before her. A man who deceived his own wife so shamelessly and threw his children's money out of the window merely to gratify his vanity was capable of anything. She sat down, the very foundations of her existence were crumbling. Perhaps he had secretly gone in for revolutionary politics, perhaps there was some truth in the charge implicating him in the Reichstag fire. And that cheap bedspread he had given her for Christmas, that was a fraud too, of course. He had paid much more than he had pretended. What could she believe now? But these doubts did not prevent her from pursuing her activities on behalf of her Markus as passionately as ever.

The summons granted to Schulze the dentist resulted in a second visit from Herr Zarnke. There were no secrets in the house in Friedrich Karl Strasse. It became known at once that Frau Wolfsohn was in financial difficulties, the difficulties were exaggerated, there was talk about a visit from the court bailiff. Yet all she would have to do would be to draw the amount out of the bank. As usual, Herr Zarnke had heard about the writ and was on the spot. He came pretty straight to the point at once. It was now practically as good as settled that he, or rather his brother-in-law Zilchow, would soon take over the flat. It would be a pity then if Frau Wolfsohn let other people have the furniture for a mere song. Some of it would be very suitable for his purpose, and he was willing to advance her a small sum with the furniture as security or to buy some of it outright with the understanding that she could use it until she moved. She was a decent woman and would see to it that furniture belonging to a third party would be properly treated and looked after. Frau Wolfsohn, in order not to irritate him, did not say no straightaway. Herr Zarnke emphasized the fact that he could not, however, go to much expense in the matter. Germany had been drained dry by the Jews and the capitalists. It was only with difficulty that people like himself and his brother-in-law could acquire furniture such as hers.

It had always been Herr Zarnke's opinion that Germany was being exploited by the Jews and the capitalists. But he had hoped that the Leader would very quickly put things straight in this respect. That was the reason why he, Zarnke, had enlisted in the Nationalist mercenaries. But it was now nearly three months since the Leader had come into power, and things were just the same as ever. Herr Zarnke was becoming impatient and more than impatient. So were all the men in his detachment. In many cities of the Reich the mercenaries were beginning to complain. They had helped the Leader to reach a position of authority, but now it was developing that the economic system of the new magnates was worse than the one against which they had rebelled.

A few capitalists had been dispossessed. But their money had not reached the masses. The other capitalists and the Nationalist leaders had divided it among themselves. The President of the Republic received a new estate in addition to his old one, the Premier of Prussia became a rich man, and Herr Pfanz, the president of the big insurance concern, became Minister of the Interior. It would be ridiculous if one had made such great efforts to produce only these results.

Such was the talk in Herr Zarnke's detachment. As troop-leader it was his duty to report such conversations, but he did not do so. Nor did the other troop-leaders. Herr Zarnke, indeed, partly influenced, no doubt, by the favourable impression made upon him by the flat and the person of Mrs. Wolfsohn, was beginning to revise his whole political outlook. If the economic promises of the Leader were so unsound, then other things in his programme were probably equally rotten. Perhaps the Jews were by no means to blame for everything. Perhaps Herr Wolfsohn had not started the war at all and, even if he had not been at home on the night in question, perhaps he had not been implicated in the burning of the Reichstag. Such rebellious views were gaining more and more control over the simple soul of storm-troop-leader Rüdiger Zarnke.

Accordingly, he was not really particularly indignant when, one day about noon, Herr Wolfsohn unexpectedly appeared again in Friedrich Karl Strasse. He was somewhat pale and thinner than formerly but, aside from that, by no means crushed and humiliated. Frau Wolfsohn, when Markus appeared at the door, gave equally loud expression to her joy and to her indignation over the sufferings which he must have had to endure. She did not seem to care whether they heard her next door or not. She darted busily to and fro. He must have a hot bath at once. Then she went and fetched provisions and, while she prepared them, she left the door to the kitchen stand open. He sat in his black wingchair and they talked; he was overjoyed to be at home again. He sat quietly and looked about him, listened but did not speak much.

She watched him eat, with a good appetite, more and more, and only worried a tiny bit about what the meal was costing. She had really intended to refrain from mentioning her accusation against him until he had finished eating. But as he took such a long time over it, she couldn't wait, and, as soon as he had completely demolished the cutlet with egg and was starting on the cheese, she began to speak of the monstrous deception which he had put over on her and the children. He scarcely defended himself. He ate the cheese slowly, with relish; he was certainly contrite, yet not very much so.

He had hardened a good deal inwardly. He had come to the decision to go to Palestine. He was a small man and not very strong. But a man who, suspected of having set fire to the Reichstag, had gone through some weeks of imprisonment under the Nationalist regime and had stood them as well as he had, such a man would be capable of learning Hebrew and of becoming a farmer in Palestine. Frau Wolfsohn merely laughed at him. But Herr Wolfsohn stuck to his intentions. He talked of fate, read the Bible a great deal, read whatever he could find about Palestine in the reading-room of the Jewish Community Centre, went, with recommendations from Martin Oppermann and Brieger, to hundreds of people to procure the necessary immigration capital; pursued, not hastily but with dispatch, the question of his departure.

He did not, however, neglect his duties in Oppermann's Furniture Store. The packer Hinkel regarded him with hatred yet with some admiration because he had eluded the clutches of the Nationalists. Hinkel the packer had to acknowledge that even the Nationalist movement was not strong enough to crush the world-wide conspiracy of the Jews. Sixty-five millions of Germans had not been able to dislodge this one individual, Markus Wolfsohn, from his position.

Herr Wolfsohn had grown wise. He recalled the nights of fear when he lay in a cold sweat next to Frau Wolfsohn and those terrible nights in the brightly lit cell. His experiences had made him more charitable too. It did not give him any particular pleasure when he learned, one day, that now Herr Zarnke —in turn—had been arrested, he and his entire detachment.

The regular troops had overpowered the mercenaries and had carried them off to a concentration camp. Markus Wolfsohn naturally felt a certain satisfaction. He had once imagined how he would give it to Herr Zarnke. Now fate had given it to Herr Zarnke much more dreadfully than Herr Wolfsohn had contemplated. For if the prison cell had been dreadful, the concentration camp was bound to be infinitely worse.

Herr Wolfsohn, personally, did not take his ease in false security. He diligently worked on his plans for emigrating from Germany to a kindlier clime.

After he had received the assurance that his application for an emigration visa for Palestine would be granted, Frau Wolfsohn told him, one day, that Frau Zarnke had called and had asked if nothing could be done for her husband. He was as innocent as an unborn babe, yet there he was in a concentration camp. The cost of his maintenance there was deducted from her relief, so that she only had 52 marks a month to keep herself and the children on. She could not even pay the rent out of that and she would have to give up her flat to the brother-in-law. Herr Wolfsohn repressed the feeling of triumph that arose in him. He only shook his head and said: "Yes, yes. That's the way things are now." Later he remarked that one could not, of course, permit oneself to criticize official measures under any circumstances whatsoever. If one did, it would be certain to prove dangerous. But as soon as he was safely across the frontier, he would assist Frau Zarnke one time to the extent of half a Palestine pound.

II

Jaques Lavendel pulled out the middle one of the unleavened flat cakes which were stacked on the old-fashioned, many-tiered silver dish and broke it into two pieces. He leaned back against the satin cushion, embroidered with Hebraic letters in heavy gold thread. In his hoarse voice, in Aramaic sing-song, he recited: "This is the bread of adversity which our forefathers ate in Egypt. He that is hungry, let him come and eat with us. He that is needy, let him come and keep the Passover with us. This year here, next year in Jerusalem. This year as slaves, next year as freemen." Then he turned to his son. "Now it's your turn, Heinrich." And Heinrich in his turn recited the age-old questions which have to be asked on this evening by the youngest of the company at table. "How does this night differ from all other nights?" Everyone at the table thought of Berthold. For if he had lived until that evening, he, as he was a little younger than Heinrich, would have had to recite that part of the ceremony.

It was the evening of the 11th of April; the 14th of Nisan, Seder Eve, according to Jewish reckoning. From time immemorial this night has been considered most sacred by the Jews. They celebrate, on this occasion, with home ritual and sacred feast, the liberation from the captivity in Egypt and the Passover Supper. The memory of this event has been kept vivid throughout thousands of years. The liturgy for this night roads: "Not Pharaoh alone hath risen against us, but in every age men have come up against us, to destroy us, but God hath delivered us from their hands."

Since Gustav's fiftieth birthday there had not been such a full assembly of the Oppermann family as on this night in

Jaques Lavendel's house on the shores of Lake Lugano. Joachim Ranzow and Liselotte were there also. They sat round the large, ceremoniously set table. The utensils required for the evening's rite included the finest pieces of Jaques Lavendel's collection. The old-fashioned, many tiered silver dish containing the thin, white, flat cakes of unleavened bread stood on the table, as well as small silver plates of all descriptions. One had some bits of meat upon it, another the remains of some salad, and one, in the shape of a cart, contained sweet jam prepared with apples and nuts. Silver goblets stood about. A very large, full one, which no one touched, was for the prophet Elijah, the forerunner of the Messiah, in case—as was always hoped—he should appear as a guest that night. Jaques Lavendel had placed before each of those at the table a book, a *Haggadah,* which gave the prescribed order of the prayers for the evening. He possessed many editions of this book, among them some which were extremely old and crudely illustrated. The entire ceremony was as curious as were these books. It was passionate, naïve, cheerful, and melancholy, full of lofty pride and equally lofty humility; childish symbols and others of profound significance alternated with one another.

Gustav, while Jaques Lavendel's hoarse voice murmured pleasantly in the old-fashioned sing-song, turned over the leaves of his prayer-book, his *Haggadah,* and looked at the crude illustrations. There was Pharaoh, sitting in a bathtub, his crown upon his head, a rigid stare on his face; there were the ten plagues and the water turned into blood. Then Pharaoh was pictured sitting on his throne, with the same rigid stare, and frogs—that meant the ten plagues again—were hopping about him. Incidentally, while counting the ten plagues, one had to dip a finger into the wine for each one of them, until all ten fingers had been dipped in succession. The idea was to remove the drops from the goblet of joy because these joys were paid for by the plagues inflicted upon the others. There were abundant references, to be sure, to the plagues inflicted upon themselves. Jews were represented, in the crude illustrations to his book, carrying bricks and mortar, under the whips of the overseers, to build the cities of Piton and Ramses. The Jews really didn't have such a bad time in those days. The overseers merely scourged them with whips; nowadays they beat them with rubber truncheons and steel rods and there were also rumours of burns inflicted upon the palms of hands and on the soles of feet. And suddenly there came to Gustav's mind again the picture by which he had been haunted incessantly since he had received that telegram. It was his friend Johannes Cohen standing on a box which, strangely enough, was triangular and had sharp edges. Johannes, however, danced about on the edge, made grotesque genuflections, sprang high in the air as though on elastic, and fell again to his knees in the marionette style of that famous dancer whom Gustav had once seen in a pantomime. He stretched out his arms and called parrot-wise, every time he made a genuflection: "I am a Jewish pig and have betrayed my Fatherland."

Gustav compelled himself to return to the pictures in his *Haggadah*. There they sat round the large table, a group of Jews, and celebrated their sacred feast. They had thus celebrated their "liberation" for some three thousand years. It was a somewhat ambiguous freedom which had been bestowed upon them. When they besought God to pour out his wrath upon their enemies, they left their doors open as a symbol of good faith, so that even their enemies would know how implicit their faith was. Prudent people, such as Herr Weinberg for instance, would send someone out into the corridor first to make sure that there was no danger near. However, they stubbornly believed in their eventual freedom. For nearly nineteen hundred years now, they had been setting out their goblet of wine in readiness for the prophet, the forerunner of the Messiah. They had done so stubbornly year after year, and the next morning the children would make the disappointing discovery that the goblet was still full, that once again the prophet had not been there to drink it.

It is upon us to begin the work,
It is not upon us to complete it.

Jaques Lavendel had finished the first part of the service. They began to eat. So far they had been speaking in Hebrew and Aramaic of the land of Egypt, from which God had freed the Jews three thousand years before. Now they were speaking in German of the land of Germany, from which they had not yet been freed. For only a small minority could escape from this land of horrors. There were many who were not allowed to leave and, if they did get out of the country, they were not allowed to take their money. If any references were made abroad about the outrages that were occurring in Germany, the authorities made that an excuse to oppress the Jews still more cruelly. Was that a reason to refrain from stirring up the civilized world against the Germany of the barbarians? No. There was perfect unanimity about the table on that point. For, with or without an excuse, the Nationalists were inflexibly determined to transfer the wealth of the Jews to their own pockets, to step into their positions, to annihilate them. One should, therefore, not allow oneself to be misled. The world must continually be told that in present-day Germany every instinct hostile to culture was considered a virtue and that the moral code of the cave-men was vested with the dignity of a State religion. But the Oppermanns were clever people, they understood the world. The world at large was indifferent; one had investments in Germany which one did not want to lose. One was interested in supplying Germany with arms, one feared Bolshevism might succeed the rule of the Nationalists. Under such conditions, humanity and civilization were weak arguments; they would have to be reinforced by something more practical if the world was to be stirred to interference.

Martin spoke of his plans. He, for his modest part, intended to assist in transplanting the good things of Germany to other soils. He had always been interested in the work of the interior decorator Bürkner. But Oppermann's Furniture Stores had not been the right place for his career, he could not have been effectively launched from there. He was now going to take him to London and there open an exclusive shop for the sole purpose of giving this man Bürkner a chance. He did not ex-expect to make large profits; whom would they benefit? But a man must have some mission.

While Martin was saying all this, Gustav became conscious of an actual physical feeling of discomfort. Formerly he had often smiled at Martin's "dignity." But now, he was startled to find that Martin had utterly and completely shed it. Never before would he have been so talkative about his position, his plans, and his "mission." That "mission"! You want to take the good things of Germany and transplant them abroad; you're making it too simple for yourself, my dear fellow. And what about Germany itself? Does one leave that to decay? Martin really hadn't the slightest idea of how lucky he was. Liselotte was sitting beside him. Though her face was not as serene as formerly and her grey almond-shaped eyes had lost their lustre, she had retained her poise and her placidity. Wherever Martin went, he would actually take with him, in Liselotte, a piece of Germany. And there were many like Liselotte, loyal and tenacious, many like Bilfinger and Frischlin. All Germany, even today, was full of them. Was one simply to leave them in the lurch? In the drawer of that inadequate little desk at his hotel, Bilfinger's papers were lying. Johannes Cohen was in a concentration camp, was being "reformed." How many in Germany knew about such things? Was it not one's duty to tell the Germans about them? Gustav felt there was a strong bond between himself and his brothers, between himself and everyone at that table. They were intelligent; he respected their superior sense of reality; yet he now found their intelligence a stale, lukewarm thing. A man who had understood the significance of Bilfinger's papers and of Johannes Cohen's torments to the extent he had, could not be guided by intelligence alone.

The meal was over. Jaques Lavendel continued the service. But he was not hard on them, he raised no objections when some of his guests gathered in a corner and conversed quietly.

Gina was there. In her worried, housewife's voice she told them what a difficult decision she had been obliged to make. Was she to accompany Edgar to Paris or Ruth to Palestine? In the end, they had seen the child off on the boat. The girl had earnestly begged her mother not to accompany her. Anyway, Ruth was so self-reliant and sensible. But even if she did not wish it, as soon as Edgar had his laboratory in Paris under way, they would take a trip to Palestine to see the child.

Edgar himself did not hear any of their low, rapid talk. He was sitting at the table, where Jaques Lavendel was chanting; he was turning over the leaves of his *Haggadah*. He had learned Hebrew when he was a boy, though not very thoroughly. He spelled out the words with some difficulty, deciphering their sense with the aid of the translation. He was a cosmopolitan, he had always smiled at the efforts of the Zionists to revive a dead language. Even little Dr. Jacoby now had to study Hebrew so as to be able to get along out there; he really had no prospects anywhere else. He, Edgar, had prospects but he got little pleasure out of them. He was no longer young, he had a hard year behind him, the one that faced him would not be easy. He, too, looked at the crude illustrations of his *Haggadah*. Egyptians were represented throwing Jewish babies into the Nile. What inadequate methods they used in those days; the present-day Egyptians were more thorough. They wanted to sterilize all Jews, as well as the Socialists and the intellectual classes. Nationalists only were to be allowed to propagate, there would be no one left to spoil their power.

The people in the corner were again talking about Germany. They did their best to keep cool. But their composure was a mask. Their homeland, their Germany, had proved false to them. For centuries they had felt secure in that homeland and now everything was suddenly crumbling to bits. They discussed, coolly, whether there was any prospect of returning. For how could the present power of the Nationalists be overthrown except through war and years of bloodshed and frightful revolution? But in their inmost hearts, against all logic, they nevertheless hoped it might be otherwise. They would return, Germany would grow great and sane again, as it used to be.

Jaques Lavendel requested them to sit down at the table again. He had arrived at the last page but one of his *Haggadah*. "You must all join in again now," he urged amiably. It was the final story in the *Haggadah,* that extremely ancient Aramaic ballad about the little lamb my daddy bought for two farthings and which the cat killed. Then begins the series of retaliations. The dog killed the cat and the stick beat the dog and the fire burned the stick and the water extinguished the fire and the ox drank the water and the butcher killed the ox and death killed the butcher and God killed death. . . . A little lamb, a little lamb. Jaques Lavendel, nodding his head, his eyes half closed, completely absorbed, chanted the simple, profound, melancholy ballad. The Aramaic words had a mysterious ring. The translation, too, which was printed opposite the Aramaic text, had a languid rhythm and sounded at once soothing and menacing. Gustav, throughout Jaques Lavendel's sing-song, heard in bitter Swabian accents: "They have smashed the standards to pieces." And he saw the hand erase the false inscription of two and one-half metres and write down the correct measurement in place of it.

And then the ballad came to an end and in the ensuing silence Heinrich observed: *"Well, daddy,* you really sing quite beautifully; but if you had played the song on the phonograph, it would have sounded still better."

They went into another room. Jaques Lavendel, transforming himself from a traditional Jew of the Ghetto into a civilian gentleman of today, spoke of his plans. First of all, he would stay here for a few months and enjoy a thorough rest. He must really thank the Leader for having induced him, a little rudely to be sure, finally to take a holiday. He was going to read a good deal; he knew far too little. He could not leave it entirely to his boy to make him up-to-date, even though his advice about the phonograph did show good powers of observation. He would travel, too. There was no relying on books and newspapers; one should see with one's own eyes what was happening in America, in Russia, in Palestine.

Martin, listening to Jaques talking like this, thought: That Jaques Lavendel has an easy time of it, travelling. The finest thing about travelling is coming home. Jaques Lavendel has this house here, where he belongs, he has citizenship, he is the only one of us with solid ground under his feet. The rest of us are homeless. When our passports expire, it will be difficult to get them renewed. Martin had made himself thick-skinned. And yet, to think that building in Gertraudten Strasse was slipping from his reach, that this casual place in Lugano was now really the only secure haven the Oppermanns possessed, hurt him. Klara, who had hitherto, as usual, been the most silent of all, was now saying in her kindly, positive way: "It seems as though, for the time being, no one of us has quite decided what he is going to do. You know that, if at any time any of you want a holiday, you will always be welcome here. It would make us happy if you would come often and meet here." She spoke quietly, as usual, but everyone realized: the Oppermanns had lost their nucleus; the story of Immanuel Oppermann, of his children and of his grandchildren was over.

Today they were still sitting together. But in future it would be, at best, chance that would reassemble them. Their homeland had slipped away from them. They had lost Berthold, they had lost the business in Gertraudten Strasse and everything connected with it, they had lost Edgar's laboratory and the house in Max Reger Strasse. That which three generations in Berlin and three times seven generations of them in Germany had built up, was gone. Martin was going to London, Edgar to Paris, Ruth was in Tel Aviv; Gustav, Jaques, Heinrich were going none knew where. They would be scattered over the four seas of the world, they would be scattered to all the eight winds.

12

Meanwhile the fog of deception was spreading more and more densely over Germany. The Reich was hermetically sealed, cut off from the rest of the world, completely abandoned to the lies which the Nationalists daily disseminated through millions of loudspeakers and printed pages. They had created a special ministry for the purpose. All the methods at the disposal of modern technique were employed to suggest to the hungry that they were fed, to the oppressed that they were free, to those threatened by the growing universal indignation that all the peoples of the earth envied them their strength and glory.

The Reich was preparing for war within and without its frontiers and was openly breaking the terms of its treaties. The highest goal of life was death on the field of battle: the great men of the Nationalists proclaimed this in their speeches and articles. War was the proper fulfilment of the destiny of the nation, proclaimed the loudspeakers. All the leisure of the younger portion of the population was spent in military exercises, the streets resounded with war-songs. Yet the Leader, in solemn, extravagantly sentimental speeches, asserted that the Reich was keeping strictly to the terms of the treaties and wanted nothing but peace. It was explained to the people, with many sly winks, that these speeches by the Leader were designed only to deceive the stupid foreigners, so that warlike preparations could go on undisturbed. The ultimate noble purpose sanctified this "play acting" born of "Nordic cunning." Such were the attempts made by the government to unite sixty-five millions of human beings in an association dedicated to sly winks and deceitful cunning.

The younger generation was educated in this spirit. They were taught that the war had not been lost, that the German people was the noblest in the world and therefore menaced from within and without by corrupting foes. The young were encouraged to explain to inquirers that their military drills were merely "sport." Children were taught that they belonged to the State, not to their parents. What their parents esteemed was derided and contemned. What appeared execrable to their parents was extolled. They were severely punished if they professed the sentiments of their parents. They were taught to lie.

In Nationalist Germany there was no worse crime than the profession of reason, peace, and honourable sentiments. The government required everyone to keep a sharp eye on his neighbour to see whether he showed due allegiance to the creed prescribed by the Nationalists. Whoever did not occasionally lodge an accusation fell under suspicion. Neighbour spied on neighbour, son on father, friend on friend. Conversations in flats were carried on in whispers, for words spoken aloud might be heard through the walls. One was afraid of one's friends, of one's employees, of the waiter who served one's meals, of the man sitting next to one in the street-car.

Lies and violence went hand in hand. The Nationalists abolished the principles which had been accepted as the rudiments of civilization by the white races since the French Revolution. They proclaimed that men were not equal in the eyes of the law. They introduced slavery again, calling it "Voluntary Labour Service." They locked up their adversaries, treating them worse than beasts, tormented them, and called it: "Physical Training." They branded them with the swastika, forced them to urinate upon one another, to tear up grass with their teeth, drove them through the streets in ridiculous processions, and called it: "Education in National Sentiment." The commandment, "Thou shalt not kill," was abolished. Political assassination was glorified as a sublime deed. The Leader referred to murderers, because they were murderers, as his "comrades." Memorial tablets were erected to murderers and the graves of the murdered ones were desecrated. A murderer, because he was a murderer, was made Chief of Police. During the first three months of the Nationalist regime in the Reich, 593 unpunished murders were committed, a greater number of such crimes than during the whole of the previous decade, and these were only the ones which had come to light and were supported by documentary evidence. Also more people were executed during the first months of the Nationalist regime than during the entire foregoing fifteen years.

Lies and misery went hand in hand. The Nationalists spoke of "Freedom and Bread," but they meant only freedom for their adherents; they meant to destroy their adversaries and supply their adherents with the bread and opportunities of those who had been destroyed. They banished able people from the country or locked them up in order to make room for their own incompetent adherents. They raised the cost of living and lowered wages. Hunger and misery increased among the people. During the first three months of the Nationalist regime, the rate of marriages dropped five and a half percent below the figure of the previous year and mortality increased by sixteen percent. Unemployment figures rose to staggering heights. Germany's percentage of unemployment became the highest in the world. But the stiff-necked Nationalists declared that they had reduced unemployment.

Lies, profiteering, and selfish indulgence went hand in hand. Anyone who belonged to the party in power could have his competitor spirited away to a concentration camp. Next to the Leader, the most popular man in Germany had been that man whose voice the people liked to hear most over the radio; he was now atoning for his rivalry with the Leader in a concentration camp. Threatened with internment in a concentration camp, Jewish creditors were forced to remit debts. Harried by the same threat, Jewish debtors were rushed into payment. Payment of rent was refused the Jewish landlord on the plea that "it would be sent after him to Palestine." Every non-Nationalist lived in constant fear. A statement that the price of meat had increased under the present government or that the programme of some Nationalist celebration had been poorly planned was enough to get a man sent to a concentration camp. The mere accusation of such a "crime" was enough, even if it had not been committed. If one of the Nationalists did not like a passerby's nose, he was permitted to aim a blow at it. If he explained that the man to whom the nose belonged had not raised his arm quickly enough when a Nationalist hymn was being sung, it was sufficient to exonerate him.

The people were sound. They had produced men and performed achievements of the highest types. The masses were made up of vigorous, industrious, and capable human beings.

But their civilization was young it was easy to misdirect their eager, uncritical idealism, to stir up their atavistic inclinations, their primeval instincts, to break through the thin veneer of their civilization. That was what was happening now. Externally, the country appeared the same as usual; street-cars and autos continued to run; shops, restaurants and theatres, many of them under compulsion, maintained their activities. The newspapers all had the same headlines and used the same type. But internally the country grew daily more barbarous, more poverty-stricken, more corrupt, more demoralized. It reeked with lies and brutality; life was fast becoming nothing but a rotten sham.

There were very many who took no interest in public affairs. They put their faith in the apparent peace of everyday life, in the celebrations and the frequent proclamations of the Nationalists which veiled the misery of the peasants and the workmen and shrouded the concentration and labor-service camps with silence. Moreover, those who had stepped into the shoes of the exiled men of ability and those who lived on the crumbs that fell from the tables of the new authorities, made a new but deceptive show of prosperity. However, the majority of the people were not taken in. There was more indignation than satisfaction. When detachments of mercenaries passed by, they fled into the entrances of houses so as not to be forced to salute. They bit their lips when they heard the vulgar song about the Jewish blood that was to spurt from the knife in order that all might go well again. But they had to hold their tongues. Whoever was caught talking was brought before a judge.

During those days people learned to lie in Germany. Many praised the Nationalists aloud but secretly cursed them. Their clothes might be of Nationalist brown but their hearts were a flaming red, the colour chosen by their adversaries. They called themselves "Beefsteaks." The "Beefsteak" party was larger than the Leader's.

But their voices did not reach the outside world, and the voice of the outside world did not reach them. There was a mercenary camp in Köpenick, Berlin, called Demuth. It was notorious for the particularly inhuman way in which the prisoners there were "instructed." While they were being ill-treated in the cellars, one of the mercenaries kept the engine of his motorcycle running in the courtyard so as to drown out the screams of the tortured and the sound of the falling blows. This engine, switched on for the sole purpose of drowning out the cries of those who were being ill-treated, was typical of the methods of the Third German Reich.

Inconsistency and deceit were the underlying characteristics of all the actions of their leaders. Their speech was deceitful and so was their silence. They got up with a lie and they went to sleep with a lie. Their discipline was a lie, their code of laws a lie, their judgments a lie, their German a lie, their science a lie, their sense of justice and their faith were lies. Their nationalism, their socialism were lies, their ethical philosophy was a lie, and so was their love. Everything was a lie, only one thing about them was genuine: their Hate!

The country groaned. But peace and order were preserved. The pillars of that order were the six hundred thousand mercenaries and its foundation the hundred thousand prisoners. The country sank deeper and deeper into misery and corruption. But those who walked on the Kurfürstendamm in Berlin, on the Jungfernstieg in Hamburg, on Hohe Strasse in Cologne, saw nothing but peace and order.

13

It was from this Germany that Anna came.

Gustav stood on the station platform at the little seaside town of Bandol in Provence and awaited her. She stepped from the train; her figure was slightly heavier than formerly but still slender. She looked at once girlish and womanly, tall and serene. It was the season of the mistral winds. Gustav noticed with pleasure that her cheeks were flushed by the fresh, pleasant breeze, but the skin around her eyes remained pale. Cheerful and calm, she sat beside him. Gustav reached for her hand; she took off her glove and put her hand in Gustav's.

Gustav was glad he had chosen this lovely, southern scene for their stay together. The seacoast was alternately sharply indented and widely sweeping. The landscape was charming but not too impressive; low hills rose in graceful lines and subdued colours, round about were greyish-green olive trees and greyish-brown crumbling cliffs, vineyards and clumps of stone-pines.

Anna explained to him, during dinner, what her plans were regarding her stay here. She was tired after her strenuous work of the past year and she was looking forward to a lazy time by the sea. It would be fine to go for walks, bathe, and lie in the sun. But she could not exist entirely without work of some kind. Her French was terribly sketchy. She had brought some books with her and a good dictionary. She spoke calmly, seriously, and cheerfully, as she always did. Her bright eyes looked critically out from under her thick, brown hair. They disregarded many things, but anything that interested them they took in; slowly, but for all time. Anna was exactly the same as when Gustav had last seen her, nineteen months ago.

He was astonished. It seemed to him that everyone who came from that land of nightmares must have undergone a radical transformation. Was he justified in his intention of banishing from that bright, serene face, from that angular brow, all tranquillity—as it had been banished, for ever, from his own? And if he were justified, would he be successful in carrying out his intention?

For the moment he did not refer to what was in his mind. Instead, he merely told Anna that, on this occasion, he would not be able to make quite such generous arrangements as hitherto. Her orderly and economical mind found this perfectly right and proper. They hired a little old car and drove out, full of the spirit of adventure, to look for a cheap house in which she could spend the few weeks of her holiday. They found one on the peninsula called La Gorguette. It was a broad, low, solitary house, standing in a little cove. It was reddish-brown, had a weatherbeaten appearance, and stood on a small cliff. Behind it rose hills covered with olives, vines, and, most of all, with clumps of stone-pines. The road led to the cliff in a graceful curve. Flowers and grass did not thrive in the salt wind. There was nothing in front of the house but the sea and a shallow sandy beach, exposed to the sun and bordered on either side by a thick growth of young stone-pines, which crept down the rocky shore to the sea.

A shabbily dressed man, with the gestures of a nobleman, showed them over the interior of the house. The rooms were large, bare, and dilapidated. The sea could be seen from every window. A few rickety pieces of furniture stood about. The man was sparing of speech and by no means obtrusive. Anna believed she could make herself comfortable there, she was intrigued by the idea of setting things to rights. The most urgent repairs could be made with very little trouble and expense. The shabby man with the gestures of a nobleman, who was a wine-grower and owned a small piece of property several hundred yards further inland, declared himself ready to help. They agreed to rent the place.

She wanted to move in within forty-eight hours. The whole of the next day she busied herself with the necessary cleaning and other arrangements. The man sawed and hammered in his calm way, sparing of speech, moving gracefully about his work. Gustav looked on. Anna sometimes asked him to tell her some French word, so she could make herself understood by the man. In other respects he was not able to give much assistance. Anna was delighted with the work, she became quite absorbed in it. If he had married her, if he had continued to live with her, everything would have turned out differently.

He was in the way; he lay down in front of the house in the sun and dozed, fanned by the light breeze. It was comforting and yet it was alarming that Anna's face was so serene and calm. This face, with its beautiful, generous mouth, the strong curve of the cheeks, and the angular forehead under the thick brown hair, this face was Germany.

The Germany of yesterday. He would have to find a way to drive the tranquillity from that face, so that the Germany of today might once again become the Germany of yesterday. The sea stretched out before him, large, greyish-blue, with little, white-capped waves dancing in the breeze. The landscape was calm, peaceful. How she did enjoy putting that dilapidated house to rights with only modest means at her disposal. He could be so happy here if only he could make up his mind to hold his tongue and not disturb Anna's tranquillity. It was a pity that it was his duty to speak.

They ate a hastily prepared collation. Eggs, cold meat, fruit, cheese, wine. It was a cheerful meal. Anna's plans of the things she wanted to do within the next five weeks began to crystallize. First of all, she would put the house to rights; she had a definite idea of how things were to look and they were going to look that way, too. They, themselves, to be sure, would have to leave almost as soon as she had achieved the desired results.

In other directions, she also had definite plans. Sport, exercise every morning. The beautiful, slightly uphill road would lend itself admirably to road work. She was a methodical girl; but she had a sense of humour, she laughed with Gustav when he teased her about her pedantic ways. She was slow, it pleased her to be pedantic. For instance, it took her rather a long time to get to know anybody. For that reason, she had recently made a systematic study of physiognomy. Gustav asked whether she thought he had grown mentally during the past eighteen months, whether she thought he had at last, at the age of fifty, become wise. Anna scrutinized him thoughtfully. He had changed, she declared. His sensual mouth had grown a little thinner; the lines about the eyes and near the nose were now more strongly marked, not as capricious as formerly. Gustav listened to her analysis reflectively, with a very slight smile.

In the afternoon they drove into Toulon to complete their shopping for the household. The amount which Anna proposed to spend for this purpose was small. They visited many shops; Anna was tireless, she chose one thing here, another there. They enjoyed the noise and the variegated appearance of the town, dined near the harbour and then Anna went off again, alone. Finally she triumphantly declared that she had everything she wanted.

The evening came, then the morning of the third day. Anna was nearly settled now. Gustav had not yet spoken of what was in his mind. After lunch they sunned themselves on the cliffs above their little cove. Anna lay face downwards, propping her chin on both her hands, and read her French book, with the dictionary beside her. Several times she asked Gustav the exact meaning of a word. She was headstrong; she often stuck to her own opinion, even when he was right.

He should not let this day, too, go by without speaking. He began to talk around the subject, discreetly. Late spring and early summer were the best seasons in Germany. He had really hoped to invite her, before she went back to her work again, to spend a week or two with him in Berlin, in his house in Max Reger Strasse. He was lying on his back, his hairy hands clasped behind his head. He gazed lazily and thoughtfully into the depths of the blue sky. "It's a pity," he concluded slowly, "that it's not possible now." "Why, not possible?" asked Anna after a short pause, continuing her reading. Gustav half rose. "Don't you know anything about it, then? Haven't you heard anything at all?"

No, she did not know anything about it. It developed that she knew nothing of Gustav's affairs, of that manifesto, of his persecution. It developed that she really knew nothing of the whole beastly situation in Germany.

She was indignant over what had happened to Gustav. But she refused absolutely to allow this one case to influence her judgment of the entire issue. In her slow, careful manner she explained her view of the matter. She spoke more to herself than to him. One national government had given place to another, which was still more national. This change was being celebrated by long, stupid speeches, and silly gigantic demonstrations were being held. But when had political speeches and demonstrations ever been sensible? That boycott was, of course, an atrocious thing and so was the book-burning. It was disgusting to read the papers and disgusting to hear the row the Nationalists made. But who took that seriously? As a matter of fact, life was going on just the same as before. In her business, for example, a new manager had been appointed, and the workmen's wages had been reduced. The new manager had, at first, tried to give himself airs. He had demanded the dismissal of seventeen Jews and Socialists. But nine of those who had been dismissed had already been reinstated. Privy Councillor Harprecht, her chief, sometimes teased her good-naturedly about "her Jew." He went through the external motions of the new cult but, when he was alone with her or any of his intimate friends, he made fun of it. She had read extracts from foreign newspapers about German atrocities. When she compared these atrocity stories with what she had seen with her own eyes, she began to wonder whether, perhaps, only a tenth part of the horrors of the French and Russian revolutions might have been true.

They were both sitting upright now, Gustav squatting cross-legged and Anna on a rock opposite him. At other times, she would have remembered to put the French dictionary carefully away in the shade of a rock. But now, it was lying in the sun and its cover was curling up. She spoke slowly, taking pains not to say too much or too little. Her bright eyes looked at him frankly and calmly. That was Anna, his Anna. She had come from Germany, that hermetically sealed country. She was one of those who lived on the top floor and did not know what was happening beneath her feet. She believed in the "Peace and Order" and she stood up for her beliefs.

He listened to her carefully, without interruption. He had often heard what she said, it was repeated in all the German newspapers. In Germany that was the only way to protect oneself; even honest, right-thinking people did it, so as not to lose their very foundations, their homeland.

Should he speak? Was there any sense in it? Was it not folly, and more than that, an infamy, to uproot this woman from her firm, comfortable tranquillity? He saw Johannes Cohen on his box—"Down on your knees, arm out"—he looked like the marionette in the pantomime. He called out in his cawing voice, like a parrot: "I am a Jewish pig and I have betrayed my Fatherland." That girl Anna could not live here in this house in southern France for four weeks without putting everything to rights. Was she to go on living without knowing anything of the rottenness and decay of her native land? No, he could not spare Anna.

He began telling her about the stories Bilfinger had related. He spoke to the accompaniment of the gentle sounds of wind and sea. He did not speak in such a matter-of-fact, objective way as Bilfinger had; his words were coloured by his feelings. He could not speak quietly, he raised his voice from time to time, and exaggerated. Yes, she had better listen. That was what had occurred in her own Württemberg, quite near to her own city of Stuttgart, while she was going about, seeing nothing but peace and order.

As he talked, he realized that he was talking badly in far too excited a manner, not credibly. He was not telling a story, he was pleading with her. What did he really want? It was clear enough what Bilfinger had wanted: he had to tell his story to one whom it concerned, to him, the Jew. But what possessed him, Gustav, to try to excite Anna about it? He did not want her to do anything. He really did not want her to take any action in the matter. But yes, he did want something. He wanted her confirmation; her confirmation that his feelings were justified. Was that selfish of him? No. They had smashed the standards, he could not sit idly by; he must have the confirmation. There were not many people he could talk to. He might have been able to talk to Johannes Cohen. But Johannes Cohen was in Herrenstein. "Down on your knees, arm out——"

Anna listened. Her bright eyes grew darker. She was indignant. Not at what she heard but that anyone could believe it. Because Gustav's house had been confiscated, he thought the whole country had suddenly turned into the forest primeval and its inhabitants into Bushmen. The waves of the sea had grown louder. She had to raise her voice. Her cheeks were flushed in spots, leaving the skin around her eyes quite pale.

Gustav was not very much affected by her anger. He had known it would not be easy to dislodge Anna from her firm convictions. She had come from the land of lies. For months the most eminent experts in the art of lying had been scattering billions of lies throughout the country by means of the most modern devices. Anna had been breathing that atmosphere of lies day after day, hour after hour. To befog people like herself and conceal the truth from them was the sole purpose of the ministry of lies. It was the most important mission of this aftermath of the revolution. Anna had been saturated with these lies; to purge her of the poison was a task requiring time and patience.

Gustav fetched the documents. Anna and he lay face downwards, their chins propped up by their hands, and he read her what Bilfinger had recorded. The waves broke with even rhythm, the mistral breeze fluttered the papers, they had to put stones on them to keep them down. Gustav read on, passing the enclosures, consisting of the sworn affidavits and the photographs, across to her. He said little of his own experiences and nothing of Johannes Cohen. She was to assimilate things slowly, just as they had made their impression upon him slowly.

When he had finished, she said nothing but gathered the documents together carefully and replaced them in their stout wrapper. She was thoughtful but not convinced. They climbed the little crumbling path to the house. Anna set about her work. Later, she called him to dinner. The sandy beach, the pine shrubs, and the sea lay before them. Night came on, and it quickly grew cool. They talked of many things, important and trivial. Anna was, perhaps, a little less cheerful but just as serene as ever.

So it went on that evening and so it was the next morning. They did their road-work, swam and walked. Anna read her French book and attended to her household chores. The day passed just as she had planned it.

There was only one incident which recalled their conversation of the day before. Anna asked whether Johannes Cohen

was coming and if so, when. Gustav had told her in a letter
that he would perhaps visit them for three or four days. He
now explained to her about his friend Johannes. He informed
her that he could not visit them and why he could not. She
seemed more affected by this information than by Bilfinger's
documents. "Can't we help him, can't we do anything for
him?" she asked passionately, after a shocked silence. "No,"
returned Gustav. "The mercenaries don't tolerate any interference with their arrangements. If a minister or any other civilian intervenes, they only make things worse for the prisoner."
He had the vertical furrows in his forehead and was grinding
his teeth a little. But he restrained himself from saying more
about the concentration camps. He realized that her calm was
shaken at last. But he had grown wise, he waited until she
had thought everything over sufficiently behind that angular
brow of hers.

The following evening she had reached that stage. He was
already in bed, reading, when she came in to him. She sat
down next to his bed and told him that she had now finished
arranging the household. Everything was just as she had intended it to be. But it gave her no real pleasure now. The
things of which Gustav had told her were dreadful things,
they were horrible, it was difficult to grasp them. Yet she was
bound to defend the country in general, her Germany, against
him. Looked at from a broad point of view, the change had
been necessary and unquestionably welcome to the people.
Former authorities, he would have to admit, had always had
a thousand scruples, especially legal ones. Instead of knocking
their adversaries on the head, they had taken the opinion of a
hundred expert jurists before they ventured to advise their opponents to practise a little less high treason. When they really
did lock a political murderer up, they set him free again after
a few weeks. And when they did deprive anyone guilty of high
treason of his pension, they cancelled the decision a fortnight

later on a technicality of law. They had never done anything but chew cotton-wool and that was how they had let the Republic go to rack and ruin. The new authorities were crafty and foolish but they did do something. That was what the people wanted and they were impressed by it. Even the Leader, just because of that crafty simplicity of his, untainted by the slightest critical faculty, and on account of his unbending, cast-iron beliefs, was the right man for the people—the necessary antithesis to the men of yesterday. A revolution had taken place and it was a welcome one. There had been much ruthlessness but this was bound to accompany every revolution, and then the victims always screamed about robbery and murder and the end of the world. Had not Gustav himself, only yesterday, read to her an ancient Egyptian author's indictment, more than four thousand years old and very similar to what Gustav was now saying? Horrible things had happened, it was true; but individuals, not the people and not the new government, were responsible. Even if there were a hundred thousand such cases, they would still remain a hundred thousand separate and individual cases.

Gustav gazed at her bright, serious countenance. It was less serene now, she had had to rummage everywhere to find even these meagre arguments. That indictment by the Egyptian writer of four thousand three hundred years ago! Gustav's excellent memory had retained the words used: "The skilled are sent into exile, the land is ruled by a few fools. Mob sovereignty is beginning. The man in the street has come to power and is making use of it in his own fashion. He wears the finest linen robes and anoints his bald pate with myrrh, he has a fine house and corn-lofts. At one time he used to run his own errands, now he sends other people. Princes flatter him and the high officials of the old regime pay court, in their necessity, to the new upstart." Gustav enjoyed apt quotations. But her reference to this one was really far-fetched and by no means a satisfactory refutation. Everything she had said was a makeshift, far below her usual level of intelligence. She was an utterly sincere person. When she was convinced of anything with her whole heart, she was very well able to express it. Now, all her present arguments were spongy and worthless. One did not need to be a very experienced student of physiognomy to see that she only half believed them.

Gustav did not have much difficulty in refuting her. He was partly sitting up, his head propped on his hand. His face stood out clearly in the circle of light cast by the bedside lamp. It was the central point of the room. It was true enough, he said, that the people had not perpetrated the atrocities. It was a magnificent tribute to the sound character of the people that it had kept its temper so admirably in the face of the government's fourteen years of incitement to pogroms against Socialists and Jews. It was not the people that was barbarous, it was the government, the new State, its officials and its mercenaries. All the atrocities had been perpetrated by the mercenaries and they had all been committed under the protection of the government. The barbarism was not only evidenced by the acts in question, it was evidenced particularly in the principles of these new men. They had smashed the old standards and had legalized caprice and violence. The charge against the government was not that such atrocities had been committed but that they prevented all investigation, locked up complainants, and thus sanctioned the continuance of further atrocities indefinitely. Gustav mentioned the shameless professions of the creed of terrorism which these people had made in ten thousand books, speeches, and decrees; he spoke of their shameless, undisguised stalking of their prey, of their ridiculous race-arrogance. They had fetched down a fetish from the attic and it turned one's stomach to look on while professors nowadays sacrificed to that fetish in their lecture-halls, and magistrates on the bench pronounced judgment in the name of that fetish.

It was a frightful comedy. A king was sitting in his under-clothes and the people were on their knees acclaiming his splendid raiment. It was true that, even now, magnificent machinery was being constructed in Germany, that conscientious work was being done in her factories, that beautiful music was being composed, that many millions of human beings were exerting themselves to keep decent. But right next to them the caveman era had begun again, tortures and murders were being perpetrated, and people had to look the other way and stop up their ears. He admitted that the atrocities were perpetrated by individuals. He admitted, too, that each individual case of ill-treatment, each individual case of slaughter, was a small item compared with the whole. He could only point out that the whole was composed of many such small items, just as the human body was composed of cells, and that, to conclude, the whole body must perish when too many of the cells were diseased.

Gustav again could not bring himself to speak calmly and he mentioned practically no figures or dates. But he spoke out of the fullness of his heart. He was not merely offering her words, he was showing her his very soul. She watched him as he talked, watched his great, excited, mobile face in the circle of light cast by the bedside lamp, every little wrinkle in it distinctly illuminated. He did not look young but he looked virile and pugnacious. He was a different Gustav from the man she knew. His conciliatory indifference was gone. Events had taken hold of him, entered into his blood, hardened and solidified the stuff of which he was made. Anna admired and loved him.

Nevertheless, she only believed half he said. What had once taken root behind that angular brow stuck there. It was uphill work, convincing her. Gustav saw in her opposition the epitome of that poisoned, hypnotized Germany, which would require a shockingly long time to recover from the stupor it was in. Here was the confirmation he needed. The task he had set himself was a most necessary one.

He had reached the point he had been aiming at. He really might grant himself a few quiet weeks with Anna now. What he proposed to do later on would be very hard work. She, though she did not say anything much more about Germany, was changed. Reluctant as she might seem, she would be bound to see another Germany when she returned.

They passed serene, untroubled days in their weatherbeaten house, the interior of which was so clean and orderly. It was difficult to imagine, in the peace of this bright, Latin seashore, that only twenty hours away lay the land of nightmares, this Germany whose great cities had suddenly been assaulted by the terrors of the forest primeval. Gustav and Anna walked about the open lovely countryside; the road ascended the cliff in a graceful curve; vineyards, olive and pine trees surrounded them; the even rhythm of the waves beat upon the shore in their sleeping as in their waking hours; the light, cool sea-breeze blew refreshingly. Herds of goats moved over the quiet hills at sunset. Life was free, serene, arcadian, in the classic manner.

He managed, for four entire days, not to utter a single word on the subject of Germany. There were actually hours when the topic slipped his memory. Then, suddenly, in all its horror, it would obsess his mind.

They were sitting in one of the bright little cafés along the shore of the neighbouring town, and Gustav was reading a newspaper. All at once, turning pale under his tan, he dropped the paper. Anna picked it up. It contained a report that the well-known German professor Johannes Cohen had committed suicide in the concentration camp at Herrenstein. Anna, as she read, turned pale too, first around the eyes, then the pallor spread over her entire face. "Let us go," she said.

They drove home in silence. Gustav went down to the

beach and sat on a rock. She left him to his solitude. In the evening she said: "You were right, Gustav. I was wrong. I looked the other way. You are right, Germany is different. Of course, it is not only because of this man's death, and not because of what you told me and gave me to read, nor because— if it were known in Germany that I had been here with you— I should have my hair cut off and be driven through the streets as a shameless creature. But if I think, now, of what I have seen in Germany and if I contemplate it from this distance with my new eyes, from the standpoint of the present hour, I must say: 'I am ashamed, Gustav. This new Germany is completely depraved.'"

Gustav thought of the yellowish-brown, shrewd, haughty countenance of his friend Johannes. "Suicide," "shot while trying to escape," "heart failure," such were the usual official causes of death in a concentration camp. Then, what was left of the prisoner, broken bones, mutilated masses of flesh, was placed into a sealed casket and delivered to the next of kin upon payment of the cost entailed and upon the guarantee that the casket would not be opened. Death announcements containing the words: "Suddenly deceased," were now also forbidden. "The great majority of my friends and acquaintances," he said, "were at the front during the war. Very many of them were killed. I have not counted the number of my friends who have died during these past months. But this much is certain: since the Nationalists came to power more of my friends have died a violent death than during the time of the war."

When Anna asked him, later, what he intended doing, he replied: "I shall not remain silent, that is all I know." Anna asked, after some hesitation: "Isn't that imprudent?" The anxiety in her voice gave him pleasure. He shrugged his shoulders. "I can't go on living like this," he said.

The summer came. Anna had to return. Gustav took her to the station at Marseilles. She thought his face looked more serious than it had formerly, yet it seemed more boyish and virile; in any case, more contented. She crossed the frontier with mixed emotions, she was proud of his new demeanour, yet she feared what Fate might have in store for him.

14

He stood on the platform and saw Anna disappear in the direction of nightmare land. The time he had spent with her had been a good time and full of profit. He now had come to a clear understanding of much that formerly, while it was still vague and unfamiliar, had oppressed him.

For the time being, he continued to live in the weatherbeaten house up on the cliff, far from all the bustle of life. The orderly arrangements made by Anna did not last long, but that did not annoy him. He did not live like a hermit: he gossiped with his neighbours, fishermen, wine- and olive-growers, a few tourists. But he was much alone, too. He maintained few contacts with his brothers and former friends. They wrote to him but he replied more and more infrequently. He led a solitary and peaceful life, sure of his destiny.

The money in his wallet gradually diminished. He could have applied to Mühlheim or to the Swiss bank where he had an account. But he did not do so; as long as the money in his wallet held out, he would stay where he was. The money in the bank was consecrated to what he meant to do later.

His habits and tastes became simpler. He walked or drove in his small, increasingly dilapidated car about the beautiful, open countryside. He could be seen lying in the sun, eating his simple repast of bread, cheese, and fruit. He washed it down with some strong country wine. He also sat about in small

inns, conversing with peasants, traders, fishermen, and bus
drivers. There were radios in the inns, everywhere there was
music in the afternoons and dancing in the evenings. Life was
gay and noisy. Gustav calmly let himself drift. At times he
was merry and extremely charming; often he seemed like the
earlier Gustav, the Gustav to whom men liked to listen and of
whose friendship women were proud. Now, too, women
turned to look after him and were sorry when he went his
way. He was often silent but seldom sad. The things that
went on in nightmare land were ever present; he did not
banish them from his thoughts, they existed no less within him
than across the frontier. But though they were ever with him,
he remained calm, almost cheerful.

In the neighbouring large city of Marseilles, in a bookshop,
he saw a new German book displayed, a pamphlet entitled:
Observations on a New Type of Humanity. "Dedicated to a
Dear Friend. By Friedrich Wilhelm Gutwetter." He bought
the book. He found some phrases in it about the Nationalist
idea, lofty, ponderous phrases; so lofty, in fact, that they only
made the idea more difficult to grasp. It was a vague idea, it
had no address, no telephone number, it did not enable one
to arrive at any definite conclusions. Even Sybil, his slim little
matter-of-fact Sybil, would not be able to make much of it.
The next day, while he was preparing the snack of food he
wanted to take with him, he found he needed some more
paper. He tore two pages out of the *Observations on a New
Type of Humanity.*

He heard from Berlin that now Jean also, the dignified old
attendant at the Theatre Club, had joined the Nationalist
party. That made more impression on him. His last hours in
Berlin and those five marks had not been well spent. Those
hours would have been better employed with Berthold.

Often, when he was lying alone on the beach of his cove or
squatting on the sandy, sloping, pine-fringed ground in front

of the weatherbeaten rose-and-brown house, he noticed a man fishing below, on the rocks. The rocks really formed part of the property which he had leased, and he could have asked the man to leave. He liked to be alone, yet the propinquity of people was not displeasing to him. The man often waded about in the water, looking for sea-urchins, and often, too, he lay on the rocks and sunned himself. Gustav was soon passing the time of the day with him and entering into short conversations. The man was heavily built, sluggish of movement, had a large head and a thick walrus moustache. He wore a baggy, dark blue suit made of some stiff, coarse material, such as many wore in that part of the country. It developed that he was one of the numerous Germans living down here and that his name was Georg Teibschitz.

Herr Georg Teibschitz had left Germany only a few weeks before. He had very little money, but enough to enable him to live frugally for three or four years where the winters were not very severe. Herr Teibschitz stretched himself in the sun, blinking his eyes. They were deeply set and looked sleepy in his heavy head. He gazed drowsily before him and made long pauses between his sentences and before his replies. He had seen much and had experienced much. He had been rich some years ago, then his money had melted away. Later he seemed to have regained his wealth. Now he only wanted one thing: quiet and few people about him. He had seen a cottage in the neighbourhood; it could hardly be called a cottage, a kennel would be a better description. It was a cosy kennel in a pleasing landscape, greyish-brown and surrounded by olive trees. The kennel was priced at fifteen thousand francs. Herr Teibschitz had left a wife in Germany who could send him the money; but he had few illusions, she most likely would not send it.

Herr Teibschitz had few wants but he was fond of fish and sea-food of all kinds and knew all about preparing it. Gustav

invited him to use his kitchen. He discovered charcoal and a
sort of grill there. Herr Teibschitz, with Gustav's expert assistance, gutted the fish, fried them in oil, and added rosemary
and thyme. He also concocted a savoury bouillabaisse. He ate
slowly, with relish, lingering over each morsel; he even
smacked his lips a little.

Herr Teibschitz, in the days of his affluence, had enjoyed
many æsthetic hobbies. His principal hobby was paintings; he
had once possessed a fine collection of them, particularly landscapes. He had a special feeling for landscapes. He could describe one in such a way, in a few words, that it became positively visible. He had travelled extensively and remembered
what he had seen. If his wife left him in the lurch so that he
could not buy the kennel here, he would probably take a walking tour through Italy and Sicily. That was what Herr Teibschitz told Herr Oppermann, a little at a time, in his slow way
while he fished, lay on the rocks in the sun, or cooked his
catch.

One day Herr Teibschitz turned up very much altered in
his appearance. He had had his walrus moustache removed.
He explained to Gustav that it had been a hindrance to him in
eating. Gustav was having a pernicious influence on him, he
added in his lazy, joking way; he'd end by making a perfect
sybarite of him. But the opposite was the case; the presence of
the other was making Gustav simpler and simpler in his
tastes. He had also bought himself a baggy, blue suit of coarse
material such as the other had. Since Herr Teibschitz had had
his walrus moustache shaved off, it became apparent how
greatly the two men resembled each other, particularly when
they sat next to each other in their baggy blue suits. Involuntarily, too, they began to acquire each other's habits. Formerly
Gustav had tried to conquer his bad habit of grinding his
teeth, now he made no attempt to do so. When Herr Teibschitz smacked his lips, Gustav ground his teeth. Once laugh-

ing, he declared: "We look very much alike, Herr Teibschitz."
Herr Teibschitz scrutinized him. "You look more distinguished than I do, Dr. Oppermann," he said in a casual, lazy,
noncommittal tone.

Herr Teibschitz did not discuss German affairs often, but
neither did he avoid doing so. He had liked living in Germany. The German climate, German landscapes, and German
people were very congenial to him. It was a pity they were
spoiling the landscapes now with their swastikas. Last year, in
Nidden, he had seen one which completely covered the largest
of the huge sandhills in that locality. It was true that three
days later the wind had blown it away. Landscapes were long-
suffering but in the end they remained the same. During the
days of his prosperity he had travelled by airplane a great deal.
That was the way to see how vast the countryside was and
what tiny portions of it were occupied by the big cities, which
made such a noise in the world. It was a pity that this beautiful
Germany was now possessed by madness. Most people were
not yet properly aware of it. They believed that, if they talked
gently to the mad dog, he would not bite them. But he knew
that mad dogs did not react in that manner; it was a pity
about beautiful Germany. He showed Gustav a photograph of
a landscape in the Lower Alps.

Yes, in view of his modest income, Herr Teibschitz now collected photographs instead of paintings. Gustav enjoyed being
shown pictures from this new collection. They were of people
and of landscapes. Herr Teibschitz also showed him photographs of the people of New Germany. Some were portraits
of the new leaders, extremely vacuous faces, expressing only
hysterical severity and brutality. Each one of them was standing in front of a microphone with his mouth wide open. Herr
Oppermann and Herr Teibschitz, in their baggy, dark blue
suits of coarse material, bent over the photographs and looked
at the faces, at one gaping mouth after the other. They did

not say anything, they only looked at each other. Then their own lips relaxed, their own mouths broadened, they smiled. And suddenly, in spite of everything that the owners of those gaping mouths had done to them, they burst into wild fits of laughter, completely losing control of themselves. And then Herr Teibschitz brought out the crowning glory of this part of his collection. It was a photograph in which several of the best known of the Nationalist leaders were seen attending a concert. Those whose mouths had been so hysterically and brutally agape now crouched in drooping attitudes, sentimentally absorbed in the music, with dreamy eyes.

That they could act in various capacities was shown by other photographs in the collection of Herr Teibschitz. He had picture postcards, such as were sold in Germany for the benefit of the mercenaries' relief fund at twenty pfennig apiece. They either represented mercenaries shaving a young Jew's head or surrounding a platform on which they were exhibiting a young girl with a placard reading: "I, shameless creature, have given myself to a Jew," or showed them wheeling a labour leader through the streets in a "cart of disgrace." The faces of the victims were alarmingly expressionless: the young Jew's head drooped to one side; the young girl had her mouth half open; the labour leader, an old, bald-headed man, half sat, half lay in the cart with his legs crossed, one hand clinging wearily to the side of the cart, his lips rigidly shut. Herr Teibschitz passed the picture postcards over to Gustav, one after another, his tanned, hairy hand looking huge as it emerged from the tight cuff of his blue blouse. Gustav took his time looking at the photographs. Must they not actually be raving mad triumphantly to sell pictures of their infamy and send them out into the world?

"Can you understand," he asked, "how people in Germany can tolerate that? Don't they get into a rage when they see it?" Herr Teibschitz, in his slow, laconic way, observed that rage certainly existed in Germany. He had heard a good deal about it when he was there. In a concentration camp in Brunswick, for example, the prisoners, when they heard of Clara Zetkin's death, wanted to show their respect for her memory. They resolved to keep silent for twenty-four hours. Their Nationalist guards were embittered by this silence. They starved them and made their "instruction" more severe. The commandant of the camp, an expert in Nationalism, resorted to the most severe of the usual methods to break that irritating silence. The only thing he accomplished was that, towards evening, twenty-two prisoners had to be removed to the infirmary suffering from dangerous hæmorrhages. They continued to maintain their silence. They were kept without food that evening too. The silence of these four hundred men resulted in doubling the number of the guards and manning the machine-guns on the watch-towers. All through the night the commandant and his troops remained on the alert. Towards morning he had three of the older prisoners fetched from the infirmary and, as they continued to keep silent, he had them shot on the pretext that they were trying to escape. Another time Herr Teibschitz told of the execution of four workmen from Altona, who had been captured during an attack by the Nationalists on the workers' quarter. Seventy-five prisoners had been summoned to witness the deaths of their comrades. When the youngest of the condemned men was asked to express his last wish, he requested to be allowed to stretch his arms. When he was released from his bonds, he struck the commander of the mercenaries in the face with his fist. Then he laid his head on the block.

Herr Teibschitz told a good many stories of this kind and mentioned such minute details that they could not possibly have been repetitions of vague newspaper reports. Once Gustav asked him: "Tell me, Herr Teibschitz, how is it that you have such an accurate knowledge of these things?" Herr

Teibschitz, in his usual way, took a long time to open his mouth in reply. Gustav began to wonder whether he would ever answer at all. It was late in the afternoon and the sky was pallid. The moon had already risen. It was a pale yellow crescent. The sun and the moon were both visible in the sky at the same time. "We received very precise information about all those matters," said Herr Teibschitz at last.

"Who are 'we'?" asked Gustav. He timidly put the question, he did not quite succeed in hiding his excitement. Herr Teibschitz yawned. " 'We' were numbers, if you want to know exactly," he rejoined. "I, for example, was Number C II 734. The job was in connexion with the intelligence service of the interior. It was a kind of home mission," he added lazily. "A troublesome business, I can tell you, that home emigration. One lives in restaurants and hotels, sleeps in a different place every night, with the police always on one's heels. Selling Oppermann furniture is probably easier." "And what sort of people are the 'we'?" Gustav questioned further. "They are," answered Herr Teibschitz, "party officials, proletarians, a good many are women and there are children, too. The waste of human material is great; but there are many to choose from. The number of discontented is great, too. One can, of course, only use those people who know what it feels like to have no money." He turned his heavy head very slightly, blinked his sleepy eyes at Gustav in a sly, joking way: "You, for instance, Dr. Oppermann, would not have very much chance in that direction."

Both men continued silent for some time. The sun set. "You must not imagine that the work was romantic," Herr Teibschitz began again. "On the contrary, it was exceedingly tedious. It was office-work done under the sword of Damocles. Tedium, with danger added, is pretty heavy going. I found it, myself, at last both too tedious and too heavy going. You have to have a good strong hate in you to stick it out. I'm no longer capable of hating to that degree. If you have let a lunatic get hold of a machine-gun, there's no sense in hating him because you can't get it away from him. A sensible man packs up and leaves."

Otherwise the two men hardly discussed politics at all. They often remained silent for hours in each other's company, fishing, watching the fishermen, observing ants, small crabs, and spiders. If they wanted to have an exciting day, they went in search of sea-urchins, which were plentiful in the little cove.

One morning, during the early summer, Herr Teibschitz told Gustav that he would soon be setting out for his tramp through Italy. He had heard from his wife in Germany. She was willing to give him as much money as he liked, but only in Germany. Therefore, it was all up with his kennel.

Gustav was startled. He felt excited. That very morning he made a proposition to Herr Teibschitz. He did not dare to come out with it quite frankly, he dawdled clumsily over it, smiling in almost childlike embarrassment. He was prepared to supply Herr Teibschitz with the money for the purchase of the kennel. He only made one condition: that Herr Teibschitz, who could get on quite well here with his identification card, should give him his passport. Herr Teibschitz merely said: "H'm." Nothing more.

In the afternoon he brought his passport with him. He looked Gustav up and down in a critical way. "Height medium; Face round; Eyes blue; Hair light brown; Distinguishing Marks none. It's a good thing I acquired my moustache later; otherwise they would surely tell us apart, even on a passport picture. Now you merely look more distinguished," he added in his lazy, rather reserved manner. "But maybe the inspectors at the frontier won't notice that. *Bon*, Herr Teibschitz," he said and handed Gustav the passport. He made him another present, too; a grey suit which he had worn a long time. Gustav hated grey suits but he was very grateful

to Herr Teibschitz for this one and he gave him, in turn, his
dilapidated little car for the balance of the period he had
rented it.

"Make a good job of it, Herr Teibschitz," said Herr Teibschitz as Gustav left. "And if you find it too tedious—I guarantee you will—then come and visit me in my kennel."

15

Gustav was not in a hurry. He broke his journey at Marseilles, at Lyons, at Geneva, at Zürich. In Zürich he met
his nephew Heinrich.

The face of the lad with its tanned, delicate skin was still
very boyish. But his eyes had grown older, more reflective;
they now often looked just as sleepy, observant, and shrewd
as those of his father. He had been thinking a great deal during
these last weeks. Words and ideas did not come easily to him,
but in the end his good, sound commonsense always triumphed
over those vague, savage instincts which had impelled him to
his abortive settlement of accounts with Werner Rittersteg. It
was not easy for so young a boy, who had been educated in
Germany and who loved Germany, to make up his mind on
German affairs during these weeks. Heinrich knew that the
Nationalists had not only driven his cousin Berthold to his
death but very many others as well. He had read the decree
ordering that gas masks be provided in schools for all boys
except those of Jewish extraction. He clenched his strong,
young fists, but he did not confuse the Nationalists with the
Germans, and when Germany was spoken of, he maintained a
reserved attitude.

He now sat in his uncle Gustav's room at the hotel, on an

edge of the fireplace fender, taking care to keep his balance so that the frail thing should not collapse under him. Gustav questioned him about his plans for the future. Heinrich had finally decided to become an engineer. He was particularly interested in underground structures. He could see many new possibilities in them. He would work for several years in England and America. However, his ultimate goal was to work in Germany. His prospects would certainly be better anywhere else but Germany remained the necessary background for his favourite projects. Nor could he get his academic education out of his mind, though it would not prove of much use to him in his profession of engineering. He wanted to work in Germany. The idea of a speedway under Berlin, from one end to the other, fascinated him, as well as that of a subway for Cologne. He was not going to be put off his Germany by a lot of fools.

His uncle Gustav was pleased with what he heard. The lad, too, wanted to make a demonstration in his own way. He was not wanted in Germany, but he wanted Germany; he wanted to give Germany what he believed was good. Gustav was deeply moved by that. And without more ado, he told Heinrich that there were other Germans who were not going to be put off either. He told him of children who, in spite of the blows they received, refused to sing the Horst-Wessel song, of magistrates who preferred confinement in a concentration camp to giving the Roman salute, of prisoners who could be shot but could not be made to speak.

Heinrich, however, was not in sympathy with such behaviour. He got off the fender and walked to and fro. "No, sir," he said. He was not in the least impressed by such demonstrations. He, too, had heard a good deal about them but he had never heard that they had done the least bit of good. He could not imagine how they ever would do any good. There had been enough martyrs; it was time that stopped. He screwed up his extremely red lips, lowered his eyelids a little, suddenly looked grown up and very much like his father, but more determined and uncompromising. "One can't make a more convincing demonstration than being willing to die," he said. "Berthold's demonstration was an example of that kind; Berthold was a great friend of mine. His death was not of the least use. And if numbers of other people die or get themselves shut up in those ghastly camps, it's no use either."

He had spoken in an earnest tone which bordered on the sentimental. He did not like that sort of thing. He quickly came down to earth again. "Well," he said, smiling and looking boyish again. "I'm a rotten speaker but there is a friend of mine here, a student who comes from the west of Switzerland; he can explain all my views to you much better and more convincingly than I can. I'm going to meet him this afternoon in the Café Corso. Perhaps you could come, too. I'm sure you'll be interested in Pierre. He's really got a head on his shoulders."

Gustav went. Heinrich's friend turned out to be a cheerful young man with fair, reddish hair and rather cheeky manners. He was nineteen years old, Pierre Tüverlin by name, a brother of the well-known author, as Gustav soon discovered. With his smooth, facetious face, his reddish hair, and his almost lashless eyes, he was not the type to attract people readily. Nevertheless, Gustav quite liked the careless ease with which he propounded his caustic, precocious views.

The café was large, noisy, and full of smoke; it was full, too, of loud music. But the two young men obviously felt very much at their ease. Heinrich had scarcely informed his friend of the subject of his conversation with his uncle that morning when Pierre Tüverlin, in his clear, shrill voice that could easily be heard above the music, burst forth: "No, my dear sir, that won't do. Romance won't help you there. All those demonstrators of yours can go and jump in the lake. They're damned out-of-date, you can bet your boots on that. Their demonstrations won't accomplish anything against machine-guns." Heinrich gazed at his friend admiringly. "Common-sense, commonsense, and—once more—commonsense," concluded the latter. "That's what we want now." And Heinrich seconded him: "*Commonsense.* Nothing else counts. Anybody who tries anything else is moth-eaten."

Gustav was amazed and almost saddened that young people could get enthusiastic about anything as drab as commonsense. The orchestra, just then, was playing a *potpourri* from *La Muette de Portici.* A hundred years ago that opera had so excited its audience in Brussels that they rushed out into the street and started a revolution. These boys would not allow themselves to get excited over such things. "And Socrates? Seneca? Christ? Were their deaths useless?" he asked.

"I don't know," said Herr Tüverlin, declining the challenge. "But what I do know is that, since the inception of experimental science, it is wiser to live for an idea than to die for it. It is also more beneficial to the idea. A few childish slanderers have ascribed the phrase, 'Nevertheless, it does move,' to the great Galileo. He never said anything of the kind. As soon as he saw the torturers' implements, he recanted at once. He was a very great man. Since he, himself, was convinced that the universe did move, what did it matter if he said that it did not? Whether he said so or not, it did move. That was the way he thought. And your demonstrators should imitate him, my dear sir. Let them shout 'Heil Hitler!' and think something different. Those demonstrators of yours, my dear sir," he concluded, emphasizing every word with a vigorous gesture of his right hand, the back of which was covered with reddish hairs, "are useless, romantic, and out-of-date. At any rate, it is mere folly to put on the airs of a martyr nowadays."

Heinrich seemed to be regretting his former impetuosity. He sat erect in his comfortable café armchair with the air of a person paying a formal call. "My parents and I," he said, "often discuss what the Jews in Germany really should do. They are in an appalling position. Most of them can't get away, for they have no money and they're not allowed in anywhere else either. They try, under the most difficult conditions, to keep their business going in Germany. Everywhere they are spat at, they are outlaws, there are notices outside the baths forbidding them to go in, their passports are stamped with the word 'Jew,' no Christian girl can be seen with them in the street, they are expelled from their clubs, they are only allowed to play football among themselves. If any of them complain to the police, the reply is that they have only themselves to thank for incurring the just anger of the people. Are they to make demonstrations? Do you ask them, Uncle Gustav, to stand up and shout: 'Look here, you're the inferior people and we're the superior'?"

"I don't ask anybody to do anything, my boy," said Gustav. "The Jews in Germany are probably quite right to behave as they do." The music was noisy, cups were clattering, people were talking loudly all around them. Gustav spoke casually and so calmly that the young men, who had both wanted to go on speaking at the same time, were silent for a moment.

Tüverlin was the first to speak, in a more temperate tone. "Certain men who had been married to Jewesses for decades and had had children by them, declared that they had now come to see the error of their ways and were ashamed of that error; moreover, they said that they had not lived with their Jewish wives for years and were, therefore, now instituting divorce proceedings. They're skunks. At the same time, it is not possible to know whether or not these statements were made in collusion with their wives, in order to make the lives of these women and their children bearable. If they did it for that reason, they're not skunks but sensible men." "*Well*," said Heinrich, "it must be damned hard to stand still and let some little weasel spit into one's face. I think it often requires a very high degree of self-control to be sensible and hold one's tongue. My school friend Kurt Baumann writes me that they now have frequent essays to write on the theme, 'What is Heroism,' and so forth. I never got more than a C in composition but I would like to write on *that* theme. It would be sure to make them sit up in class. Of course, I'd get a D but I would have deserved an A."

Gustav could say very little to refute the arguments of his young nephew. But the events described in Bilfinger's documents rose before him; he thought of Herr Teibschitz's photographs and of Johannes as he had visualized him, a marionette on a box, leaping grotesquely and elastically about—"Down on your knees, arm out"—cawing like a parrot. In meek, unshakable steadfastness he sat confronting the young people's commonsense. Thoughtfully, without reproach, he said to his nephew Heinrich: "I believe you people have developed your commonsense to such a degree that you have forgotten how to hate."

Heinrich's boyish face turned red. The delicate tanned skin on his large, broad face flushed deeply. He thought of his written accusation against Rittersteg, he thought of the woods near Teupitz, of the very young moon there had been that night when he pressed Werner's head into the damp earth, and how he had left it all half done because his hate did not last long enough. He looked angry and embarrassed. "I'm not entirely made of wood," he said at last. But after a very brief pause he went on doggedly: "Nevertheless I would stick out my hand and shout: 'Heil Hitler!' Sure," he asserted, "I'd do it ten times over." And the nineteen-year-old Pierre Tüverlin, in his shrill voice, closed the debate with: "There's no use trying to work on people's feelings by means of fine phrases and noble gestures. Change the theory and you will change the man; not vice versa." "*Yes, sir,*" said the seventeen-year-old Heinrich.

Then Gustav paid the bill for coffee, rolls, and cigarettes for the two boys and they left.

That same evening Gustav packed up everything he still had with him, including Bilfinger's documents and that bundle of private correspondence containing the admonitory postcard, and sent everything to Lugano to be stored at his brother-in-law's. Then, with a sly smile, he put on the grey suit Herr Georg Teibschitz had given him.

16

It was a fine, sunny day when the man with the passport made out in the name of Georg Teibschitz crossed the frontier. He was a heavily built, slow-moving, amiable-looking man in a worn grey suit and he carried a shabby suitcase.

He travelled about, in South Germany to begin with, in Baden, in Swabia, in small towns and villages; that merchant Georg Teibschitz, a man who had at one time been independent and made a lot of money, who had later been employed by others but who, for the time being, was without a job. His papers were in perfect order. A man in Bandol had provided him with a number of further proofs of identity. He could substantiate everything he said.

He was in no hurry. He breathed German air, gazed on the German countryside, heard German voices. He drifted along as on a calm sea, in a state of peace and happiness. He walked about the streets, travelled across country in that miraculously lovely season of early summer, breathing deeply and gazing his fill. He was more content with himself and with his destiny during these days than he had ever been before. Life glided on, quietly, evenly, strongly, and he let himself drift.

But just because the peace and order of Germany at once enfolded him, because he adjusted his tempo to that of the others and began to think their thoughts, he doubly realized the danger of this deceptive calm and the urgent necessity of revealing what an impudent swindle this apparent tranquillity really was.

He commenced his activities slowly. The fact that he had gossiped so much, during these last weeks, down there beside the southern sea, with fishermen, with bus drivers, and all sorts of people in humble walks of life, now proved useful to him. He entered into long-winded conversations with small tradesmen, peasants, and labourers. These people made no secret to him of their private affairs. But as soon as he began to talk politics, they became speechless. The times were in favour of silence. Nevertheless, he managed to make a few of them talk.

He was disappointed. The pictures which the stories of Frischlin, Bilfinger, and Teibschitz had conjured up had been wild and colourful, whereas reality had a grey and prosaic look. People shrugged their shoulders over the atrocities committed by the mercenaries. It was an old story that the Nationalists were dirty dogs. There was no need for anyone to come and tell them that. The facts that prisoners were beaten, that their miserable rations were peppered and no water supplied to quench the resultant thirst, that they were compelled to smear one another with their own excrements, all these things were ancient history and had lost much of their original power to horrify. The really important question was how to obtain the bare necessities of life with a continually dwindling supply of money. The real problem of the masses was not the barbarism of the Nationalists but how to get along without the few pennies which the government had deducted from one's income.

Now and then, in small cafés and restaurants and at the unemployment agencies, Gustav came across the agents of that secret organization of which Georg Teibschitz had spoken. He tried to establish relations with them but was unsuccessful. These people, it was evident, really did not wish to be anything but numbers, as Herr Teibschitz had explained. A man like Gustav had no chance of getting at them.

Once, unexpectedly, in the town of Augsburg, he met Klaus Frischlin. Frischlin did not raise his voice, he did not want to attract attention. That made his words sound all the more curt when he said: "Have you gone mad? What business have you got to be in Germany? How did you get here? I'll make it possible for you to disappear over the frontier again. But I insist that you must be gone within twenty-four hours."

Unforeseen as this encounter was, Gustav had long ago prepared for it. It had been Frischlin who had involved him in this business, it had always been Frischlin, from the moment he had told him on the telephone that he was coming to Berne. Frischlin had been the first to tell him what was happening in Germany. It was owing to Frischlin that Bilfinger had spoken to him. Frischlin had forwarded that card to him, which had reminded him to undertake the task, even if he could never finish it. It was Frischlin, Gustav had long known, who had turned Georg Teibschitz into Number C II 734. So, like a schoolboy voluntarily performing a task which is beyond him but for which he nevertheless expects to be praised on account of his good intentions, with a sly and roguish air, an embarrassed childlike smile spreading over his large, badly shaven face, Gustav imparted his secret to the other. "I hope you have no objection to my being C II 734?" But Frischlin's face hardened. "You are a fool," he said roughly. "What are you thinking of? We can't use you in that way. You'll only make trouble for us." He grew more and more angry. "What are you thinking of, man? What are you up to here? What sort of quixotry is this? Do you think you are a hero in a novel? Whom do you think you are going to make an impression on? The only person you'll impress is yourself. What you are doing will only arouse annoyance, not admiration."

Gustav's face looked dejected. His unshaven cheeks hung loosely, he was an old man. Nevertheless Frischlin's words did not shake his resolution for a moment. Plaintively and stubbornly, like a child misunderstood by adults and still insisting on its original point, he slowly shook his large head. "I thought that you, at least, would understand me, Dr. Frischlin."

Klaus Frischlin had intended to give Gustav a further good, sharp piece of his mind. The fellow was not only injuring himself but everyone else concerned. However, the tone in which Gustav had spoken made it clear to him that there was absolutely nothing to be gained by talking in that way. Suddenly, too, he realized how fond he had become of the slow-going, unpractical fellow with his childlike impetuosity, his gentle stubbornness, and his simplicity, which he had preserved throughout fifty years right into the Germany of today. "I should not like anything to happen to you, Dr. Oppermann," he said. Gustav had never suspected that the man could speak with such warmth and intensity. "You will inevitably be arrested if you go on creeping about here with your seditious talk. I beg of you to leave Germany. I beg of you to hurry and leave. Believe me, our friend Lessing would give you the same advice," he added with a slight smile.

"Our friend Lessing." Gustav was very pleased that Frischlin had said: "Our friend Lessing." "Do you remember," he asked, "the quotation from Lessing I intended using as a text for the Third Book? 'Pursue your inscrutable course, eternal Providence. Let not my faith in you falter because your course is inscrutable. Do not let me despair if your steps seem to retrogress. It is not true that the shortest road is always the straightest. You are confronted by many obstacles along your path, you are obliged to make many detours to avoid them.' You see," he concluded in triumph, "that's why I'm here."

"That's utter madness, my dear man," said Frischlin, again seriously provoked. "That's the very reason you must pack up and leave. What's your idea? To help Providence make a detour? Of course, people are waiting just for you to tell them what's going on. They've known what's been going on for ages. They don't want to know anything more about that. What they do want to know is, what's to be done. Have you any ideas on that subject, Dr. Oppermann? Have you a solution to that problem? But I want you to know that we have one; it is because of this fact that I can permit the people I am in charge of to risk their lives. But I can't allow you to do so," he added sharply.

The two men walked a little distance without speaking. "Are you still angry with me?" asked Gustav at last. He spoke in a pleading, dejected tone, like a boy reprimanded for some escapade, but sure in his heart that he has done the right thing. Frischlin shrugged. "It is too bad about you, Dr. Oppermann," he said. His tone was so like that which Mühlheim had often used towards him that Gustav, in spite of Frischlin's wrath, was pleased they had met.

With quiet obduracy he continued as he had begun. He was now in the neighbourhood which had been the scene of Bilfinger's reports. He travelled about the beautiful Swabian countryside. He wished to supplement the material Bilfinger had collected; for the day would come when such material would have more than a merely historical interest. However, these activities also resulted in disappointment. The people who had so far been only names, words, and type, now that they stood before him in the flesh, proved far more shadowy than the shapes of his imagination. There was only one thing that was real about them: their fear, their wretched, intimidated demeanour. At the slightest hint, they grew dumb and showed him the door. He was able to loosen the tongues of some of the eye-witnesses who had no connexion with the victims. The faces of the victims themselves, when he mentioned what had happened to them, grew stony in the pretence of having seen nothing and knowing about nothing.

This frozen fear, this deeply embedded horror, filled Gustav with an actual physical compassion. He tried all sorts of means to induce the terrified people to talk. It was not only his desire for material; he believed that the stricken people would more easily rid themselves of the terror, which had ruined their whole lives, if they could speak of it.

One day he was sitting over a pint of wine with a veterinary surgeon, a tradesman, and a mechanic. They became excited when what had happened in their town was mentioned. They let themselves go and used strong language. Gustav did the same. They attracted the attention of the people at the next table; before they were ready to leave the inn, they were arrested.

17

His papers of identification were examined in the concentration camp at Moosach. Georg Teibschitz, from Charlottenburg in Berlin, 92 Knesebeck Strasse, aged 49, entered for disorderly conduct. His head was shaved; he was made to strip—he reluctantly parted with his grey suit—and was compelled to put on striped clothing. The jacket was too long and the trousers much too tight. Gustav cut a ridiculous figure. If they made him bend his knees, every seam would burst. He thought of Johannes. The idea of the genuflections terrified him, yet he looked forward to them with secret excitement.

He was taken to a courtyard, lined up with five others, and told to stand at attention. Three young mercenaries with stolid, good-natured peasant faces guarded them.

The six men had to stand at attention, nothing more. For the first half hour, the rigid position was not an excessive strain on Gustav. Vaguely, in his heart, he had always been sure that his enterprise would come to such an end as his standing here, his body stiffened, carefully guarded by stupid, good-natured young men. Nevertheless, he had undertaken his task with enthusiasm. Frischlin and young Heinrich might consider it senseless; he knew that it was the right solution for him. Johannes Cohen had been a reproach to him for so long. Johannes, who had stuck it out at his teacher's desk in the midst of riotous Saxon students, Johannes the marionette on his elastic—down on your knees, arm out—the dead Johannes, broken bones, a mutilated mass of flesh in a sealed casket. Johannes had nothing more to reproach him with now. They were quits.

Such were Gustav's thoughts and feelings during the first half hour. From then on he only felt: "I shan't be able to keep this up." They had been given no food at noon. The man next to him had been drooping and getting shaky for some time; a rubber truncheon made him straighten up again. "If only the back of my neck would not ache so," thought Gustav. "Now, I'll shove my right foot forward a little bit. No, my left. They'll hit me if I do it. All the same, I'm going to shove my left foot forward. I must simply lift it up and give it one or two shakes." But he did not do it.

At last they were allowed to move. That was a tremendous boon; it hurt, yet at the same time it was a relief. Then came supper, a piece of bread spread with drippings. Gustav was thirsty, but unfortunately they were not given any water. Instead of that they were ordered to attend roll-call. In the ancient Roman manner, they had to salute the swastika banner which was then being furled and sing the "Song of Germany." Then at last they could go to bed.

Gustav shared a room with twenty-three others. The room was small and the stench in it sickening; it was revolting to think of how it would reek within a few hours.

Gustav was at first tormented by thirst. The straw pricked and scratched his body, the stench grew worse and worse. But his thirst made him forget the stench and his painful weariness made him forget both thirst and stench. The building was lit by searchlights. At intervals of less than a minute, their glaring rays swept over his face. Patrols returned to the barracks, yelling and cursing. From afar came the screams of a man who was probably being "examined"; he screamed without cessation. Gustav lay on his side, grinding his teeth slightly. He fell asleep. Slept soundly. Neither searchlights, nor noise, nor thirst, nor stench disturbed him till he woke, with a start, in the early morning at the sound of a shrill bugle-call.

When they had said morning prayers, standing stiffly beside their beds, Gustav had a rapturous thrill: water was brought in. It was wonderful to feel the moisture trickling across his cracked lips and running down his throat. Unfortunately, the man behind him was in a hurry. But there was further happiness in store for him: there was breakfast, consisting of warm, black water, called coffee, and a piece of bread. It consisted also, to be sure, of the Horst-Wessel song and of the "Song of Germany."

They marched into the courtyard. The prisoners stood herded together, hundreds of them, in their grotesque, striped clothing. The swastika banner was unfurled. They saluted it in the ancient Roman fashion, shouting "Heil Hitler."

They did gymnastic exercises. It was a lowering, sultry day, thick grey clouds were in the sky. Gustav's section had to do some running exercises to begin with. That lasted twenty minutes. Gustav began to perspire after the first few minutes but the running did not worry him much. Twelve hours ago he had been tired to death; it was strange what unsuspected reserves of strength a man had. They scaled a wall with ladders. Then the running exercises again. Finally they knelt, with their heads on the ground. That lasted a very long time.

It began to rain. Gustav was waiting for them to get to the knee-bending. But there was none of that. Instead, they were ordered to throw themselves down on the damp ground and crawl about there in obedience to the commands: "Leg front, arm front, backside up, other leg front, other arm front, get up, lie down, up again, down again." It rained harder; their shaved heads became annoyingly cold in the rain. Mud puddles began to appear in the wretched turf. Down, into the puddles, up again, down again, stomach in the puddle, roll. "Honour to Germany by land and sea," shouted the mercenary in command. "That's healthy exercise," he shouted. "No one can complain about that. And if the foreign Jews complain about it, we'll complain to you with sandbags." He roared with laughter. "Laugh with me," he commanded. They laughed.

They lined up for the distribution of work. There were three groups of prisoners: those due for light correction, those due for severe correction, and the incorrigibles. The prisoner Georg Teibschitz had been entered for disorderly conduct. There was nothing else against him. He was placed, for the time being, into the class for light correction. His section had light work allotted to them. In Moosach, as in many of the other camps where absolutely no work could be found for the prisoners, they had hit upon the expedient of constructing a new road. There was, to be sure, no need of such a road. The country round Moosach was swamp and moorland and was sparsely populated. The construction of a road was difficult on

account of the nature of the soil. Still, work is there to be
done for its own sake.

Gustav's job was to wheel gravel. The wheelbarrow was
heavy, the soil soft and slippery. The barrow continually sank
into the mud, in some places there were bottomless swamps
on either side. But Gustav was strong. However, his hands
soon became swollen and his palms blistered.

It took about eight minutes to push the full barrow from the
gravel-dump to the place where the work was going on. The
return journey with the empty barrow took less than half the
time. When one got near the goal with one's loaded barrow,
one looked forward eagerly to the respite of the return journey.
Gustav inspected his companions. Twenty-one of the twenty-
three in his dormitory were there. Their hair was shaved off
or cropped very short. They had, for the most part, a disorderly growth of whisker on the cheeks or even regular
beards. Two of them had tufts of hair cut in the form of a
swastika. Some of them wore glasses; most of them had the
faces of intellectuals. They all looked emaciated, exhausted,
and broken. Many seemed on the verge of idiocy; they nearly
all had blue and black bruises on their faces. Gustav now knew
what the real Johannes at the camp at Herrenstein had looked
like. Not like the marionette of his visions, much more terrifying than that in his dirty, striped clothing. Gustav, however,
had no time for such observations except when he was pushing
the empty barrow. When he was pushing the full one, he soon
had no thought but: "When shall I get there?" and "If only I
were on the way back."

They marched back to camp. They sang the Horst-Wessel
song. They said grace:

> "Come, Lord Jesus, be our guest,
> By Thee Thy gifts to us be blest.
> Guard Thou our Nation, a deserving one,
> Bless Chancellor Hitler, her illustrious son."

They ate bread and turnip soup. Washed up the plates and dishes. Marched out into the courtyard. Stood at attention. Listened dully to the roll-call. Yelled, "Heil Hitler!" when the officer in command passed along the ranks. Sang the "Song of Germany." Began their gymnastic exercises.

And then, at last, came the knee-bending. It was quite differently conducted from the way Gustav had imagined. There was no rapid, elastic bobbing up and down. Instead, it was gone through in four movements, measured by the clock, of two minutes each. First movement: up on toes. Second: bend the knees. Third: up on toes again. Fourth: heels on ground. If one didn't lift one's heels properly, or did not bend one's knees enough, a kick came to one's assistance. The mercenaries' boots were big and heavy. Gustav, as he crouched, bending his knees, thought of his grandfather Immanuel, who had once said to him when his mother had been very ill: *"Gam su letovo. This, too, may be all for the best."* He had not understood how something bad might serve a good purpose. His grandfather had explained to him that it would be "credited to his account." There was some sort of bookkeeping involved. What seemed a trial and appeared on the debit side of the earthly ledger, would become a blessing and show on the credit side in heaven. Little Gustav had not been able to figure it out at the time; now, it slowly dawned on him what his grandfather had meant. Mechanically he repeated the Hebrew words. One, up on toes: *gam*. Two, bend the knees: *su*. Three, up on toes again: *le*. Four, heels on ground: *tovo*. He tried desperately hard not to collapse; for then the boots of the mercenaries would come to the rescue. After half an hour he was exhausted. Once, he really did fall over; the kick of the peasant-faced guard was hard. From then on he thought of nothing but of the two minutes when he could rest with his heels on the ground, and during the two minutes that he rested with his heels on the ground, he thought with fear of the six minutes of strain that were to follow.

In the half-hour's recess after the exercises Gustav lay in a corner. Then they had to get into line again, and a man with stars on his uniform made a speech. One really ought to stick all Jews and Marxists like pigs, he declared. But the Third Reich was noble and generous and was making the attempt to educate these inferior people. It was only when one of them proved himself absolutely and utterly incorrigible that he was finished off. This speech was evidently part of the "instruction," the "education." For sentences out of the book entitled *My Battle* were now read to them. They had to repeat in chorus the maxim: "As well try to keep a hyena from carrion as a Marxist from betraying his country," together with other favourite sayings of the Leader. That Leader, it was then explained to them, was born at Braunau in Austria on the 20th of April 1889. Everything he said came directly from God. If any of the blockheads there present had not, by the following morning, memorized the dates in the Leader's life, and the sentences just cited, he would get three weeks in the coal sheds. The Leader's gospel was laid down in the book entitled *My Battle*. The prisoners had the right to buy this book at the price of five marks seventy in paper covers and seven marks twenty in boards. They could have the money sent them by their next of kin.

The twenty-four prisoners in Gustav's section, most of them intellectuals, were given this sort of instruction. They were professors, doctors, writers, lawyers; their teacher was a young peasant lad. The prisoners sat in their striped clothing, blue and black bruises on their faces, their hair completely shaved off or cropped short, two of them had tufts of hair cut in the form of a swastika. They sat about apathetically, with vacant looks, and in chorus babbled the sentences read out to them, nervously trying to impress them on their tortured brains. Gustav remembered vaguely that he had once read aloud extracts from *My Battle* to a man named François and that they had laughed about them.

That night, too, Gustav slept heavily and soundly. The second day passed as had the first, the third like the second. The camp at Moosach was considered humane. It was true that Gustav received kicks and occasionally a blow over the head or in the face. But in this camp the prisoners were more seldom "examined" than in the others. Gustav suffered most from the insufficient nourishment and the excessive exercises. He often felt weak, in spite of his well-trained body, and his heart troubled him.

The physical strain was severe, the hunger and the stench were worse, but worst of all was the everlasting monotony, the everlasting gloom. Talking was not permitted, and the dreariness of the exercises crushed the spirit. They want to make beasts of us, thought Gustav, they want to empty our heads and dull our brains. Soon he thought of nothing but whether there would be any knee-bending that day or standing at attention or crawling on the ground and whether he would get the light wheelbarrow that day or the heavy one or perhaps the one with the split handle, which was especially irritating to blisters.

Although he was not allowed to speak to them, he now knew his twenty-three roommates very well indeed. He knew which was the milder and which the more irascible character, who was used to manual labour and who was not, who was strong and who was weak, who would probably last a longer time and who a shorter. He knew who said "Yes, sir," in a high-pitched voice and whose voice was deeper, who sang loud and who sang low. This last distinction was very important. For if the Horst-Wessel song or the "Heil Hitler," did not sound spirited enough, the result was that the good humour of the many-starred officer in command suffered. The oddest of Gustav's roommates was a man, perhaps in the middle fifties, who blinked a good deal and who had obviously at one time worn glasses. You could still see the slight dent across the bridge of his nose. The glasses had probably been smashed during an "examination" or they had been taken away from him as a joke. This man, whatever was said to him, never replied anything except a nervous "Yes, sir," and whenever he was addressed held his arm in front of his face in terror. It was clear that his mind was affected. He was a nuisance during physical training and manual labour; he was a burden to his fellow-prisoners and even to the warders. But the latter, who themselves suffered from the boredom of their duties, found the man's stupidity a welcome relief. They preferred putting his idiocy to amusing tests to sending him to an institution for the mentally defective.

The days passed in an insipid uniformity. Once, when Gustav was wheeling his barrow in a fresh direction, he came upon a blackish pool of water. He stopped for a moment to get his breath. He saw, reflected in the water as it glittered in the sun, a large head with a dirty, curling beard and a bit of white fluff on the skull. He had not seen his face for a long time now. At one time he had often seen it. He gazed at the head with interest. It was emaciated, the eyes were dull and bloodshot; so that was what Herr Georg Teibschitz looked like now. Gustav was surprised, but he was not displeased with Herr Georg Teibschitz. Unfortunately, he had not much time to study the face, for his barrow had to make the return trip. The next day, the pool had dried up so much that he could not see the face in it any longer. He was disappointed.

Day after day went by, always in the same torturing monotony and gloom. It was not until the end of the second week that any special incident occurred.

On this occasion an officer of higher rank—one of those with an oak twig—attended the "instructions" of Gustav's section. They had to recite in chorus one of the maxims of the Nationalists: "The State above the people." They recited the sentence and repeated it several times. Suddenly the officer with the oak twig pricked up his ears and interrupted them; asked them to repeat it in groups of four. He arrived at Gustav's group. There—it could be heard quite distinctly—a voice spoke: "Hate above the people." The man with the oak twig made them repeat the sentence again. Again it came: "Hate above the people." It was the half-witted man who had lost his glasses; they all heard the words, they all knew that the poor idiot was reciting them with the best of intentions. He repeated what he had actually understood, what he believed was the idea of the Nationalists. But the half-wit was not officially listed as a half-wit, therefore he must be considered malevolent. He and his entire section were punished by having to forgo alternately their lunch and supper. However, the ringleaders, the group to which Gustav and the man without glasses belonged, were locked up in the coal sheds.

The sheds were situated next to the outhouses. They had at one time been outhouses also, now boards had been nailed across the seats to fit them for their new purpose. Each one was about five foot square and was completely dark. Gustav was locked in one of those sheds for a week, day and night. He was allowed out only for meals. To begin with, he suffered principally from the appalling stench, then he suffered more—increasingly so day by day—from the inability of moving his limbs or stretching himself. His back hurt him most.

There were hours in which Gustav crouched in a sort of doze; there were hours of the most terrible despair, hours of rage, hours of feverish meditation on the possibility of someone trying to do something for him. But there were no longer any hours in which Gustav approved of his destiny. He never thought again: *"Gam su letovo."*

He had been a fool to return to Germany. Those two young men, Heinrich and the other, had been right. The Jews who remained in Germany and held their tongues were right. What an impudent piece of conceit that had been, thinking himself superior to Herr Weinberg. Had Bilfinger ever fixed it up again with his fiancée? That cursed Bilfinger. It was all his fault. He wished he could knock his glasses off his square head for him. No, it was all Johannes Cohen's fault. He was the one who had enticed him here. Johannes had always spoiled everything for him. And he had had an easy time of it with his knee bending. To hop about like a marionette was no art. To stand for two minutes on the tips of your toes is a different proposition, my lad. Especially during movement Number Three.

What were those places called where the Romans used to lock up their slaves? Some ancient writer had described them. Silly of me not to be able to think of the word. I used to believe, in Max Reger Strasse, that I couldn't work unless I had plenty of room to walk up and down. Shall I ask them to dock me another meal and let me out for two hours instead? They wouldn't do it. They have smashed the standards to pieces! Now I have it. Columella was the man who wrote about the slaves, and the places were called *ergastula*. My memory. I still have a decent memory left.

I'm a beast in a cage. It won't help anybody if I perish here in this stench. They were right. There is nothing more ridiculous than a martyr. That Johannes Cohen ought to have been given a punch on the jaw. *De mortuis nil nisi bene.* All the same, he ought to have been given a good punch. Anna should have advised me against this. She should have shut me up in a sanatorium for nervous disorders. And now, I'm really going to give Johannes one right in the middle of his yellow jaw.

He struck out. His fist met the wooden wall of the cell. It had been a weak blow but he was terrified by it. He was

afraid someone might have heard it. He sat up erectly and said,
"Yes, sir."

One night he, too, was conducted to an "examination." He
was classified under the heading of "disorderly conduct." He
still belonged to those under "light correction," in spite of the
punishment he had undergone. If he was "examined," it was
not with any evil end in view but solely because they happened to have nothing else to do. Nevertheless, Gustav returned from this examination in such a state that when they
came to fetch him from his cell the next day, he was found
there, leaning against the wall in a fainting condition. He was
sent to the infirmary barracks for two days. Then he went back
to his original room and his days went on as before. Except
that the elderly man without glasses had now disappeared,
and it was now Gustav who, when he was addressed, held his
arm in front of his face and said, "Yes, sir."

18

Klaus Frischlin, during these weeks of his work in the central organization offices of the counter-movement, had
grown still more cool and calculating. But he received a severe
shock when he saw the name of Georg Teibschitz on the
secret list of those who had been caught.

He tried to get into touch with Mühlheim. Mühlheim's association with his Nationalist colleagues was an intimate one.
It enabled him to initiate negotiations for the rescue of many
of his friends with good prospects of success. It was true that
such negotiations were not without danger for himself, and
his Nationalist colleagues were advising him more and more
urgently to get away before it was too late. But Mühlheim

could not resist the petitions of those who saw in him the last drop in the bottle. I really am a fool, he said to himself. What is the good of continually saying: Just this once more? Whereupon, having brought one last and final operation to a conclusion, he undertook another one, which was to be the very last.

He often remembered his foolish friend Gustav. He got little news of him, to be sure. It was a long time now since he had had word from him. Gustav was probably running round in some delightful place abroad, safe and cheerful, in the company of some charming woman. If he, Mühlheim, ever got to the point of finally being able to get away, it would not be much trouble to locate Gustav. Mühlheim had long since forgotten his friend's follies; he longed more and more eagerly to meet him somewhere abroad.

Such was Mühlheim's general state of mind when Klaus Frischlin rang him up. He asked Frischlin eagerly whether he had any news about Gustav, whether he knew where he was. Frischlin answered curtly that he would give Mühlheim all such information when they met. Mühlheim, accordingly, awaited Frischlin's visit in some excitement. The latter told him, without much preamble, that in the concentration camp at Moosach there was a certain Georg Teibschitz, who was identical with Gustav Oppermann.

Mühlheim, white to the lips, lost control of himself and vented his grief and rage on Klaus Frischlin. "You were the only man he kept up relations with," he raved. "You ought to have advised him. He's a mere child." "How do you know that I did not advise him?" Klaus Frischlin asked coolly.

Mühlheim stared at him helplessly. It was extremely dangerous to intercede for anyone the mercenaries had once caught. His Nationalist colleagues would absolutely refuse to help him in such an undertaking. He had intended going abroad on Tuesday. He was going to get himself into a nice mess. The same thing would happen as in the parable of the vineyard. But he did not, for a moment, consider running away.

There were two possibilities. He would try both. In the first place F. W. Gutwetter would have to be set in motion, and secondly Jaques Lavendel would have to bring pressure to bear on the Ministry of the Interior in order that intervention might come from that quarter.

Friedrich Wilhelm Gutwetter, who was sincerely grieved when he was told of Gustav's fate, was greatly astonished when Mühlheim asked him to intercede for him. What could he do? Politics was an unexplored sphere to him. He had no idea whom he should approach and how. What reason could he give for interesting himself in a stranger by the name of Herr Teibschitz? Was it known what the Teibschitz in question was accused of? All Mühlheim's eloquence made no impression on the great essayist's childlike, impenetrable simplicity.

Mühlheim appealed to Sybil Rauch. He had little hope of her. Sybil would probably take the same attitude as Gutwetter. Perhaps she would even feel a certain slight satisfaction that things were going so badly with the man, now that he had put an end of their association. However, it turned out differently. When Sybil realized the facts, she grew very pale. Her face twitched, the whole of her slim, childlike body twitched. She began to whimper without stopping, like a child. She threw her head down upon her arms and trembled all over. Then, when Mühlheim told her he had approached Gutwetter without success, determination and anger appeared in her face. She had been enduring Gutwetter's ecstatic childishness for weeks and months, longing all the time, more and more passionately, for Gustav. If politics were an unexplored sphere to Herr Gutwetter, he would just have to make a trip of exploration to that unknown sphere, that is if he still expected Sybil Rauch to exhibit any sympathy with his cosmic feelings.

Sybil, too, had a very contrary and obstinate Gutwetter to deal with. But she had more convincing arguments at her disposal than Mühlheim. She soon possessed a letter addressed to very influential quarters, which justified favourable expectations.

Jaques Lavendel, for his part, interrupted his holiday at Lugano and went to Berlin to look up his friend Friedrich Pfanz at the Ministry of the Interior. It appeared that the latter was not making too good a job of his business. Otherwise, such things as were happening in the concentration camps, for instance, could not occur. Did Herr Pfanz believe that such things did German credit any good? Herr Pfanz did not believe so. Herr Jaques Lavendel, too, found himself in the possession of a letter addressed to influential quarters, which did not exclude favourable expectations.

19

Meanwhile, at Moosach, another commandant had been appointed. The new chief inspected the camp and the construction work on the road. The stage had been reached at which the road would have to be rolled. It was explained to him that a twenty-horse-power steam-roller would be required. The commandant had an inspiration. Twenty horse-power corresponded to eighty man-power. Hadn't they got eighty men? What was the good of going to the expense of a steam-roller? Eighty prisoners, accordingly, were harnessed to the roller. Mercenaries with truncheons and revolvers accompanied them. And, lo, the calculation turned out to be correct. The roller moved. *Hu-Hott-Heil-Hitler!* commanded the mercenaries. The eighty convicts in their striped clothing, with their bearded, emaciated, bruised faces and their cropped heads, some with the swastika coiffure, pulled and panted and pulled. *Hu-Hott-Heil-Hitler!* All the prisoners were to get a taste of the commandant's methods. Every day, therefore, a fresh batch of prisoners was harnessed. The work was not popular. The ropes cut into one's flesh. One was dependent on one's co-workers. The work had to be done precisely, in perfect rhythm. The whole affair had been given publicity.

Yes, the new commandant was very proud of his idea. The road was being built entirely by man-power, without machinery. This suited the New Age, the Third Reich; it suited the new spirit of man which is opposed to machines. He invited friends to come and see whether this road was not just as well constructed for traffic as any other. It was true that the road did not lead anywhere; it started from the camp at Moosach, crossed the moor, encircled it, and came back to the camp again. Though no one needed it, it was a good road; the friends and acquaintances of the commandant would see how good it was.

They came and saw. They saw the prisoners harnessed to the roller, and that was something they had never seen before. They told their friends. The camp was closed to the public and so was the road. But the new method of road-building excited curiosity. Very many people requested the commandant to give them permits to watch the work in progress, and he was proud of the great interest that his idea had aroused.

Meanwhile Sybil Rauch had arrived at the South German provincial capital, so as to be able to carry on her activities for Gustav's release more effectively. She had heard of the new commandant's idea and managed to secure a permit. She drove out every day to the place where the prisoners dragged the roller.

Gustav and the man of his section were harnessed on the seventh day. His health had deteriorated steadily. He suffered from shortness of breath. Although he was a strong man, the "physical training" had begun to tell on him more and more, and he was now subject to frequent fainting fits.

However, he felt fairly fresh on the day that he had to take part in pulling the roller, and as he heaved away in his harness to the shout of *Hu-Hott-Heil-Hitler!* thoughts such as he had not had for a long time came into his mind. He thought of that last Seder Eve at Jaques Lavendel's, in Lugano, and remembered that Berthold had been missing on that occasion. He should have been the one to ask: "Why is this night different from all others?" It was Berthold, not Jean, he should have been worrying about. Jean belonged to the Nationalist party. Perhaps he was one of the guards. No, he was too old for that. Jean, with that dignified head of his, really should be appointed a minister. So few of the Nationalist leaders had picturesque heads. He thought of the photographs of them which Georg Teibschitz had shown him. It is impossible to laugh when one is harnessed to a roller and has to pull, the ropes cut into one's shoulders too much, but it is possible to smile; besides one's curling beard hides a smile.

How slowly the roller was moving, how frightfully slowly. "Pursue your slow course, eternal Providence." No, it wasn't "slow," it was "inscrutable." "Pursue your inscrutable course, eternal Providence." Irritating, he knew no more of it. After working at Lessing for years, he now could not remember the rest of the quotation. Where, he wondered, did the road lead along which they were pulling the roller? They used to build cities for Pharaoh, cities like Piton and Ramses. There was some sense to that. But there did not seem to be much sense in this road here. Hurrah, now he knew how it went on: "Let not my faith in you falter because your course is inscrutable." He was glad he had remembered that. He pulled with less of an effort and had no more thoughts.

That day, too, Sybil was present. She scanned the faces of

the prisoners closely. They were all bearded faces, most of them were bruised and difficult to distinguish. It was weird to think that one of those men had lain awake one night in the house in Max Reger Strasse because he could not find the exact colour of a wallpaper he wanted; that he had racked his brain over the cadence of a phrase; that she had slept with him. She sat in her disreputable little car at the edge of the road, on the open field. The ground was damp and the car was stuck in the mud; she would have a job to get it out. She sat there, slim, childlike, and thoughtful, staring at the men with her eyes full of compassion. But she did not recognize Gustav.

She had a visitor's pass two days later. She entered the camp. She was ushered into a visitors' room. Behind a railing, escorted by two mercenaries, appeared the figure of an old, emaciated, dirty man. She turned deathly pale, struck to the heart with horror. But she controlled herself and smiled. Her smile was not as childlike as usual. The long lower part of her face trembled but, just the same, it was a smile. Then, however —perhaps it was an unwise thing to do, for this man's name was Georg Teibschitz, but she could not stop herself, she could not call him by his assumed name—she said in her small, delicate voice, full of joy, compassion, affection, hope, consolation, and good cheer: "Hallo, Gustav!" "Yes, sir," said the man with a start of terror, and put his arm up in front of his face.

Two days later he was released. Jaques Lavendel insisted that he should be taken across the frontier at once. He had made sure that no obstacles would be placed in the way of Herr Georg Teibschitz's departure. He intended to take Gustav, together with a male nurse, to his house in Lugano. Mühlheim would have liked to come with them but his positively last case still detained him.

Sybil wished to accompany them. But Gutwetter insisted on

her returning to him. Reproachfully, whimperingly, he declared on the telephone, that she had only intended to remain away three or four days and now she had been away a fortnight already. Now that she had achieved her object, she might at last pay a little attention to him. The fact was that Gutwetter had become used to her. Her sober, practical character gave his cosmic creations more substance. He needed her. He could not work without her now. Sybil saw that it was a serious matter to him. If she now obeyed the dictates of her feelings and went with Gustav, Gutwetter might slip out of her reach for ever. She resolved to visit Gustav later, and returned to Berlin.

20

Gustav's wheel-chair stood directly above the cliff which overlooked the little cove, in the tiny clearing of the pines that fringed the gentle descent of the rocky slope. The place was sheltered from the wind. There was a wide, uninterrupted view of sea and coast. The wheel-chair could be moved at will into the sunshine or shadow. Gustav, stretched out at full length, was listening to the phonograph. The nurse changed the records. They were mostly East-Jewish songs. Jaques Lavendel had presented him with the records. Gustav gave them only a part of his attention; he was watching the road that ascended the height of the cliff in a graceful curve, waiting for the appearance of the shabby little car.

He had not been able to stay at Lugano. The rose-and-brown weatherbeaten house down here had lured him away. Jaques Lavendel would have preferred to keep him in Lugano. The doctors, too, had made long faces and had talked of *debilitas cordis*. But Gustav, with gentle obstinacy, had insisted. So there he lay, a painful lassitude in all his limbs, in the bright sunshine. The phonograph played on, its sound often drowned by the noise of the wind and the sea, and he waited for the car.

At last it rattled over the hill. A man in a baggy, dark blue suit of coarse material got out, blinked in the sunshine and strolled lazily round the house. Gustav wanted to sit up but could not. The nurse led Herr Teibschitz up to him. "Well, what did I tell you, Dr. Oppermann?" he remarked. "I knew it would be too tedious for you. It did get too tedious for you, eh?" "Tedious?" returned Gustav. "Yes and no." He wanted to express himself more clearly, but talking was a great effort and he postponed it.

Herr Teibschitz perceived with regret that the resemblance between him and Herr Oppermann had diminished and that it was not only because Herr Teibschitz had grown his walrus moustache again. Gustav's face was pale, his features were beginning to shrink, even his skull seemed to have become smaller. "The course of the disease brings a complete alteration in appearance," had been the explanation of the doctors. "You look still more distinguished now, Dr. Oppermann," was the opinion of Herr Teibschitz.

Gustav was pleased to see Herr Teibschitz again. From his clearing between the pines, he could look down and see Herr Teibschitz fishing or lying in the sun. Now and then Herr Teibschitz called something up to him, but Gustav had to keep his answer until Herr Teibschitz was again beside him, he could not raise his voice to that extent. When Herr Teibschitz left off fishing, he would saunter up the crumbling path, squat down beside him at very close quarters, for the little clearing did not provide much space, and show him photographs of his kennel, talking in his slow way. His wife in Germany, now that she saw he no longer needed her, had given in. She would be only too willing to come out and join him now. If Gustav liked, he could have his fifteen thousand francs back. In fact Herr Teibschitz was now actually in a position to buy up Gustav's own palatial abode. He frankly confessed, however, that he preferred the kennel. If he paid occasional visits in this direction, that was only because Dr. Oppermann and the fish in the cove had become a sort of habit with him. Then he would saunter over to the hearth, and Gustav, lying with closed eyes, would sniff gratefully the tempting odour of the oil, the rosemary, and the frying fish. Then they dined together. Herr Teibschitz ate a great deal, with relish, chewing slowly and smacking his lips. Herr Oppermann ate little, with an effort, yet with some appetite, and ground his teeth slightly.

The long sunny days passed slowly. Gustav lay, by far the greater part of the time, in the little clearing facing the sea, painfully awake yet not unhappy. Herr Teibschitz fished. The doctor from Bandol would look in and give them the latest local gossip.

Not one of the Oppermanns ever gave notice of their intention to visit Gustav. But during the summer they all made it a point to pass through Provence. Edgar, for instance, on the way to visit his daughter Ruth in Palestine; naturally enough, he came over from Marseilles one afternoon, the day before his steamer left.

The once lively Gustav had now become very silent. Edgar noticed his brother's bluish lips and bluish fingertips. It was long before he could bring himself to leave him.

Martin, too, passing Gustav's house on the peninsula of La Gorguette while he was on a motor-tour to Upper Savoy, sat beside his brother—most of the time in silence. The clearing in the pine woods was very small. There was only just room for a single, small folding-stool in addition to Gustav's wheel-chair. Martin's position as he sat on the stool was a most uncomfortable one. The phonograph played his brother-in-law Jaques's favourite record.

> "We used to be ten brothers,
> We traded in luscious wine,
> One of us died, poor fellow,
> And then we were only nine."

The brothers got fewer and fewer.

> "We used to be six brothers,
> Our stocking trade did thrive,
> One of us died, poor fellow,
> And then we were only five."

Then:

> "We used to be three brothers,
> Tea was the trade we knew,
> One of us died, poor fellow,
> And then we were only two."

Martin sat stiffly on his little stool. He noticed how much smaller his brother's face had become. It was characterized by a certain gentle cunning which had never been there before. Gustav had suddenly taken on a resemblance to Grandfather Immanuel, except that he looked much older. Martin took out his eyeglasses, polished them, and put them away again. Berthold had gone. Now Gustav was going. Martin had often, recently, given way to his feelings. But if he allowed himself an outburst now, it would only worry Gustav. He maintained, therefore, a strained and stiff demeanour. He was the old Martin again, full of dignity and poise. The lazy speech and slovenly manners of Herr Teibschitz annoyed him.

Arthur Mühlheim, unfortunately, could not manage to make an excursion to the Mediterranean. His positively last case had aroused suspicion. He was confined to Germany now and could not get a German visa.

Gustav's visitors avoided talking of Germany. But he himself returned to the subject again and again. He did not speak of his experiences with hate but rather with amazement. With the conscientious accuracy of the philologist he attempted to reconstruct the whole thing in his memory. He longed to get hold of Frischlin so as to sift the material in his possession, connect it with Bilfinger's, and make a complete dignified and detailed record. He asked his brother-in-law Jaques to try and get Frischlin to visit him.

Frischlin was determined not to permit himself the luxury of personal feelings which might be a hindrance to his work. But Jaques Lavendel was a difficult man to resist. Frischlin made the journey. Jaques Lavendel sent Heinrich to meet him at the frontier and drive him down to the coast in the car.

When Herr Teibschitz saw Frischlin, he blinked a little, looking at him with his deeply set, sleepy eyes. "Have you found it too tedious now yourself, Dr. Frischlin?" Frischlin said: "I know you gave yourself the sack, Teibschitz, but you might at least have prevented that man from coming into the country." "It was impossible to prevent it," said Herr Teibschitz. "I disapproved of his behaviour, just as I disapprove of yours. I can sit here, you know, by the sea, for a whole day, for two days, and be patient, even if I don't get a bite. But how anyone can propose to fish without hooks, and in a sea where there are no fish either, but only policemen, is beyond my understanding." "We will get our fish all right, Teibschitz," said Frischlin.

Then Klaus Frischlin sat in the little clearing in the pines, and Gustav dictated. He found speaking a great effort. Frischlin bent down very close to him, caught and understood the most obscure expressions. Gustav was able to add about thirty pages to Bilfinger's reports. "Such is the extent of the lying and barbarism which I have witnessed myself in Germany," ran the conclusion of his dictated account. "Far worse things have happened. I leave the narration of such occurrences and that of their outcome to those who come after me." It was a great effort for him to get his breath as he spoke the final sentences. "That, too, is no more finished than the Lessing is," he said, after a pause. He looked up at Frischlin like a schoolboy who wants to be praised and consoled. Frischlin admired the expiring spirit of the man, but he was a devotee of truth, he could not speak the words of praise that the other longed to hear.

Gustav commissioned Frischlin to give his nephew Heinrich a copy of the report. He also requested him to search his correspondence and find that postcard:

It is upon us to begin the work,
It is not upon us to complete it.

He crossed out the address on the card and substituted that of Heinrich Lavendel. And to his signature, "Gustav Oppermann," he added the word, "Wreck."

Heinrich had a talk with Frischlin when the latter handed over the manuscript and card to him. "Was my uncle Gustav a useless person?" he asked. Frischlin, after some reflection, replied: "He was ready, under extremely perilous conditions, to stand up for what was right and to do what was helpful. However, he merely saw things as they were and could not devise a way in which he could be constructively helpful. He ran a Marathon and delivered a dispatch case but, alas, the case contained no message." Heinrich took a good look at Klaus Frischlin. He had expressed his opinion of that expiring spirit, Gustav Oppermann, in a manly and really very noble way. It was a good and useful opinion. The words sank deep into Heinrich's mind. If the day should ever come for him to be entrusted with a dispatch, he would be ready to run a Marathon. But he would first examine the dispatch and not until after he had examined it, would he say, *O.K.*

The next day they took leave of Gustav. Heinrich bit his lip to see him lying there, looking like a very old man with a small face and bluish, discoloured lips, fighting for breath. That was what their decency came to. Berthold, the youngest of the Oppermanns, had to go because he had behaved decently. And now this man, the oldest of them, had to go because it was a crime, nowadays, to behave decently. He, Heinrich, had once been in doubt as to which was the most important: commonsense or decency. He had not been taught the answer in Queen Louise School. Now he knew it.

Frischlin, however, as soon as Heinrich had gone, bent quite close to Gustav's ear. He addressed him in a gentle, hearty tone. "You wished to hand on the truth, Dr. Oppermann, but you did not know the truth. However, you were a good example to us. The work is going on and we know the truth. They will not crush us," he went on grimly, in Gustav's ear. "Neither us, nor our children, nor the Socialists, nor the Jews, nor the spirit of reason. They will never succeed in crushing us." Then he drew away from Gustav's ear, straightened himself up, stood beside Gustav in a respectful attitude, as though to salute him for the last time.

Gustav lay at full length in the clearing. The car, with Frischlin and Heinrich in it, climbed up the gracefully curving road to the cliff, passed over the hill, and disappeared.

Gustav watched Georg Teibschitz fishing down below. Herr Teibschitz came up the crumbling path and, without a word, showed Gustav his catch. It was a good catch. Herr Teibschitz entered the house.

Gustav was too weak to turn his head to look after him. But

it was no longer a painful weakness. He looked out over the sea. He felt the heat of the sun. He breathed the pleasant, tempting odour of the oil, the thyme, and the frying fish that issued from the house.

THE END

The New York Times Book Review
March 18, 1934

The Fate of a German Family
*Lion Feuchtwanger's New Novel Concerns the Social
Consequences Of Hitler's Rise to Power*

THE OPPERMANNS. By Lion Feutwanger. 406 pp. New York:

By Fred T. March

Events in Germany have crowded fast upon each other during the last year and a half. Feuchtwanger, in exile, his books at home consigned to the flames, is in the thick of a fight—and intentionally so. Do not expect his new novel to have the same wealth of fascinating detail, the same subtlety of characterization, the same detachment or the same dramatic effectiveness that went into the making of "Power." Do not ask for the same serenity and philosophical broadness that you will find in Thomas Mann's "Buddenbrooks"—a modern novel of another wealthy German merchant family, much like the Opper-mann family, except that the Oppermanns are of German-Jewish extraction. Feuchtwanger never loses control of his intelligence or his common sense. But he is neither giving nor asking quarter.

Technically, the new book is a topical novel. And the business of the topical novelist is to transmute impersonal political events into human terms by showing how they affect individuals—the people of the story. And such a novel is not worth its paper unless it means something and means it hard. Upton Sinclair's "The Jungle" was such a book. Feuchtwanger is writing of another jungle.

The Oppermanns are a well-to-do, cultured, respected tribe, rooted in that soil which fostered the German democracy of 1830 and 1848 and before and since—a background which has nurtured the flower of German intellectualism since the French Revolution. They are not, as it happens, very politically minded. The Junker land-holding-militarist caste, the strong German Communist movement and the Hitler rabble are all alike as foreign to them as they would be to an Slavic-Jewish extraction, now an American citizen engaged in business in Germany. Gustav, talented and reflective, a man of fifty now, still a bachelor pursuing the arts and literature and attractive women, has been working for some time on his monumental "Life of Lessing," a work which promises to be of unusual significance. The Oppermann children are in schools and already begin to develop their own youthful philosophies. The social circle and in-laws are a mixed group of several racial strains, including brilliant people and bores of varied pursuits, for the most part intelligent. The talk is of business, news, art, music, politics and philosophy. These Oppermanns are not held up as heroes of the realm. On the contrary. They are a more or less typical German group of lazy culture, or specialized interests, blind to the forces assembling for the coming Armageddon.

The Nazi cloud deepens on the horizon. But any one who has read "Mein Kampf" in one of its early editions will appreciate the witticisms a reading aloud of some of its passages arouses in this circle. When all else fails they can always fall back on "The Leader's" German prose for entertainment. They refuse to believe that such a fellow can ever come to power over the German folk. And even if, he should (through the desperation of a proud people in post-war bondage) he would be "handled," trained to harness, his absurd mouthings lost in the limbo of political shibboleths.

But political events move at breath-taking speed. The Nazi

movement rises to a peak, then sags. The Oppermanns and their circle, for all their bravado, breathe a sigh of relief. Then the Monarchists, through the aged President (who, as the joke goes, dozed off while his nods were taken for assent), betrayed the nation. The Coalition Cabinet is formed under Hitler 'and the last election is scheduled. Despite the propaganda, the ruthless terrorism, the monopoly over the radio broadcasts, the Nazis fail to win their majority—and by a fairly wide margin. But the Coalition wins.

Perhaps the most satisfying narration in the novel (several threads are followed) has to do with the hopes and miseries of the little salesman, Markus, under the Nazi terror. The story of the Oppermanns appeals to our reason, our sense of justice, our indignation. But Markus, together with his family, his problems, his humiliations, his sufferings, appeals to our emotions as well; those emotions, detached but profound, which it is the problem of pure artistic creation to arouse. The truth of documentation and argument is in the other; here, however, that has passed through the creative process. But now we are talking in terms of literature; and Feuchtwanger, no more than Voltair; or Zola (in the Dreyfuss case), is concerning himself with the literary values of his material. There is not time enough.

As for the Oppermanns: One must read this historical novel of our times to learn what happens to them. To tell the story badly in our limited space might serve to destroy the effect of what is a powerful and altogether convincing exposition. The Oppermanns lose their business: most are practically forced into exile. There are tragedies. Gustav, the dilettante, who, before the last election, has signed a protest along with other writers and scholars, scientists, artists, professors, musicians, is smuggled out of Germany. But he turns out to be the hero of the family—an impractical hero, but he wins our admiration. He does a foolish thing. Hearing of a countermovement in which an old friend of his is involved, he goes back to Germany under a false passport to play a part in the struggle. He is arrested and the story of his weeks in an internment camp from which he emerges wrecked and beaten and broken is the most bitter and harrowing and convincing portion of the novel.

But Feuchtwanger is convinced that two-thirds of the German people oppose Hitler. He leaves us this picture: They hope for improvement as a result of a strong nationalist government. They like the bold exit from the League of Nations. But they expect that the Nazi mob will be curbed or superseded. They are only bored with the mystic philosphy, the songs and slogans, the gangs of brown shirts, the parades and salutings, the rantings that come over the radio—to which they do not even bother to listen. They wince at the stories of terrorism, the full extent of which they know nothing about. They close their eyes to the degradation of German labor, the hopeless condition of the unemployed, the nullification of German culture. They hope with pitiful eagerness for the best.

And so this novel is addressed to the German people, who will not be allowed to read it, urging them to open their eyes. And it is addressed to the world outside bearing the message, "Wake up! The barbarians are upon us!"

Made in the USA
Columbia, SC
29 November 2018